BONES

■ ■ ■ ■ ■ ■ ■ ■ ■ ■

Joyce Thompson

William Morrow and Company, Inc.
New York

Library of Congress Cataloging-in-Publication Data

Thompson, Joyce.
    Bones : a novel / Joyce Thompson.
      p. cm.
    ISBN 0-688-09653-0
    I. Title.
    PS3570.H6414B66 1991
    813′.54—dc20   90-46846
                                                CIP

Printed in the United States of America

BOOK DESIGN BY A. DEMAIO

This one is for two good men—
Howard Thompson, my father,
who taught me to love justice;
and Joe Medlicott, my teacher,
who led me to love literature.

ACKNOWLEDGMENTS

■ ■ ■ ■ ■ ■ ■ ■ ■

This work has many friends. Some watched my children so I could write; some read the manuscript in its various stages; some shared their professional expertise; some gave me courage; some even loaned me money. I am indebted to them all.

Teresa Jordan, Carol Tabb, Leslie Hall, Anne Marie Thompson, Joanne and Chris Worswick, Andrew Himes, Linda Petorak, Kim Buchanan, Dan Levant, Christine Hintz-Himes, Edward Bryant, James Anderson, Andrea Carlisle, Gayle and Jim Pearl, Florita and Ervin Skov, Sylvia Duff and Marvin Miller, Morris Berman, Karen Karbo, David Millstone, Florence Weinberger, Trip Quillman, Dr. Clyde Snow, Lawson Inada, Diane McDevitt, Kim Stafford, Naomi Shihab Nye, Carol Orlock, Susan Burmeister, Ann Rittenberg, Adrian Zackheim, Ian Emmet Steele, and Alexandra Thompson Steele.

The field is no longer simple:
It's a soul's crossing time.
The dead speak noise.

—THEODORE ROETHKE

PART ONE
■ ■ ■ ■ ■

1
■ ■ ■ ■ ■

When Freddy Bascomb wakes up, sometime late in the 1980s, she has two children, no husband, and a moderate level of debt. Her career is a promise yet to be kept. Her parents are divorced, which is, from her point of view, a promise kept too late. What she wakes from is two decades dominated by hormones and compromise, twenty years of dream logic, peopled by a gaggle of incomprehensible past selves, all of whom have cashed checks using her signature and contributed their bit to the Social Security account bearing her name. When a detective impulse leads her to set out a series of eight photographs, chronologically ordered, on her windowsill, the eight female persons they represent seem discontinuous, suggesting less an identity smoothly evolved than one created through the dizzying turns of dialectic. No one image honors the past or predicts the future, but reflects a wholehearted commitment to the style and role of a particular moment. She rather likes the woman in the most recent photograph, that hard-won synthesis of all preceding selves.

The young mother, with the careless hair and tired eyes, the rumpled denim jacket, is by far the oldest of them all. Distance from parturition exhibits a restorative effect. Her *now* looks better rested, healthy, not a little amused. The sixth grader is the saddest and most frightened of all the selves. Freddy wishes she could, by some trick of time, comfort and encourage her. The high school senior is opaque and confident, the college graduate determined. It surprises Freddy to see how beautiful she was at twenty-five. That picture, on the inside of a flyer for a one-woman show in San Francisco, October 1973, was taken just a month or two before she met Jack and began the long downhill slide. There are no wedding pictures, from either time.

Only the eyes relate the images. Each of the eight female persons is watchful, meeting the world with interest and caution. As the face grows increasingly battered, the smile on it grows broader, braver, even, perhaps, a little wise. Under the circumstances, time has been fairly gentle. The internal self-psycho-portrait is less subtle and more deeply scarred. Her daughter, Paige, likes twenty-five-year-old Freddy best, probably for confirmation of her own good genes. Mothering Paige defines her biggest challenge; to enfranchise her daughter to succeed, she must succeed herself. Freddy wants Paige to know at twenty-five what she herself only begins to suspect at thirty-nine. Whether that's possible or not she doesn't know, but it's what all the best women want these days.

She loves her son as much but empathizes less easily. Being male, he seems mysterious. The old environment versus heredity question is always asking itself. What's Chaz the Human versus Chaz the Manchild versus Chaz the son of Freddy, brother of Paige et cetera ad almost infinitum. With her as mother, whom will he become?

Freddy sets out photographs and poses existential questions only after the children are in bed or when she is supposed to be painting. The rest of the time, she attends to business. Her business, of course, is the survival of the family triad, three disparate developing selves, their collective material possessions and one rented house, a mosaic business of eccentric tiles that fit together mostly because of her insistence that they must, grouted in place by a sticky mixture of necessity and dream. Only by focusing with myopic intensity, one imperative tile at a time, is it possible for the work to progress. Freddy proceeds by faith through days that put laundry next to art, art next to commerce; hustle nudges the dirty dishes, the skinned knees, and need for ethical instruction; visions of paintings never yet painted arise as she vacuums stray Cheerios from the dining-room floor; and after the bedtime story, the last bedside kiss, the need for sleep, and the desire to create wage their nightly battle for the few slim, dark hours that remain. She has a hundred jobs and no one occupation.

This job is a fluke, the result of bold but misguided extrapolation, some genius deciding that because she has a gift for drawing from life, she can do death as well. The premise was piquant, and the money isn't bad. "We hired the foremost forensic sculptor in the country to reconstruct the faces," Lieutenant Norgaard told her. "That work's all done, the best it can be. Three of the reconstructions matched up with photos of missing women, like we hoped, but we've still got these five Jane Does."

"So what exactly is it you want me to do?" Freddy asked.

"Just make 'em look alive," Norgaard told her. "Alive and up-to-date. Like you might have passed 'em on the street today."

The police call the Jane Does "Bones." Freddy is in the process of getting to know Bones 10, a white female, probable height, five foot five, her age, somewhere between twenty-four and twenty-seven. The modeled face on the table before her has all the arch unreality of a Nordstrom's mannequin and none of its charm. Her synthetic blonde hair and glassy blue eyes, the doctor says, are the results of speculation, not of science.

The doctor is wearing a brown sweater, fuzzy, over an open-collared shirt, corduroy slacks, and worn but well-kept moccasins. He's an academic doctor, not a medical one, and reminds Freddy of the moon because his face is round and lights up to varying degrees of fullness, depending. He's closest to full phase when slightly embarrassed. Probable height, six one to six three. Probable age, forty-five to fifty. Freddy met him only five minutes before and already knows a good deal about *him*. The skull in her hands is much less scrutable. The dome of the cranium is discolored in spots, and an evidence tag is tied between the eyeholes, across the bridge of the missing nose. The nose being cartilaginous, the doctor said, it decomposes.

The only bones Freddy's ever handled ere now have been in rib roast. She finds Bones 10 quite disconcerting. "Look at that smile," she says. "She knows something we don't."

"I've thought that, too," he says. "Like the bottom line is, there's only one joke."

"And it's not funny," Freddy says. "Why am I afraid my fellow K Mart shoppers will never look the same again?"

"It bothers everyone at first," the doctor says. "But you can't let your hormones get the better of your neurons. That's what I tell my students."

Freddy looks from the naked skull to the modeled head. "How can you tell how fat she was?"

"Educated guess," he says. "We weigh the bones. If we find the victim's clothing, our guesses are pretty accurate. This lady, unfortunately, came undressed. But we've got a pretty extensive data base. It lets us approximate the thickness of soft tissues at twenty different points on the face. I think it's probably fair to say Bones 10 was a mesomorph." The doctor tells her this with the enthusiasm she associates with tour guides and computer salesmen.

Not entirely sure she wants to know the answer, Freddy still can't help asking, "How the hell'd you get a data base?"

"Most of it comes from work on repatriated remains from Korea and World War Two. The army recruited a team of anthropologists to figure out who was who. They compiled a lot of useful statistics in the process."

"Oh," Freddy says. "I don't suppose you have any ideas on how to go about this?"

"You're the artist," the doctor says.

Of a hundred possible rejoinders, ninety-nine are negative. The hundredth is Carol's voice, telling her she can do anything. It's the sort of thing they say to each other often, and even if it expresses more loyalty than reasoned judgment, still, it helps. Freddy says, "Right."

"You did the sketches from the Villers trial, didn't you?"

"My kids have this nasty habit of getting hungry three times a day."

Mildly surprised, he's a new moon. Freddy sees he didn't take her for a mom. "How many kids?"

"Two." She likes him well enough to add, "My ex is an artist, too. The child support is pretty unreliable."

The little hump between his eyebrows eases, and Freddy feels a ping of pleasure. "I liked those sketches," he says. "They made me feel I knew the people."

"Thanks. It helped that they had great faces, his especially."

"You know, it was funny, but I always had the feeling I'd seen them on TV. You know, moving."

"That's the trick." She holds the skull aloft with her left hand and stares into its empty sockets. "Now, this is different."

"How did you happen to get into this line of work, anyway?" the doctor asks.

She doesn't especially want to answer, but she's flattered that he asked. "My dad was a newspaperman. He always wanted me to have a marketable skill, besides art, and I was a lousy typist. It was kind of a way to follow in his footsteps without stepping on his toes." It's a statement with a thousand small inaccuracies, most due to omission, but the doctor swallows it whole.

"Bascomb," he says. "You mean Nick Bascomb? He was your dad?"

"Still is," Freddy says. "Retirement doesn't erase paternity." More's the pity. "I suppose I ought to get to work," she says.

That launches him from his stool, a matter of long legs stretching out, assuming his weight. Uncertainty makes him a little awkward, as if he doesn't quite know what to do with those long limbs. "I have some things to do in the lab," he says. "It's down that way, if you need me. Otherwise I'll check back in a while."

"Fine. Thanks." She hears the door click shut behind him. Alone, she grimaces at her silent models. This is it, the inevitable sickening moment when she knows nothing, is nothing, when her hands feel like wood and her brain is mush and she knows she'll never be able to draw again. Her task seems quite impossible.

Carol says it's part of her process, don't sweat it, but Freddy knows it's Jack. It wouldn't surprise her to find out he had a doll that looked just like her, with pins in its eyeballs. After she left, he wrote a letter saying he'd put a curse on her. Later, of course, he said it was a joke.

"Some joke," she says aloud, addressing the skull, but Bones 10, quintessential victim, scorns Freddy's attempt to cast herself as one. Her clean grin mocks. Freddy is the first to drop her eyes. "Okay, so he didn't kill me."

Stark and disquieting as it is, the skull compels her gaze. Freddy makes herself look up, look in. The windows are uncurtained and unglazed, the house abandoned, and Freddy wants to knock there on the cheekbone and call into the vacancy, Is anybody home? Her questions echo against bone. What son-of-bitch evicted you?

Freddy feels a surge of anger, and a trickle of competence inside the surge. From her canvas bag she extracts her sketch pad and a tattered 1982 issue of *Cosmopolitan* she managed to exhume from the unintentional archive in Carol's basement. The Green River victims were mostly prostitutes or party girls, semi-professional. Freddy figures they took their grooming tips from *Cosmo*. She leafs through the magazine, studying the hairstyles and makeup on the models in the cosmetic ads, compares their vital eyes to the glazed ones of the reconstruction, posing once again that age-old question: What is the difference between the living and the dead?

Her eyes travel from skull to face, skull to face, her indignation an enlivening force, until she can imagine a young woman who resembles both, until her fingers get the message and her pencil touches down on paper. Anger and imagination fuse to make a line.

The fact is, she works by intuition. When people ask her how she does it, her answer is a shrug. She used to worry about that, having no theory to explain it, no way to break the process down analytically into steps someone else could follow. The worst part is the fear that this time, it won't happen. The fear comes every time.

And goes away. As soon as her pencil starts moving, it goes away. Something clicks in and once it does, she's okay. The doubt stops. Lately she's been trying to eliminate the ritual of fear, simply to accept her intuition as a gift and trust it.

Bones 10 probably trusted her executioner.

* * *

The doctor stands close to see the sketches, close enough to tell her he smells of Old Spice and not embalming fluid. Old Spice is one of very few after-shaves Freddy can stand.

"Very nice," he says. "She might have been in line next to me at Burger King."

"Do you like her better brunette or blonde?"

"I'm partial to dark hair myself," the doctor says. "Norgaard should be pleased to have it both ways, though. At least she looks more like a Seattle hooker than a southern matron. The sculptor's an odd old girl. Kind of a cross between a medical illustrator and a small-town beautician." The doctor laughs. "I will say this for her. She loves her work."

Freddy squints at the doctor. "Do you love yours?"

He lifts one shoulder, smile waxing broad. "It *is* pretty interesting, trying to outfox the Big Eraser."

"I never thought of death quite like that before."

"Decomposition, actually. Bacteria. It's life erasing life. The artifacts are clean and ..." the doctor pauses, then, shyly, "rather beautiful. I suppose you think that's odd."

"A little," Freddy says. "I suppose after a while you can see them as pure form."

Eyes downcast, the doctor speaks to his long hands. "Nature is the greatest artist, that's what I think. I enjoy trying to second-guess her secrets." His laugh has more disclaimer than humor in it. "Forgive me. I don't often talk about my work. You can see why."

Freddy's gaze tracks the movement of his hands, graceful but not calm. She finds herself wondering what they look like inside. "Same with me," she says. "Not many people find the relative merits of oils versus acrylics a subject of consuming interest. My daughter says I'm a real bore when I talk painting." The mention of her offspring makes Freddy consult her watch. "Speaking of my daughter, I ought to head home."

"Me, too," he says. "Would you like me to walk you to your car?"

Knee-jerk feminism almost makes her say no, but a glance at Bones 10, her open, hopeful face, changes her mind. She wasn't afraid of dark streets, either. "Yes, please," Freddy says in a small voice she hopes conveys her reservations.

The doctor flashes her a full-moon smile.

* * *

To the eternal, burning question—who cares for the children while mother works or, much less often, plays?—the answer now is Mrs. Patniak, a stout widow who lives in the basement, whose twin passions are crocheting and late-night television. Because it's possible to indulge both simultaneously, her productivity, as well as her familiarity with the talk-show citizens of the past few decades, is truly extraordinary. Her basement quarters all year long resemble a Christmas crafts bazaar. Antimacassars of every shape and pattern festoon the furniture like the webs of some mad hyperactive spider. She has many more potholders than pots, and everything from toaster to toilet paper that can be covered is, as if an object untransformed by her diligent crochet hook were damning evidence of dereliction. Since Freddy and her children have been her tenants, a matter of nearly two years, Mrs. Patniak has presented them each with not one but two afghans apiece, in colors and patterns Mrs. Patniak believes match their personalities. Paige likes the lacy yellow daisies and Chaz his choo-choo train, but Freddy has trouble accepting pink, green, and black Day-Glo zigzags as expressive of her essence. Carol, with her usual tact and wisdom, once suggested that the clashing diagonals are really a graph of Freddy's energy expenditures.

Sliding the key into the deadbolt, Freddy braces herself for the changing of the roles. If this is home, I must be Mom. On the sofa, Mrs. Patniak snoozes to the theme music from David Letterman, with Far Out the Cat snuggled in the vee where thighs meet torso. Freddy leaves her shoes beside the door and whisper-foots it down the hall to check on the children, first Chaz, who has the odd habit of sleeping with his face pressed flat into the pillow and his ass-end in the air, then Paige, who lies square on her back and has good posture even in her sleep. They'll never know if she kissed them good night or not, but she feels honor-bound to keep her promise anyway. She likes the sweet, vaguely metallic smell of sleeping children.

As soon as Freddy turns off the television, Mrs. Patniak begins to wake up. Far Out thunks off the sofa and retreats to his perch on the mantel, above an open heating vent. The sofa cushions have pressured Mrs. Patniak's curly-perm into a point, so she appears to be wearing an inverted sugar cone on her head and her eyes, slitting open reluctantly, are innocent and irritable as a newborn baby's. Once her vision is corrected by the thick trifocal lenses, she looks her age, and wary.

"How'd it go?" Freddy asks.

"The kids were fine. You?"

"Pretty weird. Did anybody call?"

"On the machine." Patniak doesn't answer the telephone, her own or Freddy's, after nine P.M., convinced that anyone calling after that hour is either a pervert or the bearer of bad news.

"Male or female?"

Patniak shrugs. "I was in the bathroom."

"I'll check it later. How was the monologue?"

"So-so. But then, I don't like disaster jokes. They're disrespectful."

"That's what makes them funny."

"Not to me. I say you should pray for the dead, not laugh at them."

"Well, I won't keep you," Freddy says. "You must be tired."

Mrs. Patniak gathers up her current work-in-progress, patchwork pastel, and stuffs it in her carpetbag, then rocks a few times back and forth to gain the momentum needed to achieve a standing position, groans on impact and wriggles her plump size-five feet into waiting pink Dearfoams. "You going back tomorrow night?" she asks.

"Probably. There's four unidentified victims to go. I'll let you know by noon."

"No hurry. I'm not going anywhere."

"You're a saint," Freddy says.

"Well, I wouldn't say that."

"A godsend, anyway," Freddy says to Patniak's back, retreating down the kitchen stairs.

The landlady's parting words waft up the stairwell. "Don't forget to lock the deadbolt."

In the dimness of the kitchen, Freddy smiles to herself. Mildly agoraphobic, Mrs. P. believes that behind every rhododendron bush and privet hedge in this modest, quiet neighborhood some dire menace lurks. The last time two alley cats indulged their mating urges within earshot of the house, Mrs. Patniak called the local precinct station to report a torture. The two policemen who responded to the call had the good grace to be amused.

As she returns to the living room to turn out lights, the red wink of the answering machine catches her eye, and she speculates briefly on who the caller is. Most likely Nick, in his cups. Divorce, retirement, and the death or reformation of his old drinking cronies, one by one, have left her father lonely and late-night philosophical. Freddy decides she isn't in the mood.

Setting the thermostat at sixty-five, she climbs the stairs to bed.

2

■ ■ ■ ■ ■

As soon as consciousness kicks in, even before she opens an eye, Paige listens for *Roadrunner* or *Mr. Rogers*, telltale evidence that Chaz has beaten her awake. The house is quiet. She stretches luxuriously, studying the stucco sky above her with its embedded glitter stars. It's all mapped out, in personal constellations—The Freddy Bear, The Corvette, The Snake. She locates them all before rising.

The next checkpoint is Mom. Until she's assured herself her mother is in place, Paige finds it hard to trust the day. Tiptoeing past Chaz's room, she heads for the stairs, pads up them. Sharp white morning light floods the loft and Mom takes refuge from it inside a cave of blankets. Paige sits beside the rumpled pink mound in the middle of the futon and not too much later, Mom's dark head burrows out, revealing one blue eye. Mom says "unh," which Paige translates as "Good morning, daughter," and retreats into her shelter.

"It's kind of chilly out here," Paige says. "Can I crawl in?"

Her mother responds by rolling onto her back, pulling the covers down just south of her chin and holding one edge of the blanket aloft. Mom's morning face is like a child's, with pink spots on her cheeks and mascara smudges under her eyes, no worry yet to etch in lines, and the advantage of being awake longer makes Paige feel adult in comparison. She slips between the flannel sheets and snuggles up close to Mom's warm right side. "How did it go last night?" she asks.

Mom presses an index finger to her lips and hisses, "Shhh. I'm trying to hold on to the tail end of a dream."

"What about?" Paige asks.

Mom squeezes her eyes shut tight and is silent for a moment, then says, "Damn. It's gone. I think Godzilla was about to propose to me. I was terribly concerned about what kind of stepfather he'd be to you kids."

"Godzilla's ugly."

"He is, isn't he? In my dream I found him very attractive."

"Do you think you ever will get married again, Mom?" This is a question Paige asks periodically, a way of taking her mother's emotional temperature. She gets the usual answer: "Don't hold your breath. Who would I marry?" Then Mom says: "How would you feel about me marrying again someday?" And Paige says again, as always, "I guess it would be okay, if he was nice."

Usually, that ends the discussion, with Paige reassured that nothing's changed, and Mom reassured it's okay if it does someday, preferably later than sooner, but this morning, Mom pushes up on one elbow and says, "Actually, I met a very nice man last night."

"I thought you were working."

"I was. He's a professor of forensic physiology, or some such thing. He's in charge of all the bones."

"What does he look like?"

"You know those pictures of the moon on grandfather clocks?"

"I think so."

"He looks like that."

"Ugh."

"I thought he was kind of cute."

"Did he ask you out?"

Mom gives her snorty laugh. "Uh-uh. He walked me to my car. That's as far as we got. But there's four more sets of bones to go."

"Mom," Paige says, in half-mock chiding.

"I figure around number three or four, we might get as far as having a drink."

"How come grown-ups always have to have drinks?"

"I suppose because it's hard to play tetherball in the dark."

Paige punches her mother's arm. "Seriously. I thought you didn't approve of drinking. Like with Grandpa."

Now Mom sits all the way up and hugs the comforter to her chest. Her face goes thoughtful, and Paige sees she's played it wrong, been too challenging and chased away the early morning whimsy that she loves. That, and she's in for a speech.

"A drink or two's okay," Mom says. "A kind of social lubricant. It helps relax you. Gives you something to do with your hands besides bite your nails. But too much drinking's a disease."

"Like with Grandpa."

"Yeah." Mom pushes back the blankets and starts to get up for real, but Paige catches hold of her hand, to restrain her. "I hardly got a snuggle at all."

"It's a new day, babe. Up and at 'em. Rise and shine."

"You were gone last night."

"So I was. Is Chaz up yet?"

"Nope." Paige tugs, and Mom lies back in her pillows. She rolls her head from side to side, neck exercise, then looks at Paige. "You're right, you know. There's no reason people couldn't get to know each other drinking Coke or Perrier water."

"Or hot chocolate," Paige says.

"Prune juice, Kool-Aid, apricot nectar."

Paige is still looking for a topper when she hears the small thud of Chaz's small feet on the steps. Gatorade dies aborning. Muss-haired, eyes pillowy from sleep, cuter in his Bugs Bunny pajamas than any sibling should be allowed to look, her brother appears at the threshold of the stairwell, embracing his blanket and sucking his thumb.

"Morning, Sweet Potato," Mom says.

Chaz takes his thumb out of his mouth long enough to smile his crooked smile and say, "Morning, Sweet Potato Mom."

In defiance of Paige's wish he disappear, Chaz advances toward the futon, his blanket trailing. Paige makes a big deal of consulting the digital and says, "Hey, Chaz. It's eight o'clock. *Sesame Street*'s coming on right now."

Chaz stays on course toward the other side of Mom, who

lifts up the blankets and stretches out her arm. Paige curses Big Bird for failing her. Chaz nests his head on Mom's shoulder. Mom says, "Aren't you going to say good morning to your big sister?"

"Good morning, Sister," Chaz says. He says it to the ceiling, his enunciation so precise it's weird. Chaz could say "psychological" perfectly when he was only two. Paige's feelings for her brother are a constantly alternating current: pride/annoyance, affection/loathing. Mom snakes her right arm around Paige and pulls both of them to her in an egalitarian hug so exuberant they almost bump heads. "My babies," she says.

Eyeball to eyeball with Chaz's happy smirk, Paige wishes she were an only child.

Freddy has a visual metaphor, not anatomically accurate, for the effects of coffee on her body. She brews it murky black and pictures it as a kind of killer cleaning compound, fast, efficient, and not altogether benevolent, that shovels the sludge from arteries and veins, then proceeds to dust away the cobwebs adhering to her central nervous system. The duster, as she imagines it, has feathers of steel. It requires something between a pint and a quart, most mornings, to get the job done. In whimsical moments, she's toyed with the idea of inventing an equivalent compound that could be injected into, say, the central-heating systems of houses with the mission of mucking out entire rooms. Sold at a price per ounce comparable to the eight dollars an hour her wealthier friends pay household help, the substance would quickly make her rich.

Now, halfway to the bottom of the second mug, her auditory sense grows acute enough that the bickering of her offspring over possession of the kitchen heating vent offends her. She turns from the frying pan, fork aloft, to growl, "Share or leave." Immediately, the kids begin to plead their cases. "Enough," Freddy says. "I don't want to hear." Turning back to the stove, she listens instead to the syncopated hiss-and-pop song of the bacon. Paige wanders off, leaving her brother crouched with his blanket in the hot airstream, and the quarreling subsides. As the bacon crisps, Freddy arrays the strips on toweling and watches the paper turn translucent with grease.

Just as she's cracking the eggs into the pan, Paige comes back. "Mom, you didn't listen to the messages."

Freddy is trying to harpoon a shard of eggshell with her fingernail. The whites are slippery; it takes three tries.

"Mom, are you listening to me?"

"No," Freddy says, guiding her catch carefully up the rim of the pan.

"I said," Paige says, "when are you going to listen to the messages on the machine?"

Freddy breaks the yolks with her spatula and swirls yellow through the pale albumen, then rains black pepper down on the marbled surface.

"It might be something important," Paige says.

"Sure," Freddy says. "The Disabled Veterans of the Spanish American War really *want* our outgrown clothes. They weave serapes out of the rags and send them to Cuba as reparation."

"Be serious," Paige says.

"Why?"

"Do you mind if I rewind the tape and listen to it?" Paige asks.

"Go ahead. If they want money, don't tell me about it." When the eggs are firm, Freddy dishes them up and hands Chaz his plate. "Use both hands and walk slow." Staring intently at his breakfast, Chaz makes for the dining-room table. "Paige, breakfast's ready." When their mealtime triangle is in place, Chaz says, "I want to say grace."

"Mom, do we have to?" Paige's first bite is already halfway to her mouth.

"It can't hurt," Freddy says. "Humor him."

Paige puts down her fork, lowers her head, and glares up at her brother. "Say it."

Chaz squelches his smile and drops his eyelids. "Thank you for breakfast, God."

Paige says, "That's dumb. It doesn't even rhyme."

Chaz looks wounded. Freddy says, "I thought it was very nice. Let's eat our eggs before they get cold."

"I think you should call the police back first," Paige says. "They said it was important."

"Who said?"

"Lieutenant somebody. I didn't get the name."

"Norgaard?"

"Maybe. Aren't you going to call them back?"

"Later."

"Mom, it was the *police*."

"Honey, I'm working for the police now. That's who hired me to do the drawings."

"Of the dead people," Chaz amends.

"Right. It's just a business call."

"At eleven-thirty-six at night?"

Freddy resolves to ask Lieutenant Norgaard to call during business hours. Then she gets up from the table. "Did you catch the number?"

"By the phone," Paige says.

Freddy picks up her mug and takes it with her to the phone nook, where she finds the phone number writ large and red on the back of an envelope in Paige's neat no-nonsense hand. She dials and gives her name and listens. When she returns to her place at the head of the table, both kids turn question-eyes upon her.

"Grandpa's dead," she tells them.

Miz Rupp is wearing her dessert suit, the vanilla skirt and jacket with the raspberry blouse and high-heel shoes the color of piecrust. She is the best-dressed teacher in the school. Paige would like to be like her when she grows up, not be a teacher but have her teacher's presence, which is crisp and delicious and feels reliable. Mom flirts with the ridiculous too much, she's always taking risks. Paige loves watching her on the high wire, admires her courage, but is always secretly terrified she'll fall. She senses that Miz Rupp's life, by contrast, is comfortably furnished with well-placed safety nets in soothing decorator colors.

It was unfair of Mom to make her come to school today. Not just unfair, but morally wrong somehow. Where could she be instead? That's what Mom said, then ran through the choices. Mom had to go to the morgue to identify Grandpa; she didn't want Paige to have to do that. So if she wanted to stay home, she'd be alone, with Mrs. Patniak fixing her lunch probably, and looking in on her. That sounds like an awful day, Mom said. You'll be much better off at school.

Paige isn't sure if this is true or not. Sometimes she slides into school, the dailiness of it, gets involved in long division or tetherball or boys and forgets about Grandpa, which would be all right if he would stay forgotten, but he won't. Every time she lets herself go into life, some strange shadow passes in front of the sun, some big tinny voice announces YOUR GRAND-FATHER HAS BEEN MURDERED. ATTENTION. THIS IS BIG. Then she feels guilty for forgetting. And sad about Grandpa. Aware that something extremely disruptive and difficult has happened. And Paige wishes it hadn't, because it's inconvenient and frightening.

So far she hasn't told anybody. When she got to school, Mandy and Katie and Joanne were talking about Kevin and Carla, and it didn't feel right to go marching up and say, "Guess what? Somebody killed my grandfather last night."

Katie was saying, "She thinks she's so cool. Her mother lets her go out on dates."

"My mom says I can't go out with boys until I'm fifteen," Joanne said.

Paige realized she didn't know how old Mom wanted her to be before she could go out. She remembered her mother's face, white and expressionless, when she told her and Chaz about Grandpa.

"Paige, I'm waiting," Miz Rupp says. When Paige focuses, she finds Miz Rupp in her waiting position, arms folded and one hip forward. Paige sits attentive and waits, too.

"I asked you to name the Mid-Atlantic States and their capitals."

"Oh," Paige says. "New York. Albany." She tries to envision the map, with its little dots and stars, but the picture seems blurry. Finally she makes out New Jersey, but can't read the name beside the capital-city star because the print's too small. "New Jersey," she says. "That's all I know."

"Did you do your homework last night?"

"Yes," Paige says. "I just don't remember."

"Please see me when the bell rings," Miz Rupp says, then lifts her eyes from Paige to scan the class. "Okay, who does remember?" Amid the thrust and rustle of volunteers, Paige slides out of the limelight into the welcome dimness of herself. Paige is sure Miz Rupp knows that something is wrong. She could tell. It isn't like Paige Winslow not to know. Paige shouldn't be at school today. Something big has happened. After the bell rings, Miz Rupp will ask her what it is, and Paige will have to tell.

3
▪ ▪ ▪ ▪ ▪

Freddy does the freeway on autopilot. So's everybody else. All the late-runners and the cowboys have gotten where they had to be by now. Traffic's moderate and conservative at ten A.M., being made up of people retired from or subpoenaed out of real life. Everybody's got time to spend and low adrenaline. Probably she's not the only one who isn't eager to arrive.

Northbound, there's a certain place the downtown skyline suddenly pops up, like the die-cut surprise inside a greeting card. This morning Freddy hates the trick, detests the city. The weather has been gray too long and the geometry of the streets climbing eastward from the bay is too eccentric. The placement and design of the freeway are an affront to the best principles of aesthetics and common sense. Everything—fire hydrants, people, parked cars, billboards—seems entirely too substantial and too other, as if reality protests too much its authenticity, but Freddy won't be fooled. It's one of those days she intuits the existence of another, less attractive version of the world beyond the scrim of this one.

She's angry, damn it: offended, affronted, mad, resentful, imposed upon, and PISSED OFF. She did not need this need this need this. She does not want to deal with death. The car is almost out of gas. The county hospital fronts on a one-way street the other way and she needs to find a cash machine so she can pay for parking and she feels bad about sending Paige to school today and she has to pick Chaz up from day care by four o'clock because Laura is going to the dentist to get—what was it?—a cap put on, and there are no fewer than three people ahead of her in line for the magic money machine and no available legal parking. A Filipino cabbie honks at her dallying, leans on the horn until she moves, forced to circle the goddamn block. She leaves the motor running in a bus zone. Her hands tremble when she feeds her card into the slit-mouth of the automated teller, and she hates them, too.

Bayview's a dump, scarred by the messy side of suffering —no carpets, no art, no blue-haired volunteers in pink smocks, smiling, just an etiolated informant with thin, pale-orange hair hunched behind the information desk, who doesn't even look up until Freddy says she's looking for the morgue. Who looks up then and says, "It's downstairs, way down, but you can't go there."

Freddy still can't guess the person's sex. She says, "I have an appointment. They're expecting me." The informer's eyes are an excessively pale blue, almost as devoid of intelligence as of color. What animation there is, Freddy attributes to hostility.

"Name?"

"Freddy Bascomb."

"You wait. I'll call." Mutters into the mouthpiece of a gummy-looking green desk phone, hangs up and says, "Someone will come up."

It's the coroner himself who does, a big square man with a mane of white hair that's yellowing like old newsprint, wearer of scrimshaw bolo ties and polo shirts with tweed. Freddy's sketched him while he testified. In court, waiting, he sucks on a half-combusted unlit cigar. Her impression is, he overcompensates for his profession, too jolly and hale. The heartiness of his handshake contrasts weirdly with the softness of his palm. A boozer's broken capillaries spiderweb his cheeks, a detail Freddy's never been close enough to see before.

"Miz Bascomb," he says, "I'm sorry about your dad. Damn sorry."

"It is him, then."

With sorrowful energy, Coroner Killgore nods. "I IDed him myself. The police didn't know it when they called you, but we were old drinking buddies, me and Nick."

It doesn't surprise her; when you're a drunk, the world drinks with you. Freddy nods.

Killgore says, "Nick was a damn fine reporter. Damn fine. The paper wasn't the same after he retired. These cubs." He pauses; she says "yes." The elegy resumes. "The police commissioner should've made him an honorary cop, all the dirt he dug up. He helped 'em put a lot of creeps away. Brave man, your dad. Nick could look the devil in the eye and never blink."

By this time they're in the elevator, a hospital double-wide, plummeting past subbasements. When they hit bottom, the doors moan open. The air down here's subarctic. Freddy wraps up in her arms. Killgore chuckles. "Folks think of hell as hot," he says. "It's not." He guides her by the elbow, down the hall. "Detective Ashford's waiting for us in my office. I keep it warm in there."

The coroner's office is filled with dry heat and stale cigar smoke. The space heater exhales white noise. There's an Oriental carpet on the floor, glass-fronted bookshelves, a mounted coho salmon, mutant-big, hung on the wall behind a cluttered dark-wood desk and a skeleton, no doubt authentic, dressed in scanty black-lace baby dolls. "Meet Eloise," Killgore says, with a nod to the remains. "And this is Detective Ashford."

Ashford pushes himself up from the cracked-leather office chair, nods without offering to shake. The detective is generic male, 50th percentile in every particular except, she hopes, intelligence. His hair's maybe a little sparser than average for early middle age. Freddy's pretty sure she's never seen him in the witness box. "I apologize for bringing you down here," he says, in a voice so bass she would have remembered if she'd ever heard it. "I didn't know until I got here myself that Dr. Killgore was acquainted with the victim."

"It's a good thing, too," Killgore heartily opines. "I'm glad I could spare you."

"I wish you'd spared me," Ashford says. He gestures at his feet. Freddy sees the bottoms of his pants legs are wet.

"I didn't know you were so squeamish," the Coroner says.

"I'm not. This is the first time I ever lost it."

"Is there something I don't know?" Freddy says.

The two men look at each other, Killgore smirking a little. Ashford grim. It's Killgore who finally speaks. "The corpse was desecrated," he says.

"Desecrated how?"

"The cranium was opened and the contents removed."

"Somebody sawed open my father's head and took out his brain?"

"Stole it, apparently," Ashford says.

"Wait a minute."

"My men searched thoroughly," Ashford says, a little defensive. "It wasn't there."

It hits her like the flu. Freddy plants both hands on the edge of Killgore's desk. Ashford slides a chair up to the backside of her knees and she sits down, grasping her kneecaps firmly to still the tremor in her hands. She didn't see it but she might as well have; her mind's eye pictures her father's head halved like a coconut, scooped out. "Did they take anything else," she says slowly, "or just his brain?"

Killgore thrusts a Styrofoam cup in front of her face. "Drink this," he says. "It's medicine."

It's whiskey, a generous shot. The fumes make her nose hairs prickle. She tips back the cup, fills her mouth, and swallows hard. A lump of heat lands on her stomach.

"His wallet was still there, with fifty bucks and all his credit cards inside. No sign of ransacking. Still," Ashford says, "we'd appreciate it if you'd meet us at the house and take a look around."

"When?" Freddy says.

Approximately three-twenty, most days, Paige plunges through the front door shouting, "Mom, I'm home," and unless she's got a trial that day or something, Mom's voice trills back, most often from the loft, "Hi, honey, I'm up here." Passing through the kitchen, Paige collects a treat—apples, cookies and milk, Doritos, whatever's there—and carries it upstairs. Mom stops painting and they sit cross-legged at the Parsons table and have a tea party. Chaz is still at day care. It's only twenty minutes, most days, but they're good ones. That's the routine.

Today she's slow to plunge, stands on the porch a moment,

feeling the coldness of the doorknob, while Far Out twines around her ankles, whining to come in. Today is off its feed, is coming down with something, is not itself. If Paige were its mother, she would make it go to bed. The house is too quiet. Far Out gives one high thin cry as he pushes past her and makes for the cat food. Paige puts a question mark at the end of her hello. There is no answer, so she asks again.

"Up here." The voice is so faint Paige is not sure if she hears or feels it. In the loft, the paints and brushes are neatly stowed, the drawing table's bare. She finds Mom sitting cross-legged in the middle of the futon, just sitting, and her hello smile is lukewarm—"Yeah, I know you're there" instead of "Wow, I'm glad to see you." Paige plops her schoolbooks on one corner of the futon and climbs toward the middle, until she's kneeling face to face with Mom.

"I'm home."

"I see. How was your day?"

Paige tilts her head to the right and raises her right shoulder up to meet it. "Good" would be lying. Even "okay," which means so-so, would be stretching it. Today was not okay. The expression on her mother's face, so mild and sad, is not okay. "How about yours?" she asks back.

"On a scale of one to ten, I'd give it a minus five." Again, that sweet-and-sour smile. "We ought to get Chaz now. Laura has a dentist appointment," Mom says, but she doesn't move. Paige wants to shake her, hard.

The hug they give each other then is sweet and frightening. Mom takes as much as she gives.

Carol's condolence casserole is dolmathes with egg-lemon sauce. She is that kind of friend. Even in a hurricane, she would not resort to tuna fish. Her fallout shelter, if she had one, would be stocked with caviar, sun-dried tomatoes, and Sara Lee. At first, the kids were suspicious of the grape leaves, as they are of any food more exotic than hot dogs, but Carol made them pretend to be rich jet-set cosmopolites dining at the world-renowned Parisian café Chez Carol, and they ate.

Now Paige is curled up on the sofa under her daisy afghan, reading, and Chaz nestles on Carol's lap, safe in its amplitude, desserting on thumb, and for Freddy this is the zenith of a nadir day. She sips the ouzo Carol brought, contemplates its loosening effect, says, "This is killer stuff," then winces.

"Loaded words," Carol says. "Bang."

"Isn't it in bad taste to pun at a time like this?"

"Why don't you write Miss Manners and inquire, my dear," Carol says, long voweled. "I'm sure she could tell you for what interval one is expected to refrain from humor following the violent demise of a close family member."

"The real irony," Freddy says, "is after all this stuff about learning to own your feelings, I find I don't have any."

"Wait'll the novocaine wears off," Carol advises.

Freddy sips again. "Actually, I lied. I feel guilty as hell. About my self-righteous little Only When You're Sober policy."

"It was still right."

"I wonder." Freddy holds up her half-filled glass and speaks to it. "The fact is, I understand the temptation."

"Forget it," Carol snaps. "There's no excuse big enough."

"And none too small."

Carol lifts Chaz down from her lap, plants him on his feet, and gives his bottom a send-off pat. "Scoot. Go torment your sister." He obeys. Carol looks stern. "Stop with the bullshit, girl."

"Why isn't there anything to ease *our* pain, goddamn it?"

"I hate self-pity," Carol says. "Besides, there is."

"One day at a time." Freddy says it with a whine of satire. "Life's a bitch and then you die."

"Oh, we're just a homily a minute tonight." Freddy hears the nasty edge in her own voice and doesn't like it. Still, tonight she's half in love with easeful angst and feels like kicking butt. Carol can take it.

Carol says, "Did you ever know anyone to embroider lies on their tea towels?"

"How about Home Sweet Home?"

Carol thinks about it, then says, "That's wishful thinking."

The phone rings. Carol reaches for the receiver but Freddy says, "Let the machine do it."

Thirty seconds of Freddy's small cheerful voice informs the caller she can't come to the phone right now but. After the beep, a male voice, also miniaturized, says, "Hello. This is Don Pankowski calling for Bones 12. The message is, she's eager for her makeover. We're here, where are you? Probably stuck in traffic, since you're not home."

Freddy grabs the receiver. "I am home. I forgot all about you. I'm sorry."

"Well," he says slowly, "are you coming?"

"No. Not tonight. I couldn't face another dead person tonight."

"Uh, are you all right?"

"You don't know, do you? My father was murdered last night."

"Jesus."

"That's why I forgot."

"I'm sorry. I don't suppose . . . Is there anything at all I could do to help?"

"I don't think so. We have a positive identification. It's really him."

"I don't know what to say."

"Me either." She hesitates a moment, then blurts it out. "They stole his brain."

"Whoo. I never heard of that."

"Neither have the police. They're hoping it's not the latest thing in designer crime."

"Let's hope," he says. "Well, I'm sure you're busy. I should let you go. I suppose you won't want to work on the reconstructions anymore for a while."

"I don't want to, but I will. I'll give you a call, all right?"

"All right," he says. "Good-bye. And good luck."

She hangs up and puts the machine back on answer. Carol's look inquires. "Would you believe I actually found him attractive, before all this started?"

"You mean last night."

"Yeah. Back when all that life stuff mattered."

Carol tilts back her head and looks at Freddy with speculation that ripens into one of her omniscient smiles. "The day they diagnosed my mother's cancer," she says. "I took a lover."

Freddy laughs at the delivery, feminist Mae West, then thinks about the message, tries to imagine the addition of a flesh and blood lover to the complexities of her life. "Frankly, it sounds exhausting."

"I think that's the point."

"Mom, will you play with me?" Chaz calls from the living room.

"I'm talking to Carol now," Freddy calls back. "Play with your sister."

"My sister is too sad," Chaz says.

"Come here," Freddy calls to him, and when he comes, wraps her arms around him tightly and strokes his soft boy-hair. The hug restores his smile. He lifts it to her, hopeful. "Will you read me a story?" he asks.

"Later, honey. In a little while."

Carol gets up and corks the ouzo, wriggles into her red down parka. "I'm going now. You need to put these two to bed." She takes Chaz's hand and pulls him with her into the living room, to the sofa where Paige is reading, and crouches down to address both children. "You two be good to your mom now, okay?"

Paige nods. Chaz says, "Because she's sad, right?"

Carol ruffles his hair. "Smart boy." She leans over and plants a fuchsia kiss on the top of Paige's head. At the door, she turns to Freddy and opens red arms wide.

The hug is soft as a feather bed and smells of Carol, spicy perfume and lemon juice. Freddy sucks up comfort un-ashamed. When they step apart, she says, "Thanks for coming, Mommy."

Carol grins and jiggles her car keys. "Good night, Mom," she says.

4

$\mathbf{F}$reddy sat at the glass-topped kitchen table, an unaccustomed guest. There was a formal dining room elsewhere. Beyond the tall glass doors Chaz, stripped to his diaper, played in the stiff trim grass with fallen lemons. Six-year-old Paige, life-preservered, bobbed in the pool. Freddy's detachment was surprising, comfortable, and so obviously reciprocated she was not even tempted to call her mother Mother.

Elsa sat, too. Even the coffee mugs were new. There was nothing in Freddy's mother's new house to remind either woman of their shared past. Elsa's husband was not only new, but young. Neither of them talked about the difference in their ages, but Freddy guessed it had to be at least ten years. While Nick was attractive in a high-colored, roughhewn way, her mother's second husband was handsome by virtue of a polished moderation, the kind male models have in upscale magazines, with features so regular and shapely they approached androgyny.

His work involved the cultivation of far-flung investments, his avocation, the nurture of exotic plants in a moist, trim conservatory that budded from the west wall of the house. In Peter's handshake, on meeting her, Freddy felt mannerly ambivalence.

From a lukewarm smile, cool words emerged. "Frederika. I've heard so much about you."

"You too," she mumbled. Next to her chiseled husband, Elsa seemed more distant and impeccable than ever. After Nick's vigor, his eccentricity, how could her mother be content with such restraint?

Elsa was, though. Over latte at the glass-topped table, she trilled his praises. "Peter is such a dear. Don't you think so? He was nervous about your visit, you know. He was afraid he wouldn't like you."

"Does he?" Freddy was mildly curious but didn't too much care.

"At first, when he saw how little you're like me, he decided you must be like Nick, so he disliked you. Then, when he got to know you better, he decided he liked you after all."

"Big of him."

"Peter saves all of his aggression for his work. He's very sensitive to other people's feelings."

Her mother's need for approval compelled her to say, "You're lucky." Freddy had forgotten how powerful her mother's needs could be.

"I am," Elsa said. "For the first time in my life, I feel lucky. And do you know why? Because for the first time in my life, I understand that we make our own luck."

Freddy tried to identify the source—Werner Erhard? L. Ron Hubbard? It didn't sound Eastern, even though Elsa was into Zen, too. Freddy equated the relationship of "into" to commitment with that of cubic zirconia to diamonds. Elsa scrutinized her face, looking for some sign of a conversion experience, but even in the interests of being a good guest, Freddy was unwilling to fake enlightenment. She did manage a nod.

Maybe to punish her stinginess, Elsa said, "How's Jack?" The visit was two days old already and nobody had yet mentioned his name.

Freddy had nearly succeeded in not thinking of him, either. Now she did. Physically, her husband was fit enough. Emotionally, he was deformed. Personally, she found him insufferable. "Jack's fine," she said.

From some dim archive, Elsa exhumed her skeptical reporter look. Once she was almost as good as Nick. Freddy was unable to decide whether it was sexism, maternity, or martyrdom that stymied her mother's career. Now, to earnest inquiries Elsa responded with stylish wisdoms in the once-a-week Living Section of the *Scottsdale Sentinel*, played goddess-guru to the spiritually inclined among the golf-club set. She and Peter patronized community theater, too. They bought Indian-inspired prints by Anglo artists at auction for charity. A garland of dried chile peppers hung near the stove and their tortillas were handmade by illegal aliens. "When was the last time you had a show?" she asked.

Anybody else might have taken it for backing off, a tactful switch, but Freddy recognized the assault for what it was. And Elsa was right, Jack was the problem. In that moment, Freddy realized how much she resented her mother rising from the ashes, preening her phoenix-feathers, while she, daughter, still burned. She said, "Give me a break. Chaz can't even blow his own nose yet. And he's number two."

"Tell me this. Are you happy?" Elsa tilted her head to the left, fixed Freddy with her resurrected gaze.

Paige's voice, addressing imaginary dolphins, rose from the pool, parted curtains of heat, and slipped inside. "Carry me to the land of the mermaids."

Freddy could only laugh.

Nick Bascomb, who could stare down the devil, had a problem seeing his only child, a daughter named Frederika, at all. Early on, the child developed a complementary disability of her own. Looking at her father, only at him, Freddy saw double, two distinct and contradictory images it was impossible to fuse. Simultaneously and side by side, she saw a kind, compassionate, principled man and a sloppy, arrogant, indifferent asshole. The champion of civic decency committed endless private crimes of omission and intent. The intrepid reporter who exposed embezzlers and challenged the hypocrisies of public officials could steal her mother's pride and kill her hope with no more thought than he invested in the act of breathing. Public Hero + Family Villain = Father. The two visions persisted, separate and coequal, on Freddy's warped stereopticon.

Even though he most often seemed quite ignorant of her

existence, Freddy came to understand that her father's behavior related in some malevolent fashion to her own. When she succeeded or something made her happy, he responded by getting drunk. When her drawing was selected for the city-wide children's art show, he got drunk. When she brought home a good report card, he got drunk. When she made a new friend or got chosen third when the class divided itself into baseball teams, he got drunk. The superstition reiterated and confirmed itself endlessly, then dogged her into adolescence. If a boy she liked asked her out, or she had a good time on a date, or a teacher praised her painting in front of the class, her father got drunk.

It never occurred to Freddy that the correlation, while statistically significant, might have been coincidental nonetheless; after all, her father did get drunk a lot. She never asked him if or why he punished her successes by getting drunk. In fact, they rarely talked at all. She scarcely knew him. When she was old enough, she left. She went to art school. After graduation, she married a young man who punished her successes by taking lovers. They divorced and she spent several lonely and productive years painting. Her work began to sell. Then she married Jack, who punished her successes by getting angry. At some point in the course of their relationship, Freddy stopped succeeding, in self-defense.

In the seventh year of Freddy's marriage to Jack, her mother, that model of forbearance and forswearing, that deep well of forgiveness, that queen of suffering, divorced Nick, moved to a city named Phoenix, and emulated one. She found an Alanon meeting, an apartment, a job, a friend or two, and, finally, a man. Postcards with pictures of cute desert rodents or Indian basketry arrived in Freddy's mailbox, reporting her mother's journey: "I love the weather," "I love the people here." After about a year, a super-deluxe-size card arrived one day, saguaros silhouetted against an Ektachrome sunset, bearing the message "I love myself."

This postal pilgrim's progress made Freddy, recently delivered of baby Chaz, unaccountably depressed. Jack surprised her with his grudging admiration: "I didn't think the old girl had it in her." He turned his grin on Freddy and saw her tears. "What're you crying about?" he wanted to know.

Freddy said, "The baby pulled my earring," but inside she

whined, God damn it, Mother, the only things you taught *me* about love were stoicism and self-denial. As if she were a tuning fork, the baby pitched his mood to hers. Chaz wailed.

Jack said, "I'm going now. Bruce Janowitz's opening. Then I'm having dinner with some people. Don't wait up."

"You said you'd watch the baby tonight so I could paint."

"I forgot," Jack said. "I promised Bruce. Some other time, Fred."

"When?"

"What do you mean, when? When I feel like it."

"When hell freezes over, you mean." It was Freddy's intention to have the last word, but Jack spat out, "Oh, fuck yourself," before he slammed the door. Chaz howled. Paige wandered in from the kitchen with traces of her peanut-butter-jelly dinner on her chin. Pointing a sticky finger at the baby, she asked, "What's wrong with him?"

"He's angry at your father," Freddy said.

Her mother moved from Phoenix to a suburb called Scottsdale. She learned to play golf. She got promoted from compiler of the calendar to counselor of the self-improvement set. With a maximum of taste and a minimum of fanfare, she married Peter. When Freddy came to visit, Elsa met her grandson for the first time. A few months later, she sent a real letter, typed, in a sealed envelope.

> Dear Freddy
>
> I am truly sorry about your growing up. Some of the fault is mine. I really believed I was doing the right thing, for all of us. I believed I could save Nick from himself.
>
> I know you bear the scars. There is nothing I can do to erase them. There is something you can do, though. Alanon has helped me more than I can say. I believe Adult Children of Alcoholics can help you. They have meetings, just like AA and Alanon. Please find one and go.
>
> Love,
> Elsa
> P.S. Part of the process of getting well is trying to make right with the people you have hurt.

"Right, Ma," Freddy said. "Sure thing."

Paige looked up from wriggling Tropical Barbie into a skintight sequined satin sheath. "What did you say?"

"Not a thing, darling," Freddy said. Carefully, she refolded her mother's letter, put it back in the envelope, then buried both under the carrot peelings in the kitchen trash.

In drizzle fine as sneezes and a good deal colder, Freddy, forcibly self-separated, not yet divorced, stood sucking on a damp cigarette outside a Quaker meeting hall and watched adult children of alcoholics assemble for their meeting. There was not much to be learned from their faces, which they kept pointed at the pavement, shrouded at the sides by collars raised against the weather. Their postures did not, she thought, look hopeful, but perhaps it was only the rain. Her own hyperkinetic pacing she attributed to a desire to prevent the live end of her cigarette from being sizzled out by one of the big drops that now and then torpedoed through the heavy mist. She knew, of course, that it was really nerves.

Every time another body turned off the street, came up the walk, and crossed the sparsely landscaped plaza leading to the door, Freddy imagined she would follow, but each time her body failed to succumb to her imagination. Her watch read 6:58. By 7:01 the traffic had thinned to a few runners, puffing and purposeful. In an interval between them, Freddy tossed her long-dead butt under a pale azalea and lit another cigarette. A big woman in a woven poncho, whose brilliant colors thumbed their noses at the sickly dusk, sailed up, head erect, and stopped in front of Freddy. "You got a light?"

"Sure." Freddy fished for her Bic, while the woman produced a skinny extra-long cigarette from the bright folds of her poncho. As they leaned together for the transaction, Freddy watched the cigarette St.-Vitus-dance toward the quaking flame. The woman inhaled deeply, then laughed a burst of smoke. "As you can see," she said, "I'm scared shitless."

Freddy had assembled a montage of small impressions—azure lids over eyes the size of giant almonds, shapely raspberry nails, expensive perfume, and tousled, sun-streaked hair, a ripe bright mouth—that suggested this woman was at least as beautiful as she was big. That she should be afraid seemed funny. "Is this your first time?"

The woman nodded.

"Me too," Freddy said. "I can't quite make myself go in."

"I drove around the block for half an hour, watching the parking places evaporate. I figured if I couldn't find a free one, I wouldn't have to come. Just as I was about to give up and go home, this old guy rolled his little red Rambler out of a place the size of half a football field. Right across the street, no less."

"I guess you're destined," Freddy said.

"What about you?"

"I was about to leave when you showed up."

"I will if you will," the woman said.

They did. As they followed Magic-Markered ACOA arrows, Freddy found it appropriate but not reassuring that the group met in the basement. A hundred people, more or less, sat on folding chairs and strained their attention toward one man up front in shirtsleeves reading from a sheet of green paper. Freddy and her companion rustled into two empties in the back row. After a while the reading, which was nearly unintelligible, stopped. The guy up front, who was trim and balding, with the mustached face of a friendly walrus, told them they had their choice of several sub-meetings: The Steps, The Book, The Struggle for Intimacy. "That sounds a little advanced," the woman whispered. "Newcomers," the man said. "That's us," Freddy whispered back.

They met behind one of those accordion-fold utility partitions, a circle of some twenty people on as many of the dimpled metal folding chairs. The man from before, the walrus, said, "I'm Jerry. I'm the adult child of an alcoholic."

Oldcomers dispersed among the new murmured in chorus, "Hi, Jerry."

"We don't use last names here," Jerry said. "We don't have conversations, either. Somebody talks, everybody listens. That's it. No talking back."

Freddy found her own surprise mirrored on other faces around the circle. Next to her, the big woman lofted her eyebrows.

"Tonight," Jerry said, "we're going to tell each other why

we're here. I started coming, I guess it was three years ago. I'd just demolished what should have been a good marriage. I was starting to hit the bottle myself. It's been a bitch," he said, smiling, "but today I'm a nicer guy with more realistic expectations of myself and the rest of the world. I even got married again, and I think I'm gonna make it work this time, God willing." He turned to the person to his left. "Okay, your turn. First tell us your first name. Then say, I'm the adult child of an alcoholic. We always do that."

The face to Jerry's left went pale. It belonged to a small man about fifty with werewolf eyebrows. "I'm Tony," he muttered. It took Tony about two minutes to say the next part and when he did, it nearly choked him. He tried to motivate the tears that washed up in his eyes by coughing harshly.

One by one, they crept around the circle, telling their tales of woe, from faces pale or flaming, all slick with sweat. Drops from Freddy's armpits rolled down her rib cage. It was at least eighty degrees in that basement and got progressively hotter as her turn approached. After each person spoke, there was a little silence and then they said in unison, as Jerry taught them, "Thank you, Tony," or "Thank you, Lydia," and the searchlight attention moved on, leaving the speaker to regroup and lick his wounds.

Freddy kept trying to think of what she would say when her turn came. Almost everything anyone said was eerily familiar, as if they'd read her diaries or watched home movies of her life. To flee was tempting. At least as often as she rehearsed her statement, she imagined a graceful exit. Slowly it occurred to her that not only was she hot, she was in pain.

Next to her, the big woman said, "Hi, I'm Carol. I'm the adult child of an alcoholic and the wife of a drug-addicted doctor. Home was always lots of fun. Basically, I'm here because I want to be thin and have a better sex life. Oh, and I have three sons."

She said it so gamely, with such fine irony, a lot of people laughed. "Thank you, Carol," they said.

With a deep grin, Carol nodded at Freddy, who looked for humor and found none in her life. Words themselves were evacuating fast. She managed to arrest her name before it got away. "I'm Freddy." The next part, being rote, came easy. "The adult child of an alcoholic." Now what? Who was she, and why had someone just yelled fire at the theater inside her brain? Her mother, her father, Jack, the kids, a cast of bloody thousands were all running around, waving their arms and shouting. The air was getting thick and hard to breathe. In the confusion, she felt Carol's hand touch, then gently squeeze her arm. "Oh, yeah," she said. "I am so sick of being a goddamn victim. I want the second half to be better than the first half was."

Apparently without sarcasm, they thanked her for sharing.

5
■ ■ ■ ■ ■

Freddy wonders what to wear. The only times she thinks about what to wear anymore are when she's cast out of character, required to do a brief appearance in somebody else's reality. Her wardrobe matches her own roles rather nicely. It has range. She can do anything from Lady to Punk, as long as you have a sense of humor. Clothes are a put-on, after all. None of her favorite outfits came off the rack ensemble. They're improvisations, all aimed slightly off the fashion bull's-eye. The best improvisations get codified into works of art, permanent for a season. Then she reshuffles, testing the look of this with that. If she were richer, she could afford to be less au courant.

She can do the soft-hard spectrum, too, send a whole gamut of messages: Protect me, revere me, admire me, wonder about me, relax with me, laugh with me, don't mess with me. Even, occasionally, want me. The two fashion statements she tries not to make are love me and pity me. Often it amuses her to mix messages. Color and shape are graphic principles, always operative. Surprise is part of the aesthetic.

This is what she *knows*, standing in front of the closet, letting her eyes rove the brights and neutrals amassed inside. Today's

role is a bitch, though. It's as if the old Sony in the living room
had suddenly extruded its tired melodrama into her real life,
or else she'd been transported by some malevolent inversion of
the video band into the land of lurid banalities. It must be
punishment for every hour she's ever wasted in front of a net-
work whodunit. Victim's daughter. A walk-on. Even if she's the
special guest star, even if she has an interesting disease or a
dalliance with the tired existential hero of the title, she won't
be back next week. You know you'll never see her again.

Downstairs, Chaz is still in the bathtub, directing a whale,
a pony, a dinosaur, a frog, and several other assorted hunks of
molded plastic in his own version of the Aqua Follies. She's
gotten as far as her pantyhose, and Detective Ashford is expecting her at ten o'clock. It was pure macha to claim she could
make it that early. Every exhortation of the self to speed produces the opposite effect, making time and will asynchronous
as Freddy rides a treadmill of endless small obsessions.

Freddy Bascomb, playing herself. What would she normally put on today? On a normal day, she'd just be getting
ready to paint, pulling on her sweats with the soft old matted-
fleece insides and the thighs colorful, paint-caked from where
she wipes her hands, no underwear, maybe some heavy cotton
socks if the studio floor was cold. She upgrades it to jeans, the
acid-washed ones, and a sweatshirt with no paint on it over a
T-shirt with just a little, heavy silver earrings, and her running
shoes.

"I want Bugs Bunny," Chaz chirrups from the tub, so she
finds the towel with the rabbit on it, snatches her son and towels
him briskly dry while he examines his pruny fingerpads and
plays with his penis, then, over his protests that he can dress
himself, stuffs damp and willfully uncooperative limbs into
sleeves and trouser legs.

"There. Where are your shoes?"

Chaz sticks his thumb in his mouth and twirls his hair.

"Think, honey. We're running late."

Chaz boycotts stress. He sings himself a little song while
she reconnoiters the premises, sometimes on hands and knees,
searching behind and under for his impish red hightops. Chaz
smiles at her ferocity. "They're playing hide and seek," he says.

Finally she spots a flash of red behind the third sofa cushion. Five minutes later, its mate turns up in the studio. She yanks up Chaz's wilting socks, stuffs feet in shoes, pulls laces, ties. "I want a double-knot, please." Freddy crimps a second bow in each. It's one of those days he wants to wear his jacket backward. She doesn't argue, just puts the hood up over his face and drags him through a dense rain to the car. While she unlocks the door, Chaz stoops to pick a dandelion from the parking strip. He presents it to her. "Because I love you, Mom."

Victim's daughter speeds slick residential streets, passing under ornamental fruit trees and huge full-bloom dogwoods tossing flower-heavy branches, snowing petals on wet grass. Destination—day care. She stops battered family import in front of a commodious, comfortably worn white house, races son up steps from curb to porch. On the front stoop, she kneels to kiss him good-bye.

Son says, Bring me a chocolate doughnut when you come back.

Impersonating the man of the house, an honest burgher, Detective Ashford opens the door, stands back to bid her enter as if she were a tradesman or some visiting official, updating the assessment, maybe, or taking census, which makes her want to say, Wait just a minute, mister. I grew up here. I have a history with this house, we've made uneasy peace. What she sees in the living room—the rusty fecal splatters on her father's oat-colored Barcalounger, on the alabaster chessboard; the beige fake Oriental, Elsa's last decorator splurge before she left, muddy with blood—makes her want to disclaim all prior knowledge of the place, to sever all connections, erase all memories, surrender title. The memories were mixed anyway. It is not a scene to nurture inner peace.

Freddy turns away, rests her forearm on the mantel for support. This way, the room's familiar.

"Uh, you want to sit down or something?" the detective asks.

"Not in here." Freddy makes for the kitchen, slides into one of the yellow pews that constitute the breakfast nook, puts her elbows on the table, and rests her chin on both fists. Ashford leans against the stove and leaves her to her deep breathing. After a while, she feels steadier, not good but better. It occurs to her that Ashford's been watching closely. Everyone is presumed guilty until proven blameless, that's the television way. Victim's daughter as suspect—it's a role within a role. Freddy wishes for a commercial break.

Ashford says, "It's a shock, huh." She can't tell from his inflection if it's a question or a statement. Probably some kind of police blotter Rorschach. Her response is probably terribly important. But as a question, it's rhetorical. As a statement, it inclines toward the stupid. On the other hand, maybe he's improvising, too. For all the policemen, plainclothes and uniform, she's encountered in her life, she's never had much sense of them as human beings. Maybe the man is just dumb.

He says, "You feel up to having a look around?"

"Sure." Freddy stands up. She misses the aroma of her father's bitter coffee, the small clatter of the pot rocking on the right rear burner. Next to booze, Nick loved his coffee. "What am I looking for?"

"Evidence of burglary," Ashford says. "I'd settle for evidence of struggle. Anything pertaining to the why question."

Maybe not stupid so much as baffled. Freddy nods.

"Do you know where your father kept his will?"

"He told me once. It's in the secret panel." Freddy navigates toward the front-hall closet. Opened, it's a domestic museum; the scent of mothballs wafts out of thirty years' worth of overcoats and windbreakers, parkas and raincoats, most Nick's but some hers, even a few of Elsa's from a long time ago. She separates the coats in the middle and pushes hard both ways until they part, revealing a small door against the back wall of the closet. "It's not really a panel. We just called it that."

It's spring-loaded. She pushes the right place and the door pops open. Inside, there's her father's strongbox and a carved redwood chest. She hands both to the detective, shuts the secret cupboard, and slides the coats back in place. He takes them to the kitchen table. There's no padlock on the metal box. "You want to open them," he says, "or shall I?"

Freddy opens the strongbox. On top there's an unaddressed business envelope, with a law firm's last-name lineup embossed in the upper left-hand corner. "This must be the will." She hands it to Ashford. "He left everything to me and my kids, unless he changed his mind."

It's okay with her if he did. Gifts from her parents always came wrapped in expectations, tied up in guilt. Avoid delivery. Open with caution. With luck, Nick's left his fortune to the Society for the Promulgation of Atheism or the Home for Yellowing Newspaper Personnel. She has no idea of the dimensions of her father's estate. He did advise her once an insurance policy would cover all the incidentals of his exit from polite society. "Cremation, probate, and the wake," he said. "I want you to be generous with the booze."

"Beer or champagne?" she asked him.

"Open bar," Nick said, "with all my friends attending."

"You better leave me a list of all your wateringholes, then."

"Anything within a ten-mile radius should do the trick."

"I'll just send invitations addressed Occupant to all contiguous zip codes. Or maybe take out a full-page ad in the *Times*."

"Being a little judgmental, aren't we?" Nick said.

"I don't like to think about you dying."

"Or drinking."

"That either," Freddy said.

"You score," Ashford says.

"I beg your pardon?"

"Your father didn't change his mind. There's a ten-grand CD apiece to send the kids to college. House, personal possessions, and remaining assets come to you."

Freddy nods.

"Let's see what else is in the box," Ashford says.

Freddy prowls, extracting the promised insurance policy, a bankbook and several CDs, title to the car. Nick's father's pocket watch is there, a smooth gold case with the profile of an Indian chief sculpted from Black Hills gold on one side, engraved intials on the other. Nick never carried it: too tempting to steal, too easy to pawn. One thing she had to say for him, he was in touch with his weaknesses. The last thing on the bottom is a small white jeweler's box. Inside, side by side on a rectangle of cotton, her parents' discarded wedding rings cohabit.

The image, so intimate and sentimental, temporarily short-circuits her defenses. Her throat goes sore with a sudden swelling. Freddy urges herself not to cry.

"What did you find?" Ashford asks.

Freddy hands him the little box. "My parents' rings. They got divorced."

"Tell me about it," Ashford says. "It's like dying."

Her cynicisms pop back up, mechanically resilient as the ducks in a midway shooting gallery. "You too?" she says.

"Thirteen years, three kids," he says morosely. "Nobody wants to be married to a cop."

With minimal encouragement, she guesses, he'll tell her all about it; divorce, like war, spins endless tales. Everybody does it. Everybody assumes you're interested, that the breakup of his or her marriage is somehow unique, the quintessential horror story. The vanity of veterans. Freddy wishes the law required mandatory lobotomies following both combat and dissolution. Still, it might behoove her to display compassion. He is a cop.

Anything with a question mark at the end will do the trick; she chooses, "Do you see your children often?"

"Jesus," Ashford says, his natural bass deepened even more by the weight of worldly pain, "No. I hardly saw them before she threw me out. That was one of her big gripes. So now it's even worse. Jesus."

"Yeah," Freddy says.

"She's got herself a new boyfriend. Sells insurance. A real nine-to-fiver, with weekends off. Safest job in the world. And you know what? I'm checking the bastard out."

Now, as the gift of numbness passes, Freddy understands she's been in shock. The scene in the living room impinges. The house does. Freddy looks at her parents' rings in their little white bed. She says, "Maybe you'd be better off just letting it go. Concentrate on your own life."

"What life? I'm a cop. Who wants to go out with a cop?"

"Gee, I'd think some women would find that . . ." What? She goes for "Glamorous. You know, exciting."

Ashford's laugh is the bark of a big dog, a Saint Bernard in the throes of self-pity. "I put this ad in the *Weekly*. The personals, you know. Law enforcement officer, mid-forties, seeks . . . Well, never mind that part. I didn't get a single letter back. Not one. I should of said I was a CPA."

The conversation marches toward quicksand. If he asks her out, Freddy can claim to be in mourning. "Things are tough all over," she says. "I wonder if you could tell me something. What are the chances you're going to catch the person who did this to my dad?"

"You bet they're tough," Ashford says. "The creep didn't leave us a thing to go on. Not so much as a flake of dandruff. We're talking a real smart creep."

"So what do you do now?"

Ashford sighs from the very bottom of his barrel chest. "A lot of legwork." He looks at Freddy. "So far, you're the only person with a motive we know about."

"Yeah. Except if you knew me, you'd know that money isn't a motive. I didn't do it."

"I know," Ashford says.

His words have a miraculous effect on Freddy. The lead cape falls off her shoulders. Her head feels light. "How?" she asks.

"Your alibi."

She didn't know she had one. Ah, Bones is her alibi. Freddy wishes she'd been exonerated by virtue of her good character, by unimpeachable evidence of her filial devotion. She wishes something would exorcise the guilt she feels. She feels it in her throat and in her joints, as neuritis and neuralgia, upset stomach, heartburn and itching. It feels like the onset of an especially nasty virus. Over-the-counter remedies are powerless against her guilt. "I wish I'd been a better daughter," she tells Ashford. "I made this rule. I wouldn't see Nick or let him see the kids unless he was sober. He wasn't sober very often."

"Nobody's perfect," Ashford says. "Everybody has regrets. Untimely death is like that."

Freddy gets it now. He's as cynical about homicide as she is about divorce. How many people have tried to tell him about their guilt? If only this, that. If only. Knowing she's predictable is not much solace. The if-onlies stand their ground. Freddy wants to go to sleep for a long time.

"About the why business," Ashford says. "We could use

your help on that. Friends, enemies, business deals. Anything that might make for a motive."

"Is there always a motive?" Freddy asks.

"I like to think so," Ashford says. "Maybe I need to think so. Without a motive, the world's a terrifying damn place."

6
■ ■ ■ ■ ■

"Hey, Paige," Ronda says. Of all the kids pooled behind her red patrol flag, Ronda picks Paige to say hey to. Ronda is a sixth grader, black, cool. All the cool sixth-grade girls wear miniskirts and have the beginnings of breasts. Some of them wear makeup to school. Some of them go out with boys who go to junior high.

"Hey, Ronda," Paige says, trying to sound cool. Cool does not jump up and down. Cool doesn't ask dumb questions. Cool rarely smiles. Paige can feel the admiration Ronda's hey directs at her from the first and second graders squirming on the curb. She is the kind of person that sixth graders say hey to. Paige hopes the flush she feels in her cheeks is invisible. Cool doesn't blush.

Finally the light changes and Ronda points her flag. The little kids spill into the street, papers gripped tight and waving in their grubby hands, Care Bears lunch boxes banging against their legs. Half of them have jackets falling off their shoulders, slips hanging down or shirttails that won't stay inside their pants. Little kids. Paige crosses slowly, with a cool stare at the cars stopped dead in obedience to Ronda's flag.

She takes the long way home because she feels like galloping. Her body wants to do something fast and funny. If she takes the alley, no one will see her. The Dobermans that live at the brown house with the deck charge, barking their brains out, but Paige trusts the chain-link fence. Standing on their hind legs, front claws poking through wire diamonds, the dogs are taller than she is. Barking, they bare those sharp teeth and slobber, they want to eat her so bad. Paige has the luxury of being scared without real danger. Waving, she gallops on, the old schoolyard gallop, front leg bent and back leg straight, dragging. Fifth graders don't whinny anymore.

Mom's home, upstairs, painting—three good signs. She says Hi-honey-how-was-your-day just like her old self. Paige considers telling her about Ronda but decides not to. "It was okay," she says. "What are you painting?"

Mom stands back from the canvas to let her see. At first all she can see is the clash—violent purple-red with violent vomit-green. There's one big blotch of yellow, slashes of black. "I know what it is," she says. "A picture of school lunch."

"Stand back," Mom says. "This one needs room."

Paige walks backward, away from the canvas. At about twelve paces, the colors take on form, the ruinous facsimile of a human face, more sickening even than school chow mein. "That's disgusting, Mom." Still, the image holds her; she stares. It's hardly a face at all, yet looks familiar. "Is it supposed to be Grandpa?"

"Sort of," Mom says. "It's more a picture of feelings than of a person."

"It looks like you had a bad dream," Paige says. She too has dreams sometimes where people you know in real life look different, where they melt or change sex. Mom says, "That, too. Actually, what set me off was, I found my high school diary."

She wags her brush at the Parsons table. A small treasure chest carved from some rosy wood sits open on it. Paige kneels beside it. "Can I look?"

"I guess so. Sure."

Paige burrows in—a dead rose, a whole sand dollar, a button that says APPLE PIE MAKES YOU STERILE and another one, with a picture, proclaiming JFK THE MAN FOR THE 60s, two picture postcards postmarked Crater Lake and Bend, Oregon, and signed Love (oh God), Michael. "Who's Michael?"

"He was my first boyfriend," Mom says. "The first boy I ever kissed. Which according to my diary was at ten-forty-seven P.M. on Friday, October thirteenth, 1963. We didn't know where to put our noses." She produces a small wire-spiral sketchbook and flips through pages. "Here." The book is open to a cartoon sketch of two nerdy teenagers, nose to nose, looking cross-eyed at each other, trying to stick their lips out far enough to touch.

"Did you ever figure it out?" Paige asks.

"It took a lot of practice."

"He wasn't very cute."

"He was okay," Mom says. "He turned me on to Mondrian."

"Mondrian is boring," Paige says. When she was younger, she liked to look at the pictures in her mother's art books. Her favorite painters are Matisse and Klee.

"I heard a few years ago that Michael had gone into banking."

Paige browses on. Mom's curlicue script snakes over whole pages and then gives way to sketches, some with captions, some without words. There are pictures of her cat, her friends, one called THE MATH TEACHER with fangs and crazy eyes. More Michaels, with a long straight nose and little dots she takes for freckles until she finds a drawing where they're labeled ZITS.

"You kissed a boy with zits?"

"It was that or go unkissed. Actually, he had fewer than most."

"I'll never do that."

"Just wait," Mom says. "If hormones don't get you, curiosity will."

Paige doubts it very much. Carson Daniels, the boy she loves, has spotless skin. Their first kiss will come, she calculates, the summer between fifth and sixth grades, probably on the way home from soccer practice. The sky will be pink from sunset, and it'll have to be a cool night, too, because in her fantasy neither one of them is sweaty. Paige has never played soccer before but plans to take it up this summer. She plans to be good at it, but not too good.

Near the back of her mother's sketchbook, there's a whole section of Dads, a few serious sketches Paige recognizes as her grandpa and a whole gallery of monsterish faces, cartoon and straight, guzzling and mumbling, belching, cursing, calling for one more drink, one asking, in a squished ballon, Freddy Who? The last picture in the book is a real Grandpa again, one that looks a lot like the picture they used to put in the paper beside his byline before he retired, only it's Xed out with gouged red lines.

Paige looks up at her mother, who stares at the picture of her father. "Did you hate your dad, or what?" she asks.

"Sure looks like it, doesn't it, babe? The thing is, I must have loved him, too. Why else would there be so many drawings?" This is Mom speculative, conversational, not knowing. This is how she talks to her friends, not Answer Woman or Mother Knows Best, more Who the Hell Knows and Your Guess Is as Good as Mine. That's how Paige takes it anyway, as license. She says, "I feel that way about my dad, too. Mixed up, like I don't know how I feel. I don't know how I'm *supposed* to feel."

Mom turns away from the painting and looks at Paige. "Forget supposed to, baby. True is hard enough."

The red pen gouges look like bleeding wounds. Paige has never drawn a picture of her father. Sometimes she is a little bit afraid of art.

Paige turns from the receiver. "Mom, it's Susanna. Can I play?"

Can Paige play? "Where?" Freddy asks.

"Her house. I'll ride my bike."

Can Paige play? Freddy feels uneasy saying yes. Isn't this a time the family needs to bond together, don't they need to talk or something, mourn, familially process death, retreat into a black cocoon, refusing to play? Paige bounces on one foot, impatient for her answer. She obviously wants to play. Freddy says, "Okay."

Into the phone, Paige says, "I'll be there in ten minutes. Bye."

"Change your clothes," Freddy says. "Wear your helmet. Be home by five."

"Five-thirty?"

"Five-thirty," Freddy says. "Wear your watch."

"Okay, Mom. Love you." Paige torpedoes toward the stairs, pausing to plant a kiss-in-passing on Freddy's cheek. Her noises

ascend—drawer scraping, toilet flushing, refrigerator recon-
naisance—then stop with a definitive front-door slam. The ensuing silence sounds as guilty—or is it anxious?—as Freddy
feels. Hard to name, that feeling. Something off-center. Colors
muddy. A morning-after feeling, or just before the fender
bends. She tries to think of what Carol would say. Ride it out,
probably, face it down. Jesus, woman, of course you're feeling
weird.

Of course she is. Witness the canvas, an adventure in gro-
tesquerie of the nails-on-chalkboard school, her chosen palette
the visual equivalent of a sinus headache, the brushstrokes
broad and crude, the whole thing spit up straight from her
subconscious with a kind of morbid fervor. Whether she'll like
it later when the paint's dry and the fever's passed remains to
be seen. Hideous as it is, she rather likes it now. And painting
it served her, gave her something to do with the manic energy
that isn't ready to resolve itself as grief.

The energy, now that's interesting. The same stuff, raw
power, no matter what the generator is. Sex, death, creation,
fear, so ostensibly different, so basically the same. Energized,
she paces. There's almost too much energy to use; she'd have
to paint and fuck and grieve and flee all at the same time, and
she'd still have some left over, for mothering, maybe, or scrubbing the tub. Since there's no one to fuck and she's not sure
what to fear, since grief comes in its season anyway, she might
as well paint. Painting, after all, produces artifacts, and artifacts
are products, and products might make money and money buys
freedom and freedom is painting.

Freddy looks at the painting on her easel, her father-paint-
ing, and winces, then smiles, a whole-face, whole-body smile.
If she keeps painting like this, she might turn into the new
Edvard Munch, Bosch-for-the-eighties, might be anointed
acrylic midwife of pre-apocalyptic end-of-century monstrosi-
ties. A dirty job, but someone's going to make his fame and
fortune from it. Dreams of a whole new career horizon out
before her.

Babies, blonde ones and brown, sprout from the deep
green pile of the day-care carpet, raising their faces to her as
if she were the sun. Among them she is big as a tree. As they

toddle toward her, Freddy drops to her knees. Little Karen swipes her car keys and makes off, jingling. Daisy-faced Annika doesn't stop coming until her nose collides with Freddy's breastbone and Freddy's arms reach round to hug her. Curious Daniel toys with her hair.

Chaz kneels in one corner, facing away and looking down at a jigsaw picture of Pleistocene times. Not until the stegosaurus is complete does he look up and see her. Then he leaps up, crying, "Mommy!" There never was a voice more happily surprised, a more joyous greeting. He does it every day. Daniel yields to his greater claim, standing aside to let Chaz tumble into Freddy's arms. "My little eggplant," she says.

Chaz wraps his arms around her neck. "I am not a eggplant," he says. "I want to be a sweetie pie."

"You can," she says. "You are."

"Your sweetie pie."

"My sweet potato pie."

Chaz burrows his face into her shoulder, making his uhhhhm sound. Freddy looks up to see Laura, drying her hands on a kitchen towel. Her smile is adult but indulgent. Freddy says, "Sometimes I envy you."

Laura sniffs the air. "Someone's made a mess in their diaper. Who is it, now? Fess up."

Freddy swivels toward the smell. "I think it's Danny."

"I changed them all, for good measure, not an hour ago."

"Not me," Chaz says. "I'm a big boy."

"I know," Laura says, "and boy, am I glad."

The truth is, Freddy isn't sure whom she envies most—Laura who spends her days with children, or the toddlers in her care. A chorus line of teddy bears frolics across the front of Laura's sweatshirt; she has curly brown hair and warm brown button eyes. Her house is snug and soothing, no harsh words or dark thoughts or big bad wolves allowed. Laura holds them at bay. Freddy wishes Elsa had been more like her. She wishes for Chaz and Paige's sake she were herself.

For a moment, Laura disappears into the kitchen, emerging with two of the fresh-baked cookies whose aroma fills the house. "Here's your snack, Chaz." She hands one cookie to the boy, one to the mother. "This is yours. I read about your father in the paper. I'm sorry."

"So am I." Freddy bites into the cookie. The chocolate chips are still warm and soft.

"If there's anything I can do," Laura says. "Anything at all." It is her standard offer. Mouthing the rich crumbs, Freddy knows now she would rather be one of the children. "I can't think of anything," she says.

"I'm praying for him," Laura says. "I'm praying for you."

Freddy composes her face and accepts the sentiment. It has always amazed her how often Laura prays, how easily she owns her prayers. At first she found it embarrassing. Now she simply says thank you.

"Mommy, let's go home," Chaz says. The melting chips have streaked his chin dark brown.

"If you ever need to leave kids here," Laura says.

Freddy says, "I appreciate it." She would probably say anything, just for the excuse to linger, but Chaz, who has been safe all day, is impatient to try his luck in broader venues. "Mommy."

"I guess we better go now," Freddy says.

"You have a nice evening." Laura says that to all the parents, every night. Freddy has always believed she means the words each time. She takes Chaz by the hand and leads him to the door, hoping Laura's goodwill extends beyond it, into the dangerous world.

Susanna's "normal" in that she has two parents, but her household feels no more reliable to Paige and maybe less so than her own. Susanna's mother stays home all day and makes a profession of being Susanna's mother. Susanna takes six different kinds of lessons after school. She has an expensive bike but her hair is always scraggly and the house is a mess—not messy like Paige's gets, when clutter periodically overwhelms a planned decor—but haphazardly, so you can tell nobody ever stopped to think about what looks good together or should go where. You can't tell how old Susanna's mother is or guess what she looked like when she was young. She and the sofa in the long skinny living room are in about the same shape. They both sag.

Still, Susanna's okay. She thinks she's a little smarter than Paige, maybe, and they both know she's not quite as popular. They're the two best readers and tetherball players in Miz

Rupp's fourth grade, natural allies more than bosom friends so far. Susanna has her own Apple computer in her room. The keyboard is sticky with Popsicle crud and a sweat sock swoons over the monitor. They're playing *Carmen San Diego*.

"Try Brazil," Paige says. It's Susanna's turn to punch the keys. In the game, you're an agent for Interpol, tracking cartoon criminals around the world. The sound effects and the animation are good enough you don't mind that it's educational.

Brazil is wrong. "It's gotta be New Zealand," Susanna says, keying. A tinny spurt of music rewards New Zealand. The suspect was sighted in Auckland. Departed by . . .

"Try freighter," Paige says.

After freighter they try plane. Plane is right. They go to Paris and catch the thief there. The program informs them they've been promoted to Detective First Class.

"Wanna keep playing?" Susanna asks.

"Naw," Paige says. "I'm getting bored."

"What do you want to do, then?"

"What do you want to do?"

"Let's get something to eat," Susanna says, but all they find, pawing behind half-empty cans and clumps of tinfoil in the refrigerator, are limp carrot sticks and half an inch of grape juice in a lidless plastic pitcher. Most of the shelf space belongs to Susanna's father's beer. "What's for dinner?" Susanna calls to her mother, who reclines on the sofa with a Harlequin romance held up six inches from her eyes.

"Burritos," the mother says. "Those frozen ones you like."

"You want to stay for dinner?" Susanna asks.

"I can't. My mom already said." Mom didn't say so, but she should have. Aren't families supposed to stick together when people die? Suddenly Paige feels disappointed, even a little bit offended, that Mom let her come at all. She looks at her watch. "I better go now."

On the way out, she remembers to say thank you to the mother, who looks surprised by the courtesy. "See you tomorrow, Susanna. Thanks." Susanna waits outside until her helmet is strapped on, then disappears. Paige mounts up, catches the pedal, and swoops into the street, into the pale gold of a late afternoon parting of gray clouds. Most of the morning rain has lifted from the pavement, leaving it pale gray, blotched with puddles. Perfume, sweet and rank, rises from blossoms in the street-side gardens, from jagged patches of seeding weeds in the parking strips she passes on her way home. From two streets up comes the staccato swoosh of grown-ups driving the arterial home. She climbs the two-block hill in lowest gear, enjoying the exertion. Home draws her with the magnetism of true north. She needs to be there.

7

"The police know squat," Freddy says.

One of Sandy's huge, anarchic eyebrows elevates into a circumflex over one pebble-bright brown eye. "Surprised?"

"Disappointed."

"I'm surprised your illusions have survived this long, my dear. You must watch a lot of television."

"It's a shortcoming of my generation. All the most attractive actors play cops or detectives."

The waitress approaches on crepe soles, squinting disapproval. What right does Freddy have to date a man *her* age? "Drinks?" The inquiry sounds grudging.

"Half a carafe of the Fumé Blanc, please," Sandy says.

"One glass or two?"

"Two."

The waitress pads off in her orthopedic shoes.

"This is lunch, Sandy," Freddy says.

"So it is. Wine with lunch aids the digestion. It's hardly dissolute. Unless, of course, you're wrestling the demon yourself."

"I'm gun-shy," Freddy says. "It's supposed to be an hereditary demon."

Sandy shakes his head, still shaggy and massive but no longer sandy. The cantankerous hair has turned dead white. "With you young people becoming so cautious and sensible, it's a mystery to me how a man seduces a woman anymore."

"To me, too."

"Come now. You can tell your Uncle Sandrew."

"There's nothing to tell."

"I find that hard to believe."

"Thanks, Sandy. Actually, I've begun to believe maybe the drought's been self-inflicted. A vacation from temptation while I sorted some things out."

"And?"

"And as of two days ago, I was feeling mildly reborn."

The wine arrives on catty little feet, is set down with a special glare for Freddy, who purrs thanks. "Ready to order?" the waitress growls.

"Come back in ten minutes," Sandy says. He fills their glasses. "There's nothing like a death in the family to complicate rebirth."

"Especially a violent death."

Sandy raises his glass. "Take it from an old man, Frederika. The fact is more important than the cause."

"I wonder," Freddy says. The wine is tart and Sandy charming. As a little girl, she had an unabashed crush on him. Maybe that was a child's subliminal insight into grown-up realities. Sandy was her father's best friend. He adored her mother. "I wonder, for instance, if you and Elsa were ever lovers."

Two beats and a flicker later, he comes back with "It would be ungentlemanly in the extreme for me to satisfy your curiosity."

"Is that a yes?"

"How is your mother?" Sandy counters.

Freddy gives up the interrogation. "Content, I think. And distant."

"I gather you don't mean that only in the geographical sense."

"No. I'm afraid I remind her of things she'd rather leave behind. Nick, for instance. If she could have her grandchildren without their mother, she'd be in heaven."

"You are your father's daughter," Sandy says. "Who could have guessed the female version would be so appealing?"

"Is that a compliment?"

"An observation. And a mystery. Your eyes, of course, come from your mother."

"My eyes are my own. As far as I know, she still has hers."

Sandy chuckles. "What is it they call the female equivalent of oedipal rivalry?"

"Not guilty," Freddy says. "We never competed for Nick. In fact, sometimes I felt like she was offering me to him somehow, not sexually exactly, but as a kind of surrogate." She's said this to Carol and no one else. She has no way of knowing if it's true. Sandy was there and might.

If he does, he isn't telling. He swaddles the notion in a tender sigh and says, "Poor Elsa. She deserves her normal life." Something in Freddy, not the noblest part, protests his solicitude. *But what about me?* Sandy says, "Your mother always felt guilty about bringing a child into a less than perfect marriage. She hoped a child would help your father stop drinking."

"Which makes me a failure from the day I was born." The words zing out, shot from guns. And they do sound bitter, yes indeed. The bullet ricochets off Sandy's tie clip and pierces Freddy's heart, its natural and deserved home. It would be bad manners to bleed to death right here. Freddy decides not to. She decides to stop bleeding this very instant.

"You hungry yet?" the waitress asks.

Sandy orders for them both, attentively, with charm. The waitress unbends a bit, exempting him from scorn. That puts all the sins on Freddy's tab. Her spirits dive. When Sandy turns back to her, he asks what's wrong. Not wanting him to think she's petty, Freddy picks another cause. "Guilt, I suppose. I was awfully hard on Nick these last few years."

Sandy laughs. "He told me. He didn't mind. In fact, he admired your spine."

"You're not just saying that to absolve me?"

"I'm no creative writer. Strictly a who-what-where man. It was the last time we played chess. He was musing what might have been if Elsa had ever put her foot down the way you did. That was just before he maneuvered me into checkmate."

"It looks like he was playing chess with whoever killed him," Freddy says.

"We hadn't played for weeks. I swear it."

"There weren't any fingerprints on the chessmen."

Sandy cocks his big head to the left, an inquisitive posture. "What did the police say?"

"Nada."

"Who's handling the case?"

"Ashford. Stocky, about my age."

"Bullnecked fellow," Sandy says. "He made his mark in riot control in the late sixties."

"I don't think he thinks he's going to solve this one."

"All their bright bulbs are on Green River. Ashford's just minding the store."

"I keep asking myself if it matters. To know."

"And?"

"Knowing the doer won't undo the deed. I understand that. And I don't think I want vengeance. I have no desire to be present at a public execution. But."

"But?" Sandy's big head thrusts forward, shaggy serif on the interrogatory form.

She pauses, herding a straggle of half-thoughts under the umbrella of but. "There's curiosity," she says. "In a way, it's the same kind that makes you slow your car down when you pass a wreck. How mangled are the bodies? How sick can someone be? But that's not all of it."

"No." Now Sandy is a comma, rocking through the pause.

She studies a patch of green Formica tabletop, three inches square. Thin clouds of white swirl through it, paling the intensity of green. "I feel as if, if I never find out who did it, I'm always going to feel like I did it myself. As if some failure of my love makes me the killer." Freddy speaks slowly, careful of the power and slipperiness of words. "I do feel guilty. Guilty of unspeakable crimes." She looks up, into Sandy's watching. "Does that make sense?"

"It does." He nods in brief, emphatic bobs. "I don't know why it does, but I understand. I've been feeling something similar myself. If not precisely guilty, at least accused."

Freddy says, "Person or persons unknown includes me. It includes everybody. A conviction absolves me."

Now Sandy's nod ticks off a slower rhythm, contemplative.

Freddy says, "Do you suppose you could learn anything about a person by how he plays chess?"

"I was going to ask you if the board was still set up."

"I'm not sure if the fingerprint people put the pieces back as they were or not. I was reeling."

Sandy says, "It wouldn't hurt to take a look."

The waitress delivers lunch as if it were an insult. "Ketchup?" she says.

The package plops down onto the pink terrain where Paige is doodling intersecting cubes. By the time she looks up, all her neighbors are focused front and center, and there's no telling whose hand dropped it. Miz Rupp is talking about Mexico. Paige sits up straighter and looks alert. At the same time, she works the note slowly across her notebook to the edge of her desk, then scoops it into her lap. Above her desk, the very model of an attentive student, she stares intently at Miz Rupp. Below it, her fingers open out a dozen crazy folds and smooth the creases on her lap.

Now she has to be patient. Miz Rupp is no one's fool. Paige waits and waits, until her counterfeit attention goes to sleep and starts to prickle like a foot does when you sit on it too long. She digs her thumbnail into her palm to keep from fidgeting. Finally, Miz Rupp turns away from the class to pull down the windowshade map of the Americas, and Paige drops her eyes.

"Dear Page, How are you? I am fine. Rup is prety boreing. Are you going to Trasy's party Saterdy? I am. Will you be my date? from Carson."

Under his name are two blank boxes, labeled YES and NO. His letters are fat and ragged, no two the same size, and the pencil lines smudge, darkening the creases, as if his hands were sweating when he wrote the note. The awfulness of Carson's spelling blunts the thrill of the invitation a little, not too much. Paige is the best speller in Miz Rupp's room, but Carson is the cutest boy. She's had a crush on him since third grade, when he pushed her in the lunch line and they both got detention, Paige for pushing back. It was the first and last time in her school career she was detained.

Paige can feel Carson looking at her from his back-row

seat, even though she doesn't look at him. She feels as if the whole class is looking at her. When Miz Rupp turns to the map, searching for Popocatepetl, Paige eases the note back on the desk top and quickly draws a third box below the other two and calls it MAYBE. Adds, in legitimate parentheses, (I HAVE TO ASK MY MOM.) Miz Rupp locates the volcano, and Paige has to wait a long time for another geographical distraction before she has a chance to refold the note and put TO CARSON on it in her neatest letters for the pure joy of writing his name.

Justine in the seat behind her is the mailbox where Paige posts her letter. Once it's entrusted to the mail chain, Paige turns real attention to the teacher.

"So the gods took pity on the two lovers, and made them into mountains, so they could be forever in each other's sight," Miz Rupp says. "That's how the legend goes. It's a very romantic story." For a beat, she smiles, then rakes her gaze across the class. "Does anybody here remember any other myths like that?"

Paige tries hard to remember a story from the library book of myths she read at the beginning of the year. Somebody got punished for looking back. It was a love story. Susanna's hand skyrockets up. Trust Susanna. Hers is the only hand. "Yes, Susanna," Miz Rupp says.

"Echo and Narcissus."

"Now there's a love story with a difference," Miz Rupp says. "Would you like to tell us about it, Susanna?"

Much to Paige's satisfaction, the recess bell nips off Narcissus. As soon as the rule of silence lifts, Justine is twitching by her side. "What did he say?"

"It's kind of personal," Paige says.

Justine, who is very popular but not too smart, links her arm through Paige's and pulls her toward the door. She says, "You can tell me. I'm your best friend."

"It was a match," Sandy says.

"His opponent was pretty good, then?"

"Nick could have deep-sixed most recreational players in this many moves."

"Unless he was being kind."

"I never knew Nick to show an opponent mercy. Not at chess."

"He used to let me win sometimes," Freddy says.

"That's different. Besides, this guy didn't need any breaks."

"What makes you think it was a guy?"

"Sexist intuition," Sandy says. "Women usually don't get this good."

Freddy says, "You're right. That is sexist. Are you telling me we can eliminate fifty-one percent of the population on the grounds of mental ineptitude?"

Sandy hedges back a step or two, pretending to shrink from feminist retribution. "It's a psychological question, not intellectual. The experts claim that the chessboard reifies oedipal rivalry. Almost without exception, the great masters learned the game from playing with their fathers." He splays his hands out, palms up, disclaiming responsibility for the hypothesis. "Women don't get obsessed enough to become masterful players because the game just doesn't feed their own particular neuroses well enough. That's how the theory goes."

"Jesus, Sandy."

"I'm not saying it's true. Besides, we don't even know for sure this is the game they played."

"Oh, right," Freddy says. "You mean to suggest that somebody would actually commit a murder and then set up a chess game to make him or *her* self look good? I mean, would you do that?"

"I wouldn't open a man's skull with a hacksaw," Sandy says. "I wouldn't kill another human being, and I was in the war."

Freddy remembers the stories, Nick's version. Both he and Sandy invoked the ghosts of Quakers in the family closet; they were legitimate COs, still working at the *Times* when most of their buddies were already in uniform, still making money, building reputations. "Feeling," Nick said, "guilty as hell.

"One night we went down to Chinatown to get some egg rolls after work, have a few drinks. Place called Tai Tung. They used to gamble in the back room and the police'd look the other way. Anyway, we got to drinking, got to talking, and in those days, every conversation led straight to war.

"After a while, Sandy says, 'You know what? I feel like shit.'

"I told him I felt like shit, too.

" 'That bastard Hitler,' Sandy says.

" 'Damn right. Him I could kill.'

" 'And feel good about it.'

" 'Amen to that. And you know what else?'

"Sandy says, 'What?'

"And I said, 'I figure this is our war. Our turn. I hate to let it pass me by.'

" 'I hear you,' Sandy said. 'I want to be a hero. At least to know I'm not a coward.' "

" 'Shit, is that what we are?'

"Sandy says, 'I keep imagining telling my grandkids Grandpa spent the war on his fat ass behind a news desk. On the other hand, I don't want to tell 'em I was a fucking killer.'

"Around midnight, we made a pact. We'd go as medics. That solved our problem. We spent the night with a couple of Chinatown whores and a couple fifths of Jack. Next morning we were first in line at the recruiter's. Those boys signed us up fast, before we had a chance to sober up."

Sandy says, "It does seem outrageously arrogant. On the other hand, it's been clear from the start we're not talking about the National Mental Health poster child here."

"Yeah," Freddy says. The egregious mental aberrations of Person(s) Unknown make her uneasy, queasy. She doesn't even want to understand. Even the Green River Killer, butcher of all her Bones, seems more congenial, maybe because she's certain she is innocent, incapable of his crimes. As a woman, she might be his victim. She is not implicated in those deaths.

Sandy says, "Are you all right? You look a little pale."

"Is that all? Good. Because I'm feeling green." Freddy makes herself look up, beyond Sandy, at her father's chair. The stains are historical now, blood dried and oxidized on corduroy, no longer shocking. Still, the room feels shocked, the air unsettled by what it's witnessed. "I hate being here," she says.

"I know. If you can hang on just a little longer, I'd like to copy this board." He pulls out his ubiquitous newsie tools, a pocket-size wire-spiral notebook, a ballpoint pen. "Okay?"

She nods.

"It won't take long. You could wait in the car, if you'd rather."

"I'll be all right. I suppose it wouldn't hurt to survey my domain. All this"—the sweep of her arm encompasses the house and all its furnishings—"is mine now." Both her voice and the gesture trail off for want of joy. Sandy kneels beside the coffee table and, using his thigh for a desk top, begins to draw the chessboard grid. Freddy plops down on the love seat and tries to inventory her inheritance. There's a decorator Kleenex box with a New England winter scene. One set of fireplace bellows with a bad case of emphysema. Brass candlesticks gone dull with grunge. What there is is too damn much stuff.

Freddy's own house is deliberately small and sparely furnished. All her life she's had a marked distaste for owning *things*. To all her father's other crimes, she adds now his posthumous generosity. What is she going to do with all these *things*? She feels unfairly, unspeakably encumbered, as if for a last joke, Dad had made her lifetime curator of the British Museum, an unresignable position, as if he'd chained an elephant to her leg. Visions of dumpsters dance in her head. A little kerosene, a flick of flame. She thinks garage sale.

Nick's library, the leavings of an omnivorous bibliophile, should be easy to give away after she's chosen a few keepers for herself. But who would take her father's papers? His daunting papers, reams and reams of them—that they survived his manic weedings, were spared the not-infrequent editorial bonfires is proof they were important, at least to him. Freddy feels incapable of the long culling, the desecration of his files. Nick's filing system was desultory, a scheme of ragged piles assembled on highly personal perceptions of consanguinity. As his daughter, she knows just enough of his obsessions to make the task beyond herculean. She needs a ruthless sorter, needs to rent-an-illiterate, immune to respect, who can discard without reading and without prejudice. Maybe Chaz could help.

Agile for an old man, Sandy rises from his crouch, snaps his notebook shut, pockets his pen. "That's done," he says briskly.

Freddy rises, eager to depart, but Sandy says, "I think we should take a look around his office. What do you say?" He takes her arm as a date might, protective and willful both, and tries to steer her toward the den, but Freddy brakes, with a strength of resistance she didn't know she felt. "Come on," Sandy says. "It'll be easier with company."

Emotions and body revolt conjointly. She will not budge. Sandy unhands her. The elevation of his eyebrows wonders why. Freddy shakes her head from side to side. "I don't want to." Her tears start softly, unexpected as a spring rain. She tries to suck them back. Sandy opens his arms to hold her, and she refuses that, too. Sandy says, "Let it come."

"No."

Sandy says, "Suffering denied becomes suffering eternal. An old man's wisdom."

"You sound like a Zen master. The sound of one hand clapping and all of that."

Sandy says, "I cracked that one when you were still in diapers. It's an amputee applauding an especially fine performance of *Waiting for Godot.*"

And Freddy weeps.

8
■ ■ ■ ■ ■

True friends know that distress has duration; one flower, one phone call, one lunch are only Band-Aids. True friendship is like a plaster cast, holding form until the bones, the frayed ends of the soul, knit up again. Carol is not a one-casserole friend, oh no. She has staying power, she's curious and opinionated, she is *involved*, so that Freddy's melodrama becomes a subplot of her own. Right now, she's center stage, playing The Voice of Reason in a highly dramatic scene called Paige Hysterical.

In a movie, having passed through the alchemies of the editing room, the scene would, finally, be short, beginning at the very peak of Paige's raging, proceeding through epiphany to resolution in a few minutes' time. In the rough cut of real life, Paige remains stubbornly immune to the truth her elders redundantly reveal. The scene goes on and on. Chaz watches from the sidelines, sucking hard on his thumb, too bedazzled by the pure fury of his sister's performance to take sides.

Freddy sits head in hands at the dining-room table, taking time out. The fact is, she's written so many checks against her energy account the past few days she's right next door to overdrawn. There's enough left to cover doing the dishes and an hour's talk with Carol before she collapses on the futon to make a sleep deposit, but Paige is asking too much. So Freddy watches, too, enclosed inside a shiny bubble of detachment, while her daughter and her friend duke it out and the scene creaks slowly on toward climax.

Carol uses her size to advantage, claiming her full height and her biggest, wisest voice to say, from some place deep in the diaphragm, "Paige, life isn't fair."

This is obviously not what Paige wants to hear. What Paige wants is not philosophy, but her own way. Nothing else will do. She wants to go to Tracy's party with Carson on the night of her grandfather's memorial service. Freddy understands she wants this badly. Paige is normally a model of self-possession. She's probably more considerate, more cooperative, more mature than your average ten-year-old. This temper, this intensity, this propensity for high drama shows itself only rarely, and thank god. The girl has talent.

First, fists clutched, eyes scrunched, she emits a high shrill scream which eventually resolves into words: I HATE YOU.

Freddy wonders how Carol will respond. If she trusted Carol less or were less tired, she'd be angry at her daughter on behalf of her friend and intervene, demanding that Paige apologize and go to her room. What Carol does is to shrug with grand indifference and sit down at the table facing Freddy, with her back to Paige.

"So when does your mother's plane get in?" Carol asks Freddy.

Freddy says, "One-thirty. Of course, Jack doesn't land until three. And did I mention that they cordially detest each other?"

Paige moves until she stands between them. Fat tears roll down her cheeks. "I know you don't love me," she accuses mournfully. "You wish I'd never been born."

This hurt a lot the first time Freddy heard it, but now her bubble is surprisingly durable, and the poison arrow fails to pierce her heart. It does make her sigh. At this moment, Paige probably believes wholeheartedly that what she says is true. She must feel terrible, and Freddy's sorry, really, but she just doesn't have the energy to play the scene; the last time she did it took twenty minutes, at least, ardently protesting innocence and love, to reach the desired tearful reconciliation.

While Paige trains a gaze of chin-out challenge on her mother, Carol raises her eyebrows at Freddy and touches her index finger to smiling lips. Paige doesn't see Carol, but does catch the flicker of a smile in her mother's eyes and realizes it's not meant for her. In danger of losing attention, she plants her hands on her hips and gives it her best shot. "You don't care about me. You never have. I wish I was dead."

Freddy looks quickly to Carol's smile for courage, then fixes her eyes on her daughter with what she hopes looks like compassion. Paige drops her arms to her sides, her shoulders set stiff at first, then slowly wilting. The tears roll on. Freddy finds this immensely more effective than any words, can almost feel the pounding of her daughter's heart and the raw throb in her throat and the high surf of adrenaline that's crashing through her veins; the storm, even if it's self-stirred-up, is real and strong, one hell of a weather. Freddy longs to comfort her.

Instead, she waits and while she's waiting, counts. By fifteen, the flow of tears has slowed and the breathing's evened out some. Around twenty-five, she risks a tiny sympathetic smile without provoking further incident. At precisely forty-five, she opens her arms to her daughter. At fifty, Paige steps into them. At fifty-five her posture softens. She crawls on Freddy's lap, rests her head on Freddy's shoulder. Freddy strokes her hair. Chaz, having held his breath for so long, exhales a little puff of audible relief and shifts from knees to bottom on his chair. The thumb comes out of his mouth. Carol reaches out to tap the tip of his nose and says, "Beep-beep."

Chaz grins and beep-beeps back.

Freddy massages the top of Paige's back, between the shoulder blades. Paige presses her face into her mother's collarbone and rubs from side to side.

"I'm thirsty," Chaz announces.

Carol says, "What's the magic word?"

"Please."

"Come on in the kitchen," Carol says. "I'll get you a drink."

Paige lifts her oh-so-pale red-spotted face and says in a solemn voice, "I'd like a drink, too, please."

"Then you shall have one," Carol says, as if nothing's happened that needs forgiving.

Paige leans back in Freddy's arms. Freddy brushes stray hairs off her daughter's forehead, kisses her cheek. Paige says, "I wish Grandpa didn't have to die."

"I know, sweetie," Freddy says. "On the other hand, I wouldn't have let you go to a boy-girl party with a date even if it wasn't Grandpa's memorial service. That's sixth-grade stuff."

"You mean I have to wait until I'm in sixth grade to go to a party with a boy?"

"Uh-huh," Freddy says. "You only get to be a kid for about ten years anymore. You'll have decades to be a vamp."

"The other kids' mothers are letting them go." Paige delivers this quietly, more information than argument.

"That's their problem," Freddy says. "You can say it's because of Grandpa if you want."

"What do I say next time?" Paige asks, fingering a lock of Freddy's hair.

"We'll figure that out next time," Freddy says.

Softly she closes off the hall so the children, now in their beds, won't hear them talking. Carol has topped off their glasses with what she deems "peasant wine, three ninety-nine." She says, "Quite a snit."

"Just what I needed."

"I'm glad I got all boys. Just wait until she gets her period."

"Yeah," Freddy says. "I just got mine."

"Of course you did. What good's a reunion between your mom and your ex at your father's funeral without a few free-floating hormones to make things interesting?"

"You were great," Freddy says.

"I was good, wasn't I?" Carol flashes her lushest grin. "Must be because I have a natural understanding of the high-strung."

"It was an act of mercy to the strung-out."

"You look like shit, by the way," Carol says.

"I know," Freddy says. "It was the anonymous phone calls. Did I tell you about them?"

"Tell me."

"At first I thought it was Jack. I hung up on him, earlier. But he's too easily bored to call three times just to hassle me."

"No heavy breathing?"

"Just pregnant silence."

"By the way," Carol says, narrowing her big eyes the way she does before she says something astute, "was that a little bit of Jack I saw tonight?"

"Uhm. I think that's what makes it so hard."

"You did fine."

"With help. When I buy in, it's all over. You're looking at three hours. When I'm this ragged, I usually buy in."

"I'm glad I was here, then," Carol says. "The kid has really got your number."

"She got it from her dad."

"I can't wait to meet him."

"I was going to ask you to be in charge of him. I'll do Elsa."

"Sure," Carol says. "I take it he's attractive."

Freddy pictures Jack's face. No adjectives come to mind. "I used to think so. I guess other women still do. It depends on whether or not you like the type."

"Which is?"

"Oh, artsy. Soulful. Terminally intense. He cultivates the outlaw poet look."

"Not hippie?"

"Not anymore. He's couthed up lately."

"Maybe I'll try to seduce him," Carol says.

"Be my guest. Just don't fall in love with him." Sipping, Freddy calls up a picture of Carol and Jack in flagrante, Carol on top, pinning Jack to the mattress with her earth-mother buttocks, the three-pounds-apiece breasts swaying above his soulful artist face, that makes her smile. "If you're going to fuck him, see if you can't work up an outbreak of herpes first."

Carol snickers. "You're welcome to a shot at Richard, you know. Turn about's fair play."

"After all you've said about his potency, I think I'll pass."

"You just have to catch him with a noseful. Then he'll stay up all night."

"Jack's got the opposite problem. Foreplay consists of one quick ear nibble, a bite of breast, then, bam, instant orgasm. Followed by a little nap."

"What he needs," Carol says, "is a *real* woman."

They both laugh. "What he needs," Freddy says, "is an inflatable doll. One with speakers. He always hated it that I didn't moan and groan."

"So who had time?" Carol says. "For the first three minutes, I'm still reviewing the shopping list. Comet. Baggies. Jesus, we're out of Absorbine, Jr. again."

"Nothing like three cases of athlete's foot in the same family," Freddy says.

"Make that four. The little bastards bring it home, you know."

"You too?"

"Itches like anything. Maybe that's what I should share with Jack."

"On his dick."

"His schlong."

"Prong."

"Poker."

"Prick."

"Ding-dong."

"His weenie," Carol says.

"What's bigger than a Tampax and smaller than a bread box?" Freddy says.

"His peenie, of course."

"His cock. His stalk. His *thang*."

"Whanger, banger, magic twanger."

Freddy giggles until her throat hurts. Carol gulps big drafts of air between haws.

After she wipes the tears out of her crow's feet, Freddy says, "You realize we're making Paige look mature."

Carol's expression fades to plaintive. "Whatever you call it, I wish I had some. You go along for months, chaste and not caring, and then suddenly you're drowning in the sea of desire, with no ships in sight."

With a quick lurch of longing, Freddy's body commiserates, remembers itself hungry and graceful, naked, smooth and strong, instead of the vehicle for work and grief it has become. Then her cramps remind her of travail; the Tylenol is wearing off. She raises her shoulders and the pain stretches with her spine. "I know what you mean," she says.

So Friday comes, not because she's ready, and it's a cold start, with sibling quibbling stomping on the diaphany of dreams, each child wanting all of Mother and Mother waking helpless as a newborn in want of mothering herself and when Freddy remembers what Friday wants from her she puts her pillow over her face and tries like an ostrich to pretend she isn't there, but then Chaz, scrambling across her to pinch his sister, knees her bladder and Freddy sits up, primal screaming, and heaves the pillow across the room, then seizes both squirmy contentious offspring in a too-fierce hug, to silence them.

Friday has every intention of being one of those days.

At Police Headquarters, numerous realities later, she finds that Detective Ashford is not important enough to have an office but occupies a provisional workspace the size of a three-person tent, three-walled by shoulder-high partitions upholstered in coarse gray. A green-plaid sport coat dangles from the back of his chair, and Freddy feels sorry for his shirt, the way it has to stretch across his paunch.

Freddy says, "About the chess game. I had a friend who plays well take a look at the board. He says whoever Nick was playing was extremely accomplished."

"Is that so?"

"Yes." Freddy hisses at the detective's indifference. "It means you're looking for somebody very smart."

"I knew that. He was smart enough not leave me any clues. Unless you found something?"

"Nothing," Freddy says. "Nothing missing or out of place, as far as I could see. I haven't tackled Nick's office yet."

The smile Ashford sends her is dimmed by long-suffering. "I wish you would."

"Sandy says Nick's opponent was good enough to be a competitive chess player. He could even be a master."

"What makes you so sure it's a he?"

Freddy restrains herself from parroting Sandy's argument. "This is your only lead," she says. "Don't you think you should do something about it?"

Ashford says, "Maybe so, but I have a little problem with it. It's called personnel."

Freddy stares at the detective. "I don't write the budget," he says. "I just live with it. The boss is very big on cost-benefit ratios these days."

"What's that supposed to mean?"

"It means you spend your time and money where you're most likely to get convictions."

A gust of indignation fills Freddy's sails. She's all set to declaim, but Ashford cuts her off right after "Do you mean to say—"

"I mean, things would be one whole hell of a lot easier if your father had gotten himself shot at Seven-Eleven. The D.A.'s real partial to things like witnesses, evidence, that kind of stuff."

Freddy says, "I don't believe this."

And Detective Ashford says, "Look, Miz Bascomb, I'll do my best, okay?"

She errands on. The Labor Temple wants her hundred bucks before they go to the trouble of setting up the chairs. Even though the notice she put in the paper said, No flowers, please, the place is already filling up with funereal displays. She peers at the facilities manager, an affable fake redhead in a bright pink pantsuit, through the stately spikes of hollyhocks.

"You want the PA, right?"

"I guess we better."

"Did I tell you you've got to move your group out by five? I've booked a dinner at six-thirty."

"We'll try to keep it short and sweet," Freddy says, handing over her check.

"We don't usually do memorials," the woman says. "If you don't mind my asking, how come you didn't use a church instead?"

"Churches made my father break out in a cold sweat," Freddy says.

At the delicatessen, she orders turkey and pastrami for a hundred, light and dark rye. "I'll need wine, too, and coffee," Freddy says.

The caterer, a slim young man in a crusty apron, says, "We have a special on California champagne by the case. It's good stuff for the money."

"I don't think so," Freddy says. "It's not a wedding."

They settle on a year-old Washington State Semillon for the drinkers, mocha java for the abstemious.

Sandy assures her, by telephone, his eulogy is almost written.

Alaska Airlines tells her Elsa's flight will be on time.

At the Hallmark Party Shop she buys black-edged white paper plates and napkins the saleswoman tells her are in vogue for fortieth-birthday parties.

On her machine, she finds two messages—Carol, saying she's got the decks cleared to pick up Jack at three; Don Pankowski, saying both he and Bones will be available at eight P.M. The rest is beeping.

En route to the airport, she picks Chaz up at Laura's. Chaz loves Sea-Tac for its escalators. With five minutes to spare, they ride them up and down. Elsa, emerging from the gate, shakes Freddy's hand. "How's my little man?" she asks her grandson, and seems hurt when Chaz takes cover behind Freddy's legs. Elsa's arrival slows the metronome from allegro to larghissimo; Freddy, nerves still racing, bounces off the walls of big elastic minutes. Wanting everything—solace, expiation, love most of all, Freddy receives from her mother small talk so small it seems to disappear on utterance. The weather. The airplane food. Apologies for Peter's absence; he's traveling on business again. Chaz fastens tight to Freddy's hand and peers at Elsa around her thighs. Nobody mentions Nick.

It's worse at home, as if time had switched dimensions and become material, so the hours are like aspic, clear and flavorless, gelling slowly around them until Freddy finds it hard to move, or even breathe. Chaz takes refuge in *Sesame Street* while Elsa freshens up. Except for Mrs. Patniak's afghans, nothing in the decor invites comment. Elsa doesn't ask to see her paintings. Nothing that matters feels safe to say.

Then Paige comes home, loose-limbed and flushed, trailing tendrils of the high excitement of school dismissal and the scent of lilacs from the afternoon outside.

Elsa, on the sofa, says, "Paige."

Paige approaches, stomach thrust out, her smile crimped between shy and willing-to-be-pleased. "Grandma?"

"How big you are. Give me a kiss, dear."

It is a puppy, sloppy and eager, embracing a distant queen. Freddy sees Elsa wipe the wet spot. "What grade are you in this year?"

"Fifth."

"Are you enjoying it?"

"Yes, Grandma."

"And what's your best subject?"

Paige's eyes stray to Freddy. Freddy raises her eyebrows slightly and smiles hard. Paige says, "I don't know."

"Every subject," Freddy says. "You should see her report card."

"What's your favorite subject, then?"

"Recess," Paige says. "Mom, I'm starved."

"There's cookies in the kitchen. Why don't you bring a plate in here?"

Reprieved, Paige disengages instantly, takes up her school-bag and skips off.

Chaz, huddled with his blanket in front of the TV, suddenly erupts with "Vegetable! Violet! Volcano!"

"What on earth's got into him?" Elsa says.

"V," Freddy says. "Today's show is sponsored by the letter V."

"Oh," Elsa says. "They didn't have *Sesame Street*, did they, when you were growing up?"

"No," Freddy says.

Paige comes back, brandishing the crescent remainder of a chocolate-chip cookie in one hand, a heaped plate in the other. She sets the plate down on the coffee table, in front of Elsa. Chaz crawls toward the cookies. Elsa takes one, studies both sides, then tries a small bite. "Homemade?" she asks.

"We got them at the store," Chaz tells her, chewing.

Sesame Street segues into *Mr. Rogers*. Today an entomologist is visiting. They watch along while Paige does her long division. Chaz says, "A spider has eight legs." Elsa says, "What a nice man." Paige looks up from her computations. "Mr. Rogers is a creep," she says. "Around five, kids turn on him," Freddy explains. "Paige used to adore him." She feels as if she's back-floating in a vat of molasses. She feels like a soft-sculpture mommy in a satirist's tableau. Maybe her father is the lucky one. When did *Mr. Rogers* turn into a ninety-minute show?

Fred is just hanging up his sweater, tying on his wingtips when the front porch shudders and the front door flies open and Carol bursts through with Jack and bags. Freddy sticks to her chair, swivel-headed to observe the scene: Paige rampant, crying Daddy; Elsa on the sofa, drawing her knees together tight and sitting straighter; Chaz's sideways scuttle toward the safety of his mother's lap; Carol an ebullient alien landed on this planet of small gestures and careful speech, in every way bigger than the rest of them as she seizes Elsa's hand, helps herself to a cookie, kisses Chaz's cowlick, gives Freddy's shoulders a bolstering squeeze. Jack puts down his suitcase and takes up his daughter, lifting her to kissing height, then, as he puts her down, nods respectfully to his ex–mother-in-law.

"Elsa," Jack says.

"Jack," Elsa says.

"Freddy," Jack says, eyes homing in at last. She gives him back a stare that's as curious, as voracious and judgmental as his own, knowing, when she drops her eyes, the photographs have been taken, are being developed, will be studied, knowing he sees the new haircut as she sees the beardless chin, takes in the shorthand of time and grief on her skin as clearly as she sees his California tan. "Hi, Jack," she says, then pushes Chaz forward, off her lap. "Say hello to Daddy, hon."

Chaz twists toward her, burying his head in her lap. Jack crouches. "Come here, son." Chaz burrows deeper, pasting himself against her legs. Freddy strokes his hair and murmurs encouragement. "Daddy's come a long way to see you." When Jack raises his eyes to hers, Freddy imagines he sees her through the cross hairs of a rifle sight. "He doesn't remember me."

Carol, merciful angel, alights, grabs Chaz under the armpits from behind and makes as if to toss him to Jack. "Here, catch." Chaz giggles. Jack reaches out and Carol zooms Chaz through the air into his father's hands. "I got you now." Chaz suffers himself to be got. "He was just playing hard to get," Carol says. Paige sidles up to Freddy while Elsa, like the cheese, stands alone.

Then Sandy comes, bringing a bottle of good French wine for dinner and Nick's eulogy inside a plain manila envelope, both of which he hands to Freddy when he sees Elsa for the first time in—how many years? She rises, and their hug-at-meeting is both subtle and eloquent, a social posture that relaxes, just for an instant, into genuine connection before they part, beginning to recite their lines into the fascinated silence that surrounds them.

"Elsa," Sandy says.

"Sandy," Elsa says.

The way they play it, the scene has style. Ingmar Bergman is banished from the set and Capra takes over, softening the focus, upping the tempo. Gratefully, Freddy slides into a supporting role, herself and Jack a subplot. A glance at Carol tells her she is watching and appreciating, in the know. Jack sits at the dining-room table, riffling through a folder of Paige's schoolwork. Chaz stands a cool two feet from his father's elbow, interested but not intimate.

Sandy says, "You look lovely."

Elsa laughs. "Your hair's so white," she says.

Freddy becomes aware of the chill dew of the wine against her chest and looks down to find she's wrapped the envelope around the bottle until it's damp and curled. As she starts for the kitchen, Jack looks to her over Paige's head with a smile less friendly than triumphant. Sandy says, "You seem to have reversed the effects of inexorable time. Or is it just the good effects of climate?"

Freddy tries not to resent Jack's claim of competent paternity. To acknowledge without empathy, that's the ticket. Of course he hates her. She can feel that, and a little wanting, too, a spark struck off their flintiness. For Jack to want her means she's strong. In the kitchen, she makes herself remember: Jack drawn to her strength for the pure joy of breaking it. The attraction is real and powerful but not benign. She stabs the cork and twists the corkscrew in a savage spiral—he is not good for me. The cork rises as the corkscrew folds its stainless wings.

"Can I help you, Mommy?"

Chaz snaps her into context; there is business to attend to. The glasses on a tray, the buzzer crying "Done!," cream-cheese stuffing bubbling in Carol's mushrooms, a whiff of warm garlic, Chaz's conspirator grin as they slide the plump hot mushroom caps onto the platter. Unexpectedly, she thinks of Nick, for a moment, vainly, listens for his voice inside the family chorus, then, bending, lays the platter on Chaz's outstretched arms. He carries it carefully away. For an instant, she has the sense of being in a painting, no more or less an object of interest than the graceful green bottle or the white mass of the refrigerator, a female figure, dark-haired and dressed in yellow, possessing mass but no responsibility. For an exhilarating instant, no mean-

ing attaches to form. There is no history, no proclivity, no
prejudice or expectation. Nothing makes the slightest bit of
sense and Freddy likes it that way.

After dinner, when she folds her napkin, smiles, and tells
them she has to go to work, the children chorus, "Not again,
Mom, not tonight," and Jack looks daggers; Elsa says, "Can't
you just call in and say you're sick?"

"Deadlines," Freddy says. "I have to," not adding that half
of what she has to do is escape. She does not tell them how
good it feels to invoke the classic, inarguable male prerogative
or how it amuses her to see their individual agendas, their
legitimate wants and unreasonable demands give way before it.
The great god work. Elsa and Jack, those masters of manipu-
lation, are rendered powerless.

Sandy says, "Well, then, let's take a drive. I'll show you how
the city's changed," and Carol offers to help Jack with the dishes
and bedding down the kids. Freddy takes up her sketch pad
and shoulders her bag. "There's clean towels in the linen closet.
Bedtime is nine tonight. Elsa, here's my extra key." She kisses
the children. "You two be good now. Mind your father." Looks
to the adults, extorting complicity, and says, "I figure it be-
hooves me to stay on the good side of the Homicide Unit these
days," which is as close as anyone comes, all evening, to men-
tioning Nick Bascomb or how he died.

Outside, after a quick hard shower, the air is damp, heavy
with dust and lilacs. Freddy rolls down her window and breathes
in freeway wind, bound for the doctor and his bones.

Stinging traces the shape of her lips, a subtle outline of
abrasion, not really painful, that makes her smile at odd times
on the trip home—as she changes lanes on the freeway, catching
sight of her all-pupil eyes in the dark mirror; as she locks the
car and eases open the front gate. The sky is clear and profligate
with stars. On the front walk, she pauses to look up and lets
the rush of traffic on the nearby thoroughfare transmute into
the streaming of celestial winds, feels the vast hollowness of joy
inside, as if she were a bubble, or a mighty cathedral delineating
grace. For a moment she is herself, a self described so strongly
in space and time no need, no pressure can deform it. Breathing
deeply, she trades secrets with the night.

Someone has left the porch light on and its circle of illumination calls her to resume. With a last glance at the stars, she climbs the stairs, becomes a woman searching clutter for her keys, passing through the door becomes the woman of the house and finds a man, her former husband, reading on the couch. Jack puts down his magazine and looks at his watch.

"You worked late."

"How late is it?" Freddy asks, pretending innocence and feeling guilt.

"A few minutes past three."

He can still do it, encode a load of accusation in neutral words. If they were still married, she would now make explanations that were truth but sounded like excuses. Even now, she turns them in her mind, compiling a detailed accounting of the hours she spent away. Just in time, she realizes he no longer has a right to audit her books. Says simply, "No wonder I'm tired."

Jack's inquisitorial eyebrow soars. Freddy goes on, "Kids get to bed all right?"

"About ten."

"How late did Carol stay?"

"About twelve."

"And when did Elsa get back from her outing?"

"Later still." Jack laughs, not nicely. "Like mother, like daughter."

It has a visceral effect. The muscles harden in her shoulders and her neck, the backs of her knees stiffen, her heart pumps something darker and heavier than blood. The feeling is familiar, unpleasantly, the Jack-feeling. Even as it takes her, she knows it's been a long time since she felt this way. The set of Jack's jaw, the prominence of the veins in his temples mirror her condition. "When are you going to stop?" she says.

"When you stop lying."

"I never lied. I never broke the rules."

His laugh. Does Jack have a laugh that's not a weapon? Freddy hates how she feels. She hates Jack's disbelief, wonders if this is the same as hating Jack, then decides it doesn't matter. With enormous effort, she manages to shrug instead of speak.

Jack says, "The two of you can compare notes in the morning, on the way to Nick's memorial."

The infusion of anger is so strong Freddy thinks she must be physically expanding.

"How terribly modern," Jack says. "How naughty."

"You're sick," Freddy says, and fears the escalation, almost expecting him to hurt her, even now. Along with the sickness of fear, she feels exhilaration at the risk.

Jack doesn't hit her, only smiles his devil's smile, the knowing serpent smile the snake flashed Eve to make her think she was impure already, so why not bite? and says, "Well, I hope you had a good time. I can't tell you how glad I am it's no concern of mine anymore. It's the children I feel sorry for."

Her stomach twists as if he'd hit her with his fist. She hates his need to sully everything. She wants enormously to find a way to hurt him back. And then decides she will not argue, will not defend. It was only a kiss, none of his business. A long and unexpected kiss, almost symphonic in its range, from tenderness to passion to compassion, surprising in its kindness and its justice and its need, a kiss arising among bones to shake its fist at death, begun in sadness, become a promise.

Freddy says, "I'm going to bed now," leaves Jack to resorb his own adrenaline and bile, climbs the stairs to her loft and consults the mirror, looking for some visible manifestation of that kiss upon her lips, but finds none. There is no way Jack could have known.

9
■ ■ ■ ■ ■

Τhe flowers of death are tall and stately, tapering heavenward as if to nudge the departing spirit toward the proper exit. They bloom absurdly in the big meeting room, too few to disguise its worn austerity, plenteous enough to embarrass it, the clash creating the kind of socio-visual joke Nick would have enjoyed. Their perfume sweetens air staled by politics. Freddy imagines that, somewhat above the pitch of human hearing, calla lilies honk wildly, trying to speed up the somber-dressed and best-behaviored traffic that snarls among the rows of folding chairs.

If anyone's in charge here, it's she, but Freddy has a strong sense of the mystery of the event. It's Nick's party; only he knows all the guests, how they chafe or fit, understands to what small constituent dramas this is reprise. Nick, are you here? Are you amused? Her gaze interrogates the airspace above the heads of the mourners. Is this as weird and funny as I think it is? I miss you. Father, I am doing my best.

Preceded by a whiff of Joy, Carol appears at her elbow, the jaunty red silk rose on her lapel taking the curse off a sober navy suit. She bends red lips to Freddy's ear. "I count one fifty and still coming. Do you think I should try to scare up some more cold cuts?"

"I had no idea I was hosting a state occasion," Freddy whispers back.

"Some people like going to funerals," Carol says. "My mother always did."

"I'm getting stage fright."

Carol squeezes Freddy's arm. "You'll be fine. What about the food?"

"Let them eat gladiolas," Freddy says. There are lots of gladioli. Her eyes range to the front row left, checking: Sandy, Paige, Jack, Chaz, Elsa, the empty on the aisle reserved for her. Everyone's in place. Her heart beats like a hummingbird trapped inside her rib cage, frantic for a way out. A silver-haired man in black approaches her, dragging his left leg behind him. The old cut and new fabric of his suit suggest a couple of decades passed in mothballs. "Little Freddy." He thrusts his big hand at her as if he were breaking earth with a spade. "It's been a long time since you used to visit me in the composing room. I sure am sorry about your dad."

His name materializes out of thin air. "Bill! How are you, Bill?"

"Not as good as I used to be. This damn arthritis."

"Well, it looks like you're still getting around okay."

"Pretty good, I guess, compared to some."

"Are you retired?"

"November, I turn seventy and they turn me out to pasture."

"That's not exactly early retirement."

"You retire, you die. I seen it happen to a dozen guys. Management would have fired all of us fifteen years ago, except for the deal the union made when they wanted to bring in them big mainframe computers. Made them promise to keep us boys in the back room until we was damn well ready to leave. That or seventy."

"It was kind of you to come today," Freddy says.

"Old Nick, he was the best."

She nods, smiling, crediting the compliment to her father's account. Hear that, Nick? The best. This day is expiation, the forgiving and forgetting of human flaws. Cast your faults and hurts, debts and regrets aside like so much dirty laundry. Leave lean and clean.

Across the room, Carol mimes a time check and Freddy consults her watch. Three minutes past the gun, but people are still cruising, shaking hands or seeking chairs. She holds up five splayed fingers. The minutes pass as slowly as last ketchup. After what feels like half an hour, Carol cues tape on the Bach and when it hits the speakers, the standers scurry to find seats, the seated rustle, settling in, heads straighten above the seat backs, a sudden blooming. Her march to the podium is the magnet that creates collective mind; she feels attention as weight attaching. Inside it, her separate self feels oddly light. The microphone crackles at her touch. She spends the last bars of the cantata regretting Nick's intransigence about religion, resenting the absence of ritual to keep her safe. Fear fevers her cheeks and a trembling takes her hands. This is one hell of a time to have to wing it.

Then silence, and eyes. So many eyes. For a moment, she makes the mistake of seeing individuals and not a crowd, senses the vast disparities of motive and emotion directed toward her—goodwill, yes, and pity, but also curiosity, judgment, envy (why?), even, from some quarter, the unmistakable sting of malice. For a moment, she's overwhelmed, then, beyond terror, finds her voice and welcomes THEM. THEY oblige by receding into collectivity. She thanks them for coming, then introduces Sandy, Nick's colleague and his closest friend. His eulogist.

The chilly metal of her folding chair gives her thighs a nasty shock when she sits down. Freddy shoots a smile up-aisle at her children, then folds her hands in her lap, trains her eyes on Sandy and is surprised to find herself incapable of listening to what he says. Only the occasional phrase accedes to meaning; for the rest, she's flotsam on the tide of her own thoughts. I'm sorry, Nick. Who are these people, anyway? Across formal distance, Sandy in his whispered pinstripes, his eyebrows disciplined for the occasion, looks reliable, important, and astute, not Sandy-friend so much as Sandy-pro, the man who covered the state legislature for twenty years. She tries to imagine how he looks through Elsa's eyes.

"A child of the Depression," Sandy says.

Childhood depression. It *was* depressing, trying always to sit on that three-legged stool—Nick, Elsa, Booze. One leg was always short. It wobbled. Maybe Sandy, too, felt like a phantom limb.

"Too busy being a reporter to be a distinguished scholar," Sandy says.

Too busy. Oh, yeah. You were a busy one, all right. I'm busy, too. Our busyness is different, though. Come to think of it, it must have been a bitch, juggling a career and a drinking habit. I know. I'm addicted to my kids. No wonder you didn't have time.

Bubbles of laughter rise and burst around her. Freddy has no idea why. Could you repeat that, Sandy? I want to laugh too.

"By the time we sobered up," Sandy says, "we were in boot camp."

That story. Nick never said much, after, drew a curtain across the war itself, except for an occasional history lesson when he was loaded, and that was always about Chamberlain and Churchill, Stalin, Hitler and Hirohito, Roosevelt, the generals—what were their names? (even now, summoned, they march)—Eisenhower, Patton, Marshall, Montgomery, Bradley. Even when whiskey hissed his esses, Nick talked about those folks so well that for a long time, Freddy believed he knew them personally, was there at every meeting, fought every battle. About his own war, nothing said.

"What makes a great reporter?" Sandy says. "Empirically speaking, curiosity. Nick always was a nosy bastard. Now, the poets may tell you there's nothing new under the sun, and in a way, I suppose that's true, but a reporter knows that it's the individual variations on the big themes that make the news. Nick was fascinated by the endless permutations of human behavior. He had more questions than a dog has fleas."

Well said, Sandy, and probably true. Except the family was exempt. He never wondered about us. Again, Freddy tries to put herself in Elsa's skin. Did Nick know Sandy loved her? Did he care? All she has are pictures of the past, a wordless documentary. Three smiling adults, one big-eyed girl child watching in the shadows. If you look closely, you can tell the taller man's been drinking. See, his cheeks are flushed, his eyes a little blurry. Almost always, there's a glass in his hand.

"Dogged persistence," Sandy says, "civic spirit, his unimpeachable integrity."

She never kissed the moon before. That's what she thought in the moment before their faces touched, and she was surprised to find him human-warm, beard-prickled, not cool and silver. She was surprised it happened, still is, yet must have wanted it because nothing happens without complicity. There is a doctrine to desire, a decorum. Yet it was just a kiss, a touch of lips, a tasting, a moment of breathing the same moist air. Freddy is glad one thing did not lead to another, that no other memory supersedes the sweetness of that kiss.

Sandy says, "I do not know what happens to the spirit after death."

Last night, her fingers tracing the contours of an unknown woman's skull, Freddy wondered about that, too. The bones were smooth, cool, shiny as a seashell when the snail that lived inside is gone. Once memory and preference, passion and confusion and particularity dwelt in that white room. Made of what? Where gone? Could so much of substance simply disappear?

"Nick always said he believed in the laws of conservation of matter and energy," Sandy says, "a kind of cosmic recycling."

A twitter passes through the mourners, appreciative of Nick's wit. Up the row, Freddy sees the silent tears that roll down her daughter's cheeks. Why is she crying now? Freddy wants to hold her daughter, to warm herself against her. It is intolerable to be so far away. She sees Chaz reach across his father's lap to pat his sister's arm. Jack, you bastard, comfort her.

"One thing we can be sure of," Sandy says. "No matter what happens to the spirit after death, Nick will find out all the whys and wherefores of it, and if there's anyplace to file his report, he'll do it."

In the rows behind her, she hears sniffing, an audible sob or two surprised out of the grief of strangers. Why? Why do they care?

"Who knows? He could be the first guy ever to win a Pulitzer for posthumous reporting," Sandy says.

Freddy doesn't think he means that; it's a mild joke in the grim face of Nick's absence. His absence is almost overwhelming. There is no substance in the father-place, only a missing piece where the gray cardboard backing of the puzzle shows, a nothingness that holds the shape of Nick. Elsa's elegantly straight posture, her clean and distant profile confirm that she is orphaned. It's that, finally, that makes her cry.

She did not mean to cry. Sternly, she accuses her tears of arising from self-pity, thinking to stop them, but her sadness is immune to criticism, and Freddy lets the tears come because she cannot stop them and besides, becomes fascinated, watching how they wetly dot her cotton skirt.

"We are better for having known you, Nick. You will be missed." Sandy grips the podium, smiling a sad smile, then, after a pause long enough to put a period to his remarks, introduces William Devins, retired publisher of the Seattle *Times*. White-haired, gray-suited, leaner by some than Sandy, Devins rises from his rear-stage seat, moves front and center. The two old men shake hands. While Sandy descends, her father's old boss smiles with his eyes at the crowd.

Sandy scuttles into his seat. Devins says, "Working for a newspaper, a writer has to curb his lyricism, and for good reason. But Nick Bascomb loved the language as much as any man. He was especially fond of poetry, and had committed much to memory. I'd like to close this afternoon by reading . . ."

Here it comes. Freddy steels herself. Reciting poetry was something Nick did drunk. She loves the poem, hates the memories unsettled by that dredge.

"Do not go gentle into that good night," Devins intones, and Freddy's tears, nearly staunched, threaten to rise up again.

Then, wham. Something hits her, intangible but real, a poison bullet that shatters peace and banishes reflection, leaving her sick and shaky with fear. Afraid, she looks first, instinctively, to the children, Chaz beginning to fidget, Paige glazed politely. Safe. Chaz feels her look and waves. Freddy smiles weakly back. Paige frowns at the exchange. If the kids are right, then what is wrong? Freddy rubs a sudden cold spot on the back of her neck, half expecting a lump to rise there, as if in response to the bite of an insect. Chill radiates from that center, a cold glow that colonizes the tops of her shoulders and reaches upward to the base of her skull.

"Wild men who caught and sang the sun in flight, And learn, too late, they grieved it on its way . . ."

Gooseflesh, an ice-cold finger caressing her skin. Freddy

presses her elbows to her ribs, rubs her upper arms for warmth. So very cold.

"And you, my father, there on the sad height, Curse, bless me now with your fierce tears, I pray. . . ."

Freddy feels the curse, her own fierce tears. It is not the poem's fault, did not arise there. This chill is an intruder's touch.

"A time of silence, to remember our friend, and say good-bye," Devins says. Closing his eyes, he clutches the podium with both hands and the silence in the hall changes subtly, from polite to profound, with the drawing in of thought.

Freddy pinches her eyelids shut and tries to compose a farewell message, but her mind will not be silent. Instead it crackles, like the television sometimes does when a neighbor's police band or ham radio cuts in and she's intercepting messages not meant for her: we tried, Nick, I did, for as long as I could . . . Grandpa, your whiskers, how you smelled . . . where you belong . . . the best, Nick . . . remember when . . . down to Charlie's . . . one for you . . . I'm sorry, Nick . . . we'll miss you . . . he's here, or she, I know it . . . think you would find it amusing . . . the news desk in the sky . . . I want to go home . . . our little secret . . . how you died . . . good-bye, good-bye, sweet Nick you'll never die.

Theatrically, Devins clears his throat, then says, "The family requests that memorials be sent to the Children's Orthopedic Hospital or to the Rainbow Coalition, whichever feels most congenial. In deference to Nick's wishes, there'll be a brief wake following the service. Thank you for coming."

In God's absence, no amen. Devins steps down from the podium. After a brief interval of quiet comes the rustling of bodies, a wave of conversation rising. Jack stands up. Elsa. Chaz worms his way across their legs toward Freddy and casts his head into her lap. Paige comes too and stands beside her, patting her mother's shoulder in a manner so adult, so other that it hurts. Freddy wraps her arms around her children and lets the last tears fall, wipes her cheeks with the Kleenex her daughter offers, then has to smile, it is so like Paige to come prepared. Her knees pop audibly as she stands up and turns and sees the throng behind her. At the back of the hall, Carol directs traffic toward the cold cuts and wine. Sandy waits, courtly, to escort her.

"Thanks, Sandy. You did a great job."

With shaggy humility, his big head dips acknowledgment. When he raises his face, a wash of tears wavers his brown eyes. The next blink spills them, one fat drop from each, into the ruddy pouches below his eyes. When she was a child, awaiting sleep in her dark room, Freddy used to try to imagine how life would be if Sandy were her father. Both of them ignore his tears. Sandy sniffs once, juicily, then in a low voice says, "Ready?"

"No," Freddy says. They walk toward it anyway, into the dense crowd milling, cautiously balancing paper plates and squat, clear plastic glasses, trying not to spill on funeral clothes. Instead of rushing and rippling, as it should, conversation trickles stingily as a feeder stream in August of a drought year. The rented server in his starched white jacket is parsimonious with the wine, filling glasses just a thumbnail past halfway. Freddy is reminded of wedding receptions where the budget shows (that's two chicken wings, one roll and half a glass of champagne per guest, ma'am), art openings of the cheese ball and Gallo school, of plastic forks and no reviews, no sales.

This is no party, not the wake Nick would have wanted, hearty and sloppy and no-holds-barred, where the booze and dirty jokes and maudlin reminiscence could flow freely until each and every mourner had pissed away his grief, no. This is a PTA meeting, awards night at the Y, a cheap institutional imitation of a party, disapproving of itself even as it pretends to be a good time. It is her fault, a fault she might attribute to bad choices—wrong time, wrong place—but knows is really the perfect, sad expression of her own ambivalence. At just this moment, Joy-scented Carol slips a plastic glass into her hand.

Freddy looks at the pale, urine-colored wine, at the disappointed faces of her father's friends, then raises her glass aloft, shouts in her loudest, child-scolding, cat-calling voice, "To Nicholas Bascomb, ace reporter. May he rest in peace. Bottoms up."

The guests stare as she fills her mouth with wine and then, like a string of caps, explode in toasts of their own. L'Chaim, she hears, and Cheers, Mud in your eye. To Nick.

With the raising of glasses, the temperature of the event rises, too, pops the bubble that surrounded Freddy, holding her aloft. Now it's people who enclose her, people with sad

smiles and avid eyes, pressing condolences upon her. Her right
hand is pumped and patted, sometimes held filling in a lingering hand-sandwich, while mourners explain how they knew her
father and how much they'll miss him. Theirs are not young
hands. The faces that approach hers, no matter how well kept,
are puckered, lined, creased, tired. She finds it possible to sort
them into categories by gross visual stereotype: Nick's col-
leagues from the newsroom all wear glasses; the noses of his
drinker friends are florid and corroded. Those with good eyes
and good noses both are public figures of one kind or
another—politicians, mostly, or television newsmen, Nick's sub-
jects or his more visible fellows.

A small but significant subgroup is female, all of whose
members, no matter what their ages or relative states of repair,
are alike in resembling Elsa in one way or another—stature or
coloring or facial structure, sometimes their blue-green eyes.
Nick's ladies, so she tags them, are vaguer in their recollections,
less profligate with anecdotes than the other guests. All, to a
woman, stare searchingly into the daughter's eyes as if these
were windows where they hoped to catch a fleeting last glimpse
of the father, and Freddy stares back her own questions. Where
did you meet Nick? Just how well did you know him?

"The killer's here. I know it." The voice, a basso buzz in
her right ear, comes from behind. One of Nick's ladies, a sixtyish
blonde with bad teeth and surprisingly good legs, gives Freddy's
hand a final squeeze and moves away. Detective Ashford, sal-
lowed by his black suit, moves into place at her side. For a
moment, they stand in silence, scanning.

Freddy says, "I felt that, too. I suppose it sounds nuts, but
I had the feeling that something cold and . . . sort of malicious
was focusing on me, trying to get my attention. It did."

"It does sound nuts," Ashford agrees. "But then, we're
dealing with a nut."

Freddy turns to look at the detective, into his big eyes with
their pale irises. "I never asked you exactly how my father died."

Ashford clears his throat first, deep rumble of phlegm.
"Heart attack."

"You mean he died of natural causes?"

"Unnaturally induced. His blood alcohol was high, and
there was a slug of morphine in his system, but Doc figures that

was just anesthetic. It probably happened when the bastard started opening his skull."

"He was still alive then?" Freddy says.

"It's just a theory. Only one person knows for sure. I'd bet my pension that asshole is in this room right now. You probably shook his hand."

How to talk about what happens then? It is more like eating than anything else, this feeling—the experience in one instant of what is made of many things. Freddy feels a flash of anger, bright and savage as summer lightning, and a pure sadness that like molasses is slow, dark, and sweet; fingers of longing stroke her, pink as last light and there is a hard black seed, too, round as a peppercorn, that wants breaking to release its taste. She fears that breaking, the bitter taste inside it that is her culpability, her guilt, proof pungent that she too is wicked in her way.

An instant, no more. Above the stockpot, drawn in steam, there rises a single image: Nick. Father. FATHER. The word cuts loose from the image then, becomes the cry of an animal speaking animal grief. Outrage at change, at endings, at the senseless hardness that is life. An instant. Ashford rocks back on his heels, as if he senses the intensity and feels the heat, yet stands close, protecting her. Freddy searches the faces that surround her, trying to read their secrets, ready to pounce and rend. In that instant, she knows she could do murder and call it revenge.

Later, necessity (or is it social inertia?) assembles the splintered family once again. The living room seems too small. Jack says, "I come to gawk at Caesar, not to love him."

Sandy says, "He was a complicated man."

Paige says, "I never knew Grandpa had so many friends. It seemed like he was always alone."

Jack says, "You could sure tell who his drinking buddies were. I never saw a funeral before that needed a bouncer."

"Fortunately," Freddy says, "you were there to fill the role."

Modestly, Jack shrugs. "Last rites, last call."

"All in all," Sandy says, "I think Nick would have enjoyed his wake."

Mrs. Patniak, who has ascended the stairs to share in the postmortem, says, "I didn't know it was a wake."

"It wasn't really," Freddy says. "Far too tame. If it had been the party Nick wanted, it'd still be going on next Thursday."

Chaz looks up from his coloring book, a circus souvenir, and the clown he has been crayoning bright, unremitting red. "Was that a party?" he asks. "Where was the cake?"

"There wasn't any cake, dummy," Paige says. "It wasn't Grandpa's birthday. Grandpa's dead, remember?"

Chaz looks from his sister to the red clown and back again. "It was a deathday party."

Paige says, "That's gross, Chaz."

Freddy says, "That's right, Chaz. A deathday party celebrating life. That's what a wake is supposed to be." No one seconds the sentiment. Her mother sits on the sofa, saying nothing, pallid and perfect. What do Pallas Athena and Little Orphan Annie and Elsa Swenson Bascomb Langtry have in common? Blank eyeballs. Inscrutable hearts. Whatever Elsa thinks, what she might feel, is inaccessible. She is a message written in invisible ink, a dark pond, smooth-surfaced and fathoms deep. Freddy wishes there were a lap she could lay her head on, feet to sit at, a hand to stroke her hair. Instead, she inches closer to her daughter, slings an arm lightly across the delicate sharp shoulders, twists a ruddy curl around her fingers. She is the instruction manual; the title is How to Mother. Elsa learns nothing from the demonstration. Her hands, pale, long-fingered, stay folded in her lap. The slow wink of a diamond on her fourth finger, left, signals her detachment from all but Sandy. Him, shyly, she keeps in sight.

Sandy watching Elsa is more explicit. His shameless eyes embrace her. Jack knows—what else could levitate the corners of his lips so cynically? The children, she thinks, feel it without knowing, as something powerful and not-quite-right; not knowing makes them restless. From the kitchen sounds the ripe boom of Carol caroling: Rock of ages cleft for me, let me hide myself in thee. Mrs. Patniak with her hyperthyroid gaze is the only innocent among them. She doesn't know a goddamn thing.

Freddy feels centuries old until the phone rings and is Doctor Don the King of Bones and makes her blush as if she were a girl. Her family-by-default is curious and she mysterious, taking the call upstairs, telling Paige to hang up before he has a chance to speak.

"How was it?" he wants to know, and she wants to tell him, but it won't come funny and the telling makes her start to cry.

"I don't want to talk anymore," she tells him.

"I understand."

"If you were here . . ."

"I understand."

"Thank you for calling."

"Sure," he says and hangs up.

Freddy considers the picture her pencil's made while they were talking. She's doodled the devil, a smiling cartoon Satan with spiral eyes, and wonders where he came from. His face is silly, ecstatically deranged; whether he means to frighten or amuse her, she doesn't know. Slowly, taking up her pencil, she sketches him a pitchfork whose five tines are the fingers of a human hand.

The devil's crude, the creature of a moment, but her pencil spares no detail as it draws that hand, shaping and shading meticulously, aspiring to a clinical reality. The task involves her so completely she slips the time-track and the voices from downstairs fade out of hearing, so wholly do she and her pencil become one instrument. The pitchfork-hand reflects the care she lavishes upon it, coming to resemble a tiny photograph. She photographs impossibility. That's what surrealism is.

Freddy hears footsteps on her stairs, the voice of Carol—here you are—but does not look up from her drawing. The knuckles are not quite right.

"Sandy's leaving now," Carol announces. "Mrs. Patniak already went."

"Fine." Should one nail be broken, shorter than the rest? If so, which one?

"Freddy . . ."

"I'm drawing."

"I can see that. But you have guests."

"I'm an artist, Carol. I want to draw."

"You have the rest of your life to draw, darling. Tonight's for taking care of business."

"This is my business."

"Freddy, I'm warning you. If I have to make small talk with your mother and your ex for another two minutes, I'm going to lose it. Besides, your children need to go to bed."

Without putting her pencil down, Freddy looks up. She sees a pretty woman, rather heavyset, whose eye makeup is beginning to smudge. The woman has a straight, haughty nose, with nostrils slightly flared, a proud chin. Her hair is light brown and gently curly. Freddy thinks she would like to draw that face sometime. Or perhaps already has. Her eyes drop to her drawing, her pencil moves, ever so delicately, suggesting veins.

Hands close on her shoulders. "Damn it, Freddy."

The line falters, too thick, too long. "Damn it yourself. You made me mess up."

"What the hell is that, anyway?"

"That?" Freddy inspects her work, seeing the whole of it now. She puts her pencil down, sensing, as she unfurls her fingers, how tight her grip has been. "I don't know. It's nothing."

"It's scary," Carol says.

"I guess so."

"Are you all right?" Carol says.

"I guess so. Sure."

"Will you come downstairs now?"

She takes a last look at her drawing and finds it ugly. "Yes," Freddy says.

Downstairs is different now. Her family is no longer a colony of chattering gibbons acting out rituals of dominance and submission but in her absence has become a random gathering of separate, tired people. Paige sits pale and still at one end of the sofa, a small replica of her pale, still grandmother across the room. Fatigue has glazed Chaz's eyes and slackened the mobile sharp features so he looks, as always when tired, a little stupid. Freddy's heart winces, to see her children looking so hard used and little comforted. Their father paces with the predatory energy she used to fear.

It means he's volatile, as highly flammable as pure hydrogen—one stray spark and Jack explodes. Automatically, she douses her own fire. The impulse to propitiate rounds her shoulders and makes her gestures small until she catches a fleeting glimpse of herself in the mirror of Carol's clear eyes; then, she tosses back her head, stands erect, feels her anger, part at her frightened self and part at him. Tonight, in her own home, she will not be afraid.

"Jack, either go run around the block a couple dozen times

or help me get these kids to bed." The voice that says this sounds strange but strong, and she's relieved when he chooses to spend his meanness on the streets.

The kids are, too. Chaz is rag doll limp as she undresses him, reluctant to remove thumb from mouth even long enough to shed his shirtsleeve. The instant his head touches the pillow, his eyelids surrender to the weight of sleep. He mews once, faintly, as she kisses him and then is gone. Paige is bruised by a long day, blue/black around the eyes and silent, with none of the whispered questions she so often poses to seduce Freddy away from bedtime imperatives, into pillow talk. The ruffles of her daisied flannel nightgown look wrong tonight, her face is so solemn, her thin limbs so deliberate as she composes herself mummylike, hands folded on her breastbone, in the narrow single bed. Freddy can't help feeling this unnatural composure, this premature adulthood is her fault.

Jack returns exultant from his walk. "I caught this black kid sorting through your tapes." He pounds one fist into the other palm. "No need to call the cops. I put the fear of god in him."

"I don't want to hear," Freddy says.

"This is a pretty shitty neighborhood," Jack says.

"That's what Mrs. Patniak says. Myself, I kind of like it."

"I worry about the kids," Jack says, something nasty in his voice invoking lawyers.

Freddy's knees lock back, her fighting posture. No fight with Jack has ever left her unscathed.

Elsa surprises both of them, her cool voice rising. "The children seem healthy and happy to me, Freddy. I think you're doing very well. I meant to mention it before."

Freddy, reeling at approbation, hugs the compliment like a bouquet. The last time Elsa praised her is beyond reach of living memory. Jack, a divide-and-conquer man, is just plain shocked by the alliance. Elsa favors him with one of her goddess smiles, then says, "Jack, why don't you use the bathroom first?"

He makes an ungracious exit. When she can hear the water running, Freddy says, "Thanks. He was spoiling for a tantrum."

"I've never enjoyed Jack's tantrums." Elsa says this with a tight smile.

Freddy remembers: Nick and Elsa visiting Jack and Freddy,

the men like two roosters, strut, peck, stab, father and husband joined in endless and annoying battle, the women treading lightly, conciliatory. It used to ruin her digestion for days. Now, for the first time, she finds it funny. Elsa laughs too, a rare and silver sound. "Your father," she says, "found Jack insufferable. He once proposed that we should simply kidnap you and Paige and haul you home."

"Maybe you should have," Freddy says. "After you left, I always had to do penance, like I owed him something for letting you come."

Elsa's smile, warming, stretches wider. "For me, it was a wonderful exercise in ambivalence. I always felt ecstatic to leave the combat zone, and sick about leaving you in it."

"Nick was never more belligerent than when he was around Jack," Freddy says.

"That's because he loved you." Elsa's ocean eyes, fixing on Freddy's, are calm and deep. "You're free now," she says.

"I am?"

Elsa nods. "You are, and so am I."

Words geyser up in Freddy, questions and declarations, a hundred things that want saying to her mother, but Jack as spoiler makes one more entrance, capping the well with his frown. "I hate to intrude, but this is my bedroom."

Both women rise. "The kids will probably wake you," Freddy says.

"Assuming I get to sleep in the first place."

"Sweet dreams, Jack," Elsa says.

They retreat to the kitchen, waiting until they get there to share a grin. "Do you want anything?" Freddy asks. "Some tea? A nightcap?"

Elsa shakes her head. "We might keep his lordship awake. Besides, I'm tired."

"You take the bathroom next, then. I'm still kind of wired."

"I understand."

It's Freddy who undertakes to close the gap between them, travels four feet with open arms. The hug is, at best, a qualified success—Elsa recoils faintly at first touch and stays stiff for the duration, but Freddy doesn't regret the attempt. "We should practice this," she says, letting go.

Elsa's hands flutter to hair, to blouse, repairing. "You have the children," she says.

Freddy steps back, sad, sad but smiling. "Good night, Mother," she says.

With a nod, Elsa sidles toward the bathroom and shuts the door.

As Freddy turns to climb the stairs to her loft, a wild sound, uncouth, nonhuman, rasps the silence, frightening for its lack of rhythm or coherence, and freezes her for the moment its source remains unknown.

In the living room, Jack is already snoring.

10

■■■■■

When Freddy Bascomb wakes
up, sometime in the dark extremities of the night or morning
following her father's last good-bye, it is to the sound of wings
beating against the window of her attic room. Of course, she
does not immediately recognize the sound as wings but first
considers other possibilities—the branches of the wine-leaved
maple, maybe, or a newspaper opened and perused by wind,
even a rain so fierce and regular its droplets merge in a single,
supple sheet, but no. *This* sound is more rhythmic, more urgent
and intimate. Behind this sound, there is consciousness, and
purpose.

Lying in bed, Freddy listens to her heartbeat long enough
to know she's not afraid, then rises and turns on light, the red
gooseneck lamp pinched onto the edge of her drawing table,
her favorite night-light for the way it circles out, dimming and
diffused, from its original intensity, so that by the time it reaches
the corners of the room, it is the gentlest of lights, barely usurp-
ing the shadows. All the while the flapping sound persists, grows
louder. For a moment she thinks it is a moth, unusually large,
at the window, then sees it is her father.

It *is* raining; his feathers glisten wetly, and he presses his face to the window, mouthing words she can't decipher through the glass. Quickly she slides back the bolt and opens the window to let him in. He has a hard time fitting, his wings are so large, but he finally works them in, then takes them off and lays them on the window seat to dry. He opens his arms and Freddy steps into them. Only briefly is the hug chaste, only briefly respects the long withholding of the knowledge of bodies, and then they press each other close, withholding nothing. With playful tenderness, Nick kisses her, from the bump of bone below her ear down to the hollows of her collarbone, and those small kisses, desired and feared, map a new road for them, detouring taboo.

Silently, smiling, her father leads her to her bed, to flowered sheets disheveled in the shadows, and she is not embarrassed as he undresses her, nor as he quickly sheds his clothing, letting it fall into a white heap beside the bed, or eases her down and backward, gently, nor when he mounts her, avidly, with an appetite some part of her has always known was so, and nothing forbids her own enthusiasm, though she remembers dimly that something used to, as she squirms and writhes and twines her naked limbs with his.

They must be quick, and quiet; she knows it. If someone were to discover them, the children, Jack or Elsa, they surely would not understand, not only would spoil the moment but turn it into something else. She is ready, so is he, and their lovemaking is all the sweeter for being secret. He is more skilled, more ardent than she would have guessed, more tender, and younger, too, than she remembers him being for years and years, his body lean and firm. There is no hint of gray in the beard-stubble that rasps her chin, none in his hair. Her heart is frantic in its pleasure, fast in its beating as bubbles rise in newly poured champagne. Amazingly, they climax together.

In the minutes that follow, Freddy tries to sort out what is her body, what his, and finds that she cannot. The smile that lilts her lips speaks for the pleasure in all her parts, and it is not the delight of the lawbreaker that makes her smile, but the delight of knowing the law no longer is.

Footsteps on the stairs—Chaz, probably, awakened from a dream and seeking comfort. At the sound, Nick draws away from her. Before rising, he whispers, "Know my killer, and you will know me," then bends to kiss her lightly between her eyes. By the time her son, trailing his blanket, burrows into the bed beside her, her father is gone, his wings are gone, the window closed and fastened.

"I had a nightmare, Mommy," Chaz says, and Freddy holds him lightly, stroking his golden hair.

11
∎ ∎ ∎ ∎ ∎

Tracy Chapman's smoky baritone suffuses the white northwest morning light with a haze of hurt and wanting. Nick Bascomb is nearly three weeks dead, and business begins to impersonate usual. Reprieved from day care, Chaz kneels on the studio floor among his Leg-O's, building a multicolored condominium on wheels, while Freddy washes color on pencil sketches of an accused embezzler, his lawyer and the prosecution, judge and jury. The defendant is just the sort of man she dislikes most, a beefy three-piece suiter complete with wingtips and a cleft chin, one of those guys whose bulk and blondness the world rewards with money and trust. She does her best to make his hale male-model face look sleazy as she knows his soul is.

"Look, Mom." Chaz clunks his improbable architecture down in the middle of her paper. Freddy's tempted to ink the wheels and run over the embezzler's wounded good-guy smile a few times, but she's got too much time invested in the sketch. "That's neat, Chaz."

"Here's your room, Mommy." Chaz points to a corner, four rows up. "See, I gave you a window. My room's right next door."

"Convenient," Freddy says. "And where's your sister's room?"

"Paige went to live with Grandma."

The thought makes her laugh and shudder at the same time. She roughs up Chaz's hair.

"She can stay in the basement when she comes to visit," Chaz explains. "Grandma, too, and my dad."

"Did you like seeing your dad?" Freddy asks.

"It was okay," Chaz says. "I'm glad he went away again."

"How come?"

Chaz peers over the edge of the drawing board at the still-damp defendant. "Because he always has to be the center of attention."

No way not to laugh. Chaz rewards his own wit with a little smile. "Where'd you hear that?" Freddy asks.

"No place. I thought of it all by myself."

"That's what your sister says about you."

"Only when she's mad at me. But Dad is bigger and he always wants to get his own way."

"Hmmm."

Knowing he's being cute, Chaz tilts his face up at her. Freddy half swallows her smile. "Don't you think so?" he wheedles.

"Hmmm."

"Paige says he used to hit you. Is that true?"

This is a conversation Freddy does not want to have. It is inevitable, she's always known that, but expected it would come calmly, when Chaz was much older, if and when he needed to know. Now he is only four and shouldn't. Paige never should have seen. The place in her stomach where guilt resides awakes and burns. "Chaz," she begins, with no idea how that fragile sentence is going to end.

Before it has to, the telephone rings. Freddy rolls her eyes, acknowledging the real if random intercession, and lets her son answer. He mimics Paige's brisk secretarial manner: Who is calling, please? Whatever the answer is, it relaxes his formal posture. "I'm fine. How are you?" Without distancing his mouth from the receiver, Chaz turns to Freddy and bellows, "Mommy, it's for you."

"Who is it?"

"I'm not sure."

"Good morning," Sandy's voice says. "This is Sandy."

"I know." Freddy grips the receiver between ear and shoulder, freeing her hands to keep working. "What's up?"

"That's what I was calling to find out. That and how you are, of course. Have you heard anything from the police?"

"Sure," Freddy says. "I heard they're waiting."

"Waiting for what?"

"A signed confession. What else?"

"You can't be serious."

"The police are. The psychology books strongly suggest the criminal will experience some deep need to claim credit for his crime."

Sandy harrumphs indignantly. "They're simply trying to excuse their own incompetence."

"Maybe so." With her pencil, Freddy thickens the judge's moustache. "They're also waiting for me to excavate Nick's office."

"You haven't?"

"No, Sandy, I haven't." Sighing, Freddy puts her pencil down. "Nobody's going to pay me to go through Nick's papers."

"I'd be more than willing to lend a hand."

"I know that, Sandy. Thanks."

"Anytime you say. I'm at your disposal."

"I appreciate it."

"Shall we set a time?"

"When I'm ready, I'll let you know. Look, I'm on deadline right now. I've gotta go."

"I'd do it myself, if that would help. You wouldn't have to . . ."

"I'm afraid it's my job, Sandy. Thanks for calling." Freddy disconnects before he can speak again. "Jesus."

"What did Sandy want, Mom?" Chaz inquires.

"Too much."

"What does that mean?"

"I was just being silly. Sandy's an old man, honey. He doesn't have enough to keep him busy, I guess. He's just real eager for them to catch Grandpa's killer."

Chaz is silent for a long time, then asks a simple question. "Why?"

"Why what?"

"Why does he want to catch Grandpa's killer?"

"Well, so he can be punished, I guess."

"What's that?"

"It's against the law to go around killing people. Besides, it's not nice. So people who kill people get put in jail, so they can't kill anybody else. That, or sometimes the state kills them."

"I thought you said it was against the law to kill people."

"Yeah, I did."

"So how come the state can kill people?"

"That's a good question."

"What's the answer?"

In this moment, intellectually engaged, her son looks like her father, the round eyes wide, chin set with similar determination. "There isn't one," Freddy says. "People argue that question all the time, they have for centuries, and nobody's come up with a good answer."

"Do you want them to kill Grandpa's killer?"

"Shit, honey, I don't know." The conundrum narrows her son's wide eyes, draws squiggles of puzzlement on the smooth skin of his forehead. Freddy wishes she could promise him a just and simple world. Instead, she hugs him. "I guess we'll have time to worry about that once he's caught. Listen, go bang on Mrs. Patniak's door, would you? She's going to watch you while I go downtown."

In his sweetest wheedle, Chaz says, "Can't I come with you?"

And Freddy, sternly: "Not today."

"Think he's guilty?" Marv brushes a fleck of black from the embezzler's cheek.

"As hell," Freddy says.

Marv's laugh rises. "I'm glad to see we can trust you to be objective."

Freddy punches his arm. "Since when is that a job requirement? Besides, pension funds are supposed to be sacred."

"You just say that because you don't have one."

Freddy shows him her sweet-and-cynical smile. "On the other hand, I don't have to come in here every day. So what's Leroy up to these days?"

"Burnt out. The agency's giving him an ulcer. "Personal life" is a concept without meaning to those guys."

"Tell me about it. I AD'ed in San Francisco for a while, before Paige was born."

"We're going to Acapulco in two weeks," Marv says. "Sun, sand, mariachis. I can't wait."

"Can I come? The weather's been getting me down."

"Only if you bring a cute date." Marv leers, then slings an arm across her shoulders. "You probably do need a vacation, don't you, you poor kid? I was going to send you a card when I heard about your dad. I swear to God, I spent half an hour in the Hallmark store on Broadway, looking for something that felt right. But death and fathers are two topics that tie me up in knots. I went next door to the Elite and had a margarita instead."

When Marv squeezes her shoulders, then releases her, Freddy misses the warmth. "I didn't expect a card."

"I am sorry, though. Consider yourself condoled, okay?" Marv checks his watch, a vintage Mickey Mouse, then says, "Since you're here, you wanna see the Sunday layout? A couple of ladies with the Bascomb byline are front page on the North-west section."

"What ladies?"

"Dead ones."

Marv leads her from graphics to layout, a matter of six feet, to where a black woman on a tall stool bends over a full-page rough. "Toni, you got Sunday? This is Freddy Bascomb."

Toni raises her eyes and reads Freddy top to bottom, a neutral scan. Freddy says, "Hi."

Toni flips through a stack of mostly-finished layouts on the top right corner of her board, pulls one out and lays it over the page in progress. Crisp, too-dark stats of her sketches stare at Freddy out of a page otherwise composed of blue pencil lines and nonsense headlines. To see them there, hard line on shiny paper, is a different seeing. The good news is, they look alive. What Freddy has not seen before is that both women look like they're in pain. "Jeez, I never realized they looked so grim."

Marv says, "I'd look grim, too, under the circumstances."

Toni says, "Marv says you drew 'em from the skulls."

Freddy nods.

"Didn't it give you the creeps?" Toni half turns on her stool.

Freddy says, "Yeah. It seemed impossible at first. But after I locked myself up with them for a while, imagination started to fill in the blanks. Maybe out of sheer boredom. They're terrible at small talk."

Toni cocks her head, holding Freddy's gaze for a moment, then says, "Weird," and turns back to her drawing table.

Freddy addresses her back. "It *was* weird. And there's three more to go." Only when she sees how weary "three more to go" makes her feel does she recognize how much the women take life from her.

Toni says, "I wouldn't do it."

Freddy hears the unspoken part—no matter how much they offered me. Her answering thought forks two ways: You don't have two kids at home, honey. Did I do something sick? The cops *are* paying well; her fee comes out of the Consultant column of the budget. When she tries to remember what she felt accepting the assignment, the best she can come up with is macha. "Shit, it *was* the money," she says.

Marv laughs. Apparently having forgotten them, Toni sweeps a busy blue pencil over the next layout. Freddy says, "I'd better get moving."

"Want me to walk you out?" Marv asks.

"Never mind. I know my way. See if you can get the dragon lady to pay me soon, okay?"

"Will do." Marv blows a kiss as she retreats.

Freddy enters the newsroom. The only big change in thirty years is the computer terminal at each desk, the soft click of word-processor keys replacing the artillery racket of Royals and Smith-Coronas. Some of the reporters she knows; if they spot her, she nods. Without deciding to, she plays the old game across the checkerboard of desks, moves like a chess knight, in ones and twos. At least twice, crossing, she lets her eyes stray toward her father's old desk.

While Freddy was otherwise occupied, the weather's been at work, so that while white clouds still fringe the horizon all around, the very top of the sky is bald and blue. The sun itself is a hazy eyeball, eccentrically placed, peering down at the city through cataracts of cloud. Its gaze is warm and mild.

Freddy's first thought, on feeling it, is: I should take Chaz to the park this afternoon.

Then, improbably, a bird sings, a sweet brief descant to the plainsong chant of passing cars, and she stops walking, surveys the street to find the bird and, failing, waits for it to sing again. A couple strolling parts to pass around her. An empty taxi slows; she waves it on. At last, a throaty five-note trill sounds, and Freddy's heart rises with it. For the first time in a long time, she is glad to be alone.

And yet, Guilt declaims. Wait just a minute, Duty shrills. Why, it's only one o'clock. There's no limit to what could be accomplished in what remains of afternoon. Ambivalence pastes Freddy to the sidewalk, threatens to detain her well beyond the death of choices, but then the bird sings again, telling her time is a treasure, and hands her the claim check. She decides to go shopping.

Shopping! It is a drug whose enticements she's disciplined herself sternly to eschew, a dangerous drug, whose promise is false, the high short-lived, and yet, once her mind is opened to the possibility, she feels all too strongly its ruinous appeal. Shopping! Under the sun's hairy gaze, she sets her course downtown. The store windows are full of impossibly thin plaster women in evening gowns, the streets with well-appointed flesh and blood ones whose every accessory is emblazoned with the initials of some enterprising designer. Attractive men in good suits stride among them, prosperous refugees from the banking blocks, the courthouse or Pill Hill. Freddy wonders why they're not at work. Meeting their mistresses, or maybe they too are an illusion, models hired, dressed, and set upon the streets by wily merchants: Shop here and sleep with men like these.

Freddy steps into a pie-slice of Nordstrom's revolving door, is ejected before a counter glittering with costume jewels. The air inside is perfumed and redolent of Bach, played live and not-half-badly on a baby grand piano set on a dais by the escalators. Cosmetics salesgirls in white coats regard her as she passes, appraisingly, as if her every flaw were not only apparent but correctible by the paints and potions on their glass shelves. All the necessities of the well-appointed woman—scarves and belts, hats, gloves, earrings, bracelets, and silken hose—whisper their promises, and Freddy, who has spent so much energy training herself not to want, feels both excited by the sweet frivolities and illegitimate among them. Wanting flowers in her, signaled by a perceptible rise in the beating of her heart.

Once the possibility of wanting is entertained, Freddy wants everything. Surely these enamel earrings shaped like hummingbirds would enhance the tenor of her days, a silk blouse would do much to ease her grief. No woman wearing such fine black boots would ever fall prey to confusion or to fear. And love. Surely love would come, easy and unexpected, if only a scarf like that one were draped about her neck. She stands bedazzled in the siren maze of merchandise, arms at her sides, made childlike by the consumer magic, until by chance she catches her reflection on a mirrored pillar. Freddy straightens her shoulders, lifts her chin, veils her mobile features with willed opacity and, *voilà*, looks rich, rich despite her unassuming clothes and tousled hair.

Looking rich, she strides past the pianist and mounts the escalator, rides its zigzag floor to floor until she spots mannequins wearing clothes that she, rich, finds worth desiring and disembarks.

Rich, she choreographs her passage among the racks, her mind full not of children and corpses, but of tuxedoed men and gala auctions for charity and what to ask the cook to make for dinner. Rich woman's fingers reach out gently to touch a sleeve, a skirt. The silk is cool and shimmery, velvet delicate and lush as the fur of pansies. Never once does she consult a price tag.

From a respectful distance, a saleswoman shadows her, observing what catches Freddy's eye. When the clerk, in her late forties and buxom, approaches and inquires if she's looking for something special today, Freddy hears in her tone that the jury is still out—the woman has not yet decided if Freddy is really rich or not.

Slowly Freddy turns from black silk, says, "I beg your pardon."

The saleswoman retreats a step, clears her throat, and asks again.

"I'm just looking, really," Freddy says.

Her demur sets the hook. The saleswoman darts among her wares, trying to warm Freddy to consumer temperature. At last and with exquisite reluctance, she consents to try on a dress of cornflower-blue silk, and the saleslady—My name is Irma—installs her in a carpeted cubicle just slightly smaller than Chaz's bedroom. When Irma retreats, Freddy strips down to her sensible K Mart underwear and for a moment regards her sensible body in the full-length triptych mirror. The light in here is diplomatically diffuse, the mirror-glass mendacious, so that Freddy, tall and slim to begin with, is elongated by its mercies to the verge of malnutrition. The dress fits and flatters her, swishes caressingly as she pirouettes, sparkles her eyes the color of the ocean at August noonday. Irma, returning to check on her, murmurs admiration.

"I don't know," Freddy says. "I'm not sure about the neckline."

"What about the neckline?"

"It might be just a little prim."

"Would you like to try something a little bit more daring?"

Freddy would, but first consults her watch. "Well . . ."

"Make yourself comfortable," Irma coos. "I'll just bring a few things in."

Five minutes later, Irma returns with laden arms. Time ceases to be measured in minutes but melts into dresses, chaste or seductive, soft or stark. It is one of those days when everything she tries on flatters her. After a while, Freddy almost believes in the life she pretends to be shopping for and Irma, believing she will make a sale, serves her willingly. When Freddy looks at her watch again, it's shockingly late. "Oh, my. I have to run."

"I can ring up your purchases while you get dressed," Irma offers.

"There just isn't time to decide. I'm afraid I'll have to come back later in the week. Maybe I'll bring my daughter. I trust her taste."

"You could take several home and show them to her. Return the ones you don't want. Our best customers do it all the time."

"How much is the blue silk?" Freddy asks.

"Twelve seventy-five."

Freddy takes a sharp but silent breath. The figure has a comma but no decimal point. It's more than two months' rent.

"Shall I ring it up?"

Freddy almost says yes. She could take it home, show it to Paige and Chaz, play grown-up dress-up. For up to three days, she could possess the fantasy.

"Well?"

"Hold it for me, would you? I really do have to run."

Irma takes the dress and Freddy resumes her true cotton-and-rayon identity. The lateness of the hour induces guilt, and the impossibility of having what fits so well, self-pity. Outside the dressing room, Irma asks her for her name. Freddy gives Irma her mother's new married name. Irma tapes it to the blue silk dress.

Music, Mozart now, grows louder as she descends. A knot of hurt expands inside her chest, throbbing for the luxury she lacks and the trouble she owns. On the first floor, in a sudden fit of acquisitive panic, Freddy buys herself a jade and turquoise scarf, too expensive at least by half, to ease the pain.

Outside, it is already growing dark.

12

The house is full of baking smells. That's good. Chaz is home before her, fondling his blanket in front of *Duck Tales* on TV. That's bad. It's Mrs. Patniak who's spooning balls of dough onto the cookie sheets. That's bad, too. Paige sticks her finger into the bowl and scoops out a clump of dough, bumpy with chocolate chips. Good. "Where's Mom?"

"She went downtown." Patniak evens the alignment of the dough balls, four rows of three, then wipes her hands on her striped apron. "There's some hot ones over there."

"She didn't say anything to me about it," Paige says.

Mrs. Patniak shrugs. "Have a glass of milk. All I know is, she asked me if I'd watch your brother and be here when you got home."

A sudden increase in the volume of the television signals the change from program to commercial. Blanket and all, Chaz appears in the kitchen. "Are the cookies done yet?"

Patniak points to the hot batch giving up their grease to paper toweling. "Help yourself, sweetheart."

Paige knows the pet name is heartfelt. Chaz is everybody's sweetheart. Not that she'd want to be Patniak's. The woman has bad breath and fat ankles. Now, in passing, Patniak pats Chaz on the head. He samples a cookie and grins up at her. "These are real good, Mrs. P."

"Do you know where Mom went, Chaz?"

"Uh-huh." As he chews, chocolate oozes from the corner of his mouth. Sometimes it's beyond her why people think he's cute.

"Would you mind telling me?"

Normally, her brother has the manners of a donkey. Now he waits until he's swallowed every single crumb before he speaks. "She went downtown."

"Was she going to see the police?"

"I don't know, but I don't think so."

"In other words, you don't know anything."

"I do too. We talked about what happens to people who kill other people. Did you know that the state can kill a killer?"

"Of course. It's called capital punishment, dummy."

Chaz licks his lips. "Do you know how they do it?"

"Not exactly," Paige says. "Sometimes they use the electric chair."

"What's that?"

"It's like a shock."

"Does it hurt?"

"How would I know?"

Mrs. Patniak checks the minutes left on the timer. "Four to go. Actually, different places do it different ways. Some states electrocute murderers, like Paige said. Some places they give 'em a shot, like poison. In the old days|in France|they used| to cut off their heads."

Paige's hand rises to her throat. She feels the smallness of her neck. "Didn't that hurt?"

"They say not much," Patniak informs them. "They used a real sharp blade, called a guillotine. It used to be like a holiday when they cut off someone's head. People packed picnic lunches and brought the kids to watch."

"Mom would never do that," Chaz says solemnly.

"It didn't hurt," Patniak goes on, "because it happened so fast. In this state, we use hanging. Only nobody's been executed here for a long time."

"That's old-fashioned," Paige says. "It's horrible."

"That's the point," Mrs. Patniak says, plucking a cookie

from the cooling pile. "It's supposed to make you stop and think before you kill somebody."

"It didn't stop whoever killed our grandpa," Chaz points out.

Chewing, Patniak shrugs. "I didn't say it worked. It's the theory, that's all."

"How come you know so much about it, anyway?" Chaz inquires, and Paige watches Mrs. Patniak's face squirm as she sucks her dentures and tries to figure out a decent answer. She looks embarrassed.

"Because it's interesting, I guess. Everybody's interested in things like that, even if they pretend they aren't."

Paige considers and decides she's interested, too. She is not sure she likes knowing this about herself. The minute timer brays, and Mrs. Patniak shoos them out of the way so she can open the oven. Chaz wanders back to the television set. Paige leans against the sink, watching Patniak wield the spatula— thrust, lift, drop—until the cookie sheet is bare. No answers here, and no point telling. A little shudder quivers her arms, as if room temperature had dropped suddenly, about thirty degrees, or a cold wind blown through, touching just her. Mom says it means somebody is walking over your grave. Paige knows it means she is afraid. She grabs a handful of cookies and heads upstairs.

Opening Mom's address book, she feels sneaky, and has to think a minute before she remembers Carol's last name. Paige dials the number. Rodney, Carol's second son, answers the phone. He's fifteen and looks like Tom Cruise. Sometimes when she's falling asleep at night, Paige imagines going out on a date with Rod. In real life, he thinks she's a little kid. Having to say when he asks who's calling heats her cheeks. Over the phone line, she hears Rodney holler, "Mom!"

Carol's voice comes on. "What's up, my dear?"

"I was wondering if you knew where my mom went."

"Haven't talked to her since yesterday. I know she planned to take her sketches over to the *Times*."

"I knew that, too. She stayed up real late last night, working on them. But she wasn't here when I got home from school."

Carol says something away from the phone, then returns. "You kids aren't alone, are you?"

"No. Mrs. Patniak is here."

"Well, I'm sure Freddy will turn up soon."

"Yeah, maybe."

Carol says, "Is something wrong?"

If Paige says yes, it becomes true. She doesn't want something to be wrong. She wants to be ten years old and not afraid. The breath she draws feels ragged in her throat. "Something weird happened at school today. Right before we got out. The secretary came to our room with a message for me."

Carol says, "What was it?"

Paige takes the memo out of the pocket of her jeans, unfolds and presses it flat against the drawing board. "It says, 'Paige Winslow. Your mother called. She wants you to go straight to your grandfather's house after school today.' That's all, except for some initials at the bottom."

The receiver amplifies Carol's soft whistle. "You're right. That's weird."

Now Paige says the really scary part. "I don't think it was really from Mom. Do you?"

Carol is quiet for a moment. "Doesn't seem like it, does it?"

All in all, Paige thinks, she feels some better for having told.

"Listen," Carol says. "I want you to make sure all the doors are locked, and I don't want you kids going outside until your mom gets home. Don't answer the phone, either. Put the machine on and listen to the messages. If it's your mother, pick it up. Otherwise, let it go. You got that?"

"Uh-huh."

"I want you to call me back in an hour, or when Freddy gets home. Whichever comes first. Okay?"

"Okay. Should I tell Mrs. Patniak?"

"Let's not upset her," Carol says. "Unless you think it would make you feel better."

"I think she'd get all uptight," Paige says, then adds what she suddenly knows is true. "That's why I called you."

"Smart girl. I'm glad you did."

"Carol?"

"Yes?"

"Do you think it was him?"

"I don't know, babe. I'll talk to you in an hour, okay? If your mom's not home by then, I'll come over."

"Thanks."

"And don't you worry. Read a good book or something."

"Okay," Paige says.

Carol hangs up then. The hum of the dial tone makes Paige feel hollow inside.

Nordie's big front door revolves her into rush and rain. Her car, parked by the paper, is a wet mile away. As Freddy's clothes grow damp, so do her spirits, chilling her mild delight in truancy. A powerful maternal tropism turns her thoughts toward home. She had not meant to be gone so long.

A soggy parking ticket waits on the windshield. Freddy pulls into traffic, dense because of the hour, slow because of the rain. The street's one way and it's the wrong one. The car heater, on to clear her breath from the windows, coaxes the sharp scent of rain repellent from her coat, and the silk scarf she lately had to have reproaches her from the passenger seat. Better to have spent her time and money on her kids. In the rearview mirror, her eyes look dark and disappointed.

From behind, an impatient driver honks her out of reverie, and it doesn't seem to matter where you hit her or with what —fists or horns—Freddy flinches democratically. Stopped at the next red light, she pries her fingers from the wheel and tries to shake the tightness from her hands. What would it take to relax her?

Her mind casts up the antidote of round-faced, round-eyed Dr. Bones, a thought that softens tendons, makes her blush and smile, remembering his warm and slippery tongue, its unexpected exploration of her own. (Guilt censors, then—what harm?—relents.) Dr. B., how big's your boner? A little to the left please, and faster faster. Ahhhhhh yes. How wonderful to wonder, to have a fantasy that somewhere in this world, this city, is separate and incarnate, real.

Rain touched by yellow light weeps down the windshield; the metronome wipers, drawing and redrawing their twin half-moons, give rhythm to desire. The bridge grille under her tires sets up an insistent hum that passes through the metal body of the car into her own, sets up a fine vibration at the tuned fork of thigh and thigh, and Freddy smiles, at the simple cunning of her flesh. And then she's home.

An explosion of questions when she enters wipes the smile from Freddy's face. Mom, where have you been? Mommy, you're late. We've been so worried. Why didn't you. Mysteriously, there's Carol, with just a whiff of disapproval in her smile.

"Hey, calm down and let me catch my breath. In case you hadn't noticed, I just got here. Traffic's a bitch tonight."

"Is that why you're so late?" Paige asks.

"I didn't know I had a curfew," Freddy says. She turns to Carol. "How come you're here?"

Carol addresses Paige. "You better show her the note."

The note, on the surface of it, makes no sense. Paige has no living grandfather. Carol says, "I take it you didn't call the school."

Freddy shakes her head. Surrendering all pretense of adulthood, Paige wraps her arms around her mother's waist. For a moment, catching the rhythm of the cradle, mother and daughter rock from side to side.

Mrs. Patniak appears from the kitchen. "Oh, there you are. Chaz and I were just trying to figure out what there was for dinner. I didn't know if you'd be home in time or not."

Freddy mumbles something about the traffic.

"It's not that I mind," says Patniak. "The kids were fine."

Freddy says, "Thank you."

"Do you still need me at seven-thirty?"

Paige stiffens in Freddy's arms. Chaz says, "Mommy, you can't go out tonight."

Freddy looks to Carol and receives only an acknowledgment of eyebrows: Yep, this is deep shit. Freddy says, "I'll have to think about it. Can I give you a call?"

Mrs. Patniak peers through her thick lenses. Astutely inquires, "Is something wrong?"

Chaz, detached from Patniak, bounces in place: "What's wrong, Mommy?"

Freddy says, "I'll give you a call, okay?"

"I'll be home." Patniak finds this witty enough to deserve a laugh. Freddy gives her a tired smile. As Mrs. P. heads for the basement door, Chaz approaches Freddy for *his* hug. He comes up to her navel now. For a moment, Freddy holds him close, then says, "Why don't you kids go play for a little while, so I can talk to Carol?"

Paige plants her feet apart, hands on hips. "No way. This is my business, too. I was the one who got the note."

Without much liking it, Freddy sees the justice of her position. And if Paige is included in the deliberations, Chaz can't be left out. This round to the enemy. Her children are implicated now.

Carol says, "Why don't we all sit down?"

On the sofa, Chaz nestles close to Freddy's side. "What's wrong, Mommy? How come you're so concerned?"

"Somebody left a note at Paige's school."

"What did it say?"

"It said Paige should go to Grandpa's house after school."

"I think you should call the police, Mom," Paige says.

"Were you at Grandpa's house, Mommy?"

"No."

"I wanted to call them, but Carol said to wait till you got home," Paige says.

"Then who would have said that?" Chaz's puzzlement is real. He dignifies it with a finger laid against his chin, a grave urgency borrowed from television detectives.

"And Mom," Paige says, "you can't go out tonight."

"I have to work tonight," Freddy says.

Chaz says, "Carol, do you know who?"

"You won't be alone. Mrs. Patniak will look out for you."

"Mom, I'm scared. I need you here."

"Was it Grandpa's killer?" Chaz says.

"We need the money," Freddy says.

"Mom, it was Grandpa's killer," Chaz says.

Paige looks at her brother with exasperation. "No duh. Why do you think I want Mom to stay home tonight?"

"I really ought to work," Freddy says.

Paige says, "Didn't Grandpa leave us anything in his will?"

"He did, but we won't get it for a long time. His estate has to go through probate first."

"I'm scared, too, Mommy," Chaz says.

Freddy captures a deep breath in her cheeks, then, exhaling, deflates them.

Carol says, "We all have to eat. I'll order us a pizza. Then, Freddy, you call the cops. Paige, is your homework done? *Cosby*'s coming on at eight."

Above the children's heads, Freddy looks to Carol. "Should I go to work or not?"

Carol elevates both shoulders. "Do what feels right," she says.

"Nothing feels right."

"Then it doesn't much matter, does it?" Carol says.

Freddy makes the call upstairs, finds Ashford working late.

"Okay!" he says, with undisguised enthusiasm. "I've been expecting the bastard to flash his cards. I just didn't know when or how."

"I don't like how," Freddy says.

"I wouldn't worry about it too much. This is just showing off. A little psychological terrorism."

"We're talking about my daughter. She's ten years old."

"I saw her at the services. Cute kid. Looks kind of serious, though."

"I want my children safe."

"Miz Bascomb, this is not a safe world." Ashford says this with studied weariness.

"Don't give me any philosophical crap," Freddy says. "This asshole is a clear and present danger."

Ashford says, "How am I supposed to know you didn't make that call yourself, just to throw us off the track? You're still the only person around who's got a motive."

"Jesus Christ," Freddy says. Her pencil rips at the drawing pad, scoring the paper with black grooves. She takes a deep breath. "Give me the name of your superior, please."

"I was only kidding."

"I'm not. Who do you report to?"

"Come on, give me a break. I apologize if I was insensitive, okay?"

"It is not okay," Freddy insists. The stress wave she's been riding all day peaks as anger, then breaks into self-pity, a great roar followed by a slow hiss of resignation. Unexpected tears fill her eyes, and she has to be silent for a moment because anything she says would be pure whine. When she speaks again, her voice is small and level. "Listen, I'm sorry. I'm under a lot of pressure these days. Which doesn't mean you're not a jerk."

Ashford's voice is wary but willing to be cheerful. "Actually, I report to Jim Norgaard."

"I'll remember that," Freddy says, "in case you make any more bad jokes. Now, tell me what you plan to do to keep my children safe."

In the bassest of big voices, Lieutenant Ashford assures her he will do everything he can.

Her freedom now feels like a dress she coveted, bought, then never wears. It's the wrong color. The waist is too short or the arms too long, the skirt's too tight. It's just not comfortable. Her stomach isn't right, either. Freddy gets her wish —to see the doctor—but is not as she wished to be. Her body feels alien, an awkward encumbrance she has to drag around. That's what happens when desire catches cold. With the sexual subplot deleted, what remains is another tedious encounter with a skull.

The ornamental shrubs, just in bloom, that beautify the campus by day look sinister as she travels from the parking lot onto unlighted paths. Rhododendron blossoms big as human faces, pale in the darkness, nod as she passes, their blind mouths whispering secrets she guesses are obscene. A clammy breeze blows in the wake of rain. As soon as she reaches her destination, her relief at arriving safely gives way to new unease. The striking of her boot heels echoes up the empty stairwell, and the corridor she climbs to sounds hollow, too. The doctor is not in his office.

Timidly, she calls out a hello or two whose second syllables rise uncertainly. In response to her interrogation of the empty hallway, his face, his body take shape in a doorway, grow bigger with his smile as he approaches. Him. Freddy realizes, watching, that she has no name to call him beyond the pronoun. She realizes, too, that her heart beats faster when he appears. He is wearing a white lab coat over his clothes.

"There you are. I didn't know if you'd make it or not. I went ahead with some work in the lab."

Freddy nods. His face is comforting somehow. Her pleasure in seeing it is less aesthetic than automatic, something like the touch of his blanket must be to Chaz. The doctor walks right up to her, stops three feet away and puts one of his hands on each of her shoulders. "How have you been?"

She smiles, feeling she is all right now, and shrugs, admitting that she hasn't been. For the second time in one unyielding day, she feels the prickle of tears at the inside corners of her eyes. His forehead puckers between leveled eyebrows. "Do you need a hug?"

That's probably, she thinks, the *kindest* thing anyone's ever asked her. She does need a hug, and now she has one. The front of his lab coat is starchy and smells of formalin. Beyond it, she feels his human warmth. The only thing that dilutes it is knowing that her pleasure is an index of her need. This makes her laugh a little, into the stiff white fabric of his coat.

"What's funny?"

She doesn't want to say. He shifts position, lowering his head, and then she feels his lips, nibbling along the right side of her neck. It tickles and gives her chills, and at first she resists the sensation because it is not pure, but his breath is warm and her skin cold and by the time he reaches that magic spot somewhere near the junction of throat and collarbone, she surrenders, burrowing her face into his shoulder.

Freddy trembles in his arms, the tremor of a driver damn-nearly crashed, of the hungover reaching for a too-needed drink. Only the tiniest fragment of her consciousness is available to appreciate the absurdity of their entanglement; the better part of her nervous system engages, without irony, in the embrace. Across the breach of skins the charge is so powerful Freddy wonders if they give off light.

His lips move in her hair now, near the crown, and his whisper raises gooseflesh. "Would you like to come to my house? I live nearby."

Against the wall of her own wanting, Freddy dutifully casts her last small stone. "I have to work."

He rests his chin on the top of her head. "I've got color photos of the model, full face and both profiles. We could bring the skull," he says. "It's a little unorthodox, but I doubt that anyone would mind."

Yes to his house is yes to everything, to whatever complications arise from everything. Yes means she will feel guilty later, for renouncing mourning and forgetting motherhood. One of the children might wake up, cross and sleepy, when she comes in and ask her where she's been. Yes means little sleep

tonight, less energy tomorrow. Can she really get up after making love and attempt to draw a living woman from her bones?
Freddy decides she is willing to try.

Finally, Paige is too tired to worry anymore. She gives up listening for Mom, and goes to sleep.

13
■ ■ ■ ■ ■

No-mind, no-thing, the original condition. Until some-time, a tiny seed of being stirs in night's dark soil and immediately knows terror, which is being without bearings, no known address in the Great Chain, but only these sensations: Black. Still. Close. As much as one cell knows.

The process of waking recapitulates the eons of evolution. It takes no more than a minute, by whose end she has correctly identified her species, if not her gender, age, or nationality. In rapid succession thereafter she acquires name, memory, a rudimentary personality. Her eyes open on the eighties, to present circumstance. There is a man beside her. The noise she took for wind is snoring.

The present seems hardly worth reclaiming. She closes her eyes, sinks back, quite willing to relinquish her identity again, but oblivion has receded meanwhile, and she's stuck.

They went the distance, she'll give them that, rewound the film all the way back past the titles, past the numbers, back to stark unimaged leader. No wonder people call it the little death. It is profoundly restful to be dead. Her traveling companion, dear Dr. Bones, still is.

Up on one elbow, she peers at his slack face. His breath has staled in sleeping and gurgles in his throat.

So, how was it, Freddy?

Nice. The first time was pro forma, awkward and funny, but that's how first times are.

More than once, then?

Oh, yes. He's got amazing staying power, really. Almost uncanny. I thought he'd never come. In fact, I'm not sure he ever did. Must have studied with a yogi or something. Weird.

How weird?

Oh, nicely. I really don't mind weird. Except for the coyote skull. That's a weird thing to have on your nightstand, kind of, isn't it? But the whole business is weird, you know, the way it seems so imperative sometimes, and so particular, as if the whole universe wants you to fuck this one man, when it's really such a simple exercise—tab A, slot B.

And variations.

Yeah, variations.

So tell me, having done it once, would you again?

With the backside of her index finger, Freddy traces the curve of the man's stubbling cheek. He stirs slightly, half turns his face away. She is not sure if their souls touched or not. She is not sure if she believes in souls.

It's five A.M., no time to ponder mysteries. Freddy rises, collects her cold scattered clothes and wriggles into them, rakes a brush through matted hair, finds his briefcase in the kitchen and extracts Bones 13, transfers her to a plastic grocery bag for the trip home, then tiptoes into the living room, one they omitted to visit in last night's heat, to check it out, finds Danish modern furniture and Navajo rugs, a Kollwitz print on one wall, a shaman's mask, and on the hearth, the bleached skull of some horned ruminant. Whether the decor is sinister or quaint, she is too tired to decide. She leaves a note taped to the coffeepot: "Good morning. Have a nice day." In place of the conventional happy face, she draws a creditable caricature of Bones 13, who always smiles.

The car is cranky, as reluctant to wake up as she was, stalls and coughs before consenting to be driven. If she doesn't drive fast, it'll be light before she gets home. On the other hand, if she drives *too* fast, some night owl traffic cop will pull her over and she'll have to explain why there's a human skull in a shopping bag belted in the passenger seat. Freddy opts for caution and gets to witness a languid dawn. In the living room, Mrs. Patniak snores louder than the man she left. Freddy decides not to wake her. That way, no one will know for sure when she got home.

Paige's digital alarm busts up whatever dream she's having. It's six o'clock and she intends to borrow two hours from sleep to put them into studying. Science and social studies, not just one test today but two. Last night, instead of studying, she let Mrs. Patniak show her how to crochet, not because she wanted to learn so much, but because Chaz is too little to. For once, she got the most attention.

Out of bed, she pulls on socks and peeks out the window. The car is there. It wasn't when she went to sleep. The house is cold and Paige wishes she were less responsible. She could count on half the fingers of one hand the number of her classmates who would actually get up early to read about the Civil War or asexual reproduction in yeast cells. The boys snickered a lot about that. Miz Rupp intercepted a note Jason sent to Eric with a picture of a yeast cell centerfold on it, complete with boobs. Miz Rupp laughed and said she was a budding beauty.

Paige cranks the thermostat, then stands over the kitchen heating vent to catch the first blast of hot air. When it comes, it inflates her nightgown, so she looks pregnant, and melts the goosebumps on her legs. Warmed, she fills a bowl to brimming with Honey Nut Cheerios and makes for the dining room, where her books await. She opens up her social-studies text. Ulysses S. Grant, it says, was the Union Army's greatest general. Whoopee. Her eyes stray from the picture of Mr. Bearded General to the Safeway bag next to Mom's purse at the far end of the table. Croissants, or maybe doughnuts. Sometimes when Mom works late, she stops at an all-night supermarket to buy something special for breakfast.

When Paige sticks her hand inside the bag, what she feels is not the expected waxy bakery sack, not a doughnut box, but something cool and hard. Curious, she pulls down the top edges of the bag. Two empty eyes stare back at her.

* * *

The sound that shocks Freddy upright in her bed is undoubtedly a scream. For a moment, Freddy listens with detached curiosity, until suddenly she understands it is her daughter screaming. She grabs her robe and, pulling it around her, races down the narrow stairs.

She finds Paige in the dining room. Bones 13 is there, too, out of her bag and grinning. Freddy grabs her coat from a chair and tosses it over the skull, then wraps her arms around her daughter. At her touch, the scream breaks into sobs. Paige trembles, sometimes shuddering between her sobs. Freddy strokes her hair, her daughter's tear-wet cheek. "Oh, baby, I'm sorry. It's all right. She isn't going to hurt you." Paige wails louder. Freddy says, "I shouldn't have left her out for you to find. I didn't know you'd be up so early," but her words have all the impact of peas on granite. Freddy is pretty sure her daughter is hysterical.

Chaz appears in his pajamas, blinking wide eyes. "What's wrong with her?" At just that moment, there comes a pounding on the basement door, and Freddy understands not when or why but that Mrs. Patniak must have awakened and taken herself downstairs. Is knocking now. "Chaz, will you open the door for Mrs. P.?"

Paige turns her face away from the intrusions and buries it in Freddy's shoulder. Her sobs do not abate. Freddy leads her to the rocking chair in the living room, sits and pulls her daughter onto her lap. She is too heavy and too long now, but Freddy rocks her anyway, to a slow and steady beat. Then Chaz and Mrs. Patniak stand before her, sleepy and shocked and wanting answers. "She's okay," Freddy says, and is looking for a simple explanation when the phone rings. "I'll get it, Mom," Chaz volunteers, and starts toward it, but Freddy says, "That's okay. The machine will answer."

On the fourth ring, her own voice, small and chipper, says, "If you are trying to reach Freddy, Paige, or Chaz, please leave your name and number after the beep and we'll get right back to you."

The machine beeps. A familiar male voice says, "Freddy, I woke up and you were gone. I hope you didn't leave angry. I found your note. My body loves your body. Call me when you can." After his hanging up, the machine warbles its end-of-message tone.

Freddy closes her eyes and keeps rocking. Apart from the thud of the rocker's runners, and the beating of her blood as it feeds a blush, a sound that only she can hear, the house is absolutely quiet. Paige has stopped crying. Freddy rocks.

Chaz's little voice, with its panpipe inflections and tidy diction, breaks the silence. "Who was that, Mother?"

Freddy opens her eyes and meets their wide ones. "It must have been a wrong number." She fakes a giggle. "Won't he be embarrassed when he realizes he called the wrong lady?"

Paige sits up straight on Freddy's lap. "Mother, the man said 'Freddy.'"

"You're right. It was a crank, then. I knew I shouldn't have put my first name in the phone book."

Mrs. Patniak says, "I heard a scream. What happened? It scared the living daylights out of me."

Freddy sighs. "Paige found a skull on the dining-room table. It gave her quite a shock."

"A real one, Mom? You mean, like in a skeleton?" A smile blossoms on Chaz's face. He bounces up and down.

"My mistake. I left it there by accident."

Paige sniffs deeply and pushes back her bangs. "I thought it was croissants."

Chaz bounces higher. "Oh, boy. Are there croissants for breakfast?"

Freddy says, "Afraid not. Only bones." She squeezes Paige around the waist. "Honey, I'm so sorry."

Paige sniffs again. "I'm sorry I woke everybody up. It's just, when I saw it, I got so scared. Not fake scared, like at movies. I wasn't faking."

Freddy squeezes her again. "I know, baby. It must have been awful."

Chaz says, "Can I see it, Mom? Where is it? Can I, please?"

Suddenly Paige stiffens and bolts off Freddy's lap. "Oh my god, my homework. I've got two tests today. That's why I got up early. I'll never get it done now." Her voice thins to a whine of desperation that's only marginally more euphonious than screaming.

"Under the circumstances," Freddy says, "I'll write you an

excuse. I'm sure Miz Rupp will let you take the tests on Monday."

"Can I, Mom?" Chaz says. "Can I see the skull?"

"Not now," Freddy says.

Paige says, "Thanks, Mom."

"I want to see the skull," Chaz wheedles, and likes the cadence of the words so much he decides to repeat them.

Mrs. Patniak says, "Well, I don't, thanks very much. I suppose I'll never get back to sleep now."

"Oh, Mrs. Patniak, I'm sorry," Freddy says.

Paige says, "Maybe if we're really quiet, and you put a pillow over your head . . ."

In martyred dismissal, Patniak waves her hand. "Not at my age. I hardly sleep anymore as it is."

Chaz is chanting, "I want to see the skull."

Mrs. Patniak turns and points her Dearfoams toward the stairs.

Paige turns to Freddy, suddenly self-possessed. "Mother, that wasn't some crank. Who is that man? What did he mean about your body?"

Freddy raises her right hand. "I take the fifth." Then slips her arm around her daughter. "I think I'll walk with you to school today."

They arrive in time to hear the tardy buzzer scold. "Mom, I'm late," Paige says in a pained whisper as they stand outside the office door.

"Don't worry, hon. I'll make it right," Freddy says.

"Can I go now, please?" Paige implores. "Miz Rupp hates it when people come in late."

"Go." Freddy swats her daughter's already receding back, watches her pump up the ramp in three-foot strides. After she's out of sight around the first of several zigs, the fast squeak of her sneakers echoes back. From the upstairs hall, Freddy hears the opening and closing of the classroom door.

The school secretary greets her with a look of friendly inquiry. She's a pale fake-blonde with mild eyes, comfortably expanded in late middle age, not at all like the squat monster who reigned in Freddy's grade school. "What can I do for you?" she asks.

"Well, first you can fix it so my daughter won't be counted tardy. She's real proud of her perfect record. It's my fault she's late."

Behind designer glasses, the kind whose bows attach to the bottom of the lens, the secretary's eyes regard her. "And who's your daughter?"

"Paige Winslow, in Miz Rupp's room."

The secretary smiles and writes herself a note on a yellow Post-it. "Was there something else?"

"Well, yes," Freddy says. "My family's in a rather unusual situation right now. I need to talk to someone about it."

"I have the free-lunch application forms right here."

"Oh, no. It's not financial." Freddy feels the cold sweat that's slicked her fingers and wipes her hands on her pants.

"Maybe you should talk to the principal."

"Yes," Freddy says, grateful. "That's what I need to do."

She sips free coffee, instant decaf in Styrofoam, while she waits, waits half a cup until the principal appears on the sanctum side of the office gate and calls for "Mrs. Winslow."

Freddy abandons her cup and rises to consummate the offered handshake. "Freddy Bascomb. My kids and I have different surnames."

The principal smiles. "I understand. I'm Chung, but my children are all Woos. Won't you come in?"

Miz Chung swings back the gate to admit Freddy. The principal wears a smart red suit, red high heels, red lips. Her black bob shines. Freddy's rumpled sweats make her feel like a slob. Meekly she follows the principal to her office where, invited, she sits on a chair of green steel and lumpy low-grade Naugahyde. Settled behind her desk, Miz Chung looks pleasant and expectant.

"We have a little problem at our house," Freddy says. "I don't know if you're aware of it or not, but my father, Paige's grandfather, was murdered a couple of weeks ago."

"How is Paige taking it?"

Freddy considers. "Pretty well, I guess. She's doing her best to keep up with her schoolwork."

"Our counselor comes to this building every other Thursday. I could arrange for him to meet with Paige."

"I really don't think that's necessary. The real problem is, somebody called here yesterday and left a message for Paige, saying she was to go straight to her grandfather's house after school." Freddy digs her fingers into already messy hair. "As you can imagine, it gave her quite a start. Me, too, when I heard about it."

Miz Chung nods sympathetically. "I can instruct the staff not to forward any more messages like that, if we get them."

"Right," Freddy says. "I'd appreciate that." Again, she wipes damp fingers on the thighs of her sweatpants. "Look, I honestly don't know if Paige is in danger, or what, but I'm worried. Whoever killed my dad is a real creep. A sicko, and probably real smart besides. He didn't leave the cops a thing to go on. And now he's calling my daughter's school." The principal's face, with its wide cheekbones, the attentive and intelligent eyes, invites confession. As hers tumbles out, Freddy realizes she sounds like a troubled child.

Miz Chung rocks back a little in her desk chair. "You're a single mother?"

"Uh-huh." Normally, Freddy avoids the label; now, angling for compassion, she embraces it.

Miz Chung says, "Me, too. It's a job that requires a good amount of grace, and a whole lot of good luck."

The phone rings on the desk then. Miz Chung swivels, punches a button, says, "Hold my calls, please. Take a message." She turns back to Freddy. "What can we do to help?"

Freddy lets a long blink soothe her eyeballs before she speaks. "I'm not quite sure. I guess if you could let people know what's going on, ask them to keep an eye on Paige. If you see anybody suspicious hanging around, let me know. Or the police."

A nod animates the shoulder-length black bob.

"There's a detective named Ashford. He's in charge. Homicide. The number's in the blue pages. I can't tell you what to expect from him, though. When I told him about the phone call yesterday, he didn't seem very concerned. Said he doubted the guy would hurt my daughter. Frankly, I don't have too much faith in the police."

Miz Chung smiles deeply. "Would it make you feel better

to know that Lieutenant Ashford was here and gone this morning before you came? We've agreed to alert the police to anything out of the way that happens here concerning Paige."

Freddy feels both redundant and relieved. "It would," she
says. "I do. I'll just go home now and feed the cat."

Miz Chung rises to see her out. "I hope they catch the
bastard," she says in farewell.

Walking home, for the first time in days, or maybe weeks,
Freddy thinks about the cat. Far Out, the boon-and-bane cat,
boon for his warmth, the softness of his fur-and-purr, for his
tolerance of Chaz's little boy rough love, for his absence of
neurosis; bane for shedding and the cat box, for being one
more being for whom she is responsible. It occurs to Freddy
she hasn't seen Far Out for a while. Was he there this morning,
watching as she rocked Paige, there on the futon when she
shocked awake? Probably he's been sleeping with one of the
kids lately. Freddy admits it; she hasn't been much fun.

Walking home, one guilt leads to another. There's Carol.
Not only hasn't Freddy been a lot of laughs, she's been all take
and no give. Friendship's supposed to flow both ways. On the
To Do list, right after *Far Out, feed and fondle*, her mental pencil
scrawls *Do something nice for Carol*. Mrs. Patniak's been a brick,
too, though her, Freddy pays. There's bills need paying, too,
and half a dozen lesser friends cut loose from contact, displaced
by death and five new acquaintances, Bones 10 to 14, those jolly
girls.

Freddy decides to stop thinking about her life—too
messy—and sniffs the still-moist morning air instead, thinks
she detects a whiff of lilac, though she can see no blooms. In
spite of everything, spring comes. Last night she took a lover,
the first in a long time. Remembering makes her smile.

Her smile broadens when she finds the gift-wrapped package on her welcome mat, the paper Monet's water lilies rein-
terpreted by Hallmark, a sateen blue bow big as a grapefruit
affixed exactly to the center of a two-foot square. The package,
when she picks it up, is heavy.

Inside, she sets the gift on the dining-room table, puts on
the kettle, spoons Friskies Stinking Liver Dinner into Far Out's
bowl. "Hey, come and get it. Here, kitty-kitty, chow down,"
Freddy calls.

The cat does not appear. Must be out mousing. Neglect has driven him to that. When the kettle whistles, she vacillates between coffee and chamomile tea. Flannel eyeballs and a severely decreased ability to make decisions argue in favor of the herb. Nap first, draw later. She makes tea, clumsily. With it steaming before her she settles at the table, to do something she never thought she would, something perverse and adult—she contemplates the package without opening it, just like her mother used to do on Christmas.

With the handle of her teaspoon, she probes the blue bow for a card. Nothing. Perhaps the package is meant for Mrs. Patniak. This Freddy believes for less than twenty seconds. Water lilies and Mrs. P. do not a match make. Besides, it was she who made love to a new man last night. Even Jack sent roses after their first time. That was, what?—thirteen years ago; no flowers since, unless you count the ones she's bought herself, or the little bouquets of clover and dandelions the children sometimes bring her.

Her fingers are quick and happy, edging the ribbon toward one corner of the box, off. With no one to laugh at her silliness, she hangs the ribbon around her neck, the way the children do at Christmas, till they're festooned in red and green and gold.

The paper next. Now she is like her mother, careful and preserving, releases the tape without tearing, smoothes the gift wrap, then refolds it according to the manufacturer's neat creases. There. Fit to keep. The box inside once held men's boots: cordovan, size 10½. Freddy would have thought the doctor had a bigger foot.

With her nails she explores under the rim of the box lid, slitting tape. Her excitement builds at the tease of virgin tissue paper, the last stand of suspense, until she spots a fragment of the gift escaped from swaddling, a tip of tortoise tail, and there's no sense pretending Freddy doesn't know, know she's been had, had badly. The only questions left are: Will she look? Will she throw up?

For the moment, her stomach's steady; maybe lack of sleep has tardied her reaction time. She tells herself there is no need to see, that not seeing would be a victory, small but the only one available; for what seems like a long time, she tests herself, not looking, but the fact is, she knows she will, and eventually succumbs to the inevitable, flicks back the tissue paper and sees the cat, its corpse, as she expected, desecrated as her father's was.

Something, fatigue or knowing, has abrogated horror. Freddy looks with pity but no terror at what remains of the family pet. Distant from the site of surgery, the cat's haunches are clean and free of blood. These Freddy idly strokes, saying, "Far Out, you poor dumb beast, you picked the wrong family to belong to, didn't you?"

Not for the first time, Freddy curses the tensile strength of her sanity. How much easier it would be to break than to continue bending. Then, knowing she's doomed to keep on coping, she replaces the boot lid on the cat box and gives herself permission to sleep awhile before she calls the cops.

14

"Chaz," Laura says, "zip up your coat."

Chaz says, "The sun is shining. I don't have to." He pushes the tow truck over bumps in the rug.

Laura's voice gets bigger and harder. "Chaz."

Chaz straightens up on his knees and looks for a place where sunshine through the prism in the window makes rainbows on the rug. He points to the rainbow. "See?"

"CHAZ. Everybody else is ready to go to the park. We're waiting for you. Would you please zip up your jacket."

There is nothing to say but no. "No," he says, trying hard to sound like he means it without sounding bratty. Grown-ups, he knows, get mean when kids sound bratty. The rest of the day-care kids are buttoned and zipped. Karen has on her pink hat with the soft white ball on top. They are all staring at him. Tony, who just turned three, toddles over to him. "Zip," Tony says. Chaz shakes his head.

"Okay," Laura says. "The rest of you go in the kitchen for a minute. I want to talk to Chaz alone."

All of the other kids march into the kitchen, except Steven, who is a baby and doesn't walk yet. He rolls on his back on the rug. Laura kneels down near Chaz. Chaz looks at the dump truck so he won't have to look at her. "Come here," she says. She doesn't sound mad. Chaz comes. She lifts his chin with her finger, so he has to look at her. "Chaz, why won't you zip your jacket when I ask you to?"

Chaz doesn't want to tell. "You'll get mad at me," he says, as sadly as he feels.

"I won't, honey. But I want to know."

Chaz hates feeling like a bad boy. It isn't fair. He drops his eyes from Laura's and tells the truth. "I can't zip yet."

"But, honey, you zip your pants when you go to the bathroom."

"No, I don't. I just pull them down. When I'm done I pull them back up."

Laura's eyes get round and she laughs her big, rumbly laugh. Chaz isn't sure if she's laughing at him or not. "I'm only four and a half years old," he says. "When I'm five, I'll know how to zip."

"I bet I could teach you right now."

"No, you couldn't. Mom already tried. I'm just not old enough yet."

"Well, then, come here." Laura catches the open edges of his jacket, works the little red tongue into the zipper slide.

"That's the part I can't do," Chaz says. "Now I can zip." He takes hold of the little tag and pulls his zipper up to his chin. "Can we go to the park now?"

Laura stands up and calls for the rest of the kids. They come tumbling out of the kitchen. "I want you in twos," she tells them. "Find a partner."

Karen in her pink hat takes Chaz's hand. Karen has big round blue eyes. She's cute. "I'm glad you're my partner," he says, and Karen smiles. She doesn't say anything, though. Karen is only two and half and doesn't talk much yet. "I'll take good care of you," Chaz tells her.

Yellow as the sun is, it isn't very warm. Raindrops sparkle the grass. Chaz counts—four pairs of two kids each. Laura pushes Steven's stroller with one hand and holds Tony by the other. She waits at street corners until everyone's together before they cross. The park is called Hiawatha, which Mom says is the name of an Indian boy who lived a long time ago. It has two sets of swings, a play structure with a built-in slide, teeter-totters, a wading pool that's empty now and fun to run around, and something else that Chaz likes best of all, two connected wooden platforms with smooth log railings he likes to pretend is his house. He invites the other kids to come visit and stay for dinner.

As soon as they enter the park, Laura lets the kids scatter. Chaz tugs at Karen's hand. "Let's swing first. I'll push you. Then we can play in my house." She makes a sound that must mean yes, because she comes along. From the drag on his arm, Chaz realizes he's running too fast for her and slows down. Usually it's him, pumping hard to keep up with longer legs. He finds two swings next to each other and helps Karen climb on one, then pushes her from behind until her swing is moving steadily. He takes the next swing and pumps like Paige showed him. By the time he's really moving, Karen's swing has almost stopped. Chaz drags his feet and jumps off. "Come on, Karen. Let's go."

He's glad the other kids are playing on the slide or swings, so he doesn't have to argue about it being his house today. "I'll be the Dad," he tells Karen, "and you can be the Mom. Here's the kitchen. Let's make some cocoa for our children." Chaz draws a pan in air, then fills it with imaginary water, stirs in the cocoa mix and, after turning on the imaginary burner, puts it on the stove. He hands Karen an imaginary spoon. "You have to keep stirring it, like this, or it'll burn." While he makes imaginary sandwiches, enough for everyone and two for Laura, Karen stirs. "How is the cocoa doing, dear?" Chaz asks, and Karen waves the spoon at him. "Good job," he says, and returns to his imaginary peanut butter jar.

"What are you making, little man?" a rough voice asks him. Chaz looks up and sees a lumpy grandmother crouching beside his house. She's wearing a green hat pulled down over her ears, a pink muffler and eyeglasses with diamonds on the frames.

"I'm making peanut butter sandwiches for all our children," he says, not stopping. "They get very hungry when they play outside."

"That's nice," the grandmother says. "Will you make one for me?"

"Sure," Chaz says. He closes the sandwich he's been working on with a second piece of bread and hands it to her. She is wearing black gloves. "Thank you," the grandmother says. "Who is your friend?"

"That's Karen," Chaz says. "She's my wife. She's stirring the cocoa."

"This is a very good sandwich," the grandma says, licking peanut butter from one black-knit finger. "I bet I can guess your name."

"I bet you can't," Chaz says. "My name is sort of unusual."

"I bet your name is really Charles," the grandmother says. "But people call you Chaz."

Chaz looks at the sparkles on her glasses. Maybe she is a magic grandmother. "How did you know?" he asks.

"I'm very good at guessing," the grandmother says. "I bet you have a sister named Paige at home."

"Do you have a crystal ball or something?"

The grandmother shakes her head. "And I bet your mother's name is Freddy. I bet you live in a white house."

The grandmother is right. It makes Chaz a little bit afraid. "Well?" she says.

Chaz takes more bread out of the imaginary package and returns to his sandwich making. "My mom says not to talk to strangers."

"How could I be a stranger when I know so much about you?" the grandmother says.

"I don't know," Chaz says. "Maybe you're a witch."

The grandma laughs, and Chaz thinks maybe he's right, she *is* a witch. "Wife," he says, "is the cocoa done yet?"

Karen nods her head at him. Chaz looks around for Laura. She's far away, standing by the swings on the other side of the wading pool and pushing Tony, who doesn't know how to pump yet. He wishes she was closer by.

"You're not afraid of witches, are you?" the grandmother asks.

Chaz tells her what he tells Paige when she's teasing him. "I'm not afraid of anything. Besides, witches aren't real. They're pretend."

"Are you sure about that?" the grandma asks, her diamond glasses twinkling, in a way that makes Chaz have to think before he answers yes.

"What about good witches?" she says. "They're different from the bad ones in the fairy tales. You just don't hear as much about them. They're shy, you know."

"Are you a good witch?" Chaz asks.

"Do you have a wish?" the grandmother asks him.

"I have lots of wishes. I make them on stars and my mom always gives me a penny for wishing ponds. My wishes don't come true very often, though. Mom says not to be disappointed. She says real magic is when people do nice things for each other."

"I'd like to do something nice for you," the grandmother says.

"Like what?"

"Well, it's a secret. You have to come with me."

"Can Karen come?"

The grandmother shakes her head. "A secret is a secret. If all your friends saw, they'd want me to do nice things for them, too, and I only have so much magic." The grandmother holds out one black gloved hand to him. "But I can tell that you're a very special little boy."

"That's what my mom says."

"Well, she must be pretty smart. Come on. Shall we see what we shall see?"

"I don't know," Chaz says. "Laura might not like it."

"Oh, she won't mind. And I'll bring you back right away. She won't even know you've been gone."

"I don't think I should leave Karen here alone. She's only two."

"Why don't you take her over there, where the other children are? Then come back, and we can have our secret."

Chaz hears two voices inside him, like he often does when he has to make a choice. One voice is usually wrong, and it's hard to tell which one. Still, it isn't every day you meet a good witch who wants to do something nice for only you. The chance, he decides, is too good to pass up. "Come on, Karen," he says. "I'm going to take you over to the slide now. We'll drink our cocoa later."

Smiling, Karen holds out her hand, and he helps her jump down from the platform. Together, they walk to the play structure. Chaz lets go of her hand. "You play here. I'll call you when it's time to eat, okay?" Before Karen can answer him, he runs back to his house. The grandmother is standing up now. Her long brown coat is buttoned clear up to her chin and she looks taller than he thought she was.

"Ready for your surprise, Chaz?" She holds out her hand. Chaz looks up, at the sunlight glinting on her jeweled glasses. He takes her hand, and they begin to walk away from the playground, toward the tennis courts and the high school beyond. "You *are* a brave boy, Chaz," the grandma says.

"My grandma lives in Arizona," Chaz tells her. "Do you have any grandchildren?"

"No," says the grandmother sadly. "But I wish I did. Maybe I could adopt you, do you suppose?"

"Well, maybe."

"Chaz! Chaaaa-aaaz!" Laura's voice, her calling voice, comes after him.

"That's Laura," Chaz says. "Maybe I should go back."

The grandma holds tight to his hand. "And spoil our nice surprise?"

"I don't want Laura to get mad at me."

The grandma says, "She won't get mad. We'll only be a minute. Come on, let's run. I bet you can run real fast."

"Chaaa-aaaz!" Laura's voice calls.

The grandma grips his hand so tight it hurts. She starts to run, pulling him after, the way Paige does when she's in hurry. Chaz stumbles and loses his footing. The grandma drags him along.

"CHAZ! Hey, what do you think you're doing? You stop right now!"

Chaz looks back. Laura is running after them. He has never seen her run before. She looks like a teddy bear might if it could run. He yells at the grandmother, "Let me go, please," but they plunge forward, and his feet barely brush against the path. He can hear the grandmother breathing hard. His shoulder hurts. Suddenly, the tight grip loosens, and his whole body falls hard on the path. A few seconds later, Laura catches him up in her arms. Brown coat flapping, the grandmother runs away from them.

"Who is that?" Laura asks.

Chaz puts his arms around her neck and cries.

Chaz sticks to her lap as if he'd been glued there. Freddy wishes she could pull him back inside her body and keep him with her always, safe. He's so big now, all arms and legs, it's almost hard to believe he was only twenty inches long when he came out.

Laura stands with both hands planted on the back of a dining-room chair. "That's all. I'm sorry. I didn't get a good look at her face. But that was no frail old lady, not the way she took off with him." She looks from Ashford to Freddy. "Jesus, I'm so sorry."

Ashford crouches beside the wingback chair where Freddy holds her son and puts one hand on the boy's leg. "I need you to tell me what you remember."

Chaz presses tighter to Freddy's chest and sucks harder on his thumb. Gently, Freddy draws thumb from mouth. "Come on, sweet potato. Nobody's going to yell at you, I promise. Tell him everything you can remember."

"She had a brown coat and a green hat," Chaz says in a small voice, without looking at Ashford. Laura just reported as much.

"And?" Ashford says.

"And a pink scarf. And diamonds on her glasses."

"What else? What was her voice like?"

"Hmmm," Chaz says. "Her voice was like Mom's when she's talking for the big bad wolf."

"How's that?"

" 'Little pig, little pig, let me come in,' " Freddy growls. "Like that?"

"Not 'The Three Little Pigs,' " Chaz says. "More like 'Little Red Riding Hood.' "

Ashford looks to Freddy. She nods. "That's wolf pretending not to be. 'Just lift the latchstring and come in, my dear.' "

Chaz nods vigorously. "She talked like that."

"Are you sure it was a she?" Ashford asks.

"I thought she was," Chaz says.

"Do you know why?"

"Her glasses and her scarf. Men don't wear pink scarfs. They don't have diamonds on their glasses, either."

"Not unless they want you to think they're women," Ashford says. "What did she say to you?"

"Lots of things. She knew my name, and my mom's name and my sister's name. She knew we live in a white house. She said she couldn't be a stranger because she knew so much about us."

Freddy is angry. She is angry enough to kick and scratch and bite and tear. She wishes Ashford would catch the pervert and give her an hour alone with him. She also wants to cry.

"She said she was a good witch," Chaz says. "She said she had a very special secret surprise for me, because I am a very special little boy."

Freddy says, "Oh, brother."

Ashford says, "Did she tell you what the surprise was, Chaz?"

Chaz shakes his head. "Uh-uh. Then it wouldn't be a surprise. That's what she said."

"You must have liked her."

It is not a question and not a judgment, just a mild statement that makes it acceptable for Chaz to have liked her. Astute enough to give Freddy a new take on the cop; he might be a good father. As a mother, what she hears is rebuke.

Chaz says, "At first I did. She talked to me. She pretended to eat my pretend sandwich. I like it when people do that."

Slowly, Chaz has turned on her lap. He faces Ashford now. The man's eyes, his attention are committed to the boy. He says, "I know what you mean."

"Mom used to do that sometimes," Chaz tells him. "But not since my grandpa died."

Truth cuts deep. Freddy chokes back excuses. Ashford says, "I bet you miss it."

"Yeah," says Chaz, "I do. My mom's got a lot on her mind. My grandpa was her father, you know."

Freddy smiles a smile that no one sees. Chaz has a way of bringing unexpected gifts—dandelions, sometimes, a penny or a special pebble he found on the sidewalk. Once he arranged the objects on her nightstand, to make it pretty. Now he forgives her. By way of thanks, she brushes her cheek against the back of his head.

Ashford puts his hand on Chaz's shoulder. "She may not have turned out to be a very nice person, but she was right about one thing. You are a special boy, Chaz. Your mother must be very proud of you." He raises his eyes to Freddy. "I think he's told us what he can right now. He's very articulate for a kid his age." To Chaz he says, "Listen, partner, if you remember anything else about this grandmother person, or if you have any dreams about her, I want you to tell your mom right away, okay? Sometimes our dreams help us remember things we forget when we're awake, you know what I mean?"

Chaz nods. "I think so. I like my dreams. Except when they're scary."

Ashford nods agreement. "When I was a boy, I used to have a dream about a grizzly bear. He was this big mean critter with ugly teeth. He'd be chasing me and I'd fall down and not be able to get up again. It was like my legs had turned to rock or something. It scared me so bad I'd scream out loud. Then my mom would come and wake me up."

"Did she give you a glass of milk?" Chaz asks. "Sometimes my mom does that."

"Yeah," Ashford says. "Or sometimes she'd sing me a song while I went back to sleep. 'Hush, little baby, don't you cry.' You know that one?"

"I'm not sure," Chaz says. "My mom doesn't sing much."

"That's because I can't carry a tune, honey," Freddy says. "You should be grateful. I do tell you stories, though."

With a sigh, to the accompaniment of popping joints, Ashford rises from his crouch. "My mother had a beautiful voice," he says. "One year at the candlelight service on Christmas eve, she sang a solo of 'Silent Night.' I remember it gave me goosebumps."

"My mom is an artist," Chaz says. "She's very good. I think maybe she's famous or something."

Embarrassed, Freddy rubs his hair. "I'm not famous, Chaz."

Her son half turns to see her face. "You get your name in the paper a lot, Mom."

"That's just on my sketches, honey boy. I just do that for money. It's my paintings that really count, and they're not famous."

"Hey," Ashford says, "let the kid be proud of you. Not everybody's mother gets her name in the paper a lot."

Freddy rolls her eyes. "Okay, okay. So I'm famous."

"Back to the office," Ashford says. "Let's hope for a quiet night."

Freddy says, "Before you go, Lieutenant, I need to talk to you. Privately."

"You're not going to yell at me again, are you?"

"Nope. I have something for you. In the trunk of my car." Above Chaz's head, she tries to make her eyes say, Urgent.

"Okay," Ashford says. "Why don't you walk me to mine?"

Chaz sidles forward on Freddy's lap. "Do you have a real police car, with lights and everything?"

Freddy squeezes her son. "I said privately, Chaz. That means you."

"No lights," Ashford tells him. "I drive a plainclothes car."

Gently, Freddy lifts her son from her lap and plants him on his feet. "You wait here with Laura for a minute. Then we'll both go home." When she stands, Chaz grips her thigh. "Let go, honey," Freddy says. "I'll just be a minute."

"I want to come with you."

Laura says, "Snacks in the kitchen, Chaz. Rice Krispie bars. I need you to help me feed the little kids."

Chaz loosens his grip without letting go. Freddy says, "Laura needs you, honey." Finally, Chaz consents to be needed. He takes Laura's hand. They go into the kitchen. Ashford says, "Well?"

"I got a present this morning. I thought you'd like to see it," Freddy says.

"What is it?"

"I wouldn't want to spoil the surprise."

Ashford puts on his overcoat. The mirror in Laura's entry hall shows Freddy her battered face, the gray skin and swollen eyes. There is no luster in her hair. The face, though it does not look like her own, looks familiar. Following Ashford down Laura's walk, Freddy realizes it was her Grandma Bascomb,

Nick's mother, she saw in the mirror. Grandma Bascomb was seventy-nine when she died.

As if he could read her thoughts, Ashford says, "You look kind of . . ."

"Like shit," Freddy says. She's so tired she has trouble fitting the key in the lock. Finally the trunk opens. "In here. I saved the paper. There wasn't any card." She stands aside while Ashford approaches the trunk and looks inside, hears the sigh of the box lid, the rustle of tissue, his strangled exclamation. When she looks at him, his face is as gray as her own.

"When did this arrive?"

"This morning. Sometime between nine and ten, I'd say."

"How?"

"I don't know. It was just there on the porch when I got home. Nice paper, huh?"

"Why didn't you call me sooner?" Ashford says.

Freddy hears the reproval. "Because I was exhausted," she says. "I took a nap. I only woke up when Laura called."

Ashford tilts his head slightly to one side, looks deeply at her in a manner cops must share with shrinks. It has the power to extort explanations. "I was out late last night," Freddy says.

"I"—she pauses, not really believing she is going to say it, hoping to sound casual if she does—"well, as a matter of fact, I took a lover last night." Spoken, the words sound old-fashioned, if not plain foolish. Freddy studies the scuffed toes of her sneakers.

"Anybody I know?" Ashford inquires.

"Not your business, is it?"

"Normally, no. Under the circumstances, Miz Bascomb, everything's my business. Who's the lucky man?"

"Not the one you're looking for," Freddy says. "Trust me."

"I don't trust anybody," Ashford says. "Not even myself."

"There's no connection," Freddy insists.

"I hope you're right." Unexpectedly gentle, the detective puts his hand on Freddy's shoulder. "Still, until we get this mother solved, I check out everything, and that includes your boyfriends."

"I'm not exactly a teenager anymore," Freddy says. "And you're not my father." Her word choice boomerangs, hurting.

Ashford says, "Did your father do that?"

"No," Freddy says. "Maybe if he had, I wouldn't have married two creeps."

"I've been meaning to ask, are you and ex number two on friendly terms?"

"Not very." Freddy looks for a motive beyond pure nastiness that might inspire Jack. "Let's see. I inherit from Nick. The kids inherit from me. If you convict me of murdering my father, Jack gets the kids. Maybe you should check him out."

"I have been," Ashford says. "You're right, he's a creep, but that's not illegal. Besides, he's got a new girlfriend."

"He does?"

"You didn't know?"

"We didn't discuss it."

Ashford says, "Does it bother you?"

"Why should it bother me?"

"I just wondered. It tore me up when my ex started seeing somebody."

"The one you checked out."

"Right. So who's your new man? I want to check him out, too."

"I take the fifth," Freddy says. "The poor guy probably never would have asked me out if he knew it would involve a police investigation." It occurs to Freddy that the doctor never actually has asked her out. Not on a date.

"Look, I can find out for myself, easy enough. And I will. How about sparing me the trouble?"

"I don't want to," Freddy says.

"I know that. I understand. I'm making you, okay? For your own good."

"Don Pankowski," Freddy says. "He's a forensic anthropologist."

"Yeah. I know the guy." Ashford looks speculatively at Freddy. "Kind of an odd duck, isn't he?"

"I'm not exactly Doris Day myself."

"More of a Jacqueline Bisset, I'd say."

"Really? Thanks."

"When you have your makeup on and stuff."

"Lieutenant, I want to go home now. I have this funny feeling my children need me. I know I need to be with them."

"Pankowski, huh?" Ashford shakes his head, then reaches into the trunk and scoops out the cat box. "Hope you don't mind if I take your present with me. Maybe the lab folks'll find a print or two."

"Lots of mine," Freddy says. "I didn't wear gloves. Are we through?"

"Yeah, we're through. Listen, take care of yourself. And be good to that little boy. He's a sweet kid."

"If you're such a hot detective, you already know I try very hard to be a good mother."

"Hey, lighten up," Ashford tells her. "Nobody said you weren't."

15
. . . . .

It's an at-home evening, brave-front and be-here-now, while Freddy tries to be easy with her children, casual, without letting them know how precious fear has made them. When Paige leaves her jacket heaped on the sofa, when Chaz forgets to flush the toilet after his daily big deposit, Freddy's tempted to excuse their transgressions and make right herself; it requires force of will to yell at them. They yammer and quarrel, tease and squeal, defy as usual, but it's hard to be annoyed, as usual, by the clamor. Beneath their chatter she imagines terrifying silence, the sound of a house without them in it. The peace and time for painting she always claims to yearn for tonight have no appeal. Give her a child-distracted mind, a house that won't stay neat, give her sticky kisses and wheedling smiles, give her shrieks and arguments, those, too. Making dinner, washing dishes, folding laundry, she doesn't even daydream but savors every wrinkle of domestic ritual.

After dinner, Paige says, "How come you're in such a good mood?" and when Chaz says, at bedtime, "Three stories, please," Freddy settles on his bed and willingly complies, bravely wrangles Dr. Seuss's tongue-tripping syllables and when she's done, says, "How about one more?"

Chaz says, "How come?"

"Oh, I don't know. Because you're special."

When Chaz is tucked in, she listens to Paige practice her clarinet, actually listens and nods appreciatively, then brushes Paige's hair and lets Paige brush hers. She brings her daughter juice to drink in bed, lets herself be seduced into a bedside chat. At ten, the clock accuses her of leniency, and she kisses Paige good night. She leaves her daughter's room with a heart full of love and steps into the emptiness she's spent all night evading.

Alone in the hall, her fists clenched, Freddy considers the available means of evasion. She could call Carol and talk about her fear, or call her lover and forget it. She could ask Mrs. Patniak to come upstairs and have a cup of tea. She could anesthetize herself with television or the unopened bottle of red wine under the drainboard, the bottle she leaves there to test her discipline and prove she's not like Nick, or she could draw herself a bubble bath and do her nails. She cannot paint. Painting is too dangerous at times like these; she's trained her muse too well to dive deep and bring up demonfish. The demons are there, wriggling and grinning, Freddy can feel them but does not want to give them form.

Be careful what you paint, lest you bring it into being.

She cannot keep them safe.

That truth is big and hard and hurts like hell.

Freddy pours herself a glass of apple juice and sits cross-legged on the blue rug in the middle of the kitchen floor. The light is yellow and the refrigerator softly intones an electrical "aum." From here she can see down the hall to the doors of both children's rooms. Her eyes keep flitting back to them. She realizes that she's keeping watch. She realizes the impossibility of always watching.

Nick's drinking she always called a sickness or a weakness, not malevolence. Jack's violence, his selfishness, were easily explained once you met his mother, and her own demons, the ones that sometimes swirl up from her subconscious and snarl on her canvases, always bear some family resemblance to known reality. They are familiar and excusable. Nick taught her to be an apologist. Good is a choice, a natural human preference; bad is what happens when people get damaged, the result of interlocking accidents.

Someone is stalking her children. Freddy can think of no excuse for that. For the first time, she believes that there is evil in the world.

Someone is stalking her children, after all.

She could call Carol, even now. My tail is in a knot, I've got the heebie-jeebies, I caught the whim-whams. Carol would say soothing, funny things. They'd end up laughing. And none of it would make the evil go away.

Knees popping, she rises. Softly, she pushes open Paige's not-quite-closed door, travels the triangle of hall light to its apex beside her daughter's bed. Paige breathes through her mouth and her face is free of trouble, the curves of cheek and jawline sweetly rounded, slack and natural. No evil shadows her, even in dream. Safe now. Freddy tucks the satin edge of the blanket closer around her chin.

Tonight Chaz sleeps on his side. Under his smooth lids, she can see the movement of his pupils that means active dreaming. One hand rests loose on his pillow, and she slips her index finger inside the soft curl of his fist. Without waking, he responds to touch, closing his fingers around hers.

Freddy is grateful for her children's safety, but takes no credit. She tries to remember what it felt like not to worry, when she had the freedom to assume the best. Damn Nick. Goddamn him. She caught this cold from him, just when she was starting to feel healthy, too. It's not fair she should be bone-cold in her own kitchen, a room she's taken pains to fill with yellow light and the scent of spices, the luxury of a rug and shining dishes and framed posters hanging on the walls. This place is meant to nourish and reassure. She should not be crouched over the heating vent, trying to bake away the shakes in the furnace's false warmth. Her heart should be light as bubbles dancing in a spring wind, not weigh three thousand pounds and reside in her kneecaps. This is not at all how she would have it be. And how it is.

If there were a pill, she'd take it. If there were a book, she'd read it. If there were a club, she'd join, a course, she'd enroll. If there were a master, she would follow, if there were a teacher she would gladly learn. If a shrink could shrink terror or make responsibility small, then gladly would she submit to shrinkage, or to magic, if witches and their spells were real.

Unfortunately, she can think of no one qualified to fix what's wrong.

The phone rings. Having decided not to answer, she eavesdrops on the machine. Sandy says: "Call me please." Freddy cringes. The machine beeps, then breaks the connection.

Maybe she can be the doctor, the teacher, the master. Maybe all that's needed is for her to say, I am. But that's absurd. She obviously is not. Next she considers the possibility of ignoring evil into nonexistence, but she's already tried that, most of her life, with poor results. The dilemma, and her attempts to resolve it, translate into a feeling of being hurled against a large dark rock, sucked back and tossed again.

Again the phone rings. The outside world must be conspiring to pull her out of the water, but it seems important to not let herself be rescued. Freddy feels as if she is supposed to keep hitting the rock until it breaks or she does. Jack says: "Freddy, I wanted to talk to you about the kids. Frankly, I'm concerned about them. Give me a call when you have some time to talk."

Thanks, Jack. I'm sure glad you're concerned. Can't wait to have you tell me what I'm doing wrong.

Maybe she really should take a bubble bath. All this thinking is getting her nowhere. Nero may have had a point; if you can't stop Rome from burning, why *not* fiddle? Freddy can't remember at the moment if Nero was responsible for the fire or not. She's not sure it matters. Bubbles, here I come.

But then the phone rings. She could unplug it, insist on isolation. She could resign from a life that's gotten too complex. A man's voice says, "This is Jim Shuster, from the West Seattle Jaycees. We're asking you to help make it possible for handicapped children to go to the circus this year. Tickets are ten dollars apiece. We need your help."

Frankly, Jim, I'd rather take my own kids to the circus. They haven't had too much fun lately, if you know what I mean. I should stop frowning so much, before my face freezes that way. I should remember to tickle my children. Maybe I should just pull Paige out of school for a week and take 'em both to Disneyland, before they get too existential to enjoy it. God knows, we could stand a vacation. Hey, don't think I didn't know it would be tough. It's just that.

Just that I can't, you know, *do* it. A person can only do so much. I mean, it's enough a person has to make a living and keep a house and raise two kids, especially if she's trying to be an artist besides, and a good friend, too, without somebody killing her father and trying to make off with her son. I need help. I really do need some help here. See, here's my application, all filled out. Help needed. Name, address, Social Security number. Nope, no insurance, I'll pay out of pocket. You bet I'll pay. Just send help. This is it. I've got my hands up, see? The white flag's waving. Send help. I don't care if it's Mighty Mouse or Jesus Christ, we're talking equal opportunity supplicant here.

Freddy waits for the next wave to break and send her crashing back into the rock, but the wind has died and the water is suddenly calm. It's still too dark to see much, but the boat's steady now and the sound of the water, gently lapping its sides, is soothing. She feels neither empty nor full, not hot or cold. She does feel grateful. It's warm in the kitchen and she's very very sleepy, so sleepy that she curls up on the blue rug and puts her head down on her arm, feeling it's safe to sleep, and quickly does, the last brief image before lights out being of a moon shining full above dark water.

Later, the voice of Dr. Bones speaks into silence: "Freddy, this is Don. You never called me back. Where are you?"

PART TWO

PART TWO

MOTHER'S LOVE

a novel

CHAPTER ONE

Clark Bailey sat at the bar, one elbow planted in its surface scum, one big hand, the opposite, encompassing a shot glass half full of what I soon learned he was fond of calling his soul medicine. "Distilled spirits," he said. "The essence." He emptied the shot glass into his mouth, wincing, as if the whiskey really were good enough for him to taste bad. That was later. In that first instant, he sat at the bar. I stood in the doorway. He was a regular, I was a stranger. He was known to me, I invisible to him. The advantage was mine.

At all times of day, the lighting in the bar of the Lucky Strike Cafe successfully simulated the dark night of the soul. The ambient air was so thick, so stationary, and so stale it seemed to both the eye and the nose of the new arrival to approximate a solid substance. Behind the bar, a radio and a television set played simultaneously and asynchronously, blending into a kind of perpetual gray noise that resembled neither music nor conversation so much as the central nervous system's wordless awareness of existential angst. Because the law required it, the Lucky Strike offered its patrons a greasy menu of greasy foods, but no one who once attempted to digest a Lucky Burger ever made the same mistake again.

Bailey possessed his barstool with the authority of a monarch, the ease of a well-mounted rider. As I watched, he took a small wire-spiral notebook from a pocket eternally distended by its occupancy, clicked down the point of his Paper Mate, and began to write on one of the small, lined pages. Quarter-turn swivels of the barstool marked pauses in his flow of thought and once, as I watched, he addressed an itch on one anklebone with the sole of the other shoe. When the bartender slouched by, Bailey ordered himself another shot of whiskey without bothering to look up.

When I felt my own scrutiny returned by a table-seated female tippler, I made my way to the bar and took a stool next but one to Bailey's, waited until the bartender, who was not busy, finished his ritual ignoring and took my order for a beer, then pulled out my own notebook and began to take notes on the state of the Lucky Strike, which I've just consulted, thirty years later, as I wrote the paragraph above. Thirty years ago, the bartender had the look of a drugged simian, and the excesses of the lady drinker's upper arms were noted as crepe draperies, dusty and forlorn.

For a while, I think, Bailey was truly unaware of me, and for a while longer, inauthentically so. He scribbled. I scribbled. Then he looked up, looked over, turned the famous Bailey eyes upon me. My notes remind me: almond-shaped, clear, light-passing brown; eyes that promised compassion, attention, understanding all at once; eyes that called to mind the Brontë sisters' brooding outlaw heroes, but managed, at the same time, to seem as reassuring as one's favorite maiden aunt's. Quick glance bespoke quick mind. If I seem to go on about Clark Bailey's eyes, remember this: I had heard about them, and their mesmerizing properties, for the better part of my life.

So, the eyes looked at me. The voice, even then roughed up by his prodigious vices, said, "What're you writing?" My notes say—downhome and hearty, not-for-publication and just-between-us. A little patronizing, as if he expected my answer to be the grocery list, or instructions to my bookie, as if, it occurs to me now, he fully expected to be the only literate person in the Lucky Strike.

I closed my notebook. "Just making a few notes. What are you writing?"

Bailey moved the hand that had screened his page-in-progress since our conversation began, to show me one surface densely filled with low-slung script. "The same," he said. "You a writer?"

"I hope so," I said. "Are you?"

"Some people think so. What kind of writer are you?"

"A novelist."

"Real or aspiring?"

"Still aspiring," I said.

"Jesus, join the club." Bailey upended his shot glass. "I've been aspiring in that direction for a dozen years."

"What's your novel about?" I asked.

"The war, of course. How about yours?"

"I'm trying to write about the places where individuals and institutions collide."

"That's war," Bailey said.

"A war novel set in time of peace."

"I'm doing war for war. I was born during the first war, tested in the second. I fully expect to die in the third," Bailey told me. "War's the only subject worth writing about. It's inexhaustible, you know, because one man's war is not another's."

About then, the simian bartender shuffled by with my beer. Simian, meaning long arms on short torso, forehead resembling a porch. Bailey ordered himself another whiskey. I asked him if it helped him write.

"It helps me live," he said. "Soul medicine. I keep myself well-dosed."

"What else do you write?" I knew, of course, but wanted to hear how he would choose to tell me what I already knew.

"Work for a newspaper," he said. "They pay me to look into this and that. Name's Bailey. I'm on the *Times*."

I shook the big hand he put out for that purpose. Notes say, Big but soft-palmed. Oval nails. Black hair sprouting from knuckle joints. Grip a hairbreadth short of challenge.

The bartender intercepted the ringing of the telephone, embraced the receiver like a prosthetic jawbone, then buried speaking and hearing parts against his chest. "Clark, you here?"

"Woman?"

"Sounds like."

"You haven't seen me."

The bar ape lipped the receiver, hung up. "If I see you, I'm supposed to tell you to call home."

"If I hear you, I will. Thanks, Tod." Bailey turned back to me. "My wife has her own notions of how I should spend my leisure time."

"How long have you been married?" I asked him.

Bailey twisted the gold signet on his betrothal digit. "I acquired my keeper ten years ago. Six years ago, via a carefully premeditated act of passion, we reproduced ourselves."

The telephone rang again, Tod answered again, to Bailey said, "She wants me to look again. Check the men's room. Are you here?"

"I just left," Bailey said.

"He just left," Tod echoed. He listened, then looked to Bailey. "She says she knows you're here."

"Then tell her I'll call her if I'm not coming home."

Tod relayed the message and quickly hung up. "I wish you'd talk to her, Clark. It makes me feel crummy, lying to a woman."

"A lady," Bailey corrected. "My wife is not a woman, but a lady." He turned to me. "You married?

"No."

"You'll never finish that novel if you do." He capped the line with an emphatic draw on his cigarette, then laughed, one of several patented Clark Bailey laughs, this one the thin chortle of the idealist unmanned by reality. "I sound like a flaming asshole, don't I? It's not my wife's fault I've never finished that book. It's not my kid's fault. The fault, dear Brutus, is in ourselves. I can't even blame whiskey."

Rather grandly, and with a sense of risk, I said, "I blame my mother."

That won me the second of his laughs, this one an unjaundiced bellow surprised out of the pit of his stomach, a laugh so unguarded and persuasive it coaxed a reflexive snicker from the lady drunk behind us, set up a twitching in the simian lower jaw, so that while one part of me felt dangerously disloyal, another was rewarded. "Mothers," Bailey said. "That's good."

Brave as a lion tamer, I took up the impudent question mark, brandished it at my companion. "What was your mother like?" Then waited, waited to see how easy a mark my opponent really was.

"My mother," Bailey said, solemn and reflective as if he were reading the title of his eighth-grade essay. "My mother taught me always to blame myself." This occasioned the lighting of another cigarette, even before the last was fully smoked. "My mother was a stewing chicken, stringy and tough. My mother was a puritan who had no traffic with God. My mother was a disappointed woman. She died about a year ago."

"I'm sorry," I said.

"Death was late for the appointment," Bailey told me. "Her mind went before her body did. If that happens to me, I hope the kid'll have the good sense to put me out to play in traffic." He looked to his shot glass and found it empty. "I miss her," he said, "the way you miss a migraine. The way you'd miss a recurring nightmare if it suddenly stopped coming back." His eyes took in the sad landscape of the Lucky Strike. "In a way, I'm still in mourning. This is my church."

It was an absurd thing to say, the grandiose pronouncement of a drunk, and yet it touched me somehow, somewhere, an unexpected power, as with the eyes "Your mother had high expectations," I said— a guess but a good one.

Bailey turned his stool slightly, front and center, so he didn't have to look at me. "The highest. Ma wanted a philosopher and got a reporter. She wanted a saint and got a sinner. I carry her legacy, a shitload of guilt, deep down in my guts, in the marrow of my bones. If sin's a snake, then guilt's a worm. It eats you from the inside out."

The vehemence of his pronouncement silenced us both. I was surprised by how easily he confessed himself, and knew by that ease how incomplete his confession was. I found I didn't hate him. That knowledge, which I experienced as the sudden absence of long-standing pain, a release, left me feeling giddy in the void. Part of me was ashamed, another part exhilarated. I knew I was in the presence of a complicated being. "My mother was very beautiful once," I told him. "Now she's quite mad."

"Hmmm." Bailey bobbed a little on his barstool, weighing the premise. "It happens with women sometimes. The prettiest ones are highest strung, most likely to snap." He sounded worldly and compassionate, as if he genuinely grieved for all the high-strung women who lost their reason, for all the hurt and baffled children of the mad, for all their disappointed husbands. I had expected treachery, but found him sad. The crust of my hard earth shifted then and I stood in a new place, understanding there was more story than I knew, more substance to the villain than I had dared imagine. I didn't hate Clark Bailey. My notes say, Confused. Intrigued. He is formidable.

Bailey turned his eyes on me, for a moment the alcohol haze lifted, burned off like morning mist, the look was deep and appraising, as if he too had glimpsed a flash of destiny. "I talk about a lot of things to a lot of people. I talk too much, but I never talk about my novel or my mother," he said. His eyes struggled to get past the barriers in mine. "What did you say your name was, kid? Who are you, anyway?"

Choosing the name I gave him, I called a new self into being, and we shook hands a second time.

CHAPTER TWO

"I'll be Katie and you be Clark," my mother said. It was my naptime and we shared her bed. The light was grainy and brown, afternoon filtered through venetian blinds and rustly beige drapes. The game frightened and excited me. Until I started school, I was not allowed the company of other children. I had no way of knowing if other sons and mothers played these games.

"This is a fine piece of writing, Clark," mother said softly.

"Thank you, Mrs. Brown," I said.

"Between artists, there is no need to stand on ceremony," my mother said. "Please call me Kate."

"Yes, Mrs. Brown."

"Kate."

"Kate," I said. My mother stared into my eyes. Her eyes were moist,

full of softness and desire. The intensity of her gaze was so unmotherly
that, in my own five-year-old defense, I made the leap and became her
Clark. "You are a very beautiful woman, Kate." That's what Clark was
supposed to say then, and I did.

My mother laughed her lilting wind-chime laugh. "And you are a
very lovely young man. Did you know that, Clark?"

"No, ma'am," I said.

There was teasing in my mother's eyes. Now she reached out and
touched my cheek with one of her long cool fingers. It was a lingering
touch, a stripe of pale fire burned softly into my skin. "You're shy," my
mother coached me. "Look away."

I dropped my eyes from hers and looked instead at dainty, stylized
pink roses, their orderly dispersion across the white terrain of sheet, and
felt her whole hand caress my cheek, then slip around, a cold soft fire,
to singe the back of my neck. Yes, Clark was shy. Kate's finger lifted his
chin. "Look at me," my mother said. "You have amazing eyes, so deep
and clear."

Clark could not help but look at her, into her own amazing eyes. I
think perhaps he was reluctant, or afraid.

Softly, mother said, "Your eyes make me dizzy. I could look into
them forever."

Clark said, "But, Mrs. Brown . . ."

And Mrs. Brown's eyes swam before him, a terrifying blue whirl-
pool becoming, at the epicenter, one huge blue eye as she drew forward
and touched her lips to his. My lips moved against my mother's. And
then we heard like prescient thunder footfalls on the stairs, and in the
hall.

We parted, Mother and I, she to her pillow and I to mine. "Pretend
to nap," she whispered, and curled away from her, I closed my eyes,
not a moment too soon, as my father Mr. Brown strode into the darkened
bedroom, booming, "What, still asleep?"

Was he the villian, or the prince? I couldn't tell. He sat on the edge
of the bed, his and my mother's, and noisily kissed my mother's hair,
palmed my shoulder and gave a hearty squeeze. His arrival reprieved
me. I was banished from the bed and sent to play with my toys. At dinner
that night, my father was expansive, my mother pale.

Small, nearly invisible to him, I sat at my father's table and felt Clark's
guilt. Kate now was wifely, her allegiance belonging once again to Mr.
Brown. With sweet intensity, she listened to his accounting of that day's
victories and troubles, stories he heaped as liberally upon her listening
as he piled mashed potatoes on his own plate, with the same gusto. I
liked the low straightforward ramble of my father's voice even though,

try as I would to emulate my mother's attentiveness, his stories failed to entertain or move me. I much preferred the fairy tales my mother read to me at bedtime, or the stories I made up for myself as I was falling asleep.

My father was a stocky man, and brusque, his good looks plebeian, I suppose, next to my mother's fine-boned, high-strung refinement, a roughly handsome man with ordinary eyes. He was energetic and well-meaning, his presence in our home was like a heavy isotope that charged the atmosphere. I wanted to accept, to reciprocate the rough kindnesses he offered me, but complicity in mother's game prevented me. No one had ever told me marriage was supposed to be sacred and exclusive, or that transgression of its boundaries wounded both heart and honor, but I must have been precocious in matters of guilt, because I knew. Because I could not love my father with a clean heart, I could not love him at all.

"And how was your day, Sport?" at dinner he ritually inquired, and I ritually replied that it was nice. He ritually ruffled my hair. That, as every night, ended our meal. From then until my bathtime, I was an innocent child, slightly bored by my toys, while father read his newspaper and mother read her book.

Bathtime. This too was ritual; I was an extraordinarily clean child. Perhaps my toys bored me because nothing I could think of to do with them approached the intensity of the game mother and I played. Perhaps her game usurped my imagination, retarding its independent growth. Perhaps becoming Clark, at mother's insistence and to her specifications, required such a leap that my imagination had no spring left over for the investment of personality in teddy bears or the creation of whimsied playmates. I write away from bathtime, my sentences commit themselves to complicated detours, as if they wished to lose their way, never to arrive in the big white-tiled bathroom with its thick red rug, the brisk red towels and big clawfooted tub. My sentences veer off in search of reasons, evading memory. Essaying to write about bathtime so many years later, I feel much as I did then, waiting for it to come.

That is, excited and afraid and disbelieving.

Excitement, in retrospect, is easy enough to understand, if somewhat harder to admit; my mother *was* a beautiful woman, her touch was skilled and gentle, her smiles and soft voice thrilling. Even at five, I sensed I knew her more intimately than my father ever would. Must I be blamed for my excitement? I think not. It was not I, after all, she undertook to excite.

What I feared I have more trouble naming, from this vast time-distance can only guess. Discovery, certainly, even though the bathroom door had its own brass bolt, which mother almost invariably re-membered to secure. That leaves us locked in together, safe. Yet I did not feel safe then and do not now, which suggests that perhaps mother herself, her high white breasts and plushy apertures, was fearsome to me. Mother, or perhaps my companion, *mon ami de coeur*, my old familiar, Guilt. Consider this, my friends: In the absence of fear, can Guilt exists?

Which brings us to the third leg of my uncertain psychic stool. What was it, exactly, that I disbelieved? That bathtime with its naughty dan-gerous delights had ever happened, or that it would again? Each alone, and both together, I suppose. Suffice to say, it was at bathtime I discovered the talent for outbehaving the furthest reaches of my disbelief that has characterized so much of my life from bathtime on.

White tiles, white walls, white porcelain, rugs and towels the dis-quieting, purpled red of pomegranate. Mother said, "There's no need to be shy. See, I'll go first." With that, she began slowly to unbutton her blouse. Her blouse was silken, it whispered in a soft, suggestive voice, shone in the clean white bathroom light. It parted to reveal more silk, thin and fine, lace-trimmed. When the blouse came off, revealing moth-er's long white arms, she cast it aside, saying, "Now it's your turn, Clark." When Clark's fingers faltered at the buttons of my little cotton shirt, Kate's tapered ones came to their aid, undoing, purposeful, inexorable, exposing my smooth white chest, teasing the garment from my shoulders, sending it to join her own in a careless heap on the floor.

Did mother see my body or his? Memory and imagination carry me out of my body, granting me an image of myself, and I'm amazed at the integrity of the small shirtless body, surprised how still and solid it appears to be, because my senses recall a heart-tumult so violent I wondered if it might crack my rib cage open, that and my skin's sensation of diffusing, dissolving, which was a kind of joyous ache. I wonder if children's bodies were meant to feel such things? Then it was Kate's turn again, and her skirt slumped, sighing softly, to the floor.

And then? I can't tell you. I can't tell you because the scene goes dark and I can't see. The darkness always comes now, and I have always believed it is my friend, holding my best interests at heart. It's only with great effort I've held it back this long, have seen so much this time. It is the light that frightens me. The darkness is my friend.

Sitting on his barstool, Clark Bailey peered intently at my face and said, "You know, there's something familiar about you. You must remind me of somebody I once knew, but I can't think of who it is."

The moment felt interesting, dangerous. My face felt naked. For an instant, I was afraid he would be able to see inside my brain, to ferret out my secrets, but the instant passed. Clark was unable to recall my mother's face from mine. "The longer you live," Clark said, "the more that happens to you. By the time you're ninety, you probably think you've met everybody in the world before."

"There's something vaguely familiar about you, too," I said.

CHAPTER THREE

"Show me yours, I'll show you mine," Clark Bailey said. He was drunk by then, feeling the world was harsh. "Hell, who else can I show it to? Not my wife. She's in it."

I gave him my address, he gave me his.

"Next week?" he said.

I told him I was going to be out of town. I told him I was going to visit my mother. "Two weeks," I said. "Will you remember?"

"I remember everything," he said. "It's my curse."

I wondered if he remembered Kate. "Don't be too hard on me," I said. "I'm new at this."

"Same," Bailey said.

"But you're a professional."

"It's not the same thing," Bailey said. "A monkey could write the shit they put in the paper." He tongued the dram of whiskey pooled in the bottom of his shot glass. "Speaking of new, have you heard about that war novel some kid wrote? What's his name? Miller? The critics can't stop raving."

"It's Mailer, I think. Norman Mailer."

"He wasn't even in the war," Bailey said. "Was he?"

"They say it's an impressive debut."

"Damn brat's ten years younger than I am," Bailey said. He looked at me with pinking eyes. "So're you, for that matter." He laughed. "I hope to god you're not better than me. You're not some kind of child prodigy like this Mailer kid, are you?"

"We'll have to wait and see."

"At least *you're* not writing about the war. Are you?"

It was the second time I told him no.

"Good. I like to think of it as my war." His laugh then knew he was a fool. "Funny how people do that, huh? Like they own nerve gas, or the depression."

"John Steinbeck owns the depression," I said, and Bailey laughed again. "I like you, kid," he said. "I even hope you're good."

I liked him less than I had earlier. Shot by shot, the whiskey he steadily consumed had coarsened him, robbed his language of wit and thickened both his features and his voice, flattened and simplified him, somehow, into a caricature: Drunk on Barstool Bemoans Inscrutable Fate. When he dismounted and made for the men's room, his legs were unreliable, as if they belonged to an animal not entirely used to walking upright. He was unlovable and not worth killing. I was disappointed and relieved.

Since I decided not to kill Clark Bailey that night, I was forced to become a writer. My notebooks for the next two weeks suggest I did not fully understand my own impulse toward clemency, whether it sprang from pity or attraction, but in either case, sparing my victim, I gained an audience, and the notebooks in which I'd previously addressed only myself began to fill up with torrents of prose I variously hoped would seduce, impress, infuriate, or unnerve him.

In those two weeks, I tried to write everything. No sooner would I get myself the beginnings of a setting and a cast of characters, no sooner create a compelling situation or light upon a premise with promise than I would think of another story I wanted more to tell, so that a black grandmother rocking on her porch in Alabama gave way to a professional gambler in Las Vegas, with a system to beat the system, the gambler to a servant of the Medicis', the servant to a hunter in the Yukon, stalking polar bears, the Yukon to Brazil, Brazil to Transylvania. What was it I told Bailey I was writing about? The collision of individuals and institutions. I wrote about a werewolf who embezzled millions and a prosititute who refused to remove her dark glasses, about a nun who, for status' sake, counterfeited a transcendent encounter with St. James the Younger, and a bus driver who wanted to become a showgirl. None of these works progressed beyond six pages.

It being interdicted, I had of course to try my hand at war, not Bailey's but the one that we Americans, so short on hindsight, quaintly refer to as the First. My father served in France; I drew upon his stories, became a doughboy, discovered in the trenches the fruitful anarchy of fear and, under fire, turned my weapon upon those among my fellows I disliked. No sooner did the shelling start than my soldier claimed the right to define "enemy" by his own lights; it simply happened, it took me by surprise, and yet, upon reflection, I was fascinated by the ethical implications of his act. Once a government issues a license to kill, can it be qualified, or made selective, as myopic drivers are required by law to wear their glasses, or homeowners with particular addresses restricted to watering their lawns only on even-numbered days in time of drought? By what dance of reason can we presume to distinguish the heroic from the criminal?

The story, as I told it, was the confession of an old man, wanting to make his peace with truth. In a sense, his impulse to deconstruct the fiction by which he'd lived was not unlike Clark Bailey's near the end. Perhaps my story was prophetic. Art is as capable of anticipating reality as of reshaping what is real. When he was in France, my soldier wrote letters to his sweetheart at home in Minnesota. In them, he accurately reported the tally of his kills, always letting her believe Germany was homeland of his victims. At war's end, he received a medal. His sweetheart's name was Katherine.

I spent four fevered days on the attempt, which later grew into the second of my published novels. I had to abandon it then. Time squeezed me tightly. I wanted Clark Bailey to like my writing, as fervently as a younger Kate had admired young Clark's work. For the first time, I understood the subtext of desire in the relationship of a writer to his audience, for the first time sensed how erotic that might be.

With my deadline closer than the next breath, I returned to the story of the prostitute with the need to hide her eyes. When she was a child, her father beat her for lying. She had stolen her great-aunt's music box, which played Brahms' lullaby. When her mother discovers the music box in the child's drawer, the girl says the great-aunt gave it to her as a gift. I did a particularly good job, I think, of evoking the child's obsession with the object, of tempting her with it beyond her capacity to resist. It was her eyes, of course, that confessed her sins of covetousness and theft. Bailey and I had agreed to trade first chapters only. By the end of mine, Kathy, the prostitute, has been offered a thousand dollars by an ardent client, if only she will reveal her eyes.

The day I mailed my effort to Bailey, his first chapter arrived in the post. This many years later, I remember vividly the tremor in my hands as I opened the manila envelope, not cleanly, but with crude impatience. Ashamed of my avidity, I straightened my desk, I brewed and drank a cup of tea, walked a brisk mile through afternoon drizzle before I allowed myself to sit down and read Clark Bailey's words.

How was it? His authentic war reduced mine to a comic strip. His hero was appealingly unheroic, a convincing human who housed a dozen subtle contradictions. The sharp blade of surreality pared all that was extraneous from the narration; one had the sensation of watching not a film but its negative twin. The effect was deeply unsettling. I was sure the book, if the rest was as good, would take its place on the shelf of the greatest novels arising from that war.

More than anything I had desired in my life before that time, I wanted to have written it myself.

CHAPTER FOUR

My reasons for visiting my mother were never simple. The usual maternal bait, money and nurture, did not apply. What hooked me, reeled me in was her intensity. Madness had simplified my mother into something essential and irreducible. Mother's world was no larger or more dangerous than the Victorian wood-frame house that defined it, a private "guest home" kept by two retired nurses, Miss Lavender and Mrs. Swanson, whom my father Mr. Brown paid handsomely and trusted to be both decent and discreet. Within the walls of Lavender Haven, my mother had achieved an enviable freedom from convention and constraint. Unthreatened there, her personality was undefended. She wore no more flesh than was necessary to cover her bones.

When mother was melancholy, at the low ebb of her mania, she could be silent and immobile for days, not leaving her bed except to relieve her bladder or her bowels, not touching her food. When the tide turned, when her emotional surf pounded and churned up foam, she engaged in a frenzy of fantasy, costuming herself as a girl child dresses dolls, starred in a play of her own devising, with only one role manifest, although Mrs. Swanson, who was devoted to mother, was sure Miss Kate could see and hear the rest of the cast. Riding the arc between extremes, mother was relatively normal, reading books and writing love poems which compared favorably, I think, to those of Elizabeth Barrett Browning.

The evening of the afternoon Clark Bailey's manuscript arrived, my mother's tide was nearing high. She wore an evening dress of deep blue satin. It had been years by then since her skin had felt the sun, and it was white, almost transparent. Sharp and piquant, her collarbone rose childlike above the soft folds of the dress. Her hair, a deep brown frosted silver, fell loose and thick over her shoulders, pinned back over one ear and garnished with a black silk rose. Excitement rouged her cheeks. She was eating her supper in the dining room, wearing her white silk gloves.

"My dear, I've been expecting you. I'm so glad that you came."

Between bites, she inquired about the state of the world. I assured her that the world was well.

"And you?"

"I too."

"Mother will be so pleased you've come," my mother said, from which I took my cues for that day's role. Her mother was alive, dowager duchess, Kate was the princess. I was a sibling, or perhaps her cousin. I was free to help create the drama. What I said was, "You're looking lovely, Kate."

"Why, thank you. This is my favorite dress. Dorothy didn't have time today to put my hair up, though."

Dorothy was Mrs. Swanson. "It's pretty down," I said.

"The roast beef is quite tender. Would you like some? I could ask Dorothy to set another place."

"I've already eaten, thank you."

"I can't wait until it's time to go to the ball. Dorothy says we must wait until it's dark. I want to dance all night."

"I didn't know there was a ball," I said.

"Oh, yes. And I believe my friend is coming. My special friend." As Mother leaned closer, satin dipped close to roast beef gravy. Her white gloves were spotted brown. "He dances beautifully, you know. So strong and graceful. We dance so well together that other people stop to watch us."

I nodded, smiling.

"He's younger than I, you know. But I don't think it shows, do you?" She sat erect, taking a formal pose. Still smiling, I nodded no. "Would you like a glass of wine?" she asked.

"Yes, please."

Mother called for Mrs. Swanson, who brought me a wineglass. Mother poured. I watched Cabernet Sauvignon fill the glass and exceed it, staining the tablecloth. When she saw what she'd done, Mother laughed. "Dorothy says I must learn to pay attention."

I dried the glass with my napkin, sipped off the excess and raised it to her.

"To the ball," my mother said. "And to love."

"To love," I said.

When Mother was done with her supper, Dorothy Swanson put a record on the phonograph, one of the Viennese waltzes that Mother loved. Usually Mrs. Swanson partnered Mother in the dance, but that night the honor was mine. I took my mother in my arms. Mrs. Swanson sat in a wingback chair to watch us. One two three, one two three, we swept around the little clearing in the parlor. "Remember," Mrs. Swanson said, "she loves to dip."

We dipped and swirled, Mother light and brittle as a paper doll. She whispered to my shoulder, and it hurt me, hurt deeply to see that lovely face, used up by hope. When the needle reached the label of the record, Mrs. Swanson told my mother that the ball was over. Mother kissed me good night. "You go to your room now, Kate. I'll be right along to help you get undressed."

Meekly, Mother obeyed. Mrs. Swanson rose to see me to the door. On the porch she said, "It's been a happy time. I feel a bad one coming."

"Has my father been to see her?"

"No, dear. It's painful for him, and he's busy. He writes her every two weeks, though."

"Does she remember who he is?"

"I'm not sure," Mrs. Swanson said. "Sometimes after she reads one of his letters, she says she's heard from Clark." Mrs. Swanson flattened her lips. "I wish I knew who he was, don't you?"

I thanked Mrs. Swanson for the good care she was taking of mother and said good night. Leaving, I knew the visit had accomplished its purpose. My hatred was revived.

Notes say: Visited Mother. The forge where Mother baked was too damn hot. There is a shatter-pattern to her glaze. She is sublimed. And what to say to Clark. I want to make him dance with Mother, dance and dance and dance. Dance, Clark. Dance in the air and in the flames of hell. Dance with words. Dance with Mother. Dance with me.

The only thing changed about the Lucky Strike, besides Tod's shirt, was Bailey's posture on his stool. Before, he curved toward the bar but now sat upright. Before, he pretended to be unaware of my arrival. That night he was waiting, his stool turned subtly so his eyes could watch the door. When I walked through it, in that first unguarded instant, his gaze was avid, requited, and then became opaque. As before, I left a stool unoccupied between us. Tod appeared at once and took my order for a beer.

"Still raining?" Bailey said.

"Slowed to a drizzle. I hope I haven't kept you waiting long."

"Not too." Before him on the bar, a shot glass and a coffee mug stood side by side. Each was half full. A manila envelope lay beside them, on his right. I opened my briefcase, took out another envelope, and set it to my left.

"How've you been?" Bailey said.

"Well. You?"

"Fine. I've been great." He sipped his whiskey. "You go to see your mother?"

"I did."

He put the shot glass down, took up the mug and sipped his coffee. Tod brought my beer. I waited for the head to flatten before I drank. Bailey watched Sid Caesar on the black-and-white screen. "Funny guy," he said.

"I don't watch television."

"I like the fights," Bailey said.

I sipped my beer. It was Rainier, a sturdy local brew. Caesar yielded to Philip Morris. Bailey stared at the screen.

I said, "I wonder if people will still read books in fifty years."

"Don't bet on it. People are lazy," he said. "I'm lazy."

I let the pause lengthen until the thought lay dead. "Give me some chips, will ya?" the woman behind us called to Tod.

"Comin', Dottie." Tod ripped open a new bag, filled a wooden bowl and carried them to Dot. A little pile of bills and coins sat before her on the table like a poker stake. From it, Tod picked up the price of the chips. She pushed a quarter toward him. "For your trouble." Tod tossed the quarter in the air, caught it and slapped it down hard on the back of his hand.

"Tails," Bailey called.

Tod lifted his palm and looked at the coin. "It's heads."

"It's always heads," Bailey said.

Dot cackled. Tod said, "Want to try again, Clark?"

Bailey said "why" and sighed. To me: "Damnedest thing. I beat the odds. I'm always wrong."

"I'm not much of a gambler myself," I said.

Bailey looked at me closely, appraising, then flicked one shoulder up. When he spoke, it was to the coffee in his mug. "So," he said, "we going to talk or not?"

I took a swallow of beer. "Talk," I said.

He picked up the envelope to his right, moved it front and center on the bar, splayed his big hand, palm down, on top. "What made you want to write about a whore?" he said.

CHAPTER FIVE

Bailey cared. His caring was my power. My notes say: Big, round. Power a shining silver ball. I held it in my hands. It was as if I held his soul.

His eyes were hungry. He was ashamed of his hunger, I think, but could not conceal it. Desire's tremolo betrayed him when he spoke. "So, what do you think?"

"You know what you have."

"Yeah. Writer's block." His laugh was a small explosion, too weak to fell that wall.

"You're blocked?"

Teeth of a savage comb, his fingers plunged into his hair. "Shit, yes." Fingers took flight from hair, poised on the bar, and then rose up to summon Tod. "Hold the coffee. I need a drink."

Tod said, "Sure."

Bailey lit a cigarette.

"Tell me," I said. Power became a question mark, my silver scimitar.

"What's to tell? I wrote and then I stopped."

The tip of my curved blade touched temple, touched breastbone, probing. Where did the answer lie?

His eyes. Through them, I glimpsed his pain. I understood: There was no pain in Mother's eyes. Her beauty was ruined, her mind ravaged, but she was not in pain. Madness is refuge, my notes say, a safe house. For Bailey, there is no haven. "I'm a hack and a drunk," he said. "Not to mention my shortcomings as husband and father."

His chapter lay before me on the bar. I touched it. "This is very good. It might be great."

"Might is my least favorite word in the language," Bailey said. "Especially when combined with have and been."

I thrust again. "What stopped you?"

Bailey inhaled the question, blew it out as smoke. "Fear," he said, and flicked his ashes. "That's an hypothesis."

"What are you afraid of?"

Bailey closed around his manuscript like a flower at dusk, like a crab, a mother. "Back off, kid," he said.

"You chose to show me. I didn't make you."

"So?"

"So."

"That doesn't mean I wanted to be psychoanalyzed."

"What does it mean?"

"Fuck it," Bailey said.

I thought of clams, still alive in their shells. Plunged into fresh water, they open. They open before they die. "Okay," I said, unlatching my briefcase, putting my own manuscript inside. I stood down from my barstool. "Fuck it," I said. I tossed a couple of dollars on the bar, turned toward the door.

"Wait," Bailey said. "You're right. I didn't have to let you read it." I kept moving toward the door. "I was an asshole," he said to my back. "This is hard."

Slowly, I turned, returned. Sat. Said nothing.

"I'm afraid it's no good," Bailey said. "I'm afraid of failing. The shape I'm in, I'm afraid of even trying."

The shell was opening. With fresh silence, I encouraged it.

Bailey said, "In case you hadn't noticed, I'm a fucking drunk. Booze is a jealous mistress. She doesn't want to share me. Every time I make a date with the muse, booze lures me back, seduces me. She uses me up and throws me away. I spend half my life hung over. I'm only as good as I need to be to do my stories for the *Times*." Arms crossed over his manuscript, he turned and looked at me. Each word he spoke then was equally emphatic. "I can't make myself do it."

I let his words drift, sink, disappear, gave them the space a last chord needs to die. I said, "When would you write, if you could?"

"Nights," Bailey said. "That's all I've got. I have a study at home. I have a typewriter. I also have a wife and kid. When I lock myself inside, somehow they're locked in with me. I hear their footsteps and their whispers. I hear them wanting me, wondering what I'm doing, when I'm going to come out. I hear them wanting so loud and clear I can't hear my own thoughts. Then I want a drink so bad, I just get up and leave."

"I can help you," I said.

"Sure."

"I have a large apartment. I have a room that's not being used. I think it was the maid's room once. It's not spacious, but it should be adequate."

"Adequate for what?"

"For you to write in. I have a table and a chair and a wastebasket. I even have an extra typewriter. It used to be my mother's. She used to write."

Push me, pull you. Bailey was interested, torn. "You'd do that for me?" he said. Then, "What's in it for you?"

"Lots of things. Not least of which, I want to read your book."

"Hey, Tod, come here," Bailey called, and when Tod came, pointed at me and said, "Tell me, is there someone sitting on that stool?"

Tod's eyes slid back and forth, Clark to me, to Clark to me. "Yeah, somebody's sittin' there. You want another beer?"

"Sure," I said.

"Good," Bailey said. "I thought maybe it was the DTs."

"How about you, Clark? You're slow tonight. You want another shot?"

Bailey nodded yes. Then he said, "No. Not tonight. Bring me another cup of coffee, would you?"

One of Tod's apeish eyebrows raised and he cocked his head. "You okay, Clark?"

"I am. I'm practicing restraint."

"Good for you," Tod said, and went to draft my beer.

"I couldn't tell Olivia," Bailey said. "She wouldn't like it, not after she let me have the spare room for a study."

"How many nights are you home now?"

"I don't know. Oh, I get it. I don't go home, she thinks I'm drinking."

"Something like that. What she thinks is your problem."

"It might work," Bailey said. "It just might work." He was quiet for a moment, then said, "I like the irony, you know? She thinks I'm debauching myself, and all the time I'm being the best of good boys." For the first time, hope flickered in his eyes. "You sure you want to do this? Hell, you hardly know me."

"I know good writing when I see it," I said.

Bailey slapped me on the shoulder then. His eyes roved toward the ceiling. "Maybe there really is a God."

"Maybe so," I said. "I should warn you, there's something I want in return."

"What's that?"

"Writing is lonely. I want a friend."

"A friend of the work. You got it, kid."

The silver ball expanded, throbbed in my hands.

CHAPTER SIX

Bailey was tense and grateful. He arrived ten minutes before the appointed time and spent them apologizing for his eagerness. His eyes were clear as I had seen them, and instead of whiskey, he smelled faintly of soap. In the Lucky Strike, his gestures were constrained, scaled to the setting, but in the greater space of my apartment, his body language grew louder and more eloquent. He paced, long-legged, his long arms swept and dipped through air, almost as if he were conducting an invisible orchestra with an equally invisible baton. My apartment was high-ceilinged, gracious, languid. In its staid precincts, his energy was palpable.

I showed him to his room, the perfectly appointed writer's cell: a sturdy oak table, with matching typing stand, the swivel chair strong and padded, grainy type-erasers, one end a broom, a ream of good white bond. There were yellow legal pads and sharpened pencils if he cared to use them, and a wastebasket big enough to accommodate numerous false starts.

Bailey touched Mother's Smith-Corona upright lovingly. "My brand," he said. "A workhorse."

"There are fresh ribbons and platen cleaner in the drawer."

"You're an optimist," he said. "Hell, tonight even I'm an optimist. I'm going to do good work here, kid."

"I'm sure of it."

Bailey took off his jacket and hung it on the back of the chair. "Well," he said. "To work."

"To work."

The premise was, he would write his novel while I worked on mine. I settled at my Underwood in the dining-room alcove, rolled in a sheet of paper, listened. Footsteps first, Bailey pacing. At last he sat, and I could hear the ball-bearing feet of the swivel chair skating across the floorboards, finally the shelling of paper with words, rat tat tat tat. When he typed, he was fast. Silence stretched long between the blasts of language. I was far too excited to make fiction. On my own white bond, I wrote: Typing now, typing, typing, the quick brown fox is doing calisthenics, leaping the log, what is he writing, now is the time for all good men and bad ones too to come to the aid to the aid to the aid to the aid. To come to the aid of their souls.

An hour and a half later, Bailey wandered out of his room, called out, found me diligently positioned in front of my machine. Now is the time the time is the time, I typed as he watched, pretending it was a meaningful sentence being composed before his eyes. "How's it going?" he asked me.

"Pretty well. You?"

"What've you got to drink?" Bailey said.

"There's a fresh pot of coffee. I could make you tea if you like."

"Got any whiskey?"

"No whiskey."

"Gin?"

"No gin."

"Vodka?"

I shook my head.

"How about wine?"

"I had wine with my dinner, but it's gone."

"I knew I should have brought my flask," Bailey said.

"I've made myself a rule. No alcohol until the night's work's done. Five good pages buys you a drink."

"Jesus," Bailey said. "What happened to *in vino veritas?*"

"That's fine for poets," I said, "but novelists can't afford too much *vino*. Besides, we're writing lies."

Bailey clenched and opened his fists, clenched and opened. "You're a tough taskmaster, kid."

I shrugged.

"Nobody ever thanked another person for saving him from himself. Don't you know that?"

"I'm not looking for thanks," I said.

"Olivia tries to save me," Bailey said. "Pleas and sermons, liberally salted with tears. When she runs out of steam, she sends the kid in as reinforcements. Please, Daddy, don't get drunk anymore. She tries to make me promise. It's enough to break your heart."

"Do you promise?"

"Hell no," Bailey said. "I tell her I love her too much to make a promise I've got a snowman's prayer in hell of keeping. I tell her there is honor even among scoundrels. I don't know if she understands or not." He opened his palms, looked at them, then at me. "What say we pop around to the Lucky Strike. Just one drink. That's all I need. With a drink under my belt, I'll be set to write all night."

"Five pages," I said. "How many do you have?"

"I've thrown out three already."

"It's the starting up again that's hard," I said. "That's why we're going to do this every night until we're done."

Bailey looked at me and shook his head. "You're crazy."

"You're lazy."

Bailey laughed. "Damn right. Lazy and weak and easily distracted. The Irish have never been known for self-discipline."

"Five pages," I said. "I'll pour the coffee."

"Jesus." Bailey returned to his desk. I brought him coffee, black and strong. "Why be so fucking arbitrary? Why five pages, anyway?"

"Because you're too out of shape to do ten."

"You're a fucking puritan," Bailey said.

"I like to think of myself as a hedonist with discipline."

"I want a drink," Bailey said.

"I know. So you want a drink. So what."

"All right, kid. Five pages, and then my liver's my own."

We shook on it, and returned to our work.

For the next three weeks, omitting Saturday and Sunday, Bailey came to my apartment every night, and I was right; once he established the habit of working, his productivity increased until he could easily create, though not exceed, seven pages in the five hours we spent at our respective desks. The more Bailey bent to the task, the more restless I myself became, finding it difficult to apply myself to any one story for more than a page or two. I indulged myself, hopping from plot to plot, letting my imagination rove. Bailey took great satisfaction from the growing pile of pages. I knew this because he often fingered their edges, feeling the thickness of the stack, often tamped and straightened until it was absolutely flush.

For those three weeks, things proceeded so smoothly I began to believe that salvation was an easy job, began to calculate, multiplying numbers of pages by numbers of days, how soon the novel would be completed. Bailey had some two hundred pages when our vigil began, and anticipated he would need about five hundred to tell his tale. Three months, I estimated, and the novel would be done.

Our relationship deepened as our manuscripts grew fat. Sober, Bailey's mind was acute and original, his discourse rigorous. Sober, he was a stringent moralist, the most ethical of men. It often pleased me to advocate the devil's interests, insofar as I understood them, in our debates.

The *Times* had assigned Bailey to investigate the alleged sexual misconduct of the mayor's executive secretary, and the case was building nicely. Three lobbyists were willing to be quoted—the lady in question expected to be wined, dined, and satisfied in return for unimpeded access to her employer. She had an appetite for luxuries beyond her salary, for power exceeding the limits of her job description. There was a hint of bribery, a whiff of blackmail. Clark was alternately uneasy about exposing the woman, and sanguine that the story would win him an award. I found it paradoxical, how successful I was in the reformation of what I sought to destroy, but didn't let the ambiguity of my position distress me too much. My notes say I was happy. I believed that Clark was, too.

Then it happened, the high wind in the house of cards; the mayor's executive secretary, exposed, swallowed an abundance of sleeping pills and declined to wake up. When I heard the news, my thought was: Clark has succeeded. I was pleased, proud. For the first time, I had a sense of his influence in the world at large. I expected we would celebrate that night.

He didn't come. I walked down to the Lucky Strike, but he wasn't there. I called the city desk, got the newsroom, but Clark had left there early in the afternoon. I called his home. His daughter—the kid—offered to take a message. For three long days, he disappeared. I tried to imagine what false oasis he'd found, in what disreputable part of the city. I continued to hope he would turn up. My notes say that I was worried, angry. They suggest that I was hurt.

Three days. In them, I learned something of the relationship of time to desire, something of the emotional alchemy that mixes the two to make minutes dense as lead and hours long as days. I thought about my mother, at bath time and out of time. I thought about myself, and the dangers of my enterprise. I thought about alcohol, deeply, not simply as weakness or predilection, but as the muse's evil twin. Most of all, I thought about Clark Bailey, about the larger-than-life-size space his sudden absence left in my apartment and my self. All of my thinking marbled through that long and heavy time, as smoke through air, oil through water, swirled restlessly, yielding little insight except for this: In the supremely serious game Clark Bailey and I played, my own life was as much at stake as his.

Called the paper, my notes say. Called the bar. Called his home. I filled pages upon pages with speculation, spleen, and longing. I called and called, disguising my voice each time, trying to hide my urgency. At last, on the morning of the fourth day, Bailey's daughter told me that her father was ill. He was resting. He could not come to the phone. After a moment's relief at knowing he was found, was alive, my anxiety returned at even greater force. I would feel no peace while he remained inaccessible to me. I resented his wife and daughter, the shallow legitimacy of their claim to him.

The fifth day, a Sunday, was the most difficult of all. I had no hope of Bailey escaping the prison of his home; he was captive and obliged, cast in a domestic drama of remonstrance and remorse. He would not come. There was no reason to stay home. I sallied forth into the city, daring it to distract me, amuse me, to make me forget, even for a moment, the existence of Clark Bailey. No city, no Sunday can deliver so much. I hated the streets as I drove them, hated the oysters I swallowed and the beer that washed them down, I despised the art museum with its placid Oriental scrolls and its worst-of-the-Renaissance oils, hated the carp in their pools and the squirrels with their rodent busyness, oblivious to my wanting. A raw wind slanted the incessant rain. Consciousness was a burden I could not put aside. The city disgusted me. I disgusted myself.

On Monday morning, a weak sun teased vapor from roofs, trees, lawns, an uprising of mist that bore my spirits with it. I shopped for groceries, answered correspondance, cleared my quarters of the clutter accumulated during my vigil, when I had no appetite for order. I willed myself to sit at the typewriter, to work the keys, and after an hour or two, will was transformed to willingness; I finished a chapter in the World War I novel that had been hanging fire since Bailey's last night in residence. All the while I assured myself I didn't care if Bailey came to me that night or not.

Promptly at seven, his knock sounded on my door. I let him knock twice, three times before I answered, a small repayment in kind for my long season of waiting. A massive bandage was affixed to his left temple, and his smile when he saw me was abashed. "How you doing, kid?" he said. "As you can see, I had a little accident."

I kept my voice level. "What happened?"

"Got coshed," he said cheerfully. "Mugged, coshed, and left for dead. Fortunately, somebody went out in that alley to take a piss. Found me before I drowned in my own blood."

My insides lurched. He might have died. For something as meaningless as money, he might have died. Without the novel finished. I had almost been cheated of my revenge. "The coffee's ready," I said. "Would you like some?"

"Coffee and aspirin," he said. "My head aches like a son of a bitch."

"Can you work?"

The flesh around his left eye was purple-green. Inside this grisly socket, his brown eye winked. "Damn well better, don't you think? I spent the weekend realizing I don't want to get myself killed before this book is finished." He held up both hands and flexed the fingers. "I'm ready."

Recriminations rose in my throat; I wanted to spit them at Bailey's readiness. He'd offered no apology, no explanation. He had not said he missed me. All my deceits, all my conceits commingled, becoming the petulance of the spurned lover. The bitterness of that bile surprised and warned me. Involvement was not my ally. How could I hope to control Clark Bailey if I could not even control my own feelings? I swallowed my anger, asked no questions, brought coffee and aspirin. I was a friend of the work. I was an enemy of the man.

Bailey said, "Hangovers are great for contemplation. I'm going to make that old typewriter sing tonight."

"I'm eager to get to work myself," I said.

Bailey took his coffee mug and headed for the spare bedroom. As soon as the typewriter began to speak, I slipped the skeleton key from my pocket and locked the door.

16
■ ■ ■ ■ ■

Freddy lays the last page facedown atop the others and finger by finger pulls off her Isotoner driving gloves. Her eyes, excused from reading, seek distance, gaze past the drawing table, the work bench, and the bookshelves to the far wall, where narrow rectangular windows frame odd compositions of the world outside: Holly Tree with Second Story; Fir Tree, Power Lines, and Sky. Nick told her once that good writing makes pictures in the reader's mind. Most of what she's seeing is inside her head.

The most vivid of the pictures arises where her memory intersects with what she's read. It's midmorning, a Saturday. The house was quiet when she woke up. For the first time since Wednesday her father's car is in the driveway. The last three days have been a strange combination of anxiety—her mother's—and relief—her own. When her father is gone, her mother pays attention to her, needs her. There are no fights. When her father is gone, her mother never cries. When her father comes home, her mother withdraws into silence and tears, weeps until her eyes are nearly swollen shut. It may take days before she speaks above a whisper. Her father is always sick when he comes home.

Freddy knows she should be glad her father's safe, and tells herself she is, but her stomach, tight and uneasy, says otherwise. She wishes it were a school day, so she wouldn't have to watch the painful minuet-on-eggshells her parents do. Sometime after ten, her mother, pale and rumpled, emerges from the bedroom, heads to the kitchen to brew the morning coffee. Freddy follows her.

"Your father's awake now," Elsa says. "I want you to talk to him."

"Shouldn't it wait until he's feeling better?" Freddy says.

"I want you to talk to him now. I want you to ask him to stop drinking. Ask him to promise."

"Mom."

"Do it," Elsa says. "Please. Nothing I say makes any difference. Maybe he'll promise you."

"Can I have breakfast first?"

"He almost got himself killed last night," Elsa says. "Do it now. For me."

"I have to go to the bathroom," Freddy says, and spends a long time there, sounding out every syllable of every chemical ingredient in the foot powder, the toothpaste, and her father's Brylcreem, knowing her mother is too fastidious to open that closed door. At last, resigned, she flushes and comes out.

Almost stealthily, she opens her parents' bedroom door. The light is dim. Pillows propped against the headboard posture her father nearly upright from the waist and he dozes turned to the right, so that she sees in silhouette the sickening distortion of the upper left part of his face, temple and eye grotesquely swollen, bandaged hugely in tape and gauze. For a moment, she simply stares. Then her father opens his right eye, smiles weakly at her.

"Hi."

"I must look pretty scary," her father says.

Freddy nods, mirroring his faint, embarrassed smile.

"It's still me. And it isn't catching." He points to the padded chair. "You can sit down if you want."

"Okay." Freddy moves deeper into the shadows and sits beside her father's bed. "How do you feel?"

"Not so good. I feel like somebody parked a truck on my face last night."

"Headache?"

"Uh-huh. Although that word hardly does justice to the sensation."

"What happened?"

Her father's right shoulder lifts against the pillows. "Not surprisingly, I don't exactly remember. When I woke up, I was in the emergency room with some teenage medicine man doing embroidery on my head."

"What hospital?"

"The county hospital. Your mother was upset that they didn't find a plastic surgeon to sew me up."

"Mom says you might have died."

"I might have died in the war," Nick says. "I might have died crossing the street."

"I'm glad you didn't."

"Me, too. How are you?"

"Okay. Mom wanted me to talk to you."

Her father sighs. "Yeah."

"She really worries when you don't come home."

"I know."

"She wishes you'd stop drinking."

"I know that, too," Nick says. "Do you really want to have this conversation?"

"No."

"Me either. Not that I don't deserve recriminations. Please accept my abject apologies. I am a piece of shit."

Freddy's begun to get used to her father's voice emerging from the monster face; he seems less frightening now. What does frighten her is the resignation in his words. "No, you're not," she says.

"Don't contradict your elders, little girl," her father says. "I know whereof I speak. Will you tell your mother that I'm genuinely contrite?"

"She wants you to promise to stop drinking," Freddy says. "She thought you might promise me."

"Ah-ha," Nick says. "Your mother doesn't understand me, then. You are the last person on earth I'd make that promise to."

His words surprise her; they make her feel diminished.

Her father says, "Because I might break my promise. And I can't make it, knowing that. Do you understand?"

"I think so."

"I love you, Freddy. It hurts me to think that I hurt you."

She wants to deny the hurt, to absolve him, but she can't. "I love you, too," she says.

"Have we talked long enough?"

"I guess so. What should I say to Elsa?"

"Invoke filial ethics," Nick says. "This was a privileged communication."

Thirty years later, in her loft, Freddy says, "Sure, Nick." The hurt in her chest surprises her; she would have thought her heart had broken too many times to break again. How often, growing up, she wished to be an orphan, the child of possibility, with no known antecedents. Nick's power to hurt her, even after death, takes her breath away. From her deep sense of betrayal rises a desire to root the bastard out. She calls downstairs to her son.

Chaz responds to her summons, padding up the stairs. He hands her a sheet of stiff white paper. "I made you a picture, Mommy." He points to two stick figures of unequal height. "That's you and me. And that's a rainbow."

"So it is. It's lovely, Chaz." Freddy wraps her arms around him and squeezes tight. The embrace clarifies her priorities, restores identity; she is mother, with all that entails. Then she remembers the mother in the story, and drops her arms.

Her son regards her solemnly. "Is something wrong, Mommy?"

"Put on your shoes and socks, honey. We have to go downtown."

"Are we going shopping for new shoes?"

Freddy shakes her head. "Not today. We're going to the police station."

"Oh, boy!" Chaz says, then asks how come.

"You know that big envelope we found on the porch after we walked Paige to school?"

"What was inside it?"

"Clues, I think."

"About Grandpa?"

"Yeah." Freddy stands up and gives her son a gentle shove toward the stairs. "Come on. Let's go."

"Why didn't you call me as soon as you found it?" Ashford says.

They sit in his illusion of an office, Chaz on her lap. Freddy says, "It was addressed to me."

"You knew it was evidence."

"Not until I read it."

The envelope and its contents have already been dispatched to the lab. Ashford looks to her across his desktop. "So what does it say?"

Freddy dips her chin toward the top of Chaz's head, raises her eyebrows. Ashford stands up, the change in his pockets clinking as his pants fall straight. "Hey, son. How'd you like a tour of the station?"

Chaz slides down from Freddy's lap and takes the policeman's extended hand. At the door of the cubicle, he turns toward her. "Is it okay with you, Mom?"

"I guess you're safe here. Sure."

"Sit tight," Ashford says. "I'll be right back."

While he's gone, Freddy studies his children, school pictures in a triptych frame. The girl has braces. The larger of the two boys looks like his father. When Ashford returns, he says, "Nice kid."

Freddy points to the pictures. "Yours, too."

"Yeah," Ashford says. "That was last year. Pete started junior high school. They all look different now."

"It goes fast."

"Damn right." Ashford sits. "Tell me about the package."

"It's a book," Freddy says. "Part of a novel. I think at least some of it's true."

"I was hoping you were going to say confession."

"Maybe it is," Freddy says. "A slow one. Everything in it so far happened at least thirty years ago."

"Motive?"

"Maybe," Freddy says again. "If Clark is really Nick, then whoever wrote it was in love with my father."

"Crime of passion." Ashford squints, trying the idea on. "You can usually rule that one out if the victim's elderly."

"Nick wasn't always old."

"What didn't you want the kid to hear?"

"Incest."

"Jesus," Ashford says. "Something for everyone."

"You better read it for yourself. Sandy, too. He knew my father as well as anyone."

"Unless it is Sandy."

Almost automatically, she laughs. "I've known Sandy all my life."

"I got the impression the man was hiding something."

"He's always had a crush on my mother. They may have been lovers at one time. I'm not sure."

"Better and better," Ashford says.

"I don't think so. He really wants to help. Maybe he can."

"Okay. I'll send him a copy. The three of us can get together tonight and compare notes. Say seven o'clock, here?"

"I'm not leaving my children. It was hard enough to let Paige go to school today."

"Your place then. You mind if I bring a sandwich?"

"Come for dinner. I'll make a big pot of something."

"Since it's a party," Ashford says, "why not invite your friend? The big one."

"Carol?"

"Good-looking woman. Is she married?"

Freddy thinks about it. "In name only, I guess."

The detective can't hide his smile. Freddy has a strong sense of life rushing on about her, of herself as a rock in the streambed, unmoved by the current. Her father's death exempts her from the pageant; Ashford's mating urge seems quaint, and touching. Freddy thinks of Carol, her vitality, how lonely she really is. "You should ask her yourself," she says.

"Maybe I will." Changing modes, he fades the smile. "Meanwhile, I'll dig into our baby's book. Let's hope he gave us something to go on."

"Actually, I couldn't tell if it was a he or not," Freddy says.

Freddy's heart lurches with something like wonder when she sees her son, perched on the reception counter, swinging his legs, chattering at the uniformed policewoman on her tall stool. No shadow darkens his delight in being who and where he is, quick-minded, in a new place, a little bit promiscuous with his charm. Her son is whole and healthy and still safe. "Hi, Mom," he sings to her.

The policewoman, won by the child, smiles warmly at the mother. "Your boy was just telling me about the life-size dinosaurs at the science center."

"I liked the pterodactyl best," Chaz says.

"Would you like a souvenir of your visit to the police station?" the woman asks.

Chaz looks to Freddy. "What do you say?" she coaches.

"Yes, please."

The woman hands Chaz her ballpoint pen. "See? It says Seattle Police Department on it."

"I'm going to write you a ticket, Mommy," Chaz says.

"What do you say to the lady?"

Chaz flashes one of his rewarding smiles. "Thank you for the pen."

"You're welcome, son. You come back and see me again, all right?"

Freddy lifts Chaz down from the counter and sets him on the floor. He puts one hand in hers, using the other to wave good-bye. On the front steps of the station, Freddy consults her watch. Just short of one o'clock. For a moment, she imagines going home, a test of her willingness to be there; today, in her imagination, home resembles a small white fort, embattled. She asks Chaz if he wants to eat lunch out.

He leaps beside her. "Yesss!"

Seeking out a downtown storefront McDonald's, standing in line, Freddy finds her mind divided. What she's read cleaves her, claiming the darker part. McDonald's is clean, well if somewhat sterilely lighted. Chaz orders a Happy Meal—burger and milk. Freddy asks for a Quarter-Pounder. She wonders how any mother could corrupt her own child. She wonders what becomes of the corrupted child.

Ketchup for her fries? Cream for her coffee?

Her father had a hidden life. She saw no more of him than leaves above ground. There was a deep and secret root.

That's five oh seven, please.

Paige will be home at twenty after three.

Mommy, look. It's Big Bird on a scooter.

Daddy, look. The kid's a woman, mother now. Chaz, will you share your fries?

Mommy, I can't open the ketchup.

Redder than blood. Did Elsa suspect? Why did she stay? She stayed so long. She must have known. Chaz, honey, drink your milk.

And yes, no use pretending, she feels it, a kind of malevolent suction, strong and greedy, tugging at her clothes, her skin, trying to swallow up her mind. Paige has promised to come directly home from school.

Look, Mommy, Big Bird can jump over three french fries. Will you read me the riddles on the box?

What's dark and strange and mean all over? Ashford likes Carol. The world would be a safer place without so much wanting in it. The answer is: Oscar's Garbage Can. You know, Chaz, I'd feel better if we walked over and met Paige after school.

Big Bird crashes into the happy meal box and falls off the scooter. Chaz looks at her and says, You're really worried about us, aren't you, Mommy?

Freddy wedges the yellow plastic bird back onto the yellow plastic scooter. How easy some things are to fix. Yes, Chaz, she says, I guess I really am.

17

■■■■■

10:30 A.M.

Having reached the answering machine at her own home
number, Paige tries Mrs. Patniak. The school secretary swivels
her chair back and forth in short annoyed arcs, as if she's expecting a call from the President of the United States or something. Finally, Mrs. Patniak answers, wheezing.

"Hi, Mrs. P. This is Paige. I forgot to bring my clarinet to
school today, and my mom's not home. Are you going to be
there around lunchtime?"

"Well, I suppose I could be. I was planning to pay my light
bill and my phone bill up at Olsen's Drugs, and then meet my
friend Myra at the bakery. We try to get together at least once
a month."

"Don't stay home," Paige says. "How about if you hide your
key to our house where I can get it? The problem is, I forgot
mine."

"I could call Myra," Mrs. Patniak says. "We could do it
tomorrow instead."

"Could you just put your key in the hanging basket closest
to the door? I'll bring it back to you as soon as I get home from
school."

"You mean the begonias?" Mrs. Patniak inquires.

"I guess so. The one that's closest to the door."

"Begonias."

"Yeah," Paige says.

"In the begonias," Mrs. Patniak says. "I'll just write myself a note so I won't forget."

"Thanks, Mrs. P."

"I'll bring you and your brother a treat from the bakery. You know, the begonias aren't doing as well this year. I wonder if it's air pollution, or maybe the weather. I should pick up some plant food at the nursery."

"Right," Paige says. The school secretary has started to tap the eraser end of her pencil against the desktop. Her eyes are fixed on Paige. "Look, I really appreciate it. I've got to go now. Say hi to Myra." She hangs up before Mrs. P. can say anything more and turns to the secretary. "Sorry that took so long. Thanks."

"Next time," the secretary says, "remember your clarinet. Write yourself a note and tape it to the front door. That's what I do." She walks her chair toward the desk until her whole lap disappears beneath it.

Paige nods thanks for the advice. Just then the bell rings and two overcoated teachers thrust open the double doors, herding a mass of fourth, fifth, and sixth graders, rowdy and red-cheeked from playing, back inside the school building. No tetherball today. Forgetting her clarinet has cost her all of first recess. Paige spots her friend Susanna upward bound against the far wall and squirms sideways through the crowd, across the ramp, to join her.

"Where were you?" Susanna wants to know.

"I called my mother," Paige says. "Only she wasn't home."

12:07 P.M.

Paige raises her face to the sun. There's just enough breeze, today, to play in her bangs. Two sets of doors muffle the sound of lunchtime, and she pauses on the sidewalk to imagine herself inside, on line, grabbing a chocolate milk, griping about the grody corn dogs. If she were inside, she'd be calculating where to sit and who to play with after lunch. Being outside when she normally is in feels wicked, even though she has special permission to be going home. Someday maybe she'll skip school, just for the pure excitement of it. Mom told her she and her friend did that once, went to the beach and spent the whole day flying kites. The wind today's too gentle to keep a kite aloft. Without thinking about it, Paige swings into her usual route, unusual at noon because there is no crossing guard.

Traffic's intermittent, and she considers dashing across against the light, but her responsible self, the one who does her homework and gets straight As, talks her out of it, punches the signal change button the three times custom says it takes, and waits with the toes of her tennis shoes square on the edge of the curb until a switch to warning yellow slows the lone approaching car. It's sometime in the course of crossing, at some point in the vast concrete desert of the crosswalk, that she notices the stranger, lurking against the phone pole across the street.

This is the city, of course, and she's a city kid, no stranger to strangers, since most people are, and "lurk" is in her mind because it was one of this week's spelling words and she had to use it in a sentence, properly, on Tuesday's homework ("The stranger lurked in the park"), but something in the way this particular person leans against that phone pole pastes the two words tight together in the present tense and makes her just a little bit afraid. Maybe it's because this stranger is really strange. Paige knows the color red his hair is is not one of nature's shades. His sunglasses are really two big mirrors stuck in aviator frames. And his coat—it's baggy, checkered, obviously used to belong to somebody else. Is that an earring? Something besides his glasses is spiking back the sunlight.

Paige has the feeling the stranger is watching her. Before she reaches the curb, she changes course, cutting out of the crosswalk and angling up the street so she won't have to walk right past him. This way's no longer, just not the way she usually goes. She resents the stranger a little, for being so strange he makes the usual seem wrong, and walks how she thinks a soldier or a tough guy would, with long strides, swinging her arms, head up, eyes straight ahead.

Half a block, and the street draws a broad arc, swooping

west toward the park, the ferry dock and sound; Paige eases up on the power walking once the curve carries her out of the stranger's sight and brings her own house into view. The house is white and trimmed in gray, an unembellished bungalow with the tidy charm of the houses in fairy tales—Grandmother's cottage, or the Seven Dwarves'. It is the sort of house people live in before the adventure begins and come home to when it is over. Two pink rosebuds on the bush beside the front gate are just ready to unfold.

With a metal on metal clash, the chain-link gate closes itself behind her, and Paige bounds up the front walk, noting with pleasure the pastel geometry of her last spray-painted project, a yellow-pink-orange box, and the rain-paled ghosts of her last chalk drawing. So those are begonias, closest to the door. Mrs. P. is right, they do look a little sickly. Paige stands on tiptoe to reach under their waxy leaves, feeling for the key, and the stretch half turns her, so that she sees. The red-haired man leans against the bulkhead across the way, his checkered coat obliterating C in the graffitied FUCK YOU, the mirror panes of his sunglasses trained so directly on her she can almost see her two small reflected selves across the street. Her fingers find the key and drop it.

She has it now, but it doesn't want to fit the lock. Fear makes her fingers spastic. She drops the key on the porch, it bounces. She retrieves it. He watches. He does not move.

Steady now. The key knows how. She trains her eyes on the slot and slides the key into the lock. Turn *away* from the door frame—that's Mom's voice, instructing her. See? That draws the bolt. She hears it move, thunk into place. Thumb on the door handle, down, push, step, and slam. Paige locks the door and leans against it. The house is warm and smells slightly stale, as if the air has settled in their absence, mixed a new smell that matches silence. How long will the man stand there? On tiptoe, she peers out the window set high in the door, a rectangle made up of squares of glass, and sees he has not moved. F U STRANGER K, the wall says. Paige doesn't know what to do. She wants to cry.

The silence is too absolute. Paige dispels it with a game show, turned up high. A top-heavy blonde woman in a bathing suit and high heels spins a big wheel. The audience oohs and aahs. Paige grabs the afghan from the back of the sofa, draws her feet up, tents her knees, wraps herself tight in dusty pink wool. One of the contestants, a man who looks like a stuffed rabbit missing its ears, jumps up and down, clapping. The fat woman who was his rival stands quiet and looks disappointed. Paige tries to imagine all the places Mom might be right now, but the list is too long, especially since Grandpa died, and the exercise succeeds only in making her mother seem more distant, less accessible.

Paige thinks of Chaz, wishes he were with her now. She shouldn't wish that, since she's in danger and if he were here, he would be too, but if he were, she would have someone besides herself to think of, and that would make her brave. If Chaz were here, she would know what to do.

What would Chaz do if he were here? Paige managed birth and babyhood, tootled through toddlerhood without the slightest desire to put her thumb in her mouth, wasn't like Chaz, who flaunts his need for comfort and doesn't care who knows, and she likes it when Mom tells people that she, Paige, never did suck her thumb, but right now, right this minute, she's willing to give it a try. Her thumb tastes of sugar from breakfast and salt from sweat, a little soapy and a little dirty. With her tongue, she explores the whorls of her thumbprint and the ridged, cool hardness of her nail. She swallows once, and her thumb tastes only of itself.

On the television, a gray cat dances beside its bowl.

2:47 P.M.

Last one's a rotten egg. Mother and son race for the door. Freddy hangs back a little, not so it's obvious, to give Chaz's short legs the advantage over her longer ones. He wants to be golden; she doesn't care. Chaz touches her out, crows, "I win."

"I'm rotten," Freddy says. "Once again." Unlocking the door, she hears music emanating from the house. "Chaz, did we forget to turn the television off?"

Inside, the volume's high enough to make the floorboards vibrate. Freddy punches the off button, welcomes ensuing silence. As it settles, so does uneasiness. She *knows* the TV wasn't playing when they left. "Mommy, look," Chaz says. She turns toward his voice. He is pointing at a big lump on the sofa, swaddled in afghan.

Freddy touches the lump, feels more than fabric, knows it is her daughter. Tremulous hands lift back the soft wool to reveal Paige's eyelids clenched, her mouth set in a grimace. Her skin is warm. At Freddy's touch, Paige contracts, tightening the ball her body makes. She whimpers softly.

"Paige, honey, wake up. It's Mom."

Paige frets, twitches, fighting the nightmare. She does not wake. Behind Freddy's shoulder, Chaz asks, "Is Paige sick?"

"I don't know, honey," Freddy says. Not knowing frightens her. She takes her daughter's hand, speaks her name sharply, hoping to wake them both.

As Paige moves, Chaz stands back. Paige opens her eyes. Freddy waits the seconds it takes her to focus, recognize, relax. "Are you sick?"

"I don't think so," Paige says.

"What are you doing home from school?"

"I came to get my clarinet." Abruptly, Paige rises up on one elbow. "Is he still there?"

"Is who still there?"

"The man. The man in the checkered coat."

"Where?"

"Outside. Across the street. He followed me home from school."

"I didn't see anyone."

"He was leaning against the cement wall. Right in the middle of FUCK YOU."

"Ah, yes. Fuck you."

"Is he still there?"

"I don't think so."

"Please check."

"Okay, I'll check."

Chaz says, "I'll check, too." Together they go to the window, look out, across the street and up and down it. "Nobody," Freddy says.

"Nobody," Chaz echoes.

"I didn't imagine him."

"I never said you did. What did he look like?"

"Fake. Like he was wearing a disguise. Red red hair. And he had on sunglasses, the kind with mirrors, so you can see out but nobody can see in."

"He followed you?"

"Yes. And then he stood outside, just staring at the house. I didn't know what to do. I turned the TV up loud so I wouldn't be so scared. Then I guess I fell asleep."

Freddy puts her hand on Paige's shoulder. It is a tiny, fine-boned shoulder. The wind could break it. Freddy says, "I'm so sorry."

"It's not your fault, Mom."

What Paige says is entirely reasonable and feels untrue. Who else is there to blame?

"He didn't hurt me, Mom. He just scared me. I didn't know where you were."

"We were at the police station," Chaz says.

"There was a package on the porch this morning," Freddy says. "I had to take it downtown."

"Like with Far Out?"

"No, not like that. This one wasn't bloody. It was a book. I think it's a book about your grandpa. I think whoever killed him wrote it."

"This is just like television," Chaz says. "Maybe we're really on television."

"I wish," Paige says. "I wish we could just go away some-where, for a long time."

"Disneyland!" Chaz says. "Let's go to Disneyland."

"I'd like that," Freddy says. "A lot."

"You mean you'll take us?"

"No. I'd like to, though."

Paige touches Freddy's arm. "Mom, do you think the guy who followed me home is Grandpa's killer?"

"I hope not, baby, but I don't know who else it could be. We've lived here for three years with no witches in the park and no creeps hanging around across the street."

Paige pulls the afghan close, like a shawl, around her shoul-ders. "Mom, I'm scared."

"Yeah," Freddy says. "Me, too. Did you have lunch?"

"Uh-uh."

"Are you hungry?"

Paige closes her eyes briefly, consulting her stomach. "Now that you're home," she says.

18

Chili the color of old brick gurgles in her biggest kettle. Ashford appears in the kitchen. "Smells good," he says. "Your daughter's real sharp. She makes a good witness."

Freddy stirs the pot. "I want police protection," she says.

"Yeah. I wish I could give it to you."

"You wish?"

"I did get the guys over at South precinct to put you on their cruising route. A police car'll circle by here three, four times a day."

"What the hell good is that going to do?"

Ashford shrugs. "We might get lucky. At worst, it's a presence. Might warn the fucker off."

Freddy lifts her wooden spoon out of the pot, holds it before her. "It seems to me if you just watched us day and night, you'd catch him." A large glob of chili sauce plops to the floor. Ashford grabs the paper towels, crouches to mop up the splatter. "The brass says there's no hard reason to believe you or your family are in danger."

"My father was murdered. We're being harassed. What does it take to convince them?"

"Everybody downtown's all tied up in this television thing." Ashford aims, shoots the balled paper towel. It misses the garbage can.

"What television thing?"

"It's called *Crimebusters*. One of those things where they get some over-the-hill movie star to play host, and they ask the public to call in with tips. The producers decided they wanted to do Green River. The chief was desperate enough to agree."

"That guy hasn't killed anybody in years," Freddy says. "He's probably dead himself."

"The case isn't. It's still number-one priority back at the ranch. A department can only stand so much bad publicity."

"Is that what it takes? Do I have to stir up bad publicity? I probably could. Nick worked for the paper."

"Suit yourself," Ashford says. "I hope you tell them I've been doing my best."

The detective's shoulders droop and his arms hang straight at his sides, a bad-boy-chastened posture that makes him look young despite hair loss, and forlorn. When Carol appears in the doorway, he straightens miraculously.

"I brought a salad. Is it time to eat?"

"Thanks, Carol," Freddy says. "We were waiting on you and Sandy. Do you remember . . . ?"

Ashford strides forward, offering his hand. "Mike Ashford."

"I remember," Carol says. "Hi, Mike."

"We were just discussing the case. Your friend here isn't too pleased with my progress."

"Can you blame her?" Carol's words take Freddy's side, but her tone, flirtatious, is all on Ashford's.

"I never knew your first name," Freddy says.

"There's a lot you don't know," Ashford says.

"I bet there is," Carol says.

Freddy says, "Why don't you two set the table? Please." She requests this less to promote their flirtation than to spare herself witnessing it.

Carol transfers a stack of bowls into Ashford's waiting hands. Bright-voiced, she says, "I'll get the silverware."

At the stove, Freddy feels neglected. Carol should know better. Ashford should go courting on his own time. She calls to the children, "As soon as Sandy gets here, it's time to wash your hands."

During dinner, for the children's sake, they speak in trivialities. The conversation skitters on the very surface of what is, by media consensus, the world's reality today. They ride the news, respect the weather. Chilly for this time of year, Carol observes. Solemnly, they all agree. They talk about Central America, about the Pope, about Liz Taylor and Dr. Ruth. Sandy has always excelled at this sort of slightly-more-significant-than-small talk. With Carol as audience, Ashford exhibits a facility of wit Freddy never once suspected he possessed. She finds it impossible to think of him as Mike.

After the table's cleared, Carol retreats with the children. Sandy and Ashford set their copies of the manuscript before them on the table. Freddy fetches three sketches from her drawing board upstairs and, a little timidly, lays them out. One is a picture of Chaz's grandmother witch, one a sketch of the man who followed Paige. "The kids say these are pretty accurate," she says. The third sketch shows a young Nick Bascomb on a barstool in a grimy tavern. Behind the bar, a slightly Neanderthal man is drying glasses. Freddy says, "That's supposed to be the Lucky Strike."

"A good likeness," Sandy says. "I think the Lucky Strike is really the old Superior, on Madison. That was one of Nick's haunts."

Ashford records this information in his notebook. "What else is real?"

"The mugging, of course," Sandy says. "It left a nasty scar. Do you remember that, Freddy?"

"Too well. Nick looked like Frankenstein's monster. Elsa hardly spoke to him for weeks."

"Do you remember how old you were?"

"I think I was in third grade. Eight, I guess."

"So we're talking late fifties?"

Sandy says, "*The Naked and the Dead* was published in 1946."

Ashford says, "So?"

"So I don't think we can trust the time sequencing. Freddy, do you remember what year your father's mother died?"

"Two days before my sixth birthday. Elsa canceled my party. She said we'd have one later, but we never did."

"Maybe we're getting ahead of ourselves here," Ashford says. "Let's start small. Do you think Bailey is Bascomb?"

"I never doubted it," Sandy says. "Freddy?"

"It sounded like Nick. I saw him in my mind."

"What about this other guy?"

"Guy?" Sandy says. "I had the impression the writer was a woman."

Ashford says, "Jeez, I was sure it was a guy. A woman never even crossed my mind."

"I couldn't decide," Freddy says. "I think whoever it is didn't want us to know for sure."

Sandy turns pages, his eyes zigzagging across lines of type. At last he looks up. "I guess there is no real evidence to support my assumption."

"Who were Nick's friends then, besides you?"

"A few reporters," Sandy says. "Old sots and Young Turks."

"Names?" Ashford's pen is poised.

"Don't bother," Sandy says. "None of them could write like this."

"What about you?"

"I was based in Olympia for most of the fifties, so I didn't see the Bascombs on a daily basis. If I was in town, I was more likely keeping vigil with Elsa than carousing with Nick. We used to play Scrabble, Freddy. Do you remember?"

"I always lost."

Sandy smiles at her. "You played well for your age."

Ashford says, "Was Bascomb a ladies' man? Did he ever have a mistress that you know of?"

Curious, Freddy trains her eyes on Sandy. "Women were always drawn to Nick, understandably so. He was a handsome man. Virile but gentle. He may have succumbed to the occasional seductress, but I doubt he ever kept a mistress. Despite his foibles, Nick adored his wife."

"How could he treat her the way he did then?" Freddy's

voice is fiery, accusing. Her anger has awakened from its nap.

Sandy says quietly, "That was the problem, not the man."

"Uh, what about other men?" Ashford inquires.

"Elsa Bascomb was a faithful wife," Sandy says. His laugh sounds slightly rueful.

"I didn't mean that," Ashford says. "Was Bascomb attracted to other men? Did guys come on to him?"

Sandy colors slightly under their gaze. "Not to my knowledge," he says. "I wouldn't think so. No." He straightens the stack of pages in front of him. "Though if the writer is a man, I suppose that becomes an issue, doesn't it?"

"It does," Ashford says.

"Of course, it *is* fiction," Sandy says. "We have no idea what's literally true, what's metaphorically true, and what's just made up. Do we?"

"I was hoping you could tell me," Ashford says. "What about the guy's crazy mother? You think that's true?"

"It has the ring of truth, doesn't it? But that's the trick of fiction," Sandy says. "I have a dim recollection of Nick once telling me he was initiated in the art of love by someone older and more experienced than he. Those were close to his exact words. A lot of men would have been liberal with the details. Even drunk, that's all Nick said."

"Mama *was* crazy," Ashford says. "That part gave me the creeps."

"It made me feel sorry for him," Freddy says. "Or her. I can't imagine a mother doing those things to her kid."

Ashford laughs gruffly. "Motherhood and sainthood are not the same thing. Spend some time down at headquarters, if you don't believe me. Kids can't fight back."

"I wish I hadn't read it," Freddy says. "Every time I pat one of the kids on the head now, I wonder if I'm being a pervert."

"I doubt it, Miz Bascomb," Ashford says. "Here's one more question. Did your father ever write a novel?"

Freddy shakes her head. "I never saw one."

Ashford looks to Sandy. Sandy says, "Right after the war, he said he wanted to. He may even have said he tried. But I also remember Nick saying that fiction couldn't hold a handle to fact. Novelists are limited by probability, he said."

"But he might have?"

"I suppose so."

"It's time you went through your father's study," Ashford says.

A knock sounds on the door, stops, then resumes. The two men look startled. Nobody moves. Chaz comes trotting out of the bedroom, calling, "I'll get it, Mommy." Before anyone can intercept him, he opens the door, converses briefly with the caller, then closes it again. "It's a man, Mommy. He wants to see you."

Freddy crosses to the door. "Tell Carol and Paige it's about time for dessert." She opens the door, the screen door, expecting the paper boy.

Don Pankowski hands her a single yellow rose.

"Who is it, Mom?" Chaz calls from behind her.

"The Roto-Rooter man." Freddy steps onto the porch and closes the door behind her. "What are you doing here?"

"You didn't call me back."

"I'm sorry. Things got crazy."

"Oh."

"Yeah. This probably isn't the best time to be starting an . . ."

"A relationship?"

"Whatever." Freddy lifts the rosebud to her nose. "Yellow ones smell best. Thank you."

"You're welcome."

"Would you like to come in?"

"It looks like you're having a party. I wouldn't want to intrude."

"It's not a party," Freddy says.

"Do you have a date?"

"No." He *is* tall; she has to lift her face to see his. Some part of her resents his greater height. Freddy says, "There's two friends, two kids, and a cop. Come in, if you want."

"It doesn't sound like you care."

His disappointment accuses. Freddy is not aware of having promised him her unconditional enthusiasm. "Your choice," she says.

Above her, his face looks perplexed and, maybe, tender.

Looking into it, she resists the propitiating impulse to smile. Something in her would not mind fighting.

He puts his arms around her. One Freddy is indignant, wondering how he dares. Another, simpler woman welcomes the embrace. Behind them, the screen door whines on its hinges and her son, stocking-footed, appears beside her. "Mom, what's a Roto-Rooter man?"

Freddy's impulse is to pull out of the embrace, to refute it. Her son has never seen her in the arms of a man. Chaz was too young when they left to remember her with Jack, and her few adventures since have been both brief and meticulously discreet. Don feels her panic but won't permit her flight. With surprising grace, he manages to keep one arm around her while he extends his shaking hand to Chaz. "My name is Don, and I'm not the Roto-Rooter man. Your mother was kidding."

"What are you then?"

"A friend."

"How come I never heard of you?"

"Does your mother know all of your friends?"

Chaz thinks about it, then looks to Freddy. "Do you, Mom?"

"Probably not."

Again, Chaz addresses his mother. "Is he going to come inside?"

"Are you?" Freddy asks.

Don bends toward Chaz. "Is it all right with the man of the house?"

Chaz looks befuddled. No one has ever called him that before. Freddy says, "He means you, Chaz. Can he come?"

Chaz says, "If you want him to, Mommy, it's okay with me."

Freddy herds them both into the dining room, where Carol and Paige have joined the men in her absence. "This is Don Pankowski," she announces. One by one, she names the others. Carol is warm, Sandy cool, and Paige cooler. Freddy says, "I'll make the coffee now."

Despite the dirty dishes, the kitchen feels like refuge. So does the mindless task of changing filters, grinding beans, the long wait for a full kettle to come to a boil. She watches it the way she used to watch the children sleep when they were babies, with infinite patience and a little bit of wonder, listens for the sound of molecules excited, steam expanding inside a finite space. After a while, how long or little she couldn't say, Carol joins her. "I like him," she says.

"Which one?"

"Don."

"Really?"

"I liked the rose."

The rose lies where she put it down, already beginning to droop over the edge of the cutting board. Another ten minutes and it will be beyond resuscitation. The rose accuses her of criminal neglect. When Paige was a baby, Freddy sometimes dreamed she had misplaced her, lost her for hours. By the time she found the baby, Paige was starved past saving but had miraculously acquired speech, in order to rebuke her. After Chaz was born, Freddy was too exhausted to dream.

Carol industriously spoons sugar into the pewter bowl. "Are you okay?" she asks.

Freddy gives her head the dumb brisk shake of a dog annoyed by fleas. Breathes out a sigh that sounds like an unformed question. She says, "Everything's coming at me with equal force. There's not even time to recognize what's okay and what's not before the next thing hits me."

"Right," Carol says.

"You know what I mean?"

"Sure," Carol says. "This is when the nice boy doctors give us pills. If we didn't burn out in the sixties, we can fade out now."

"Shit," Freddy says. "So what do you do about it?"

"You hang on tight. You go with the speed and forgive yourself for not knowing anything. Once in a while, some bell rings and you get a ten-minute recess to figure things out." Carol smiles. "If you can work it in, you exercise."

"Don't tell me to exercise, damn it. Tell me everything is going to be all right."

The kettle's whistle has risen to a scream. Carol turns off the burner, moves the kettle to a cool place. "I don't know that," she says. "How the hell can I tell you that?"

They look at each other, squarely, coolly. Bitch, Freddy thinks. She says, "I love you." She does not say this because she feels it, but because she believes it. Carol's stance softens and the sharpness leaves her gaze.

"I love you, too," Carol says. "The coffee's ready."

Wedges of store-bought apple pie silence their tongues, but eyes continue to converse. Don looks to Freddy, Ashford to Carol, Paige to Freddy, Sandy to Chaz. Chaz, chewing, swivels his head, regarding everyone in turn, as if he sees but doesn't understand the subtexts.

Something besides the detective catches Carol's eye. She lays her fork down and reaches for Freddy's sketches, the witch and Paige's stranger, aligns them side by side. Her eyes move back and forth between them. By now, the rest of them are watching her.

Carol looks up, smiling. "Now I know what it is. I thought these faces looked familiar. Can't you see it, Fred?"

"See what?"

"They look like Jack."

Freddy gets up from her place and stands behind Carol, to share her point of view. For the first time, she sees a slight but real resemblance to her former husband. Everyone looks expectantly at her. If she stood before them naked, Freddy would not feel more exposed.

It's Ashford who says, "Well?"

"Well nothing. It must have been a Freudian slip." Freddy snatches up the drawings, turns them facedown. She avoids looking at the kids. "Would anybody like more coffee?"

Ashford says, "Sometimes the subconscious—"

"Makes mistakes," Freddy says. "It was a mistake, okay? Eat your dessert before it gets stale."

Sandy is the first to finish with his pie. He wipes his lips and sets his neatly folded napkin beside his plate. "I should be heading home. At my age, one sleeps best before midnight." He stands, then pauses behind his chair. "By the way, I should tell you, I called the library and asked for a list of all World War One novels published between 1950 and 1960. It might turn up something useful."

"Can you do that?" Carol says. "Just call them up and ask them to do your homework?"

Sandy grins. "Of course. In fact, most librarians love a

quest. And most newspapermen avail themselves of that enthusiasm from time to time." He looks at the children. "The Quick Information number is listed in the Blue Pages. But you must never ask for information you could as easily find out yourself."

Paige nods solemnly.

Ashford is the next to rise. "I want to get to gym by six tomorrow morning." He pats his stomach. "I need to atone for my sins. Good chili, Miz Bascomb. And don't worry, all right? I think it's going to be a quiet night." When he turns to Carol, his smile brightens by a hundred watts. "Nice seeing you again."

"You, too," Carol says. "I had no idea policemen could be so civilized."

"I'm going to take that as a compliment," Ashford says. "Night, Doc. Night, kids."

"Night, kids," Freddy echoes, rising. "Come on. I'll tuck you in." The children, pale and tired, suffer themselves to be tucked. Freddy returns to the dining room to find Best Friend and New Man locked in competition for last-to-leave. Freddy produces a Christmas-gift bottle of Drambuie and pours all three of them an after-dinner drink.

Don tells Carol that most of his work is for archaeologists and anthropologists, not the police.

Carol admits to persisting in a shitty marriage for the sake of her children and her charge cards.

Asked point-blank, Don confesses to a previous marriage. His ex-wife and his child, a daughter, live in Virginia.

Carol tells Don that as soon as her baby starts junior high school, she's going to get a job and maybe ask for a divorce.

Don asks if Carol and her husband have tried counseling.

Carol laughs.

Don says it didn't work for them, either.

Freddy says Jack wouldn't do it.

Carol says Jack is an asshole. She says that although Freddy is a wonderful person, she has a certain disability when it comes to choosing male companions.

Freddy says she hopes her luck is changing.

Don asks Carol if he passes.

Carol laughs, out loud and rudely, which means, at least provisionally, he does. But, she says, as her grandmother was fond of remarking, you have to eat a ton of salt with a man before you know him.

Don professes to appreciate this bit of wisdom.

Carol says it's time she was leaving. She tells Don to be good to Freddy.

Carol and Freddy hug, fondly. Freddy wonders what Don makes of this.

After Carol leaves, Don says, Nice woman.

Freddy says, The best.

Don suggests that Freddy sit beside him on the couch.

Freddy's not sure she wants to, but she does. Don puts his arm around her. He tells her to relax. She tries.

Here we are, Don says. He sounds content. Freddy asks him what his mother is like.

Don says, Was. She was a character. Wrote poetry and liked to feed the birds. Knew everything there was to know about the birds.

Freddy says someday she'd like to know about birds. She says she's exhausted and ought to go to bed.

Don suggests she lie down and put her head in his lap. He says it's all right if she falls asleep.

Freddy says she doesn't want to fall asleep and have to wake up later and get ready for bed.

Don says, Ah, bed.

Freddy says, I can't ask you to stay.

Don toys with a strand of her hair. He says he understands.

Freddy says, Thank you. For the first time, she begins to relax.

After a few moments' silence, Don says, Why not?

Freddy grabs for the language that's begun to slip away. She says, The kids. I have no bedroom door.

He says, I like your kids.

Freddy says that's good. Time, she says.

He says he knows it will take time.

Time for myself, she says. The timing's tough, she says. Too much is happening inside too little time.

Don strokes her hair.

To silence his fingers, Freddy takes his hand in hers and holds it tight. His hand is almost twice the size of hers.

He asks her if something's wrong.

She tells him almost everything is wrong.

Was it just sex? he says.

It was sex, wasn't it? Freddy says. She smiles. I liked it. I needed it. Thank you.

Don says he hadn't had sex for a long time before the other night.

Freddy says, It didn't show.

Don smiles, and then his face goes grave. It wasn't just sex for me, he says. I want to know you for a long time.

Freddy says that's nice.

Don asks her if she feels the same way.

Freddy examines what shards of feeling remain distinct inside her. She tells him she doesn't know.

His face saddens. I thought we were on to something good, he says.

Freddy says, Maybe we are.

Don squeezes her shoulders, then begins to collect himself, withdrawing.

Freddy says, I like you, Don. I'm sorry that my life is such a mess. Can you be patient?

He pushes to his feet. I guess I have to. Sure. When can I see you again?

Freddy can't envision her calendar or imagine her immediate future. She says, Saturday night, because traditionally men and women get together on Saturday night. They have a good time.

Don says he'll see her on Saturday night. He says he'll call her soon.

Freddy gets up and walks him to the door. They kiss. He leaves. She locks the door. For a moment, regret and relief achieve a perfect equilibrium inside her.

Freddy hears his car start in the street. She goes down the hall, to check on the children. There they are.

Returning to the dining room, she finds it full of moving cold blue light. A police car sits at the curb, its motor running. The blue light rakes the walls, the ceiling, dispersing and creating shadows. It streaks across the empty mugs and crumpled napkins, the flatness of her sketches on the table. When she turns them over, the blue light startles the faces of her drawings into a moment's life.

Carol was right; they do resemble Jack.

19
·····

Once, when he was drunk and Freddy not much older than Paige is now, Nick showed her a full-page cartoon in one of his *Playboy* magazines. Kirk Douglas, big-chinned and dressed as Spartacus, stood on top of a hill with six crippled followers, surrounded by Roman legions so numerous and dense they bled off the page in all directions. The caption said: "They can't stop men who want to be free."

Nick jabbed at the page with his index finger. "You know what this is about?"

Freddy had learned young that conversations with drunks were always endless, often pointless, and usually rhetorical. She shook her head.

"That," Nick said triumphantly, "is the American ideal of hero. You see? It's really not about Spartacus at all."

"Oh," was all she said then, but she remembered. This morning she feels like Kirk Douglas, holding the hilltop, indomitable despite the odds. Her troops, small but wily, are eating their morning ration of Cheerios with milk. They look renewed. A police car cruises past on the street outside. Freddy waves to it with her spoon.

"Listen, you two," she says. "From now on, we have a new

policy. I need to know where you are at all times. As much as we can, we stick together. You understand?"

Chaz nods agreement. Paige is silent and looks resistant.

"I'm not criticizing you, honey. You forgot your clarinet. Under ordinary circumstances, what you did would make perfect sense. Only these aren't normal times for us. Whoever's following us around is not nice and not sane. From here on out, we take no chances."

"Why does she want to follow us around for anyway?" Chaz says.

Paige says, "He wants to hurt us, dummy. Especially you."

Freddy feels wounded by this little flash of cruelty. It means Paige is more frayed than shows. She says, "Please don't talk to your brother like that."

Paige surprises her by apologizing to Chaz.

Chaz says, "Is it true, Mom?"

Is it? Until now, Freddy's always censored her thoughts before they reached Paige's conclusion. Slowly, she says, "I hope not, but your sister may be right. Maybe he or she just wants to frighten us. I don't intend to find out which."

"It's a he, Mom," Paige says. "I know it is."

"It's an old lady," Chaz protests.

"It's a creep and a crank and crazy," Freddy says. "Paige, I'm driving you to school and picking you up after. I want you to stay inside during recess and lunch."

"You might as well put me in jail," Paige says.

"I'm sorry, babe, but I want you safe. Chaz, I have to go to Grandpa's house and start sorting through his papers. You can come with me or be at Laura's. Your choice."

"Will you pay attention to me?" Chaz asks.

"Not very much. You'll have to entertain yourself."

"You haven't paid attention to us since Grandpa died," Chaz says. "I liked it better before."

"Me, too," Freddy says.

"I want to go to Laura's."

The children look at her, solemn eyes in pale faces. What made her think they were refreshed? Below the speeding currents of adrenaline and caffeine, the doggedness of pure dumb duty, Freddy feels for a moment her own deep exhaustion.

The kids have finished their cereal. Freddy looks at her watch. "Bus leaves in half an hour," she says. "Meet at the door."

Freddy stands on the porch and tries to remember living here. The holly tree's much taller now. Moss carpets the stone steps, and neglect has released the shrubs from symmetry. The rhododendrons and azaleas are leggy and eccentric, the two dwarf cedars shaggy, no longer twins. The rockery was Elsa's project. After she left, Nick let it go wild. Only the rank rich smell of city dirt is still the same. She breathes it deeply, remembering homecomings and leavings, teenage good-night kisses under the porch light or simply sitting, thinking, under the summer stars. Soon the house will belong to strangers. Freddy tries to decide if she minds or not.

She has no words adequate to describe the smell that greets her, grabs and engulfs her when she opens the door. The house stinks, it reeks, is dead and decomposing. The smell is so present and insistent it becomes her. Freddy is sure she is its source, will never be able to wash the stench out of her clothes, her skin, her hair.

It's strongest in the kitchen. Freddy covers her nose and mouth with a hand towel and cautiously opens the cupboard under the sink. Next to sacks of neatly sorted bottles and cans, the organic garbage ripens into slime. Trying not to breathe, she carries the pail into the backyard and leaves it there, opens windows and sprays Lysol freely through the house.

The house is as he left it, testifying that he didn't plan to leave. Cans half full of pork and beans, creamed corn and Kadota figs, topped with tinfoil that looks several times recycled, bear witness to Nick's frugality and his intention to keep on eating. Several plastic containers, their contents unidentifiable by now, host prosperous colonies of mold. The milk's gone sour in its carton.

What did she expect—that some benevolent domestic genie would appear to clean up her father's mess? If she were richer, she'd hire one to do just that. As it is, she searches until she finds the Lawn and Leaf bags, empties the refrigerator into one, sweeps the contents of the shelves into another, with no thought of saving for herself Nick's half-used cylinder of Morton's salt, his shredded wheat or Minute Rice. A coating of scum on the spice containers suggests that Elsa bought them before she left. Inside the percolator, Nick's last grounds have hardened into brown cement. Two bags, and everything that once resembled food had been discarded. Freddy deposits them in the garbage cans outside the kitchen door, then goes to the bathroom to wash her hands.

Where she finds Nick's soap, Nick's shaving cream, his hair tonic, his razor, his red toothbrush and uncapped Colgate, his comb, his Ban Roll-On and a styptic pencil stub. The towel from Nick's last shower is tossed across the curtain rod, his paisley pajamas, a pair she gave him once for Father's Day, dangle from the hook on the back of the door. The hamper, full of Nick's dirty underwear, emits a smell that's stale but Nick-ish. Perched like a slight white butterfly atop the bathroom trash, a little square of toilet paper frames a single spot of blood shed shaving. When Freddy was Chaz's age, she used to like to watch her father shave. Mornings he was hung over, he used to cut himself a lot. Seeing this last innocent drop of her father's blood, Freddy puts down the toilet seat that Nick left up, sits on it, and cries.

In the silent house, Freddy breaks silence, gasps, moans, wails, coughs, howls her sorrow, gives voice to every wordless feeling that wants out and doesn't stop until her aria diminuendos to a whimper. She reaches for a Kleenex then, wipes up her tears, the molten mascara, and is amazed, really amazed how much looser and lighter she feels inside. The mirror, freckled by Nick's last splashes, says she looks terrible, but Freddy doesn't care. The cultures that make a ritual of noisy, messy mourning must have it right. At last, she's ready to confront her father's study.

Either Nick disbelieved the homily equating a clean desk with mental order or had a very messy mind. His desk top suggests a topographical map of the Rocky Mountain States in winter white. Paper mountains and paper buttes rise high and jagged above paper caverns; there are plains of paper and crumpled paper boulders, everything speckled with a fine coating of ash and house dust. Freddy empties the overflowing ashtrays, moves the coffee mugs with their evil-looking dregs, then begins to excavate the paper landscape. Her father, it appears, was not given to discarding anything that arrived by mail and he must have been on every mailing list in the United States and Canada. There are form letters from Social Security, urgent pleas for support from half a dozen liberal candidates and twice that many liberal causes, invitations to subscribe, to attend, to invest, a flyer urging you to prepurchase your burial plot and spare your loved ones, another offering no-questions-asked health insurance for people over sixty-five.

Several eons deep, Freddy finds the first letter that wasn't computer generated. Signed Elsa, it opens tersely: Nick—. Freddy acquits herself of invasion of privacy, by virtue of extenuating circumstance. The letter reads

> I know you're pleased that Freddy's come back to town since she left Jack, and I trust you'll do what you can to offer her support, but knowing you, I also want to remind you that our daughter needs her own life and isn't on this earth to make yours easier. I think you owe her the gift of distance. She has two children to raise, and doesn't need another dependent. I hope, of course, that you've taken steps to control your drinking.
> Best wishes,

The letter must be three years old by now. Freddy wonders if Nick saved it on purpose or by default. She's tempted to save it herself, as proof of Elsa's concern, then decides the past is best called trash. She crumples the letter and throws it away. The next stratum consists mostly of empty cigarette packages and the little translucent rectangles with colored plastic tails smokers remove when opening them. She finds a handful of flashy color brochures for upscale retirement homes, one for a cruise of the Greek islands Nick never took. Approaching bare desk top, she finds a square of notepaper with a telephone number scrawled in Nick's hand. Hopeful, she dials. "Steve's Foreign Auto," a gruff voice answers. Freddy hangs up.

Bedrock's unappetizing. There are no fossils, only a paste of ash and time scumming the scarred wood, a litter of tobacco crumbs and something else, grayish and granular, that might be eraser-leavings, or the droppings of mice on a literary diet. Down to the sorry surface, and Freddy's learned nothing that might help. Where did Nick hide his secrets? The desk has three drawers. Before she opens them, though, Freddy decides to clean her father's desk top. She finds furniture polish, the shake-first spray kind, under the kitchen sink and sacrifices two worn hand towels to the polishing, permanently matting flat their terry roughness with desk-top sludge, turning their mild yellow a gummy shade of gray. Done, she tosses them down the laundry chute. Someday she'll do her father's wash.

After the surface chaos, the desk's innards are surprisingly well ordered, the contents commonplace: a ream of the ground-wood paper Nick used for drafting, another of letterhead, second sheets, printed envelopes and manila ones, new typewriter ribbons, scores of pencils short and tall, carbon paper, White-Out, a stapler, a staple remover, paper clips. The drawers are full of tools, not clues. The only thing that makes Nick's desk distinct from the desk of any secretary with an aversion to high tech is the pint of Wild Turkey in the bottom drawer.

Freddy feels the backs and unders of the drawers, the inside structure of the desk, finding nothing more startling than the roughness of wood not meant to be seen, and left unfinished. Having interrogated the desk and found it innocent, Freddy coasters around the study on the ball-bearing feet of Nick's favorite chair, swiveling between the floor-to-ceiling book-shelves and two metal filing cabinets, each six drawers tall, her father bought at government auction. Freddy stares at each in turn, dizzied by knowing how much language, how many words, what a prodigious number of periods and commas and mysterious semicolons waits to swamp and maybe drown her.

The files seem more promising, the bookshelves safer. She wouldn't have to read the books, after all; her father merely owned them. A quick riffle of the pages, and she'll find their secrets, if they have any. She begins near the floor, impiously grasping the volumes spine up by the covers and letting the pages fan out toward the floor. The shelves must measure fifteen feet across. Three yards of opened books rain down two empty matchbooks, one of her father's business cards, and a triangular scrap of paper blank except for the yellowing of its edges. The telephone ringing startles and reprieves her.

"Frederika?"

"Sandy?"

"Yes, my dear. When you weren't home, I figured you'd be there. Have you found anything of interest?"

"No. Have you?"

"I'm at the downtown library now. I believe we've found our mystery author."

Freddy says, "Tell me."

"K. M. Bayliss."

"I think I've heard of him."

"I wouldn't doubt it. The fiction librarian found our World War I novel. Except for a few details, remarkably close to the plot described in our unpublished manuscript. Bayliss has written no fewer than eleven novels in the last three decades. Several have been made into movies. According to the critics, none has lived up to the promise of the first, a book called *Hero Time*."

"So we're close to catching him?"

"Closer than we were. Bayliss is one of those notably reclusive writers. No photos on the book jackets. That, along with initials, could constitute an attempt to disguise gender. The author has never been known to give an interview."

"Still," Freddy says.

"Indeed. I've already spoken to the police. Lieutenant Ashford should even now be contacting Bayliss's New York publisher. An arrest, as they say, may be imminent."

"You're a hell of a detective, Sandy."

"No medals yet, my dear. As Ashford sensibly pointed out, our manuscript could be the work of some third party. A ruse. A red herring. Perhaps a frame."

"You're giving me a headache, Sandy."

"The possibilities *are* rather baroque. Enough to whet an old man's appetite for intrigue."

"I just want it to be over," Freddy says.

"I understand, my dear. You know, I can't help thinking Nick would have enjoyed this chase. *Mutatis mutandis*, of course."

"Speak English, would you, Sandy?"

Sandy chuckles. "Latin. It means, the necessary changes having been made. I meant by it that if Nick weren't the victim—"

"Yeah. Nick told me once that good newspapermen wrote simple but talked fancy."

"A shrewd observation."

"Do you think I can give up on the study now?"

"I wouldn't think so," Sandy says. "Literary coincidence doesn't constitute hard evidence, especially in a murder case. You'd best keep digging."

"I was afraid you'd say that. Thanks for the news."

"There should be more soon. Good luck, Frederika."

Freddy thanks him again and hangs up before the conversation can meander round another bend. Maybe there are books by K. M. Bayliss on her father's shelves. She brings a stable chair from the dining room, mounts it, and beginning at the upper left-hand corner, scans the spines. There is no more order to Nick's bookcase than to his desk top, unless the organizing principles elude her. Wittgenstein is shelved next to Camus, who stands shoulder to shoulder with Joyce, Thomas, Rolvag. Halfway through the second row, Freddy's eyes are swimming and her neck aches from reading sideways. Every now and then she has to climb down and advance the chair. Jefferson, Thoreau, Voltaire, Kafka, Bradley, More, Aquinas. Did Nick read all this stuff? No wonder he drank too much. She moves the chair again. Bellow. Heller. Mailer. Parker. Cerf. Roth. Buchwald. Wiesel.

Muffled by distance, she hears chimes. High noon at the local church? The ringing stops, then starts up again, sounding the same four notes. When she recognizes the ringing as the front-door chimes—one of Elsa's gentrifying innovations— Freddy's heart sounds an erratic note or two of its own. Again the summons comes. Since no one but Sandy knows she's here, it must be a peddler, selling aluminum siding, maybe, or encyclopedias. Yes, she is the woman of the house. She wipes book dust from her hands on the thighs of her jeans and climbs down to answer the door. Not today, thank you. Unless they're selling candy, she isn't buying.

The security porthole with its two-way glass fails to reveal the caller, showing her only the holly tree and, beyond it, a power line so beset by starlings it droops like a necklace strung of birds. The porch is empty when she opens the door. She calls out, hel-lo, and listens, but gets no answer, hears no footsteps on the mossy stairs. Her eyes tell no more than her ears until she drops them. Obscuring WELCOME, a fat manila envelope rests on the mat, its high-yellow color already dimmed by the faint drizzle that's arisen while she worked. Her pulse catches then, her hands are trembling as she stoops to pick it up.

CHAPTER SEVEN

Although he taught me the rules, the names of the pieces and their ways of moving across the board, I never enjoyed playing chess with my father Mr. Brown, perhaps because I felt, between us, so little stake in the game. Whether I wanted her or not, the queen was already mine. When Clark Bailey asked if I played, my interest sharpened exponentially.

The first night I began my practice of locking him in his room, I was too exhilarated even to pretend to work myself. Instead I paced, I browsed through art books, played opera, too softly to disturb him, letting my spirits soar and sink with the voices of the singers. Most of all I listened. His brush with death must indeed have fortified his dedication, because almost as soon as I turned the key, I heard the desk chair sigh under his weight and the small squealing of its ball bearings as he wheeled himself into position at the keyboard. The first sentence must already have composed itself in his mind, because the keys began immediately to clatter, which they continued to do in fitful bursts for the next hour or more.

At last he rose; I heard his footsteps as he made toward the door. The knob swiveled, once and civilly. Even in the next room, I could sense his surprise as the expected failed to happen. Thereafter, the doorknob, which was in need of oiling and always chirruped, began to squeak like a frightened mouse as he turned it back and forth, pulled it toward him, performed a dozen small tests and adjustments. When he understood the door was not about to yield, he pounded on it, not a knuckle rapping but flat-palmed, and called my name.

"Yes?" I inquired.

"Door's stuck," Bailey said.

"The door is locked," I replied.

"There's no key," he said, after a moment's pause during which I imagined he looked for one.

"It's in my pocket," I said.

"Let me out," Bailey said.

I smiled, although of course he couldn't see me through the door. The door was solid, an inch-thick slab veneered in mahogany. Bailey struck the door again—the lack of resonance must have taught him about the imperviousness of wood—and then said, "I told you to open the door."

"I don't think so."

"What the hell do you mean, you don't think so?" he thundered.

"I mean," I said, "it isn't time."

Silence as he absorbed this. Then, "Just when will it be time?"

"When you've written"—I considered—"nine pages."

"Jesus Christ. You know how long it takes me to write nine pages? That's a night's work and then some."

"All the more reason to abjure distractions."

"I need to take a piss," Bailey said.

"Use the vase," I told him. "I'll empty it later."

"What gives you the right to hold me captive?" Bailey said.

"You did."

"I did no such thing."

"You told me," I said, "that you wanted to finish your novel. You told me you wanted that more than anything."

"Right now I want more than anything to take a leak."

"You might use the window, if you prefer it to the vase."

"You insufferable snot-nosed brat."

"I prefer to think of myself as a friend of the work."

"When I get out of here, I'll show you friend."

"Think," I advised him. "Last week you spent at least three nights drinking when you could have been working. You're a writer with a great deal of talent and too little discipline. Under the circumstances, I'm simply bolstering your discipline."

"Let me out of here."

"No." I left the door then, returned to the living room and turned up the volume on *La Traviata*. Bailey pounded some more and shouted, I'm not sure what or for how long. When the record ended, he was back at work, the keys furious in their assault on platen. It was nearly eleven o'clock before he called my name again.

I responded pleasantly.

"I've done five pages, almost six," he said. "I need a break. Do you play chess?"

"Not very well."

"Do you have a chess set?"

"Yes, I do. It was my grandfather's."

"I'll teach you," Bailey said. "Just let me out of here."

I was too curious not to comply. "No tricks?" I said.

Through the dense wood, I could hear him sigh. "No tricks."

When I opened the door, I was surprised to see his bruises and his bandages. My imagination had healed his wounds. He stepped heavily over the threshold and laid his hand on my shoulder. "I don't know whether to beat you up or thank you. I've gotten five good pages."

"Thank me, then."

"Shit," Bailey said. "Where's the chessboard?"

I set it up while he went to the bathroom. The set was fine, and old, having belonged to Kate's father. The pieces were ebony and ivory, smooth and heavy, the ivory yellowed with age. I was amazed how my adrenaline rose at the prospect of joining battle, even knowing that to-night, at least, my defeat was foreordained.

"Under the circumstances," Bailey said, "I'll take the black." He told me, as my father had, about the bishop's diagonals and the cunning indirection of the knights, the king's weakness and the queen's dominion. He explained castling and the transvestism of pawns and told me that the best player was always the most longsighted. We began classically, advancing pawns.

"Do you play much?" I asked him.

"Not anymore. My brother and I fought out our adolescence on the chessboard. We played for blood."

"You never mentioned a brother before."

"Didn't I?" Bailey said. His knight snared mine, with no reprisal possible.

"No," I said. "Who was the better player?"

"Frank was. The little bastard. I never felt better than when I beat him. It didn't happen often."

"Where is he now?"

"Down under," Bailey said.

"Australia?"

"Dead." Bailey's offensive net swooped up another pawn. The POW camp on his side of the board was growing populous. I fixed my con-centration on the board, looking for ways to minimize the damage. "Frank was a brilliant kid," Bailey said. "If you think I lack discipline, though, you should have seen him. No staying power."

I moved a pawn that seemed safe. It was. Bailey's knight took my remaining bishop. "Check," he said. "Demon rum bit Frank's ass a long time before it got around to mine. He crippled a kid with his car. Couldn't live with it. He killed himself."

"I'm sorry," I said, and I was. My quarrel was not with Frank.

Bailey shrugged. "You gonna move or what?"

Having my king in mortal danger sharpened my powers of projection. "I'm new at this," I said. "Give me time."

"Sorry," Bailey said. "I forgot."

Where I had only been able to foresee the next move, and then imperfectly, my vision extended, suddenly, to encompass a hypothetical future. It was not rosy. I saved my threatened king. He took my pawn. I took his knight. He cursed. "That's what I get for thinking about Frank," he said. Three moves later, I was in check again. Desperate, I decided to try castling. Bailey took my queen. "Check."

My powers of prediction were acute enough by then that I conceded. Bailey was an expansive winner, assuring me I had played well for a beginner and would soon improve. I knew this was true; my rout then only whetted my appetite for future battles, battles in which I, general of ivory, commander-in-chief of ebony, a cunning strategist, would decisively prevail. It occurred to me that I would not take Bailey's life until I was capable of capturing his king.

Bailey thanked me for the diversion, then looked at his watch. "Not quite midnight. If you don't mind, I'd like to get back to work for a while."

I emptied the vase, which he'd used, and filled the thermos, which he'd drained, while he read through the night's work and pronounced it "not half bad." As I retreated to the door, Bailey called over his shoulder, "Are you going to lock me in again?"

Inside my pocket, I toyed with the key. "Would you like me to?" I asked.

He laughed. "Sure. It makes me feel like the princess in the fairy tale, supposed to spin gold from straw."

"Don't talk to any little men," I told him. "They drive hard bargains."

"Rumpelstiltskin's a piker compared to you," Bailey said, and with that, began to type.

More to keep Bailey out than shut him in, I locked the door once more and went to the bookshelves, where there were several volumes about chess, also my grandfather's, which I had never opened, much less read. Selecting the most promising of these, a book of problems, I sat down at the board and undertook to study openings.

My excitement carried me easily through the first problem. When the second was set up, though, my exhilaration turned on me, becoming as irresistible a weariness as I'd experienced since childhood when my mother's voice, spinning stories, seduced me into sleep. My will to waking was powerless against the gentle gravity that pressed my eyelids down, and it was useless to struggle; when I managed to keep my eyes unlidded, all they could do was stare. Thought was impossible, too taxing. I lay back on the sofa and let sleep claim me.

In my dream, Kate was the ivory queen, her gown more stiff than sibilant, and the floor of the bathroom was a mosaic checkerboard of black and white tiles, the winy towels banners of the queen.

I knelt humbly at her feet, a pawn.

"My knight is coming," said the queen. "I must bathe."

I rose and attended as she removed her robes, rich garments so heavy I could scarcely bear their weight as she laid them in my arms. At last the queen was entirely naked except for the emerald in her navel which, she told me, it would be bad luck to remove. I laid her clothes carefully in the bottom of a deep chest that smelled intoxicatingly of cedar. When I returned to assist her, the whiteness of her skin was startling, an apogee of white that seemed to be lighted from the inside, and hurt my eyes. She had grown in my absence both larger and more female, transcending the proportions of a mere woman to attain those of a goddess, her breasts deep and intelligent, her hips monumental, smoothly curving as the aged mountains of Vermont. Her sex was a shrouded valley, a chasm plump and thickly forested, along whose floor a sweet and secret river ran.

"Draw my bath," the queen commanded.

Jewels shone between the talons of the tub's clawed feet and the spigots were gold, fashioned to resemble the sex of men. When I turned the gold scrotum handles, blood thick and furred as tomato juice flowed from the faucets. Smiling, the naked queen, my mother, stepped into the bathtub and after a moment's crouch as she accommodated to the heat, sat and reclined, her breasts and shoulders a blinding brightness rising from the red, the green jewel in her navel winking, a beacon in her belly, above the tide. Her bathtub toys were inflatable ecclesiastics and the shrunken heads of men, which must have been hollow, since they floated easily, faceup.

"Join me," Mother invited.

I knelt beside the tub and wept.

It was Bailey hammering for release that woke me. I wakened sticky and disgruntled. My face was wet with a salty amalgam of sweat and tears. Before I freed Bailey, I washed it with cold water. Again, I was startled by the swellings and discolorations of his face. He was tired but in high spirits, pleased by an honest night's writing. I did not confide my dream to him but after he left inscribed it in my notebook.

So many years later, I find it has not lost the power to frighten me.

CHAPTER EIGHT

"Forgive me for bothering you." Dorothy Swanson, a flutterer, picked at my sleeve. "I know you're busy, but your father's traveling again, and we've been so worried. It's been two weeks."

"How bad?" I said.

"Very bad. The worst. She hasn't spoken. It's all I can do to get her to take a little water."

"No food?"

"She's skin and bones, poor dear."

"Poor dear indeed."

"I hoped that seeing you might snap her out of it."

"Maybe," I said. "Although she doesn't always know me at the best of times."

"No, dear. But somewhere deep inside she knows she know you, don't you think?"

"Have you had the doctor in?" I asked.

"Oh, yes. He's been here twice. If she doesn't eat by Friday, he wants to take her to the hospital so they can feed her intravenously. If we can't reach your father, you'll have to sign her in."

Swanson's kindly dried-apple face was puckered with concern. The better part of Mrs. Swanson's life had been expended in concern for others, but her devotion to Mother exceeded the disinterested affection of nurse for patient, resembling more the way a mother will love her retarded child above its normal siblings, as if its very helplessness exerts a special claim on her heart. She assumed I felt as she did, only worse, having lost the wonderful mother she imagined mine to have been. She didn't know, nor did my father Mr. Brown, just how long my mother had been gone. Swanson took my right hand between both of hers, using the top one to give mine pats she intended to be comforting. I couldn't evade the awareness that those plump old hands, like mine, knew Mother's body. I suffered myself to be patted, then pulled away. "The poor, sweet thing," she said. "So talented, too. Do you suppose there ever was a Clark?"

I told Mrs. Swanson I didn't know. I asked her if she knew of anything that might have set this episode off or made it more dramatic than the others.

"Oh, yes," she said. "She told me he'd written her, a cruel letter. She said he said it was all her fault. He said he was just a boy when she seduced him, too curious and flattered to resist. He thanked her for initiating him, told her he was married now, with a child of his own. He thought of her sometimes, fondly." Swanson looked up at me, her blue eyes wavering.

"Did you actually see the letter?" I said.

"I asked to, but she wouldn't show me. She said she was too ashamed."

"Has she received any mail lately?"

"Oh, yes. She still gets letters now and then. Your father writes, you know, and several of her old acquaintances. She writes back when she's"—here the voice came close to breaking—"when she's better."

"So there may have been a real letter?"

A deep intake of breath expanded Mrs. Swanson to her full height and girth. "It's our policy to respect the privacy of our guests. Lavender House is not an institution, it's a home."

"Of course," I said.

Exhaling, Swanson collapsed into her short and portly self. "I can't bear to think of her in an ordinary hospital," she said. "Those young nurses they have today, they think more of their paycheck than their patients. They wouldn't understand how special Kate is."

"We've been grateful," I said, "that you do."

At that, Swanson brightened a bit. "Oh, yes," she said. "Would you like to see her now?"

"Now" was the moment I had been postponing. I never liked to see my mother, yet I was dutiful to a fault, for reasons that escape me still. If more than a week or two elapsed between my visits, my sense of omission, which was not abstract at all but an actual physical sensation, grew so great it blighted all my other senses, making it difficult, finally impossible to smell, hear, taste, or to sleep properly. Seeing Mother brought me no joy, but did restore me to myself. I followed Mrs. Swanson to Mother's room and remember thinking, of her massive, tightly corseted backside, how little it resembled living flesh.

She opened the door a slice and turned to face me, with a hopeful, artificial smile. "There she is," Swanson said, as if Mother might have been anywhere but in that bedroom, the largest in the house, with its busy and oddly martial wallpaper, the vertical columns of small pink roses in their endless forced march from floor to ceiling, pervaded with the scent of lavender, which the proprietors found more pleasant and as effective as industrial disinfectants. Mother's bed, a mahogany fourposter as grim and formal as the prospects for spontaneous bliss on the wedding night of an arranged marriage, had once belonged to Miss Lavender's maiden great-aunt. Mother lay back in a bank of pillows, eyes fixed on the pink ceiling.

"Someone to see you, Kate dear," Mrs. Swanson said. Again, her ersatz nurse's smile revealed her dentures. "I'll leave you two alone now." With a little bob, she retreated backward and I stepped into the room, closing the door behind me. Mother, who had no weight to lose, was nonetheless diminished, slighter and more transparent, too, as if she were no more than bones wrapped in chamois. Beneath the delicate high cheekbones, her cheeks hollowed alarmingly. In such a thin face, her eyes seemed huge. They didn't leave the ceiling until I sat on the edge of her bed, my weight disrupting the perfect stasis of her pose.

I lifted her pale hand from the rose satin comforter and held it in mine. "Hello, Mother." Her eyes, which had brushed over me, now studied the shiny terrain of the coverlet. Her expression was fixed as a statue's, those eyes blank as the Apollo Belvedere's, or Little Orphan Annie's. The ivory queen on her father's chessboard was no less animated.

Having been inoculated so thoroughly and so young, I truly believed I was immune to the vagaries of emotion, and prided myself on my detachment, but beside my mother's, mine was a paltry thing. In spite of myself, surprising myself, I felt. Thinking of it today, I feel again: as if all my life I had carried a balloon inside me which now expanded and, displacing all my organs, pressed hard against my heart. What its thin skin enclosed was nothing, Nothing, a nothingness that defied its dictionary definition by having inside me a terrible mass and which felt as endlessly expansive, as cold and full of missed connections as the universe itself. My balloon filled with the aching loneliness of the winter sky at midnight, with its inherent knowledge of the distance between the stars, nothingness an absolute condition, like a disease with no known cure but death. I wanted not my mother, but to be mothered. I longed to die.

I do not describe my feelings well. Words chip away. To shape them makes them small. This is not precisely what I felt, is less than I felt, then and in memory; my words, my metaphors embroider Nothing until it is almost a pretty thing and I, who am committed to tell the truth at last, am tricked by language into more and graver lies.

For a long time, I sat beside my vacant mother, holding her scrawny alabaster hand, myself grown fat on emptiness and scarcely more present than she. Then a small thing, a minute thing happened, or I simply noticed that it had. In our silence, in our separation, Mother and I had begun to breathe in unison.

We drew breath and expelled it in the same measure, as if a single metronome governed our somatic rhythms. The intimacy destroyed by birth was now restored. Our reunion was wordless, absurdly subtle, yet as we performed that simple, essential transaction, trading new air for old, subsisting on common substance in common rhythm, I felt somehow elated, and redeemed.

I don't know how long we sat there, breathing, before Mother broke her two-week silence. Her voice, hoarse from disuse, startled me. What she said was "Clark?"

"Yes, dear," I said.

"You came." Her voice did not exceed a whisper. "You said you'd never come."

"I'm sorry. I was wrong."

"Your letter hurt me. I cried."

"I'm sorry," I said again. "I didn't mean it."

"I've waited so long," Kate said. As her voice revived, so did her eyes. Fixed on mine, they glittered.

I said, "I know. So have I."

Kate's hand, inert ere now, stroked mine. Her skin was thin as paper, a fine sheet, her blue veins the watermark. There was exquisite tenderness, forgiveness, in her touch. Then, quite abruptly, she dropped my hand and lifted hers to her hair, felt it curiously, as if her fingertips could see. "I must look dreadful," she said. "I wasn't expecting you."

"You look lovely, Mrs. Brown."

Her laugh was a girl's. She reminded me to call her Kate. "I've been ill," she said. "No strength. Lie down beside me for a while."

"Wait," I told her, and stood, removed my shoes, went to the door, which had no lock. I tilted a heavy chair under the doorknob. If it kept no one out, it would at least buy time. Mother had fluffed a pillow for me when I returned to the bed. We lay facing one another, as we had when I was a child. Kate's face was changed; I could not tell if it was lovely or grotesque. There were silver hairs in her eyebrows, as if a morning frost had not yet melted. She reached across the little space between us and touched me delicately, feature by feature, curve by curve, as if my face were a book she was reading in braille. "So long," she breathed. "Why did you write that letter? It was unkind."

"I wanted to free you," I said. "I hoped to free myself. But it was a mistake. I know that now."

"So long," she said.

"Do you still have the letter?"

For a moment, something like defiance shone in her eyes.

"Give it to me," I said. "I want to take it back."

She struggled to rise up, a vast effort, reached under her pillow, produced the letter. I took it from her and stuffed it in my pocket, never taking my eyes from hers. "Gone. Withdrawn. Forgive me."

"I forgive you," Mother said. Then, "Kiss me, Clark."

It was back then, the old vertigo, as I reeled between two beings, my own and Clark's. I was afraid that Mrs. Swanson, in the kitchen, would hear the frantic pumping of my heart. Mother's eyes, approaching mine, were no brighter or madder than they had ever been. Clark kissed his Kate. Her lips were hot and dry, her mouth, once sweet, now tasted sour. Her hands played in my hair. After our lips parted, her breath, warm, moist, and foul, still kissed me. In that moment, I did not know who I was, or where I was, or how old.

"Love me, Clark," Kate whispered.

"I do."

"Love my body," she said.

I was excited and felt ill.

"Please."

How often had I pleased her? She arched back now, anticipating pleasure, exposing the awful, undefended whiteness of her throat. Her breath came fast and shallow. She was sure of her power. I understood then that a child can be forgiven. An adult cannot. My mother drew my hand toward her breast. With the other, I lifted up my pillow and pressed it against her face. I did not know how long it would take, so I pressed for a long time. She scarcely struggled. The excitement in my body resolved as tears.

Leaving, I turned her head to one side, smoothed her hair, crossed her hands over her diaphragm and pulled the covers up snug to her chin. She looked serene.

I straightened my clothes, put on my shoes, withdrew the chair. In the dining room, Mrs. Swanson and Miss Lavender were serving supper to their other "guests." Mrs. Swanson put down the bowl of mashed potatoes and followed me into the front hall.

"Did she know you?" she asked. "What happened?"

"She knew me," I said. "We talked. She's sleeping now. I think she'll eat tomorrow."

"I knew it," Mrs. Swanson said. "Our Kate will be all right."

She flung out short thick arms and caught me in a hug. "Bless you, child."

I squirmed out of Mrs. Swanson's embrace. "Please call and tell me how she is," I said.

CHAPTER NINE

It was close to midnight when Bailey appeared at my door. The blurred look of his irises suggested he'd been drinking. His breath confirmed it. "Can I come in?" he said.

I stepped back to let him enter. He moved as if the gyroscope that balanced him was winding down to wobbles. "Planning to write?" I asked him. "Or were you looking for a place to sleep it off?"

He struggled out of his wilted raincoat, tossed it on the sofa, then sat beside it, his long arms drooping down between his knees. He mumbled something.

"What?"

"Said, don't know why I came." His voice was slow as thick syrup and the words came out coated, with none of the sharpness of his sober diction.

"Since you're here," I said, "you're having coffee." It was made, hours before, in anticipation of a night's writing. Waiting, it had grown strong and muddy. He winced at the first sip. Groaned. "You could have a shower," I said. "It might help."

"No," he said. "I've got a grief."

"What? Did you lose your job? Olivia kick you out?"

He swung his head shoulder to shoulder in long pendulum arcs. "Somebody died," he said.

"It happens every day," I said.

"Couldn't tell Olivia," Bailey said. "The kid, though, she was sweet. Knew right away that I was off my feed. 'What's wrong, Daddy?' she said. I could have told her, except she's too young."

"Are you going to tell me," I said, "or do I have to guess?"

Gravity tugged his features into a sad frown, made jowls, predicting what age would later make irreversible. "Shit," he said. "Who are you, that I should tell you?"

"I'm here," I said.

"Yeah. Yeah, kid, you are. You want to hear a sad little story?"

"Sure," I said. "I've got time."

Bailey moved his hands to his thighs and leaned back on the sofa. "I was sixteen years old," he said. "Great beginning, huh? Once upon a time I was sixteen years old." He sighed.

"Go on," I said.

"I'm embarrassed," he said. "You believe it? She was just a little younger than I am now. Twice my age then. She had a kid, two, three years old."

"Who?" I said.

"Kate," he said. His voice caressed the name. "Kate Brown. I hadn't seen her for nearly twenty years. I saw in the paper this morning she was dead. Not old, either. Fifty-two."

"What did she die of?" I asked.

"Paper said heart failure."

"It happens," I said.

"Yeah. You know, I always figured I'd see her again. Call her up one day and say, Remember me? Let's have lunch."

"Who was this Kate to you?" Did I sound casual? In my own ears, the words had solemn weight.

Bailey raised his head and looked me in the eye. "My boss's wife. Maybe she was my boss. Her husband signed my check." His pause accommodated sighs. "Remember that paper, the *Imago*? Came out every other week. Supposed to be a journal of arts and culture. Seattle hasn't had anything quite like it since. Kate's husband bankrolled it and made her editor. The woman could write. A little highfalutin sometimes, but solid stuff. Paper never operated in the black, but that didn't matter to Brown. He did it for her."

He paused for a long time, looking back. I held my questions. It was his story I wanted to hear, told his own way. "Kate grew up back east," he said. "Had a fine education, one of those Seven Sisters schools. She met Brown back there. He was on his way back from Europe, after the first war. Stocky, gruff guy, full of energy and opinions. Fell madly in love with this lady intellectual. Hell, she *was* beautiful. He was going to make his fortune in the West. She didn't want to move to some god-forsaken backwater like Seattle." Here he laughed. "Brown set out to make bucks, and he did. Manufacturing. Widgets for the folks at Boeing. When he got rich enough, Brown laid siege to Kate until he wore her down. The *Imago* was her wedding present." Bailey looked at me. "You bored?"

I shook my head. "It's an interesting story so far. You want more coffee?"

"Yeah."

I refilled his cup.

He said, "So it was the Depression. Hard times. My folks were scraping bottom. Crash didn't touch Brown, though, except to make him richer. He bought up real estate. The guy may have been crude, but he was smart. Only kept petty cash in U.S. banks, and he thought the stock market was bullshit. Did his banking in Europe. Bought into mines, gold and diamonds, in Africa and South America. He had an eye for quality."

"Sounds like quite a character," I said.

"Yeah. He even looked solid, brick shithouse kind of guy. Anyway, the *Imago* had this apprenticeship thing. 'For young writers of exceptional promise,' the notice said. They gave you money and experience. I'd graduated high school early and couldn't afford to go to college. I wanted to help out the folks. Frankie'd just started high school. So I joined the Longshoremen's Union. Spent most of my time waiting around, but I was down there every day, so when there was work, I got a piece of it. Hard fucking work, too. Every dime I made, I gave my mother a nickel and put the other one away for college. It was a friend of my mom's, a schoolteacher, who saw the notice in the *Imago*, about this apprentice thing. She knew I'd been a reporter for the high school paper, and she sent us the clipping. I thought I'd died and gone to heaven." Bailey put down his coffee cup, the bottom full of sludge. "You got anything stronger?"

His speech had cleared in the telling. I wanted to keep him drunk enough to talk, sober enough to talk well. A delicate balance. "Brandy," I said.

"Straight up."

"That's the only way it's served," I said. I poured a generous amount into a snifter and handed it to him. His big fingers looked awkward on the fine stem. "You savor it," I said. "This stuff is twelve years old and has a pedigree."

Bailey tilted his head back and tossed off half the shot. When he lowered the snifter, his eyes were watering. "Potent."

"I gather you applied for the apprenticeship," I said.

"Yeah. They wanted you to submit an essay on the real and potential role of the arts in northwest culture," Bailey said. "I worked like a crazy man on that mother. It was a good piece. I also lied. You were supposed to be at least eighteen years old and enrolled in college." He made as if to gulp, then remembered my admonition and sipped the brandy. "This stuff does funny things to your nose hairs," he said. "Anyway, the rest is history, as they say."

"Kate," I prompted softly.

"Kate," he said. "Ah, Kate. It took me about five minutes to fall in love with her. Only it wasn't really love, you know? More like a crush. I was in awe. Not only was she lovely, really lovely, but she could write better than I dreamed of then. She knew things I didn't. Lots of things." He lifted his snifter. "Things I still don't." He laughed. "Hey, I grew up poor. Sit me down at a fancy table and I still get nervous about the forks." Affecting elegance, his little finger arched, he sipped the brandy.

"Kate," I said.

"She was the best teacher I ever had," he said. "In more ways than one. She'd assign me stories and then go over them word by word, phrase by phrase. Taught me the difference between good enough and good. Maybe I could have figured that out for myself, but it would have taken years. Seattle *was* a backwater. Good enough was plenty good for the locals.

"When we'd be sitting at her desk at the paper, huddled over one of my pieces, I started to realize that I felt something more than admiration for this lady. I'd smell her perfume and forget all about the dangling modifier in paragraph three. Then one night it happened. It was a Friday. Brown was out of town and their kid was staying with Brown's mother for the weekend. We'd all been busy proofing copy for the next issue. By the time we were done, it was well past six o'clock. Kate asked me to come into her office. She picked my latest essay off her desk. 'I'd like to talk about this,' she said. 'Perhaps you'd like to join me for dinner.'

"We ate in the dining room at the Olympic Hotel. I'd never seen anything like it. I ordered a steak. Kate had to coach me through the silverware. I amused her, but somehow she didn't make me feel stupid, just young. Then she asked me to drive her home. I was a bus rat, but the family had a Ford, so I knew how. When we pulled into her big driveway, she suggested I come in for a drink. We'd talk about my story.

"Maybe this is the same stuff she gave me to drink, I don't know. My mother was WCTU. I'd never had a drop of alcohol. It went right to my head. Kate sat beside me and said a lot of nice things about my piece, which also went to my head. She told me to call her Kate. I wasn't sure but what I was asleep and dreaming. Then she asked me to kiss her." Bailey reverted, draining what remained of his brandy, and asked for more.

I poured it. "How did you feel?" I said.

"Jesus. I felt as if I'd never really felt anything before. My whole body was alive and singing. It didn't stop with a kiss, either. Seduction isn't the right word for what she did. Enchantment, maybe. It was like being in a ballet, something graceful and beautiful. You never saw anything like Kate's body. At least how I remember it, it made those *Playboy* centerfolds look like Russian peasants. She was built, for sure, but somehow she reminded me of a fine instrument, a violin or a baby grand piano. She taught me how to play it.

"We practiced all weekend. I didn't get home until Sunday night. My father was worried sick and my mother was pissed off. I told them I'd heard a ship was coming in Friday night so I went right from the paper to the union hall. Worked straight through, I told them. My mother asked where were my wages. I said I lost them playing poker."

Something in his tone put a period to the telling. "What happened then?" I said. "How long did it go on?"

"It didn't," Bailey said. "Sunday night, there I was back in the bedroom I shared with Frankie. It was smaller than Kate Brown's closet. He wanted to play a game of chess. I said I was too tired. Went to bed early. I hadn't bathed. Wanted to keep Kate's scent on me as long as I could. Forever. I was afraid Frankie would be able to smell it. I knew I could never explain what had happened to me. I lay awake for hours, thinking. Sometime that night, I understood that I couldn't let it happen again.

"That doesn't mean I didn't want it to. But I wasn't a total asshole. She was a married woman, with a child. I was a sixteen-year-old kid with a hundred and eleven dollars in a coffee can under my bed. I felt like, well, life blessed me once, beyond my wildest dreams. I accepted the gift. To have expected it again, or taken it for granted would have been pure greed.

"I thought a lot about Brown, too. Here was a guy richer than I'd ever be, more powerful. It was obvious he adored his wife, even though Kate said he couldn't please her in the sack. Hair-trigger type, I gathered. Still, there was no joy for me in making him a cuckold. I pitied the guy. And I also knew I'd never be able to look him in the eye or take his money again. Monday morning I mailed in my notice. Told my parents I got fired. It took me three more years to save up my college tuition."

I said, "What about Kate? Didn't you feel you owed her something?"

"I never saw her again," Bailey said softly. "Besides, there's no way to pay for that kind of gift. I suppose you could say I gave her my silence, my absence. That was my gift in return."

"And now she's dead," I said.

"Yeah. Now she's dead. Funeral's on Tuesday. It's not lunch, but I guess I'll go anyhow, and say good-bye."

There were tears in Bailey's eyes, tears I wanted to attribute to booze and Irish sentimentality. He dug at them with his knuckles. "I hope I pleased her," Bailey said. "Olivia has Kate's delicacy, but not her passion. I know it's never been that good for me again." He drank up the brandy still in his glass. "I should get out of here," he said. "Thanks for listening. I feel like you confessed me."

"Maybe someday I'll ask you to do the same for me."

"Sure. I must really trust you. Thanks, kid."

He rose to go. I rose to see him out. At the door, he thanked me for the brandy. In the hall, he said, "You know, I've been thinking. Maybe I should dedicate the book to Kate. Don't know how the hell I'd explain it to Olivia, but it feels right somehow. What do you think?"

Too little too late, is what I thought. "Why not?" is what I said.

CHAPTER TEN

Since my father Mr. Brown was abroad when Mother died, it fell to me to make the funeral arrangements. While his secretaries barraged two continents with cables bearing the bad news, I met with undertakers, clergy, florists, and caterers. The family plot in Lakeview Cemetery had, despite the burgeoning population of the departed, room for two more Browns. I ordered Mother's headstone in a style compatible with the ensemble. Of the Episcopal churches in the city, I chose the parish with the highest per capita income, the best organist, and the most off-street parking. Because Mr. Brown was so eminent a citizen, both of the daily papers ran Mother's obituary at full length under headline type. At last I received a cable saying my father was homeward bound. He would arrive in time.

I alerted Customs to his bereaved condition; they agreed to readmit him without the usual delays. A porter was on hand to witness our reunion. Solemnly, we shook hands, then proceeded to the waiting car, parked with official blessings in an illegally convenient spot. Once we were on the road, my father took a flat silver flask from his briefcase and consoled himself with a shot of good scotch. I told him that his black suit was cleaned and pressed, his black shoes shined, a fresh shirt waiting. I had not presumed to choose his tie. A limousine would call for him at eleven o'clock the following morning to take him to the service.

"You'll stay at the house, won't you?" he said. "We'll go together."

I told him I didn't plan to attend the funeral.

Instead of arguing, as I expected, he simply said, "Why not?"

There were several reasons, I responded—my distaste for funerals; my wish to remember Mother as she had been during our final interview;

grave doubts that my composure would hold up. "There's been so much to do, I haven't had the chance to mourn. In fact, I'm not sure I fully understand yet that she's dead."

Mr. Brown said, "The Kate I married has been dead a long time. This is just a formality, long overdue." He turned to look at me, to see if his words gave offense. My features were, I think, inscrutable. "I do appreciate how attentive you've been to . . . well, to what she became. It can't have been easy."

"I simply never thought of her as Mother," I said.

"And I could never forget," my father said. He tipped his flask again. "Frankly, I'm glad it's over." I heard him swish the whiskey around his mouth before he swallowed. "Time comes, a man has to cut his losses. In the case of your mother, I did that some time ago." Again he looked directly at me. "After a decent interval, you're going to have a stepmother. Fine woman, made of sterner stuff than Kate."

I said nothing. He asked if I was shocked. I shook my head. The woman I pictured was thick and common, hardy, like Mr. Brown himself.

"I hope you'll like her," he said. "But I don't expect it. Her entering the family won't damage your prospects. I've instructed my agents to transfer half of my estate at the time of Kate's death into your trust. You'll never want."

"That's very generous," I said. "I wish you happiness."

"Thank you," my father said. "I'm sorry I wasn't a better father to you. I guess I didn't know how. You always seemed so much your mother's child."

"Sometimes I wonder if I ever was a child." This may have been the most honest thing I ever said to Mr. Brown.

He laughed. "You used to be smaller, anyway. I can vouch for that." He punched my arm, awkwardly. "Hell, let's let the past be past. All right? You're rich. I'm free. The world's our oyster." He laughed again. "Let's eat it raw."

I wanted my oysters cooked in a fine sauce, served with champagne. I didn't say so. We finished the drive to my father's house in Broadmoor in a silence he thought was companionable and I found preferable to speech. The guard saluted from his watchhouse at the gate. I parked my father's Mercedes at the apex of the cobbled drive and helped him carry his bags inside. Mrs. Kramer, the housekeeper, would return from her sister's later that afternoon to make his evening meal.

We stood awkwardly in the foyer. "I guess I won't see you tomorrow, then," my father said."

"No. I hope you understand."

"Where will you be?" he said.

"The coast," I said. "Or maybe I'll go to the mountains for a few days. I'll decide when I get in the car."

"Call me when you get back."

"I will."

"There'll be papers for you to sign."

"At your convenience."

He raised his arms, as if to hug me, then let them fall back to his sides. "After flying halfway round the world, I probably smell pretty ripe. Kate never liked to welcome me home until I bathed."

I smiled, lightly touched his shoulder. My father was shorter than I. "Everything should run smoothly tomorrow. The funeral director's a fellow called Butterworth. He'll see to protocol."

"Thank you," my father said.

I said, "Good luck."

I attended Mother's funeral as Miss Simpson, a spinster schoolteacher. She was the first of my older ladies, plain and severe, not terribly imaginative but quite convincing. Miss Simpson wore a drab brown crepe dress to the funeral, lace-up oxfords, black, with stocky heels, opaque stockings meant to approximate in color generic Caucasian flesh and a brown tweed coat. Since Miss Simpson, as I conceived her, was a member of the Audubon Society and fond of birds, I chose a hat without feathers, a flat brown felt creation with a coarse mesh veil. She wore a dull goldish brooch shaped like an acorn, and ecru gloves.

Before changing to philosophy, I studied drama in college, so my makeup skills were serviceable. Miss Simpson's skin had a yellow cast. So did her mostly white hair. She wore sensible wire-rimmed bifocals and Yardley's lavender cologne. In her brown handbag, she carried a white handkerchief embroidered with the initial S in case she felt the need to weep. She had taught fifth grade for thirty-seven years, and had been the first to encourage Kate's promise as a writer. Miss Simpson was troubled by arthritis, and had corns.

As soon as I rose, the morning of the funeral, I put on Miss Simpson's sturdy underwear, her dull clothing and sensible shoes. I read the morning paper through her spectacles, turned the pages with the stiff fingers I imagined were hers on rising. I practiced walking on her tired feet, perfecting a gait that, short of a limp, still had a sort of wince to it. Miss Simpson drove downtown in my Jaguar, parked in the Washington Athletic Club garage and proceeded to the church by bus. I was flattered when a gentleman much my senior stood up and offered her his seat.

Miss Simpson arrived at the church some twenty minutes early and took up an inconspicuous position near the bottom of the broad steps that aproned the wide front doors. To my delight, my speculation proved correct; elderly women are the least remarkable of humans. Any flaws in my costuming were amply compensated by others' assumption of Miss Simpson's insignificance. In her shoes, I was not merely incognito, I was invisible.

Mrs. Swanson and Miss Lavender, garbed alike as stout crows, arrived in tandem, arms linked for mutual support. Mrs. Swanson's eyes were puffy and looked small as raisins. I recognized several of my father's business associates, his lawyer, his accountant, numerous of his employees, two city councilmen and one superior court judge. A special city car delivered the mayor and his wife. The turnout was good, and most of those attending looked prominent and prosperous.

At five minutes to the hour, Clark Bailey appeared, well groomed in a dark blue suit, wearing a gray felt fedora. Miss Simpson sidled across the steps and fell in behind him, followed him into the church, received a program from an usher wearing a boutonniere, slipped into a pew immediately behind the one Bailey chose, sat slightly to his left so she could see his face. Bailey scanned the program, refolded it, wiped his palms on his trouser legs, fidgeted with a sleeve button, settled his hands in his lap, and flexed his fingers. His hat sat beside him. The organ played "Jesu, Joy of Man's Desiring." Bailey studied the crowd. When an usher escorted Mr. Brown to his position in the front pew, Bailey averted his gaze. Mother's coffin, the most ostentatious available, lay in state before the altar, flanked by extravagant, easel-mounted wreaths resembling giant floral lifesavers. The organ played on.

After the concert came prayers. The color drained from Bailey's face till he resembled putty, damp and shiny. After prayers, the eulogy. I had supplied the minister most of his information, including, about the late lamented *Imago*, a liberal quote from young Clark Bailey's essay about the real and potential role of the arts in the city of Seattle, which I'd found among Mother's personal effects. Halfway into the second sentence, he seemed to recognize his own words, drew a handkerchief from his pocket and wiped his brow. His hands were trembling. Bailey grasped his kneecaps and endured, sitting through the prayers, rising but not singing for the hymns.

At last it was time to view the body. My father did so decorously, standing a full minute or more beside Kate's remains, then allowing himself to be escorted down the side aisle toward his waiting limousine. Two pews by two, the congregation was permitted to advance and file by the coffin. When the ushers reached mid-nave, Bailey rose, and I behind him, edged toward the center aisle, emerged almost in unison. At first he thought to flee, but I bumped against him from the rear, a believable lack of grace in an old lady. Bailey reached out to steady me.

Together we turned toward the altar. Hat in hand, he walked up the aisle. I could not read his expression as his eyes passed briefly over Mother's face. On her pillow of pink satin, she looked pretty, much younger than she was, no more like her self than I looked, at that moment, like mine. She was too pale, too still. Still, the undertaker was a worthy cosmetician. I was too fascinated by his skill; by the time I left Mother's side, Bailey was gone.

Suddenly I was ravenously hungry. I climbed into a waiting cab and treated Miss Simpson to lunch at Rosellini's Six-Ten, where she tossed back two martinis and ate a rare steak. The challenge of staying in character buffered me, I think, from the letdown I would otherwise have felt. My premiere deception seemed to have been an unconditional success; I began to see the life-enhancing potential of disguise. The only negative consequence was to my feet. By the time I hobbled back to the garage to claim my car, I had developed blisters from the mile walked in Miss Simpson's unyielding footwear and the wince in my step was quite genuine. As soon as I was settled in the Jaguar, I unlaced the oxfords, tossed them over the seat, and drove home barefoot.

Later that night, when Bailey came knocking at my door, Miss Simpson was safely dismembered in the back of my closet. I was myself again, and very rich.

CHAPTER ELEVEN

One night some months later, during our by-then-customary eleven o'clock chess break, Bailey said, "You know, this book is longer than it would have been if I hadn't met you in the Lucky Strike that night."

We'd been discussing chance; he still believed our meeting was. I said, "There wouldn't be a book if you hadn't met me."

Bailey said, "Maybe. Probably. I concede that. But what I meant was, I find myself putting off the ending. I've enjoyed this." He waved a hand, encompassing with it me, the apartment, chess, conversation, and creation. He was not a man to blush, but his color rose then. "I consider you a friend," he said.

In terms of chess and friendship both, it was my move. I responded by sweeping my arm across the game-in-progress, scattering all our warriors, without prejudice, to the floor.

Bailey stared, his expression unresolved between anger and amazement. "What the hell'd you do that for?" he said.

"Surprise," I said.

"Like hell. We had the better part of an hour in that game."

"So much for conventional warfare," I said. "That was a nuclear weapon. I just dropped the bomb. I win."

His anger gave way before my logic. He laughed. "You're crazy," he said.

"Is it so crazy to make new rules if you're about to lose by the old ones?" I said.

Bailey said, "Ask Harry Truman."

I said, "Be warned."

My notes say, He dismissed the warning. I wonder why I felt compelled to give it. Is it because I never had a friend before? We did not set up the board again. He's gone now, and I feel another headache coming on. These grow more frequent and more debilitating. Have I inherited my father's migraines along with Mother's weakness? The book is nearly finished. The time draws near. I too am reluctant. Like C.B., I have enjoyed "all this." The pain in my head is intense. I picture a viper inside my skull, slowly devouring my brain. I begin to feel sick to my stomach. I should lie down in a dark room. He took my warning for a joke.

Sometimes I thought he'd never finish writing. The nearer the end drew, the slower came the prose. Proximity to ending correlated positively, inexorably, with propensity for drink. By the end of February, Bailey's sick leave for the coming year was already spent and the paper warned him: Any day passed nursing a hangover was a day without pay. The editor in chief took him to lunch and suggested he visit a psychiatrist. Olivia was almost hysterically opposed. "She's afraid they'll say it's her fault," Bailey told me. "I don't think so, but she doesn't want to chance it. Olivia'd rather I drank myself to death than think I drink because of her."

Respecting her druthers, drink he did, whiskey by preference, but lacking that, scotch, gin, vodka, rum, beer, wine, schnapps, brandy, or, in extremity, syrupy sweet-flavored liqueurs. In those weeks, he remained professionally functional by never being wholly sober, drinking the better part of the night, sleeping a few hours, boozing enough with breakfast to see him through till lunch, refueling then for the afternoon, until five o'clock quitting time signaled the start of another all-night cocktail hour. He appeared at my apartment only sporadically, then only for as long as he could bear to be without a drink, which wasn't long, no more than a few hours at a time.

I knew he was avoiding home even more diligently than the home-away my back room had become, and so I held my tongue, plied him with coffee and the sweets he needed to resupply his blood with sugars, left him to his typing, if he seemed so inclined, or listened, when he was in the mood to talk. An heroic battle, no-holds-barred, was being waged in those weeks, that I knew, but I was unable to discern with any certainty who was fighting whom, for what. I do not believe it was so simple as Good Clark versus Bad Clark, Strong versus Weak, or even Man against Addiction. Perhaps it was not a battle I witnessed at all, but a courtship, Bailey in love with death, with failure, pressing suit for oblivion. If so, the seeds of his undoing lay in himself, his constitution and his muse alike too strong to succumb before the ardor of his self-abuse. Not wanting to be perceived as adversary, I offered no advice, pled no case, let be. I stopped locking the door while he was writing.

Sometime in early March the tide turned, inexplicably as a cancer goes dormant in remission, leaving Bailey sober as the second vice-president of the Women's Christian Temperance Union, and nearly as humorless. His color was bad—if old ivory could sweat, then he resembled it—his face was bloated and his eyeballs looked as if they'd been soaked in brine. He had the shakes; his cup danced in his saucer to a Latin rhythm, like castanets. His mood was remorseful, and grim.

"I've got to finish this fucker," he told me. "It's the only thing in my whole fucking life I've ever been sure I was supposed to do. I can't afford to fuck up now."

"Your vocabulary seems to have fallen on hard times," I said.

"Fuck you," Bailey said. "Fuck you to hell. How can you know what it's like for me? Do you have any idea what's at stake? But I'm ready. I am. I can take whatever they dish out. Adulation, derision, it doesn't matter. What matters is that I finish the fucking book."

"Being a little grandiose, aren't we? The usual response to a first novel is mass indifference. That or a hung jury."

"I can take that, too," he said, then, as a new doubt struck, looked sharply at me. "It is good, isn't it? I haven't been fooling myself about that too, have I?"

"It's good," I said.

"How good?"

I shrugged. "Good. I think it's very good. But what do I know?"

"I trusted you," he said.

"Only because you didn't trust yourself."

"I'm too old to trust myself," Bailey said, "and too smart. There's too much conflicting evidence. Christ, I'm a hick drunk from the ass end of nowhere. Who gives a shit what I think?"

"If you don't finish the book, I guess you'll never know."

Bailey spread his arms across the back of the sofa, squeezed his eyelids shut, emptied his lungs. For a moment, he looked crucified. Then he leaned forward, saying, "You're right, kid. I know you're right. I just want to say one thing, once. Then I'll shut up. It's   fucking   hard."

The three words had equal weight. I gave them room to mute, then said, "I think it's supposed to be. And you only have to trust me another—what, a week or two?"

"Less," Bailey said. "Less than that, if I can just keep working. I need to stay obsessed. I wish there was some kind of pill I could take."

"Writers have always wished that."

"It ain't booze," Bailey said.

"It might be coffee."

"I'm starting to hate that stuff. Sleep in a cup. I feel like shit."

"You deserve to feel like shit," I said. "You went out and asked to feel like shit. You probably even want to."

Bailey said, "Maybe. So tell me, you really think it's any good?"

I wondered what he'd do if I said no. There have been a few times in my life, of a few seconds' duration, when my power over another being has approached the absolute. This was one of them. I considered long enough to let him think I might be lying, then didn't. "I know it is," I said.

He put the final period to the last sentence on the Ides of March. We joked about the date. After the manic chatter of the keys, the silence in the apartment seemed vast. Bailey didn't emerge at once from the back room. By the time he did, I had the whiskey ready.

He came out stocking-footed, doing a little dance, pleased as a ten-year-old who's hit his first home run. "It's goddamn done and it's god-damn good," he chanted. When he saw the bottle, he said, "What's this?"

"A little celebration. Unless you'd rather go out someplace."

"Here's fine." He looked around him. "I like it here."

"You want ice?"

"Straight up. I'm surprised, though. I thought you disapproved."

"Everything in its season. Tonight you deserve to relax."

We raised our glasses, clinked them with spirit. "To a long and prosperous literary career," I said.

"To a friend of the work," he said. *"Sine qua non."*

"I wonder."

"I know. I'll pay you back rent for the office out of my first royalty check."

"I'll settle for an autographed first edition."

"God, I like the sound of that. At least I owe you a steak dinner. You hungry now?"

"It's the middle of the night. If you're hungry, I have cold cuts."

"I'd rather drink. This is good stuff."

"Hundred proof." I refilled his glass.

"Seriously," he said, "I feel ten years younger. Ten pounds lighter. I feel terrific."

"You look better," I said.

"You know, I thought maybe I wouldn't drink, after. Go on the wagon, see how I like the ride."

"Tomorrow," I said.

"To tomorrow." He drank. "Lord, that's good." I filled his glass again. "For the first time in years, I look forward to tomorrow. The door of the cage is finally open."

"What cage?"

"All of them. Maybe I don't have to be a fucking newspaper reporter until I die. Maybe there's life beyond who, what, where, when. Maybe Olivia'll be so impressed by the novel she'll let me sleep with her again. If she doesn't, maybe I'll get out."

"Would you really do that?"

"By the cold light of day, probably not. But tonight's for dreaming, right? The cash is cold and hard, the women warm."

I filled his glass again.

"You know, I wouldn't even mind having another baby. I think my kid is lonely. It'd do her good." As the bottle emptied, Bailey swelled toward drunken eloquence, that state where consonants eroded and feeling soared. "Poor kid," he said. "Caught between a drunk and a hard face. Sometimes I wonder what she makes of it all. You know what I hope? I hope that this novel is going to make it up to her, at least a little. Not this year or next, but someday maybe she'll read it and say, well, maybe my old man wasn't so bad after all. Look what he did. I want her to be proud of me."

"You can certainly be proud of yourself."

"It's not the same," Bailey said. " I wish my folks were still alive. I wish Kate was. They got to see my byline in the *Times*, sure, but it's not the same as this. Reporting I do for the money. That and some do-good sense of justice my mother fed me with her milk. There was righteous indignation mixed in my pabulum. The world is full of crooks and swindlers, right? S'my job to catch the bastards and see 'em hang. Miz Bailey's good boy Clark to the rescue of a rotten world. And who cares, anyhow? Who cares?" Reflexively, almost as punctuation, he drank. The whiskey was doing its work. I could almost hear the hiss of elation escaping, dissipating. Bailey drooped on the sofa. I poured the last of the fifth into his glass and rose to get another bottle. The eyes he lifted to me when I returned were pink and sad.

"Y'know what scares me most? That nothing's going to change. I'll still be lonely."

I put the fresh bottle down on the tray and this time sat beside him on the sofa, put an arm, companionable, across his shoulders. "Are you lonely, Clark?" I asked him.

His voice was small and choky. "Bone lonely," he said.

With an acute sense of risk, I closed my arms around him. He hugged me back, fiercely. His solidity, his warmth, his need engulfed me. Consolation passed between our skins. Our breathing, too, fell into unison. I had imagined this moment a hundred times without imagining that I would like it. Touch had never brought me comfort before, this trembling peace.

I knew I would have to move, swiftly and subtly, move right, before self-consciousness set in. How? I could smell the whiskey on his breath, could feel its damp warmth on my shoulder. How? I thought of Kate. Gentle as a whisper, I lifted up one hand and began to stroke his hair. He didn't pull away. Slowly, I raised my other hand and touched his cheek. "You're a very talented young man, Clark," I whispered. "A very attractive young man, too."

Bailey moaned, but did not resist me. My hands grew bolder, as if, set free, they were wiser than my mind. Fingers confirmed by sense what eyes had seen, and I was frightened by the tenderness I felt. Still, he did not resist. "You shouldn't be lonely, Clark. Not now."

Slowly, one of his hands began to rub a circle on my back, between the shoulder blades. The spot grew warm and radiant. I stroked his neck and arms, his chest. His body wakened slowly, began to reciprocate my touching. The circle widened on my back, grew generous and purposeful. Suddenly, I understood; thought was the enemy. If mind did not intrude, defining context, our bodies would proceed. Our bodies knew. To achieve my purpose, it was necessary only to trust my flesh.

At what point compassion turned to passion, the sensual to sexual, I could not say. The body, long starved, learns to forget its hunger. We had first, Clark and I, to know that we were hungry. There was no one moment that we knew, only a quickening of breath, an acceleration of pulse, a slicking of the skin, a dedication of the blood that made us impatient with the interventions of clothing, a diffuse hunger that focused slowly, sharpening to appetite and, finally, desire. What began for me as the means to an end was transformed into the end itself. Never else in my life have my intention and my delight so wholly coalesced.

There was a moment when, like Mother, I whispered, "Love me, Clark." And Bailey did.

In the morning, he didn't remember. That was all right. It was 1955, Clark Bailey was a married man, a father, and I had pictures. I knew the book was mine. You see, dear Frederika, I am a man.

20
. . . . .

Freddy juggles the soap cake palm to palm, whips up a high white lather, scrubs diligently, which is about as effective, under the circumstances, as treating stomach cancer with Tums. The dirt is in her mind. Already the words are gone, lost as the wax is when a sculpture's cast, but the pictures are here to stay. In her mental movie, Nick plays Clark. She hates the villain. Almost as much, she hates the occasional wisps of pity his story teased out of her. The last grown-up book she finished, at Carol's insistence, was something called *The Road Less Traveled*, about stern love and serendipity. What she's just read, she would never have chosen to know.

Can reading make you sick? Her insides don't feel as they're supposed to. Some foreign substance has invaded, making her shoulders rigid and her knees loose, seeding a headache in her temples, thickening breakfast into a nasty lump, yet it's nothing the doctors at Group Health could diagnose or treat. It's okay, Doc, just something I read.

Back in the study, Freddy stares at the army of Nick's books and sees them differently, not as the *things* they were an hour past, but as weapons, deadly mushrooms, blood parasites, coccus and spirochete, fungus and virus, able to invade, infect, disrupt, and overcome. It makes no sense that books should have such power.

Before her father's wall of books, Freddy feels powerless. She feels tired, confused, abused.

Above all else—it comes as revelation—she feels angry.

Like a stream undammed or a clogged toilet overflowing, like tsunami pounding on the puny shore, so anger breaks in Freddy, a high red tide. Without regard to authorship, she seizes the first volume that comes to hand and hurls it with all her might across the room, toward the floor. It lands open, dust jacket torn, facedown on its splayed pages and has, it pleases her to note, the broken look of a bird the cat has played with. She takes another book and pitches differently; this one hits the wall first, then plunges to the floor. Tossed underhand, she finds, books try to fly and, given aeronautically poor design, crash nicely. Some she grasps by one board cover and hears the spine give as she flings. Book by book, she bares her father's shelves remembering how, at home, at school, and in the library, she was taught to handle books as if they were sacred objects, with respect, and trashing the reliquary now, she feels the vandal's high, the iconoclast's delight in defiance, the anarchist's lonely and violent love.

Twenty minutes, and Nick's temple is strewn with fallen gods. She's made one hell of a mess. She rotates her shoulders and shakes her hands, briskly does a couple deep knee bends. Freddy stands among the ruins and smiles a rueful smile, almost frightened by how much better she feels.

At three-ten, Freddy finds Paige sitting primly on the bench in the school office, waiting to be checked out, then proceeds to Laura's to fetch her son. White morning has turned to yellow afternoon, bright and cool. The kids are pink-cheeked, chattering, and Freddy likes the way the little car encloses them, a family safe-deposit box on wheels. To the unexamined assumption that she must go home immediately, call the police, do the laundry, a little truant voice says, Why? It takes the kids a couple of blocks to notice she's driven past the house. "Where are we going, Mom?" Paige wants to know.

Freddy spins a destination out of sunlight. "Winchell's."

"Oh, boy! Doughnuts," Chaz says.

Paige says, "How come? Did something good happen?"

"We're here, aren't we? The sun is shining. I figure we're due for a treat."

"Oh," Paige says, and after a moment's thought, "Can I have two things, Mom?"

"Sure."

"Me, too?" Chaz asks.

"We'll see."

"That's not fair," Chaz whines.

"If you finish one and you're still hungry, you can have another."

"He won't eat his dinner," Paige warns.

"I read an article just the other day that said kids who have sweets for dinner one night a week get better grades than kids who always eat their spinach," Freddy says.

"Is that true, Mommy?" Chaz says.

Freddy shrugs.

"Come on," Paige says. "That isn't what my health book says."

"You musn't trust everything you read in books."

By now they're at Winchell's, eyeing trays of doughnuts inside the glass case, Chaz humming his little deciding song as his eye travels from chocolate-dipped to cruller to a white-frosted doughnut spiked with multicolored sprinkles. Freddy orders coffee. Paige asks for two maple bars, please. Chaz hums. The counter woman says, "Haven't seen you folks around for a while."

It's true. The last time they came, Molly was pregnant but not showing. Now her lower belly blooms expectantly under a loose yellow smock. "We've been busy," Freddy says. "What'll it be, Chaz?"

He points to the chocolate, and Freddy nods assent.

Receiving his doughnut, Chaz says, "My grandpa died. That's how come you haven't seen us around."

"I'm sorry," Molly says, as she counts out Freddy's change. "My dad died when I was twelve."

"My mom is thirty-nine," Chaz says.

Paige takes her brother firmly by the arm and pulls him to a table. "You don't go around telling people about Grandpa, dummy. Or how old Mom is, either."

Chaz bites into his doughnut. "Why not? It's true."

"And you don't talk with your mouth full."

"Leave him be," Freddy says.

"He's so rude," Paige says.

"He's little."

"I never did stuff like that."

Freddy smiles at her daughter. "You were always pretty discreet, Paige, but you did use to chew and talk at the same time."

"Hnh. Until I was about two, maybe. He's almost five."

Chaz sticks out his chocolate-covered tongue.

Freddy says, "Watch it," but her voice lacks edge. There is no place she would rather be right now, no voices she would rather hear. In the dusty sunlight of the doughnut shop, her children's bickering sounds natural, a grating music so familiar she finds it sweet. Chaz swivels his rooted chair, which squawks with every arc. Paige tells him to cut it out. Winchell's coffee is always strong and they serve it with real cream.

Halfway through the second maple bar, Paige looks across to Freddy. "So how was your day, Mom? Did you go to Grandpa's, like you said?"

"Uh-huh."

"Did you find anything?"

"I didn't, but Sandy did. He thinks this thing is going to be over soon."

"Good," Paige says. "Then I can go outside at recess again."

Chaz says, "Then Mom will be fun again."

Paige turns sternly to her brother. "It's not Mom's fault she hasn't been any fun, dummy. You don't have to make her feel bad about it."

"Sorry, Mom," Chaz says.

"You can't just say sorry all the time," Paige says. "You should think before you talk. That's what Miz Rupp says."

"Sorry, Mom," Chaz says again.

"I accept your apology. Maybe when you two stop fighting, I'll be more fun."

"As long as we have to be together all the time," Paige says, "we're going to fight. I never get to spend any time with my own friends anymore."

"Me, either," Chaz says.

"You don't have any friends, dummy."

First Chaz wails, and then, finger by finger, begins to enu-
merate his friends. "Mommy's my friend. Mrs. Patniak's my
friend. Laura's my friend."

"Grown-ups don't count."

Freddy finds a quarter in her pocket and stands up. She
points across Winchell's parking lot to the Texaco beyond. "Listen, my darlings. You sit tight. I'm going to use the pay phone."

"I'm in charge," Paige says.

"Each of you is in charge of yourself. Don't draw blood."

"Karen's a kid and she's my friend," Chaz says.

Winchell's glass door closes on contention. The car engines
snarling up Admiral Way, being nonverbal, with nothing to
grind but their gears, sound pleasant and pacific. Freddy feeds
her quarter to the telephone and dials her own best friend.
Rodney answers on the third ring.

"Hi, this is Freddy. Is Carol there?"

"I thought she was with you. That's what her note said."

"Oh. Uh. Well. I wasn't where I was supposed to be. I
thought I might catch her at home."

"She's not here."

"Too bad. Listen, tell her I'm sorry I screwed up. Ask her
to give me a call when she gets home."

"The note says if she's not home by dinner to go ahead
and feed ourselves."

"Well, maybe she's at my house. I'm heading there now."

"If you see Mom, ask her to call home, would you? They
think Anthony sprained his finger at basketball."

"Did you put ice on it?"

"Yeah. Coach says we ought to get it X-rayed."

"You want me to come over and take him to the doctor?"

"Just tell my mom."

"Right. Maybe you should call your dad. He is a doctor."

"We tried that."

"Listen, give him Tylenol if he's hurting."

"Sure."

"Take care, Rod."

"Yeah."

For this she paid a quarter. If she had another and rang

up Ashford, Freddy'd bet a dozen doughnut holes she wouldn't find him in. Back in Winchell's, she finds Chaz gnawing the last third of Paige's second maple bar. He shakes it at her and, chewing, announces that his sister is his friend.

Her father's house looks better than her own. Without vigilance, the kids have backslid. The living room's a welter of socks, toys, papers, half-empty glasses. A cereal bowl perches on top of the TV and she hasn't exactly been a saint herself. Unopened mail and unpaid bills cover half the dining-room table, her sweaters hang from chairbacks and the plants look sad. The red light on the answering machine blinks persistently. "Hang up your coats," she orders. "Pick up your junk. When I can see the rug, I'll vacuum it."

Paige turns on the television.

"No TV. Not until this place is clean."

"I can watch television and clean up at the same time," Paige says. "I'm not stupid."

"I better see some improvement in here. Soon."

"Don't worry, you will."

"Chaz, all your toys belong in your room."

"Mo-om."

"Now." The kitchen, her turf, is daunting. A faint sour smell emanates from the dishes stacked in the sink. The last clean load still sits in the dishwasher. Freddy tosses out a decomposing half tomato, puts away the bread, then goes to the phone nook and rewinds the tape.

"Freddy, this is Sandy. I'll try you at your father's."

"Freddy, this is Carol. Listen, if my boys call there for me, I just left. Okay? I've got a lunch date. [Giggle.] I expect it's going to be a long lunch. Talk to you later."

"Miz Bascomb, Lieutenant Norgaard. I know you've been under pressure, but with this television special coming up, so are we. I'd like to have your sketches of all the unidentified victims by next Tuesday. Call me, please."

"Freddy, this is Don. I'll try again."

"Ashford here. Your friend Sandy's hot lead turns out to be lukewarm. Nobody who does business with this Bayliss character has ever laid eyes on him. Royalties get paid into a bank account in Zurich. I called Interpol to try to find out what to do next, but with the time difference, I won't hear anything until tomorrow. I'm going to be out of the office on [throat clearing] personal business for the rest of the afternoon, but I'll check my messages. Well, bye."

"Freddy, this is Elsa. Give me a call."

"Frederika Bascomb? This is Miss Wilson from Citibank Visa. Our records show that your account is overdue. My number is—"

Freddy hits STOP. There is no call she would rather return than do the dishes. Later tonight, she'll pay the bills. Later tonight, she'll call her mother. Everybody else is on his own. She rolls up her sleeves and ties a dish towel around her waist to keep splashes from the low sink from wetting her jeans, then begins to melt, chip, scrub, or otherwise detach dried food from her neglected plates and bowls, taking a certain satisfaction in visible results, so much so that when the sink's in order, she moves on to the refrigerator, spooning moldy leftovers into the garbage until it's full.

"Paige! Hey, Paige. Time to take out the garbage."

Freddy shimmies the full sack, supposed to be biodegradable in less than eons, out of the can and handle-ties the top in a neat bow. "Paige, do you hear me?"

Paige hears but doesn't move. Sometimes, if you ignore her long enough, Mom will either forget what she wants or do the job herself. *Ghostbusters* is on. If Mom keeps yelling, Paige will respond at the next commercial break.

"Paige!"

Paige kicks her shoes off. Mom can hardly expect her to take the garbage out in stocking feet.

Chaz says, "Hey, Paige. Mom wants you."

"I know that, dummy."

"I don't think she's in a very good mood."

"What else is new?"

"Paige?"

"Coming," Paige calls back. The show segues into an ad for a kind of breakfast cereal that Mom won't buy. Paige rocks to her feet, trots to the kitchen. Mom is loading the dishwasher. "Did you want me?" Paige asks, innocently as she can.

"I want you to take the garbage out."

"I'll do it after *Ghostbusters*."

Mom looks at the wall clock: ten past four. "It just started. Do it now."

"Touchy, touchy," Paige says, picking up the sack.

"I'm sick of this mess."

"Missis Clean."

"Damn right," Mom says. "So move."

"I'm moving." Paige carries the sack to the living room, where Chaz sits cross-legged in front of the TV. "Hey, Chaz."

"Yes?"

"I'll give you a quarter if you take out the garbage. I don't have my shoes on, see?"

"How much is a quarter?"

"Twenty-five cents. One quarter of a dollar."

"Is it bigger than a nickle?"

"Lots."

"What can I buy?"

"Three Hershey kisses or two gummy worms. Besides, I'll be your friend."

"You already are."

"For the rest of the week. The sack's not heavy. Come on, Chaz."

Still watching the screen, her brother rises, hikes up his jeans. "Can I have the quarter now?"

"When you get back."

"Okay." Chaz takes hold of the bow tie and drags the sack across the carpet toward the door.

"Careful," Paige says. She opens the front door and holds the screen door open until he's out, then drops back to the floor. This episode is about how the Ghostbusters adopted Slimer. There's a certain comfort to a show you've seen before, just like with chicken-noodle soup and tuna sandwiches for dinner, or rereading a favorite book. No surprises. If you liked it once, you will again. Paige has always been fond of Slimer, with his green ectoplasm skin and goofy smile.

A little while later, Mom comes into the living room carrying a cup of coffee and sits down on the sofa. Paige can hear the dishwasher sloshing in the kitchen.

"What are you watching?" Mom asks.

"*Teenage Mutant Ninja Turtles.* You'd like it. They're all named after famous artists."

"Is that so?"

"Yeah. There's Raphaél, and Leonardo and Michelangelo."

"You're right, I like it," Mom says. "Where's your brother?"

"I don't know," Paige says. "He probably went to his room."

"Check, would you?"

"Mom."

"Just do it."

So Paige bellows her brother's name, "Chaa-aaa-aaz! Hey, Chaz, come here."

Chaz doesn't answer.

Mom says, "Go see."

So Paige gets up and goes down the hall and into her brother's room. She doesn't see him, not even in the closet. The bathroom door is closed. Paige knocks, then opens it, expecting to see her brother on the toilet, looking at *Fox in Socks* or something while he takes a dump, but he isn't there. Back in the living room, Mom is watching *Teenage Mutant Ninja Turtles.* "Find him?" she says.

"Nope. He's probably hiding." As soon as Paige says this, she remembers. Did she hear her brother come back in? Mom laughs at the cartoon. Paige says, "I think Chaz went outside."

"When?"

It hurts Paige to say, "When *Ghostbusters* was still on."

"Holy shit." Mom's on her feet now. "Just where did he say he was going, anyway?"

Hurts even more to say, "I said I'd give him a quarter if he'd take the garbage out."

"That was a fucking half an hour ago."

"I'm sorry, Mom," Paige says. "He's probably riding his trike."

They reach the door together, Paige and Mom, bump hips but don't smile. Mom races down the front steps, down the walk and out the gate. Paige wills Chaz to be there, pedaling, when she looks up the street. Except for a stray cat and the old guy two houses up trimming his roses, the street is empty. Mom says, "Oh, God." Paige says, "Maybe he's in the alley."

They run up the side street, turn into the alley, where the

garbage cans are. When Mom lifts the lid, flies rise up buzzing. Mom pokes at the garbage sack. "I think that's the one. Can you see him?"

More than she ever wanted to see Santa, Paige wants to see her brother, but the alley, too, is empty. "Oh, God," Mom says again, then, "Paige, you check at Amy's house and Leroy's, down at the corner. I'm going to take the house apart. Okay?"

"Oh, God. I'm sorry, Mom," Paige says.

Mom gives her hair an automatic ruffle. "He's probably up in my room," she says. "Maybe he didn't hear us call."

Glad for a mission, Paige starts to run up the alley, top speed, but then Mom calls her back. "Wait. I think we better stay together." She takes Paige by the hand and holds on tight. "Come on."

They ask the old man pruning, but he hasn't seen Chaz today. They ask at Amy's house, but no one has seen Chaz this afternoon. At Leroy's, no one is home. Chaz's trike is still in the garage. When they pound on Mrs. Patniak's basement door, she says Chaz isn't there. Paige can't help it. She starts to cry. Mom pulls her close against one hip. "There's still the house," she says.

They look in the closets and under all the beds, calling his name. They look behind doors. They even look in the dryer. They look in rooms they've already looked in, just for good measure. Then Mom sits on the sofa and presses her fingertips against her eyebrows, hard. Paige is almost afraid to breathe.

Mom says, "Let's think this out. He knows he's not supposed to leave this block. He wouldn't, would he?"

"I don't think so," Paige says.

"Unless he went somewhere with Leroy's family. But he wouldn't do that without asking permission, would he?"

"No."

"Is there anywhere else he could be?"

Paige can't tell if it's fear or guilt that makes her cry. Maybe it's both. Big sobs rise up and make her shoulders shake. "It's all my fault," she says between them. "I'm so stupid. I never thought anything bad would happen."

In a flat voice, Mom says, "I wish we could rewind the last hour."

"Me too," Paige says. "I'd take the garbage out, first time you asked."

"Then you might be the one who's gone," Mom says.

Paige looks melted, the way she droops. Streaks of red scar her pallor, and her pupils have nearly swallowed up her irises, so that her gaze is deep and black. Trained on Freddy, it reminds her that she's the mother, supposed to be in charge. "I think it's time to call the police," she says, wishing there were something more immediate, something more hopeful she could do instead. Freddy wishes she still thought of the police as she once did, with a capital P, as a force to be invoked in time of need, a source of righteous power waiting to be tapped by troubled citizens. She picks up the phone, waits for the dial tone, then puts it down. "No. We better leave this line open. I'll call from Mrs. Patniak's. You stay by the phone."

Paige sits down at the desk, her eyes fixed on the instrument. Freddy starts through the kitchen toward the stairs, and then turns back. "What am I thinking? I can't leave you here alone. Come on." Paige stands up. "Turn the machine on, okay?" She does. Paige precedes her down the narrow stairs, knocking on the woodwork to signal their approach. Mrs. Patniak meets them in her smaller kitchen, where a kettle full of potatoes is boiling on the stove.

"Have you found Chaz?"

"No, we haven't," Freddy says. "May I use your phone? I need to call the cops."

"Is yours out of order?"

"I'm afraid   someone   may have   taken him." The words squeeze out past Freddy's reluctance to say them and cause Mrs. Patniak to tie her hands into a prayerful knot. "I think it's best to leave mine open."

"Of course." Mrs. Patniak's hands flutter to Freddy's shoulder. "You poor thing. Can I make you a cup of tea?"

Thirsty for the kindness if not the beverage, Freddy accepts. Mrs. P. takes Paige's arm. "Let's see what's in the cookie jar. You help me make your mother's tea, all right?" To Freddy, she says, "The phone's in the bedroom. Make yourself at home."

Mrs. Patniak's wrought-iron bed is covered by a patchwork

afghan, a riot of deep color. Freddy sinks down on the soft mattress and reaches for the phone. Downtown, they tell her Detective Ashford is gone for the day.

"I know that," Freddy says. "He said he'd check for messages. I need to leave one. This is an emergency. Please ask him to call Freddy Bascomb immediately. I don't care how late it is. Please."

"What is your number?"

Freddy recites the digits. The woman recites them back. "Is that correct?"

"It is. Now would you please check and see if Lieutenant Norgaard is there?"

"Lieutenant Norgaard is in an important meeting."

"This is an important emergency. Could you page him?"

"Actually, he's at a dinner meeting, with the *Crimestoppers* producers. I don't know where they went."

"Will he be back tonight?"

"I have no way of knowing that."

"Please give him the same message I left for Ashford."

"Could someone else help you, Miz Bascomb?"

"I have reason to believe my son's been kidnapped," Freddy says.

"Oh, my," the woman says. "Have you been contacted by the kidnapper?"

"No."

"How long has your son been missing?"

"About an hour. Maybe a little more."

"We don't normally consider someone missing until they've been gone longer than that, Miz Bascomb. Have you called his friends? Have you searched your neighborhood?"

"My son is four years old."

"You must be terribly worried, I understand that. Usually, though, we advise parents to sit tight awhile. The child usually turns up."

"This isn't usually. Ashford knows that."

"Actually, Miz Bascomb, I see by your phone number that you don't live in the downtown precinct. You should be talking to South precinct. That's in Holly Park. Would you like their number?"

"I'd like my son back," Freddy says.

"Why don't you give South a call, Miz Bascomb? They may be able to help you there."

Freddy smashes the receiver into the cradle. The small violence gives no relief. She picks the receiver up again and dials Carol's number. Again, it is Rodney who answers. His mother isn't home.

"Listen, Rod. Chaz is missing. I need to talk to your mother. Leave her a note. Leave her a dozen notes. Tell her to call me the minute she walks in the door. You understand?"

"I thought she was going to your house."

"I must have missed her. Don't worry, she's all right. But Chaz isn't. Please have her call."

"Okay," Rod says.

She hangs up gently this time, and holds the phone in her lap. So far, reaching out, she's touched thin air. Freddy's not been conscious of not thinking about Chaz, but now an image rises in her mind, of him at Winchell's, chocolate-doughnut tongue protruding from his grin, hair grown shaggy since the last cut, a smudge of chocolate on his chin, that steals her breath. Tears come stinging into her eyes. Through their waver, she punches up her mother's number.

Elsa, at least, is home.

"Freddy, I'm glad you called. Sandy expressed me that material. The chapters, you know? He thought I might remember something useful."

"Did you?"

"I've tried so hard to forget those times. It brought them back, though. Clark certainly seems like Nick, don't you think?"

"Yeah, I do."

"I always wondered if there wasn't another woman."

"What did Nick say?"

"I never asked."

"It wasn't a woman," Freddy says.

"What did you say?"

"More stuff came today. It was a man."

"I find that hard . . ." Elsa interrupts herself. "Well, maybe not. Nick was a hard man to know." She makes a dry sound that might be a laugh. "Maybe we all are."

"Mother," Freddy says, "Chaz is missing. Gone."

Across the miles, she hears Elsa exhale. "You think . . . ?"

"Yes. I don't know what to do."

"I don't know what to tell you."

"Oh, God, I love him." Freddy did not mean to cry, but love twists her voice and forces out tears.

"Freddy, I'm so sorry," Elsa says. Then, "I could come, if you want me to. I don't know what I could do to help you, but I'm willing. Peter's away again, on business."

"You'd really do that?"

"If you want me to."

"I don't know."

"I'm not exactly the sort to come in and take over the kitchen, like your friend Carol. Crises aren't my cup of tea. But I suppose I could get a flight tomorrow morning. Or anytime. Why don't you think it over and let me know."

"Thanks," Freddy says. "I don't know if it would make it easier or harder. I can't imagine anything right now. Maybe I'm afraid to. Does that make any sense?"

"How do you think I got through all those nights Nick was out drinking? Or whatever he was doing."

"I want my baby back."

"I know you do. You call me anytime, all right? Let me know what's happening." After a little pause, she says, "He *is* my grandson."

"If you still pray," Freddy says, "please do."

"I will."

After they hang up, Freddy puts the phone back on the nightstand and stares at the wall, where hangs a framed photograph of Mr. Patniak, deceased, a round-faced, scant-haired man with a faintly embarrassed smile.

"Mom?" Paige speaks from the doorway. "Your tea was getting cold. I brought it to you."

"Thanks, honey."

Paige carries the cup and saucer carefully across the room and sets it on the nightstand. Freddy pats the bed beside her and Paige sits down. "Are the police coming?"

"Not yet. There's one more call to make."

"Are you going to tell Dad?"

"I hadn't even thought about it. You suppose I should?"

Paige says, "No."

Freddy says, "When it's over maybe. When we get Chaz back."

Paige says, "I wish I was dead."

Freddy puts her arm around her daughter. "Don't say that."

Paige says, "I do. You're just being nice. You know it's all my fault. You probably hate me."

"Baby, I'll never hate you."

"I do. All those things you say when you're mad at me, they're true. I *am* lazy and thoughtless and selfish."

"No, you're not. That's bullshit. That's just the stuff a mother's supposed to say when a kid won't clean her room. I never mean it."

Paige leans into Freddy shoulder. "I just feel so bad, Mom."

Freddy puts her arm around her daughter. "I know," she says.

21
.....

Paige is asleep at last, a matter
of nearly an hour spent seated on the edge of her bed, stroking
silky bangs back off her forehead, a gesture whose soft redun-
dancy soothed them both. South precinct has come and gone
—two beat cops in a cruiser, a twenty-minute explanation
Freddy still isn't sure they understood, the conclusion, finally,
that the case properly was Ashford's and not theirs. They left
with a snapshot of Chaz and a few scrawled notes, advising her
not to worry: "The boys downtown know what they're doing."
She did not remind them of Green River. No one has called
her back.

Freddy stalks the house now, not knowing what to do.
There is wine in the cupboard, dope in her sock drawer, but
she'll not resort to either; on this, the worst night of her life,
the vigil must be pure. The phone crouches on its stand and
sometimes tempts her, another drug. She could call Don or
Sandy. They would come, would comfort her, would try to
assume some of this weight that's rightly hers. Her comfort,
her diminishment in seeking it would not help Chaz. Somehow,
perhaps irrationally, she believes her strength might. Besides,
Freddy's not sure how wholly she trusts either man. Her father
had a secret life.

The feeling of something askew, of something absent and perhaps at risk she has when Paige sleeps over at a friend's house tonight is magnified ten thousand times. Time is no longer measured in minutes but by her footsteps as she circles room to room, by each breath she takes in the absence of her son. Her prayers are sporadic, automatic, and unrelieving; Freddy is not willing or able to turn over the case. Like the police, god is lower-cased and full of foibles. Past midnight, she cannot avoid considering what she will do if Chaz is not restored to her. How she will live.

How many times has she stood in the doorway of his room, how often wished that this time, she would find him there, asleep, and know this terror to be dreaming. This time she enters and lies down stiffly on his empty bed, clutches his pillow to her chest, willing it to turn into her baby, which it does not. Freddy hates the world for lacking magic. Chaz sleeps hot; his pillow smells of tearless shampoo and little boy sweat. His green dinosaur piñata hangs above the bed. There is a Leg-O castle in the corner, a pair of his small Levi's with the knees out on the floor. His picture books, his stuffed animals, his rock collection, unremarkable to anyone but Chaz. Reaching under the covers, she finds his blanket and pulls it out, fingers its sateen edges, then puts it over her face the way he sometimes does. The tears flow freely, rolling out of the corners of her eyes and down her cheeks, into her ears, and her body remembers, more than her mind does, carrying and giving birth, the nursing and changing and napping, teething, toddling, talking, the little hands, bony legs, big eyes, the smells and sounds and touches of her son. When she was pregnant for a second time, Jack wanted her to get an abortion, but Freddy wanted Chaz.

The phone rouses Freddy and her pulse. She runs to answer.

Brightly, Carol says, "Good morning. I hope this message is either a mistake or history now."

"It's not. He's gone."

"Shit. When?"

Freddy tries to remember. Her brain is slow and her voice thick. "Afternoon. Sorry. I'm a mess."

"Do you want me to come over?"

"No. Anthony sprained his thumb. Just call Ashford, will you? You were with Ashford?"

"He just left. He should be home in half an hour."

"Call him. Ask him to please call me." More awake, Freddy feels the headache thudding in her skull. "What time is it?"

"After three. It was a very long lunch."

"Maybe he should wait till morning. First thing, huh?"

"Fred, if there's anything I can . . ."

"Just get your boyfriend. I want my baby."

"Oh, honey," Carol says, and then, "I love you. Get some sleep."

"You too."

They say good night. Freddy returns to Chaz's room. This time she crawls under his covers. Reality quickly melts into the impossible. She is too exhausted to resist the nightmares that wait to claim her.

It's dark where Chaz wakes up. Even though he doesn't have to take naps anymore, he sometimes falls asleep in one place and wakes up in another, usually in his own room. Chaz doesn't think he's in his own room now. Even on nights Mom carries him in from the car and puts him to bed sound asleep, she takes off his shoes and remembers to put his night-light on. Wiggling his toes, he finds he's still wearing his sneakers. He feels around him in the dark for his blanket, but it isn't there.

Chaz puts his thumb in his mouth to help him remember. When he's five, he plans to give up thumbs and sometimes practices thinking or going to sleep without one, but right now he wants to concentrate. Besides, there's no one around to see him. He remembers going to Laura's and playing dump trucks with Tony in the sandbox, he remembers corn dogs for lunch and watching *Peter Pan* while the babies took their naps. He thinks he remembers Mom picking him up, Paige being in the car, but that might have been yesterday, or even Monday. Chaz knows the names of all the days by heart, but he still has a little trouble putting them in order. Usually he doesn't forget so much unless he's getting sick. He checks the places he gets sick—his head, his throat and stomach. They all feel pretty good, except he's getting hungry.

Chaz takes his thumb out of his mouth and wipes it dry on his pants, then calls for Mom.

Pretty soon he hears something and then he sees something, a stripe of light with a black silhouette inside it, then dark again. Mom cut silhouettes of him and Paige out of black paper, glued them on white paper, and hung them up framed in the bathroom. He likes the word. "Hey, Mom," Chaz says, "I just saw your silhouette."

Mom doesn't say anything, just moves toward him in the dark. Chaz thinks he can hear her breathing. "I'm awake now, Mommy. It's okay to turn on the light."

No answer. Mom must be making up a new game. She does that sometimes, and he plays along. They surprise each other. He hears her come closer, then feels her sit down on the bed. He leaps toward her. "I got you now," he says.

But what he's got doesn't feel like Mom, feels thicker, strange, rough and hard. Suddenly, for the first time since he woke up, Chaz is afraid. "Who are you?" he says.

A big hand settles on the top of his head. It doesn't hurt him. "Who are you?" he asks again.

A man's voice says, "A friend."

Chaz says, "All my friends are grown-up women and little kids."

"A friend of the family," the man's voice says. Chaz thinks he might have heard that voice before. He tries to remember where. Instead he remembers going to Winchell's for doughnuts. "Paige said she'd give me a quarter if I took out the garbage," he says. "You stole me."

"Borrowed is a nicer word, don't you think?"

If you borrow something, you're supposed to give it back. Chaz says, "Can I go home now?"

"No," the voice says. "Not yet."

"When can I?" Chaz asks.

"When your mother comes."

"Is she coming now?"

"Not yet."

"Why did you steal me?"

"Hmmm," the voice says. "That's a very good question, Chaz."

"Don't you know the answer?"

"Every question has many answers, Chaz."

"I know who you are. I can tell from your voice. You're the grandma from the park."

"Very clever, Chaz."

"But you're not an old woman. You're a man. I can tell that even in the dark. How come you dressed up like an old lady?"

"Don't you like to play dress-up, Chaz?"

"Sometimes. But I'm still a kid."

"Don't you get bored with just being yourself all the time?"

"I can be anybody I want to. Sometimes I pretend I'm George Washington. He's the father of our country. Sometimes I'm Mighty Mouse. Sometimes I'm this bad kid named Ralphie who lives in the tree stump in our yard and breaks things."

"But that's just pretend. When people look at you, they see Chaz."

"I guess so."

"When you disguise yourself, people treat you as if you were the person you look like. That's much more interesting, and more useful."

Chaz thinks about it. Last Halloween, he was a pirate. People acted like they were scared of him, but that was just pretend, too. They treated him like a little kid in a pirate suit they pretended to be scared of.

The man's voice says, "It amuses me to dress up. I like it when nobody knows for sure who I am."

"Do you know my mom?"

"I first knew your grandfather when your mother was just about your age."

Suddenly Chaz has the same feeling he gets when he puts the last piece in the puzzle and he can see the picture whole. He's not sure if he should say something or not. When he does, he makes it into a question, just in case. "Are you the person who killed my grandpa?"

"It was his own fault, Chaz."

That means yes. "That wasn't very nice," Chaz says.

The man laughs. Chaz doesn't think he said anything funny. Suddenly he's not hungry anymore. "Are you going to kill me, too?"

"I don't know."

When Mom says she doesn't know, it means maybe. Maybe means maybe yes, maybe no and you have to wait to find out.

The man says, "I'm improvising."

"What's that?"

"It means I'm playing it by ear. Making it up as I go along. Life is much more interesting when one can improvise."

"So you might not kill me?"

"Death is nothing to be afraid of, Chaz. Living is much more terrible."

Until now, Chaz has thought of death as something that happens to old people, not as something that might happen to him. Until now, living has not seemed terrible to him.

The man says, "I want you to go to sleep now, Chaz."

"I don't want to," Chaz says. "I'm not tired."

"You will be."

A hand comes out of the darkness and takes his arm. Something stings him, like a bee. Chaz tries to pull away. An arm circles him and holds him tight. He does feel tired. The stinging stops. His eyelids are so heavy he can't hold them up anymore. The arms lay him back on the bed. Fingers brush against his cheek, as gently as Mom's. From a great distance, he hears a voice say, "Such a charming boy, Nick. Such a love."

Six men hammer the lid on a big crate. If they drive the last nail, something awful will happen to Chaz. Freddy screams at them to stop. Her own voice startles her awake. On this side of dreaming, the hammering goes on. Freddy hits her head on the green dinosaur when she stands up. Morning sunlight shrinks her pupils and makes her squint.

She's still fully dressed for yesterday. Smoothing wrinkles from her shirt, patting flat the renegade clumpings of her hair, she makes for the front door. Mike Ashford stands on the porch in jeans and a sweatshirt, with the promising start of a beard.

"Your phone's disconnected," Ashford says. "At six A.M. they cut you off."

"Oh, shit."

"I talked them into hooking you back up so I can tap it. They want your check first thing Monday morning. You'll have service back sometime this afternoon."

"I think I need a cup of coffee," Freddy says.

Ashford follows her to the kitchen. Freddy puts on the kettle, grinds the beans. Ashford says, "Your friend is great, by the way. Carol."

"What about my son?"

"We'll find him," Ashford says. "Alive, too. I'm not even looking for a body yet."

He says what Freddy's not allowed herself to think. She leans against the refrigerator for support.

"Take it easy," Ashford says. "That means I'm optimistic."

"You're sure as hell not much of a diplomat."

At that moment, heralded by a quick flurry of knocks, Mrs. Patniak in her glen-plaid housecoat emerges into the kitchen. "Freddy? Freddy, dear, have they found Chaz yet?"

"Not yet."

"Well, they will, I'm sure. I've been praying hard."

"Thanks, Mrs. P."

" 'Suffer the little children to come unto me.' That's what Jesus said."

"Was there anything else?"

"Yes. Do you know that there are two strange men in the alley? They're poking around the garbage cans. Do you think I should call the police?"

"They are the police," Ashford says. "They're with me."

Mrs. Patniak says, "They didn't look like officers."

Freddy glances out the kitchen window. "Right. No uniforms."

"It should've been done last night," Ashford says. "Cops are so damn territorial. I hate this hierarchy bullshit."

Mrs. Patniak peers up at Ashford. Paige pads into the kitchen, attaches herself to Freddy's side. "Have they found Chaz?"

"No, honey. But Detective Ashford says they will."

Paige looks at Ashford. "How?"

"We're doing everything we can."

"I've been laying in bed thinking," Paige says. "About how big the city is."

Freddy pulls Paige tight against her.

Ashford says, "You're right. It is big. But what I think is, we don't have to search it. I think he's going to contact your mother."

Paige says, "You don't even know who he is. All we know about him is he killed my grandpa and my cat."

Freddy wishes Paige would stop talking, especially because what she says seems to be true.

Paige says, "You don't know anything. Maybe he's going to kill our whole family, one by one."

Freddy says, "Baby, stop."

"That's what I've been laying in bed thinking, Mom. I can't stop. I'm scared." Paige buries her face against Freddy.

Mrs. Patniak clears her throat. "Well, I think it's about time for *Saturday Sermon* on Channel Twenty-two. Would you like to watch it with me, Paige? We could make cocoa."

Into Freddy's stomach, Paige says, "No."

"I'll just be going then," Mrs. P. says. "If there's anything I can do, you know where I live." Her attempted laugh sounds more like gargling.

Over Paige's head, Freddy says, "Actually, we do know a little more than we did before. I got another installment of the book yesterday. Delivered at my dad's."

"And?" Ashford says.

"Paige, why don't you watch Saturday cartoons for a while?"

"You're trying to get rid of me."

"Only for your own sake."

"You can't protect me anymore, Mom. I already know there's no Santa Claus and the police aren't perfect."

"Hey, I resent that," Ashford says.

Paige favors him with the fraction of a smile. "It's still true," she says.

Yet another score to settle with her father's killer. Her daughter looking ten and thinking forty. "It isn't pretty, Paige."

"Nothing is," her daughter says. "Not anymore."

"So," Ashford says, "what more do we know?"

"Assuming it's true."

"Assuming," Ashford says. "What?"

Freddy puts her hands over Paige's ears. Paige pulls them away. Freddy's sigh accepts and regrets the impossibility of holding her aloof from ugliness. "Okay. First of all, it is a he."

"I knew it," Paige says.

"Second, he killed his own mother."

Ashford whistles.

"Three," Freddy says, "he got Nick, or Clark, real drunk and then seduced him. He took pictures. That's how he got Nick's book."

"Blackmail," Ashford says. "I hadn't thought of that one."

Paige says, "What book?"

Freddy says, "Only Nick was the victim."

"Doesn't matter. It's still in Motiveland."

"What book?"

"This book that's been appearing on the doorstep," Freddy says. "In pieces."

"Is it a real book?"

"It's typed."

Paige turns to Ashford. "Then you can trace the typewriter. I've seen that on TV."

"Right. We're talking a Hewlett-Packard Deskjet printer. Retails for about eight hundred bucks. Four thousand some odd owners in Seattle have sent in their warranty cards in the last couple years."

"That's a lot, huh?"

"Uh-huh. HP's sending us names and addresses. All of Seattle, plus all the Bascombs, Baileys, Baylisses, and Browns in their files. From everywhere. We'll check them out, but it's going to take a while. The Browns are a bitch."

"I'm impressed," Freddy says.

"Yeah, well. It's labor-intensive and slower than corn syrup, but it's one of the better leads we've got."

"What about Zurich?"

"Like I said, I'm trying to get some advice from Interpol. Frankly, I'm not too hopeful. There's a reason crooks bank in Switzerland. To all intents and purposes, we're looking for the invisible man."

"Or the invisible woman," Freddy says. "I just remembered. He went to his mother's funeral dressed like an old lady, so neither his father nor Nick would recognize him. 'The first of my old ladies' is what he said. He said nobody really looks at old women."

"Is that true?" Paige says.

"I don't know. Do you?"

"Not except Mrs. Patniak," Paige says. Then, "Hey, Mom. Maybe the killer is really Mrs. P."

Freddy says, "Paige, really," but she laughs a little at the thought.

Paige says, "Seriously, it could be anybody. It could be Sandy." She points at Ashford. "It could be him. What do we know about him? It could be your new boyfriend."

Ashford says, "Not it."

Freddy says, "Damn. It's Saturday. I made a date for tonight."

"You're not going out tonight, are you, Mom?"

"Of course not. But Don doesn't know about Chaz. I need to call and cancel."

"The kid's right," Ashford says. "There is something kind of creepy about that guy. Who wants to work with dead things all the time?"

"That's a fine thing for a cop to say."

"Contrary to popular belief, most of police work concerns the living."

Paige says, "Maybe I should be a detective when I grow up. This is really sort of fun."

Ashford puts his hand on Paige's shoulder and looks at her sternly, straight in the eye. "No, it's not," he says.

He might as well have slapped her. Paige looks as if he had. Freddy holds her breath, watches her daughter's short, frayed fuse burn through, the implosion that taps her reservoir of tears and self-recrimination. Paige sobs. "I didn't mean it. Not like that. I'm such a rotten person." The sentences come out chunky, broken by the necessity to breathe. Freddy looks around inside herself for some calm corner she can stand in to offer comfort. Before she finds one, Ashford drops to his knees in front of Paige.

"You're not a bad person," he says. "I'm sorry I snapped at you."

"I love my brother. I really do. I wish I could take back every mean thing I ever said to him."

"You'll get the chance," Ashford says. He catches one of Paige's limp hands and holds it in his own. "I'm doing everything I can, okay? Every police station in the county has your brother's picture by now. Every cop on every beat knows that we're looking for him. And you know what? You're right. Sometimes it is kind of fun to be a detective. I just get frustrated."

Paige struggles to get the better of the storm. Her sobs mute to sniffles. Ashford pulls a white handkerchief out of his back pocket and hands it to her. "Here. Blow." Paige hesitates. Ashford says, "It's clean. I guarantee it. I just don't do ironing."

"Neither does Mom." Paige makes a tiny smile, then buries her face in the big handkerchief and blows like a tugboat. Solemnly, she holds the handkerchief out to Ashford. "It's yours," he says. "Keep it." Paige finds a dry space and blows again.

Ashford pushes to his feet. "Give me the book stuff, will you? I'll have the boys run it into the lab, just in case Mr. Clean slipped up and forgot to wear his gloves." He snorts. "Jesus, what I'd give for one clear print." A little awkwardly, he touches Freddy's arm. "How're you holding up?"

Freddy tells him what she's been telling herself. "Okay, I guess. There really isn't much choice."

"I guess not. Carol says you're one tough lady. In the good sense." He combs his fingers through the thinning hair. "Jesus. I better stop talking, before somebody punches me out."

"It's hard to know how to behave," Freddy says. "Even how to feel."

"I feel exhausted," Ashford says. "I'm going back to my place and try to get some sleep, so I'll be worth something later. As soon as the phone's working, I'm going to monitor the tap myself."

"What happens when he calls?"

"Depends on what he has to say. You keep him talking as long as you can. Ask questions. Ask to speak to your son."

"What happens if he doesn't call?" Paige asks.

"We go to the news, for one thing. Get the whole town looking for your brother."

Paige says, "Oh."

Freddy retrieves the manuscript from the dining-room table and hands it to Ashford. "I'm sorry this happened," he says.

Freddy says, "Yeah." She walks with him to the door. Outside, a squat Oriental man stands spraddle-legged, his hands against the top frame of the chain-link fence. The two cops from the alley stand behind him. The one in the red sweatshirt calls to Ashford. "We caught this guy sizing the place up. He was carrying these." The cop holds up a pair of long-bladed grass clippers.

Freddy follows Ashford down the walk. When they reach the gate, the prisoner nods toward the house. "You live here, please?"

Freddy says, "I live here."

"Not steal. Forty dollar, mow lawn." He points at the shaggy grass.

"I know. It needs it," Freddy says. "But I can't afford forty bucks."

"Big job. Forty dollar."

Freddy shakes her head, then points at her chest. "I'll mow it." To Ashford, she says, "We've had this conversation before. He's a gardener. Comes around every couple of weeks in spring and summer."

"Let him go," Ashford says. The two cops step back. Ashford takes the grass clippers and hands them to the gardener with a little bow. "Sorry. There's been some trouble here."

"Trouble?" The gardener looks to Freddy. She nods. "I come back other time."

"Sure. Take care."

The man walks backward until he's beyond reach of the law's long arm, then turns and hurries away up the street.

"Laotian," Freddy says. "He's got a couple of sons. I hired them once last summer when the lawn was bad and I was feeling flush."

"You boys find anything?" Ashford says.

"A lot of flies. That's about it. The alley's paved. Gets a fair amount of traffic. Nobody saw a thing."

Ashford hands them the manila envelope. "Run this by the lab. Same tests as before. I'll call them later." He turns to Freddy: "Hang in there." The cops disperse.

Inside, Paige has settled with a bowl of cereal in front of the TV. She looks up at Freddy. "So, Mom, what are we going to do today?"

For a moment, Freddy lets herself be mesmerized by the little cartoon figures cavorting on the screen. The animation's crude but zippy. Freddy feels the burden of being human and existing in real time. How the hell to live through the day?

The change to a commercial, also animated but in another style, releases her attention. Paige says, "Well?"

"Well, first I'm going to use Mrs. Patniak's phone to cancel my date. After that, baby, I just don't know."

22

■ ■ ■ ■ ■

Now he wakes up in a dim brown light, sees a bowl of frosty pink glass stuck to the ceiling, and the places where the ceiling meets the walls. Sees the shape of windows covered up with thick curtains, where the light sneaks in. Opposite the windows, he sees a door, in the same place the light was coming from the last time he woke up. He sees a chest of drawers, a nightstand, the bed he lies on, all made of the same reddish wood. He is uncomfortable. At first he's not sure why, then feels and smells and sees that he has wet the bed.

His pants and the bottom part of his shirt are wet. A big wet circle surrounds him, darker brown than the rest of the spread. Since he stopped wearing diapers at night, Chaz has only wet the bed once. Once in almost two years, and that was a long time ago. Two of the things Chaz likes best about himself are his vocabulary and his nighttime dryness. Mom says he is precocious in both things. Now he's gone and pissed away half of his self-respect. It makes him want to cry.

When he thinks about it, Chaz has other reasons to want to cry. He is hungry, for one thing. Scared, for another. He misses Mom so much that missing hurts, almost like being hungry, and Paige a little less but still a lot. He wonders if Mom got mad at her about the garbage. Usually he enjoys it when Mom yells at Paige, but this time he hopes she didn't. If it wasn't a bad dream, and he doesn't think so, the man in the dark said he was maybe going to kill him. Chaz lies in his puddle and thinks about dying. People do it on TV all the time, usually the bad guys though. When Grandpa died, Mom said dying was peaceful. You don't feel anything and you don't worry anymore. If he was dead, he wouldn't feel hungry or wet or even scared.

Still, Chaz thinks he would rather be alive. He looks forward to being five. When he is five, he will stop sucking his thumb and start tying his shoes. He is going to learn how to read, write, button, zip, swim, and ride a two-wheel bike. He has already given some thought to who he wants to invite to his birthday party. He hopes Mom will come to get him soon. He is a little angry that she hasn't come already.

Chaz wonders if it is possible to escape from this room. He knows his address. If he could get out, all he would have to do is find a policeman and tell him the address and the policeman would take him home. He sits up on the edge of the bed and takes off his tennis shoes so he'll be quieter. Even his socks are wet. He slips off the bed onto the floor and tiptoes to the door first, tries the knob. The door is locked.

He tiptoes to the windows and pulls back the curtains, finds venetian blinds underneath them and opens up a slat so he can peek out. What he sees is the top of a tall tree, which he can tell by its needles is an evergreen. Another thing he wants to do is learn to recognize the different kinds of evergreens by name. The ground is a long way down. Even if he could get the window open, he's not sure he could make himself jump from that high up. If he was Mighty Mouse or Superman, he could fly.

His wet pants, cold now, stick to the skin underneath them, rubbing, and hunger pinches like fingers in his stomach where food should be. The fact is, he can't fly, can't tie, can't even, to his shame, stay dry. Chaz is so lonely he would almost welcome a visit from the man in the dark, just to take his mind off his own misery. There is a little rug beside the bed that looks like the magic carpet in one of his picture books, with fringes on the edges and flowers and vines and strange shapes woven into it. Chaz sits down on the carpet he is pretty sure is not magic because nothing else is and because he has nothing else in the world to do, he cries.

Chaz is not used to crying by himself. Usually when he cries, Mom or maybe Laura or even Paige comforts him, washes the scrape, bandages the cut, repairs the insult, or quiets the fear. Crying by himself is only half of crying and not the best part, either. After a while, because it does no good to cry, he stops. He wonders if Mom and Paige are missing him.

Chaz looks around the room. There is nothing in it to suggest that it belongs to someone—no pictures, no books, no toys, no clock, no mirror, no television set or radio or record player. It is a boring room. In addition to being hungry, wet, cold, and scared, Chaz is bored. He plays with the fringe on the little carpet and wishes that he knew how to braid, like Paige does.

And then suddenly Chaz is much more scared than bored, because he hears something, which makes him realize that until now there has been nothing to hear. He hears sounds of opening or closing, hears floorboards creaking, hears a big voice made small by distance singing, and most of all, he hears the race of his own heart, telling him that boredom is over and fear is back. He does what any sensible boy or goat or rabbit in any of his books would do. He hides. Chaz presses his belly flat to the floor and slides under the bed, which is the only place he can see to hide, and keeps sliding until he is way up under the headboard, against the wall. Under-the-bed dust tickles his nose but he swallows his sneezes and keeps silent. He is pretty sure that no one but him can hear the pounding of his heart.

After a while, the sound advances, getting louder, and he hears the door to this room open. Hard shoes walk toward him. When they come in sight, he is surprised by them, not man shoes but the thick-heeled black lace-up shoes old ladies wear.

"Chaz!" a voice trills. "Are you hiding from me? Come out, come out, wherever you are."

In his hiding place, Chaz hardly breathes, and hopes he is well enough hidden that the threat will pass, until a hand gropes under the bed, explores among the dust motes, then finds his ankle. The hand pulls him easily out of hiding and when it does, he sees that his captor is not the man in the dark at all, but the old grandmother from the park. "There you are, you little rascal." She is smiling and seems to be in a good mood. She helps him to stand up and brushes dust off of his pants. "Wet and dirty, aren't we? Well, never mind." The grandmother unfurls the dark red towel she's carried over her arm. "It's your bathtime now," she says.

First, hoping to wash off fear, they shower, Freddy in the bathroom while Paige sits by the phone, then the reverse. Freddy puts on no makeup, no earrings, no perfume, as if the slightest hint of personal vanity might offend the gods of missing children and so jeopardize Chaz's safe return. The instinctive choice of a black shirt tells her she is in mourning. Paige dresses brightly, in white pants, a sunflower yellow sweatshirt, and this too seems appropriate; between them, they bear witness to solemnity and hope. How to wait is a huge question until Paige produces two decks of playing cards, red and blue, and proposes that they play double solitaire.

Freddy recognizes genius when she sees it. The game interlaces their separate solitudes, it gives them something to do with their hands, is mindful enough to require attention and prevent deep thought. Paige is quicker but Freddy's more foresighted; first one wins, then the other. The orderly outcome, putting eight stacks of cards, by suit, in perfect series, seems entirely just and worthwhile. They do it again and again.

Every once in a while, between games or when they're temporarily stumped, Freddy says, "Check the phone, will you?" and Paige leans over, picks up the receiver, listens, hangs up. "Still out."

"There's a red queen for your black jack."

"Put the three of spades up, Mom."

"Ha. I beat you."

"Ready? Go."

"That's cheating."

"Check the phone, will you?"

"Dead."

"I see a place for your nine."

"Let's go through them one more time."

"Bathroom break."

"Get me some juice since you're up, please."

"The phone's still dead."

"I win again."

"Mom, when do you think we'll hear something?"

"It beats me, babe."

"I hate this."

"Me too."

"Let's play again."

The phone surprises them by ringing. Paige looks at Freddy. Freddy nods. Paige answers, Hello? Passes the receiver to Freddy. Freddy raises her eyebrows. Paige shakes her head.

Don says, I called back as soon as I got your message.

Freddy tells him about Chaz.

Don offers to come over.

Mindful of the gods of the missing children, Freddy says no.

"Another game, Mom?"

"Why not?"

The phone rings, heart leaps, hands tremble. Paige shakes her head.

Freddy tells Sandy about Chaz.

Sandy offers to come over.

Freddy says no.

"Ready?"

"Ready."

"Red eight on black nine."

Ring.

Freddy tells Elsa there's nothing new. Mindful of the jealous gods of missing children, Freddy tells her not to come from Arizona. She'll call with news.

"I almost liked it better when the phone was out."

"I know. Me too."

"You got a two of diamonds?"

"It's buried."

Phone. Carol. No, thank you, no. I will, I will and thanks again.

"Mom."

"Yes, honey."

"What if he doesn't call?"

"He will."

"Will he ask for ransom?"

"Sweetie, I don't know."

"What if he does?"

"Let's not think about that yet."

Paige climbs on Freddy's lap and Freddy holds her, loves her, wishing her lap felt full with just one child. Touching Paige makes Freddy long for Chaz, sets her imagination traveling the awful darkness of not knowing. Oh Chaz, I want another forty fifty years to love you.

"Mom, I don't feel so good."

"You getting hungry?"

"No, just sad."

Freddy holds her daughter as close as she can.

Mrs. Patniak knocks and enters at the same time. "I could hear the phone ring. I wondered . . ."

"Nothing yet."

"Oh, dear. Well, I'm sure that everything will be all right. Have you two eaten lunch? I've just made sandwiches."

"How about it, Paige?"

"Yes, thank you, Mrs. P."

So Mrs. Patniak brings not just sandwiches but potato salad and pickles, sweet and dill, and a pan of brownies still warm from the oven. Mrs. P. as is her habit asks a blessing, adds to it today a little special pleading, and the three of them have a picnic by the telephone, Paige wolfing down her food and Freddy, mindful of those wrathful gods, just nibbling, no one saying out loud that tuna sandwiches and brownies are Chaz's favorites but everyone remembering.

The telephone rings again, this time is Miss Johnston from US West Communications reminding Freddy of her overdue bill, to which will be added a twenty-five-dollar fee for reconnection.

"I'll bring the check," Freddy tells her. "First thing Monday morning."

"Was that him?" Mrs. Patniak asks when she hangs up.

"Bill collectors," Freddy says. "I owe you money, too. Rent and child care. You should have said something."

"I know you're good for it, dear."

Freddy gets her checkbook and a tally of the hours Mrs. P. has watched the kids. "Look at this. I haven't paid bills since before Nick died." She signs Mrs. Patniak's check and passes it to her.

Mrs. P. folds it in half and puts it in the pocket of her

housedress. "If I could afford to, I'd pay you to live here," she says.

"You're a good soul, Mrs. P."

Again, the phone rings. This time, Freddy's sure, it will be him.

"Norgaard," Lieutenant Norgaard says. "I take it you got my message."

"I take it you got mine."

"I need the last two sketches by Tuesday morning. The show's live on Tuesday night."

"You'd better hire somebody else then."

"Look, Miz Bascomb. You've done nothing but drag your feet since you took this job. It was unfortunate about Nick, but it's been what? At least three weeks since then. And Nick told me you were a pro."

"You talked to my father about me?"

"You think I picked you out of the phone book? I was having a drink with Nick, we got to talking about Green River. I told him I had a problem with the sculptures. He suggested I give you a call."

"I didn't know that."

"He asked me not to mention it. Look, the work you've done is fine. I just need two more sketches. How hard can that be."

"My son is missing. Since yesterday afternoon."

"I see." After a little silence, Norgaard says, "Ashford's handling it?"

"Yes."

"He's a good man. Thorough."

"I hope so."

"Maybe the time would pass faster if you were working on the sketches."

"If you get my boy back, I'll do them for free."

"Has Ashford talked to the papers yet?"

"Not yet."

"So how do you want to leave this, Miz Bascomb?"

"I can't think straight right now. How about I'll call you back in twenty-four hours. I'll either do the stuff myself or find you another artist who can handle it."

"This is important to us, Miz Bascomb. The show's running nationally. Live."

"Lieutenant, I'm getting nervous about tying up the phone. I'm going to hang up now." Freddy does. She considers, not for the first time, that her troubles didn't really start until she undertook to draw the dead. A door opens in her mind; beyond it lies the valley of the bones. She slams it shut before she can see detail. Chaz is so small still, so delicate.

While Freddy was on the phone, Mrs. Patniak's cleared up the artifacts of lunch. Now, about to leave, she opens her stout arms and encircles Freddy in them, drawing her to the pillowy bosom, patting her back as if to burp her, emitting the scent of Emeraude. "God is watching over Chaz," Mrs. Patniak says.

"And you're watching over us. Thanks, Mrs. P."

When the landlady is gone, Paige says, "You want to play solitaire anymore?"

"Do you?"

"Not really."

"I suppose we could finish cleaning up the house."

"What I really want to do is ride my bike."

"I can't let you do that."

"I know. I don't suppose I could have a friend over either."

"I'm afraid not."

"I feel like we're prisoners, Mom."

"We are."

"It's almost three o'clock."

"We could try to take a nap."

"Go ahead," Paige says. "I'm not sleepy."

"I can't tell if I am or not." Reflected in Paige's eyes, Freddy sees her own bewilderment. There is a truth beyond the interventionary net the world weaves to obscure their trouble, and Freddy suspects the truth is small and stark, terrifyingly simple, a domestic arithmetic that says three minus one leaves two, frightened and heartsore, missing one. Freddy doesn't want to live in this imbalance.

This time it is the shudder of the porch that intervenes. Mother and daughter, startled, break their reflexive gaze and turn toward the door. Metal strikes metal, the porch trembles once more and after several beats of silence, they hear the clang of the front gate closing—a pattern of sounds that, factored with the hour, means mailman. They converge on the box. Excitement speeds down Freddy's arms, making her fingers clumsy as she reaches for the thin white envelopes, turns them address side to, finds that today's messages all pertain to finance and propaganda. Even the seven-hundred-dollar check, long overdue, brings her no joy, especially since the bills arriving coincidentally swallow it whole.

"Well?" Paige says.

"Nothing."

"What now?"

Sunshine slips under the eaves to touch them on the porch and the day spreads out before them, high spring beckoning, throaty with the purr of lawn mowers, the warmth fermenting cut grass into a dizzying perfume, triggering in Freddy's limbs the wish to stretch, in her lungs, the need to blow, making her whole body want to go, to blend and meld with the sweet air, spring with the season. Resenting the invitation, her mind says no. From the tops of the neighborhood cedars, the local crows cry, "Maw! Maw! Maw!" Freddy's never understood before that crows call for their mothers.

Paige says, "If Chaz was home, we could all go to the park."

"Or the beach. I miss the beach."

In unison, reluctantly, they turn away from the day and return to their confinement. The house seems close and cluttered. "Maybe we should leave the door open," Freddy says, and it seems like a hard call, to let in or shut out, as if their peace of mind, even their safety hangs in that balance. Door open, Freddy sits on the sofa. A minute later, feeling uneasy and exposed, she gets up and locks it. Paige stares at the dark screen of the TV. Freddy is amazed how loudly the telephone does not ring.

The grandmother's bathroom is much bigger than theirs at home, and nicer, too. Her bathtub is big and white. It stands on the feet of beasts from fairy tales, gnarled curves and claws, each clutching a round white ball. The sink spreads like a flower on a thick white stem. Everything matches—the washcloths, the towels, the rug, a deep dark red.

Grandmother witch reaches out one long thin finger and strums Chaz's ribs. Normally that would tickle. Instead it makes him cold.

Grandmother witch says, "What a lovely boy you are, Chaz. But so thin."

Chaz thinks about the witch in the story who wanted to fatten Hansel up before she ate him. His witch is smiling now. Her big old teeth remind him of mountains with seams and pockets of gold.

"Doesn't your mother feed you enough?" the grandmother says.

Chaz doesn't like to hear Mom criticized. He says, "I eat a lot. My mom says I have the metabull of a hummingbird."

"Metabolism?" The witch laughs. "That's good." Once again her finger descends his rib cage, coming to rest on his blue elastic waistband. "And who's this on your underpants, little hummingbird?"

Chaz squirms a few inches backward. "That's Charlie Brown from *Peanuts*. They have Lucy for girls."

"So Charlie Brown's your friend, eh? I don't know him."

"He's just the picture on my underwear. I don't even like *Peanuts* that much."

Grandmother witch hooks her pointing finger under the waistband. Chaz sidles back again, this time into the cool lip of the tub. The grandmother pulls his underpants down around his ankles. Chaz puts his hands over his private spot. The witch laughs as if he's made a joke.

Her big finger pokes his shield of hands. "Hummingbird. I like that," she says. "Now let me see what you've got there."

Chaz holds himself tighter and looks over the witch's shoulder, past her sparkling earring and gray hair, to the white wall. Even kneeling on the rug, the witch is taller than he is. Her finger pokes harder. "Come on now. Let Grandma see."

Chaz looks at the wall and says, No. He's disappointed by how little his voice sounds.

Suddenly the witch's voice is as big as a lion's. "Do as I say," she roars.

Her roar startles Chaz so much he drops his hands. When he looks at the witch, she is smiling at his penis. He moves his hands to cover himself, but the witch catches his wrists and holds them apart.

"Please let go," Chaz says.

The witch laughs softly. "But you like it, see?" She nods at his penis.

Chaz is embarrassed and surprised to see it sticking out. "I have to go to the bathroom," he says.

The witch crawls back a knee's worth and sweeps out her arm toward the toilet. "Please."

Chaz is afraid to turn his back to her. He moves toward the toilet sideways, like a crab. There, with one hand, he lifts up the heavy seat, then stands in peeing position, but nothing happens. "Please don't look," he says to the witch. "I can't go when people watch."

Humming a tune he doesn't know, the witch turns her face away from him. Once it starts coming, Chaz thinks the pee is never going to stop. The witch hears when it does. Her hands on his waist turn him toward her. The witch's eyes are bright and shiny as the sparkles on her glasses. He thinks it is important to watch them closely. Then he feels something warm, alive, move softly under his balls. The witch fondles him gently.

For a moment, while he figures out for sure just what is happening, Chaz freezes. It's true. The old woman is touching him *there*.

Chaz raises his right leg and kicks out as hard as he can, striking the witch somewhere between her stomach and her chest. Chaz wishes there were more than thirty-seven pounds behind the kick. Still, it surprises the witch, knocks her off balance, so she sits back on her heels and lets him go. With her head tilted toward her shoulder and half a smile, she says, "Now what was that all about?"

Chaz clenches his fists and calls forth his biggest voice. "Don't touch me there." Ever since Mom explained to him about strangers and bad men who like to do bad things to little boys, Chaz practiced saying this sometimes, inside his mind. In his rehearsals, the words have magic power. The bad men disappear.

Grandmother witch says nothing. Her hand reaches out for him. Chaz slaps it with all his might. "I said don't do that. My mom says nobody but me is allowed to touch my private spots."

"Doesn't your mother touch them?" the witch asks dreamily.

"Now that I'm a big boy, I take baths by myself."

"How can a little hummingbird be such a big boy?" Grand-mother witch says.

Chaz says, "I don't know, but I am."

"My mother touched me," the witch says. "She touched me all over."

To his relief, Chaz sees her eyes have changed. Instead of burning him, they've got the look that grown-ups get when they think about things that happened a long time ago, like they're watching a movie you can't see. "Even there?" Chaz says.

"Here, there, everywhere. My mother touched me all over."

"Weren't you scared?" Chaz says.

"Scared?" The witch's eyes drift back toward him, without quite catching. "Scared of my mother?" Again for a moment she hums her little tune. When she speaks again, her voice sounds different. "I love my mother. My mother would never hurt me. She's a good mother."

Does the witch remember him? Glad to be out of the spot-light, Chaz waits for the movie to be over. After a long time, the witch blinks, almost as if she's surprised to see him. Chaz doesn't want her to come all the way back to here and now. "Is your mother still alive?" he says.

With her pointer finger, the witch pushes her glasses up higher on her nose. "Mother's dead," she says. "She wanted to die. She didn't say so, but I knew." Her gaze is earnest, as if she wants to convince him of her truth. "I loved my mother. I would do anything for her."

To Chaz's amazement, he sees tears in the grandmother's eyes. When she blinks, her eyelids push them out and down her cheeks. The tears blaze little trails of paleness through her heavy powder and the witch's cheeks look like sandpaper. Whenever people in his real life cry, Chaz puts his arms around them and gives them love. He reminds himself that this is not a nice person crying. He folds his arms across his chest and waits.

The witch's back curves and her shoulders droop. She sits back on her heels and cries. Pretty soon her whole face is wet and slack and she just keeps staring past him at the wall. Chaz knows he would feel sad if Mom was dead. Sometimes he's dreamed she was and woken up crying. With a great rattle, the witch sniffs up the loose snot in her nose, then gives a little cry, almost a whimper. Even Paige, who is an impressive cryer, never cries as long and hard as Grandmother witch. Chaz finds it hard to not feel sorry for her.

"My mother loved me, too," the witch sobs. "She was a good mother. She loved me."

Chaz has never felt it necessary to tell anyone that Mom loves him. Why wouldn't she? Chaz thought all mothers loved their kids. Yelled at them and even hit them sometimes maybe, in the mysterious way of mothers, but always smiled again eventually and washed their socks and made them dinner. He doesn't think the witch is sure. And the witch is old. It frightens Chaz to think that mothers matter for so long.

Not sure he is doing the right thing, Chaz reaches out one hand, slowly, and touches the witch's shoulder. "Maybe you should blow your nose," he says.

The witch's eyes look drowned, like bright pebbles in the bottom of a dirty fish tank. She raises her lank arms and wraps them around Chaz, pulling him so tight against her it's hard to breathe, so close he feels the secret padded swellings under her dress and smells her makeup and her sweat. The witch mumbles something into his hair. The hug goes on so long that Chaz thinks they both might die in it or still be there when his mother comes to get him. He stares at the witch's earring and tries not to think at all.

At last he feels her straighten. Still holding to his waist, she pushes him away, then looks at him. Chaz holds his chin up and tries to meet her gaze. "So," she says, "you don't want to have a bath with Grandma?"

Solemnly, Chaz shakes his head.

One of the witch's hands closes tighter around him. The other disappears into her skirt. "Well, then," she says, "I guess it's bedtime." This time he sees the needle before it stings him, on his bottom where the doctor gives him shots.

How long would it take to knock on every door in the city? She could probably skip the poorer neighborhoods, unless of course he was trying to trick her. And what about a psychic? Why haven't the police tried that? No fingerprints doesn't mean no evidence. Those envelopes could be radiant with psychic vibrations. What about bloodhounds? Don't they have dogs?

First thing Monday morning, she's going to hire a private detective. Never mind the money, he can wait through probate. Or she can sell her car and drive Nick's. The police are probably giving her second-rate service because she doesn't own a house and pay property tax. Maybe she should explain how it's factored into the rent. If her father were alive, he would call city hall. Maybe she should put on black tights and her purple cape and sunglasses, jump off the roof and fly. She's never been able to fly before but she might be angry enough to stay airborne now.

Freddy dreams of action while she sits on the sofa and lets Paige brush her hair. Her hair's short, so the brushing is therapeutic, not cosmetic. The bristles of the hairbrush scratch her scalp. When she thinks about it, it feels good.

Freddy feels bigger inside than her body is, something like the way a snake must feel before it sheds its skin. She imagines splitting open to let a larger self emerge. Freddy remembers pushing her babies out, Paige's whimper greeting the world, Chaz's offended yelp. She would rather work that hard every day of her life, giving birth with the same awful regularity that the fire bringer lost his liver or that other Greek guy pushed his rock uphill, over and over again with no rest, than be condemned to wait like this.

"Your hair is shiny, Mom," Paige says.

Freddy would cheerfully go bald for something positive to do. She's smart and she's strong; motherhood has taught her that. She can do anything that's required, if only life would be generous enough to ask it of her, anything but to sit here with her hands folded in her lap. Again, inside her head, she shouts Chaz's name top volume, willing her inner voice to spread, to echo until it reaches every hidden improbable mousehole in the city, until Chaz hears her calling. She stills her thoughts to listen for his answering call.

When she thinks again, it is a kind of praying, addressed without prejudice to any spirit inclined to listen, powerful enough to help her. Here's my collateral, one soul. Let's make a deal. Yes, she would forgo success, would give up sex, relinquish any hope of being mated, could probably make do without a limb or two, if it came to that, even her sight. Of course, deal makers always want what's most important. She would try to give up painting.

Freddy's trying to draw up a formal contract—Chaz must be returned to her alive, unharmed, with any psychic damage reversible—when Carol comes through the front door.

"There you are," she says. "I used my key."

Paige says, "Hi, Carol," and stops brushing Freddy's hair.

Freddy feels the crackle of her friend's vitality, her grand expansiveness, which lets her know by contrast how small and maimed she feels. It occurs to her that Carol's gotten laid since she last saw her.

Carol sets a casserole on the coffee table. "Dinner. Yours and mine. I made a double batch. You hear anything?"

"Nothing."

"Anthony's finger isn't sprained, just jammed. He's fine."

"Good," Freddy says.

"Shit, honey, I feel just awful for you. I wish there were something I could do."

"Yeah," Freddy says. "I know."

"I talked to Mike about an hour ago. He's doing everything he can."

Freddy wonders, not for the first time, how much that is.

"He says it's real promising that no body's turned up."

"He told me he wasn't looking for one."

"He didn't want to scare you, hon. But he figures if Chaz has been alive this long, he's going to stay alive."

"That's comforting."

Carol arches her eyebrows and, at the same time, turns down the corners of her mouth. "I don't know how to be comforting. I keep imagining if it were one of mine."

"Then I'd be saying the same stupid things to you. Except I wouldn't be dating a cop."

"Am I hearing a complaint?"

Carol unburdens herself of keys, purse, sweater, settles at easy attention in the armchair while Freddy thinks. Her movements are charged with a grace Freddy dimly remembers feeling in her own limbs. On several counts, Freddy pleads guilty to envy, jealously, self-pity, and a persistent desire to whine. She says, "Not really. I was just promising God I'd be celibate for the next thirty years or so if I could have Chaz back."

Carol's laugh makes light of a serious transaction. On the sofa, Paige rustles and Freddy, turning, sees her daughter is avid as a sparrow, watching for crumbs. "Go put the kettle on, honey, would you?" Freddy says.

"Oh, Mom."

"Let the big girls talk a minute," Carol says. "Scoot."

Paige's passage to the kitchen is painfully slow. Freddy says, "Actually, she's been wonderful."

Carol says, "Hang in there. I know it's hard to believe right now, but one of these days, you'll get your own life back."

"What's left of it."

"Life is full of grand surprises," Carol says, spreading her arms to echo the chair's embrace. "Fred, this might be it. The prince."

"In an unmarked cop car?"

Carol's shrug is big enough to shuck off worlds of trouble. "Anyway, he's thinking about getting out. Going back to school, maybe. Finding something more healthy to do."

"Tell him to stay away from medical school."

Carol laughs. "Right. One doctor per lifetime is enough." Vees forward over her thighs to say, "I feel a little opportunistic, I guess. Up while you're down. Profiting from your bad luck. Forgive me?"

It's her blessing being asked. If she gives it—and she must—Freddy wonders what she'll have left. She tries to picture a rich life, ten years hence, a bigger house, a studio without her bed in it, a new car in the garage. A view? In ten years, Paige will be gone. Chaz should be starting high school. She conjures a kitchen, spacious and welcoming, tries to put Chaz, a hungry teenager, there at the table. Will he be home?

"You're slow to forgive," Carol says.

"I'm sorry. I was just thinking. Of course you're forgiven."

Paige, bringing them coffee, says, "Forgiven for what? Did you guys have a fight?"

Freddy holds Carol's gaze while she tells her daughter, "For being happy."

Paige gives a ten-year-old's frisson of headshake—the ways of adults are weird. "Okay," she says.

And the porch gives its admonition of arrival, impact shuddering the old boards, passing as a smaller current into the house itself, so Freddy feels it in *her* feet and rises before a knock sounds on the door. A thin teenager in a WAZZU sweatshirt holds out a long white box tied with green ribbon. At the curb, a station wagon idles, its advertising message interrupted by the driver's open door. The kid consults his clipboard. "Bascomb, right?"

Freddy nods and the boy thrusts the box into her arms. "These are for you." He sprints back to the wagon, climbs in, and slams the door.

A cool floral perfume rises from the box in Freddy's arms. Paige and Carol gather round as she sets it on the coffee table, works the crisp ribbon off the end, lifts the lid to reveal, bedded in florist's thin green waxed paper, a forest of long green stems, leaves bordered with tiny uniform serrations as if a seamstress had trimmed them with her shears, the tender claret heads of roses, a dozen.

"Wow," Paige says. "They're beautiful."

Above the roses in their cardboard catafalque, Carol beams at Freddy. "See what I mean about surprises?"

Freddy rises from her knees. "I better get these in water." Friend and daughter follow to the kitchen. Freddy scouts the high shelves and finds her biggest vase, green factory-molded glass, rather ugly and so long unused that dust drifts in its ridges. Carol takes it to the sink for washing, while Freddy looks for scissors to put fresh cuts in the stems. Over her shoulder, scrubbing, Carol asks, "What did he write on the card?"

Freddy feels under the crinkly florist's paper, searching. What she finds, on the very bottom of the box, is not the customary two-by-three-inch gift card, but a plump white envelope with her name, given and unabbreviated, inscribed on the front.

"Don, right?" Carol says.

Knowing somehow that Don is wrong, Freddy slips the envelope unseen out of the box, up under her loose sweatshirt, where she secures it in the waistband of her pants. "Right," she says.

"Well?"

"He says he wants a rain check. We had a date tonight."

"Did he sign it love?"

"He's holding good thoughts," Freddy improvises. "The bottom says XOX."

"Nice," Carol says. She rubs the vase dry and fills it with

water, adds the packet of preservative the florist sent, lifts the first blossom from the box. "Do you want to do the honors, or shall I?"

"I'll supervise." The sharp corners of the envelope prickle her stomach. She tells herself she's not withholding evidence, just buying time.

"When was the last time somebody sent you roses, Mom?"

"A dozen red ones? Two boyfriends back before your father. The kid was rich."

"Did you like him?"

"Not very much."

"How come?"

"We're talking ancient history."

"So?"

"So the most interesting thing about him was his bank account. His father owned a company that manufactured men's underwear. My roomates used to call him the Crown Prince of Jock Straps."

"How come you never told me about him before?"

"You never asked."

Carol makes the minutest of adjustments to her arrangement, turning a blossom here, lifting a leaf. "What do you think?"

"Lovely."

"Marry him, Mom."

"Don't be hasty," Freddy says.

"I've got to run," Carol says. "Saturday errands. I júst wanted to come by and give you a hug." Carol seizes Freddy in a brisk embrace. Today her optimism, her energy will not transfuse; instead, pooled on the surface of Freddy's resistant skin, they evaporate into the sunlit kitchen air. Carol hugs Paige in her turn, collects her possessions, dives past them off the porch, into the still-golden afternoon. Left behind and longingly, they watch. Beside her, Freddy hears her daughter sigh.

"You know what, babe? I am exhausted. I think I'm going to go upstairs and lie down for a while."

"What about me?"

"Maybe there's a decent movie on TV."

"Fat chance."

"You could read."

"How long are you going to sleep for?"

"Not long. I may not be able to get to sleep at all." Freddy locks the front door, kisses the top of Paige's restless head, and climbs the tall stairs to her room to read her mail.

23

■ ■ ■ ■ ■

My Dear Frederika,

First, I hope you will forgive the somewhat unorthodox means by which this letter reaches you; I'm sure you can appreciate the need for subtlety. Please accept the accompanying flowers with my compliments.

As I am sure you are eager to learn, young Charles is, if not enraptured with his present circumstances, nonetheless enduring tolerably well. Yes, my dear, your son lives and doubtless misses you sorely.

Please dine with me this evening in my home, at 8:30 P.M. I would extend this invitation to your charming daughter, too, but alas, I fear you would not let her come.

I am sure you've been in contact with the police; it is not they I invite to partake of my hospitality. Should they come with you or in your stead, it is your son who will suffer my displeasure. I trust you know enough of me by now to understand that I am not unwilling to perform acts others might find distasteful or abhorrent. I hope I make myself clear.

A volume has been left in your name at the front

desk of the Elliott Bay Bookstore at First and Main. When you call for it this evening, you will receive instructions on how to proceed. Once again, I regret that the need for caution requires me to be less than direct.

Anticipating the pleasure of your company,

I remain

A Friend of the Family

Freddy leans back into her bank of pillows and closes her eyes, trading the stark planes of her attic ceiling for a vision of the inside of her mind, which right now resembles an anarchist's shooting gallery where the target ducks fly freely through a web of ricocheting bullets and it is not quite clear to anyone what winning is. The place is loud and smells of sulfur. Freddy aims for clarity and explodes in doubt.

The image is not useful. She opens her eyes to the simpler landscape of the ceiling, breathing deeply, lets her vision reach and blur. Now, to reason. What does reason say?

If she calls the police, do the police become responsible? Not a soul would blame her for surrendering her burden to higher authority. If something terrible happened to Chaz then, it would be their fault.

Or it would be her fault, for surrendering. Knowing what she does of them. Ashford, exhausted. Norgaard, stagestruck. All of them overworked and underpaid and given to self-pity. All of them ordinary one-leg-at-a-time humans.

Their greater experience.

How often can this happen?

Their expertise.

You seen one madman, you seen 'em all.

Their bigger weapons.

Her love.

Are these her thoughts, or someone else's. Reason does not come easy. She is an artist, one who feels.

Not a decision to be made alone.

Lord, strike me with answers like lightning. Illumine what is right.

Why, why alone?

A week ago she would have talked to Carol, but Carol has

gone over to the other side. She is the last person Freddy could talk to now.

Mrs. Patniak is too pat. Too frightened.

Don even if he is safe is still too new.

Jack. Chaz's father. Jack who has a chromosomal stake in each of her children. Why did his face invade her drawings? She can imagine him stealing the children if it suited his purpose, but won't believe she lived so long or tried so hard with a man who would do murder. Still, Freddy knows she cannot ask his help. Jack goes to the bottom of the list, moving Carol one notch up.

Sandy. Makes sense but feels wrong. Why?

Paige is too young.

Ashford. No. Yes. Think. Think hard. She has seen the glimmer of intelligence, a flicker of compassion. What are his motives? Where is his justice? Dead or alive. What does he think of that? The bottom line is this—would he be capable of telling her to go alone if it were right for her to go alone.

What would her mother do? She tries but can't extrapolate. Elsa. What would you do? Help me exonerate me love me take me back into the simple waters of your womb. Share the weight of this decision. More and more it seems to be a reasonable demand.

Freddy reaches for the bedside phone, then drops her hand. Reason, assuming she has used it properly, says talk to Elsa, but reason is only half a mind. And she is tired, so profoundly overtaxed each of her cells is aching, their microscopic depletion organizing itself into aching muscles, tissues, tendons, bones. Even her hair hurts. It is four-fifty-five by her bedside clock. She can afford to sleep for half an hour, surrender consciousness that long, consign her problem as she does when painting to the other half of mind, letting nonreason have its turn. If not always often when painting she wakes up knowing what to do.

Freddy sets the clock for half an hour hence, lies limp and straight to court unconsciousness. She holds the image of the green glass vase. When it turns violet, pulsing with a yellow light, when it begins to melt and swirl and tumble like a waterfall, the divide has been crossed. She floats, then sinks. She rides the fast toboggan down the chute of dreams.

Thirty minutes later, the beeper calls Freddy back to the starting gate. She brings one souvenir. Sandy. Of course. Who else?

Which makes it even more important to talk to Elsa. Again she reaches for the phone, and then, sleep lifting, remembers that the phone is bugged.

Mrs. Patniak's is not. Freddy charges Paige with minding theirs and explains to Mrs. P. she musn't tie it up. Again she sits on the bright bedspread afghan to make her call.

Elsa is home, news-hungry. "Have the police found anything?

"Nothing."

"Let's hope no news is good news."

"Maybe."

"When Peter called this morning I told him about Chaz. He was terribly concerned. He sends his love."

"Thank him, okay? I want to ask you a couple of questions. About Sandy."

"Dear Sandy. How is he?"

"Okay, I guess. Was Sandy ever jealous of Nick?"

"Sandy always acknowledged Nick was the better writer. I never felt he was jealous."

"When I was little, I used to think Sandy was in love with you."

"If he was, he never mentioned it to me," Elsa says. "He was married once, you know."

"I didn't."

"Her name was Martha. We were all in school together. She was a lovely girl. Sandy adored her."

"What happened?"

"Leukemia. She was only twenty-six years old when she died. Sandy nursed her himself, right up to the end."

"I didn't know."

"Sandy was devastated. He moved in with us for a while, after. We were his lifeline. That's how we all got so close."

"Could there have been more to Nick's relationship with Sandy than you knew about?"

"No, Freddy. Sandy is a dear man, but Nick never found

him very interesting. Sometimes when he'd been drinking, he'd say as much, call Sandy an old maid. Nick could be cruel when he was drinking."

"I know. Didn't Sandy ever get angry?"

"Sandy is incapable of anger on his own behalf. If he caught you kicking a dog, that would be different. But he never thought of himself as a dog."

"He makes a good suspect. The best."

"The worst. For your father, choosing to be a CO during the war was entirely a moral choice. With Sandy, it was an expression of his nature. He's naturally a gentle man."

"People keep secrets," Freddy says.

"Nick kept secrets, but Sandy has always been an open book. A good book, mind you, well written, but with very little suspense."

Almost against her will, Freddy says, "What about Jack?"

Elsa is silent for a moment before she answers. "I've always thought that Jack was troubled. Nick thought so, too."

"I don't want it to be Jack. No matter how I feel about him, he *is* the children's father."

"Freddy, you're sounding like *your* father. This is the police's problem now, not yours."

"We're talking about my son."

"Nick could never understand how arrogant it is, to assume that every windmill is yours to tilt at, every injustice yours to redress. Try to be my child, for once. Living one clean, quiet life is quite enough."

"What if it was your baby missing?"

Elsa sighs. "I used to think about things like that. What would I be capable of, to save my child? I suspect every mother wonders that."

"What did you decide?"

"I was never put to the test. But you've heard the stories. Women do extraordinary things." Elsa laughs. "Maybe it's hormonal. In my case, I'm sure the capacity for heroism passed with the menopause."

Freddy laughs, too. "Thanks, Mom. You've helped."

"I hope so, though I don't know how. I wish you were closer, Freddy, so we could practice hugging."

"Me too," Freddy says, and then good-bye.

24
......

R. E. A. D. One by one,
the letters pulse red to form the neon exhortation. At twilight in
Pioneer Square, those exhorted are straying tourists, lingering
bums. The yuppie couples striding to chic dinner destinations
along the skid row upgrade are immune to storefront pleadings.
Freddy enters the bookstore at the corner and joins a gaggle
of customers fanned around the front desk. Help is plentiful,
if stern. She advances quickly to the counter. The clerk she
draws looks from the neck up as if he might have signed the
Declaration of Independence—straight carriage and a studious
pallor, high forehead, half bald, a ponytail that looks more
distinguished than rebellious. Neck down, plaid flannel, he is
a lumberjack. How may he help?

"I believe you're holding a book for Bascomb?"

"I'll check."

He spins gracefully toward a span of open shelves marked
by the letters of the alphabet, retrieves an object and spins back.
Behind the counter, six people step and sidestep through the
dance of commerce without colliding. "Here you are. Campbell.
The Hero with a Thousand Faces."

Yellow and black is what she sees. "What do I owe you?"

The clerk extracts a receipt from between the pages. "Already paid." He inserts a free page marker and tucks the book into a bag. "Enjoy it."

Freddy nods. She backs out of the buyers' circle, a little tremor in her fingers rustling the paper sack. A sign points to the café downstairs, and she descends, discovers where the lonely bookish come on Saturday night. At a swarm of blue-topped tables, single occupants eat and read at the same time, wearing a common, concentrating scowl. The room is lined with books and quiet as a library. Freddy finds a small empty table near the back wall and takes her new book from the bag.

She cracks the virgin cover, colors of bumblebee, and begins to turn pages, looking for further instructions without knowing what form they will take. She hopes there is no code to crack or riddle to be solved. She's speeding, scared and excited at the same time. To ask her to be clever would be too much. Maybe he knew that. When she finds the answer, it is straightforward, a typed address.

Freddy sets the slip of paper before her on the blue table and feels an unexpected satisfaction, as if some important task has been completed. Everything is as much in place as she could put it: Paige and Mrs. Patniak safely ensconced downstairs, among the antimacassars, believing it is the police she is going to meet; herself showered, made up, dressed, and accessoried as if she were going to an opening or on a date, as if grooming might hone the edge of her determination; the letter re-addressed to Carol and placed in keeping of Mrs. Patniak. "If I'm not home by midnight, call Carol and read this to her, please." This is the hedge she plants around her bets. The odds aren't posted. If she's not home by midnight, Ashford can have his turn.

The solitary diners around her are sipping wine. The inside of her mouth, palate and tongue, tighten, wanting. A glass of cold white might steady her. A little gush of saliva approves the premise. Freddy rises and joins the short line at the beverage counter. It is only seven-twenty. The person in front of her, young, with hair gelled into ragged peaks, wearing a long black coat despite the season, orders capuccino. The expressionless counterman asks without much interest what she wants. In a desperate flurry, she scans the posted menu.

"Lemon seltzer, please." She plops a quarter in the IT'S HIP

TO TIP mug and returns to her seat. The seltzer is unsugared, tart, setting up small convulsions on the back of her tongue. How easy it would be. She applauds the censor's intervention even as she deplores its tardiness. Her mouth, not privy to the moral fine points, is disappointed by her choice. Tough chicks drink booze. Freddy lets the bubbles in the seltzer sting her tongue before she swallows.

Nothing is irreversible, she tells herself. She could call Ashford still. Bail out of folly. Freddy tries to believe she believes this, but the thought does nothing to brake the momentum of her metabolism. Her body knows. It must have known all along, knew at the moment she hid the letter, unopened, instead of announcing its arrival. Yes, she knew. Freddy laughs softly, to herself, and at the same time, wants to cry.

If she finishes the seltzer, she'll need to pee. Maybe, given her jumpsuit, should anyway. In their ability to urinate casually, ubiquitously, while remaining erect men do, Freddy concedes, enjoy a biological advantage, one of few she recognizes as innate. To the coming encounter, she wants to bring a clear mind and an empty bladder. Elliott Bay's bathroom reading matter is on the walls, a heated felt-tip dialogue between Jesus freaks and radical feminists, both sides trading in blunt cliché.

Fresh lipstick and no more excuse to linger. The three wall-mounted pay phones she passes leaving invite her to recant. Upstairs and almost out the door, it strikes her that she needs to leave a trail. Using the table of new arrivals for a desk, she copies the address onto a scrap of paper torn from the bag, then finds the same tall clerk who found the book for her. "Excuse me, I hate to bother you, but I called my friend and she didn't really want me to pick this up for her do you suppose you could put it back in will call I'm really sorry." She thrusts her package into his long pale hands. "The name is Bascomb."

The tall clerk cocks his head, receiving it, tall forehead ridging with his question: "Are you all right?"

Freddy spreads her hands in disclaimer, emits a shrill approximation of a laugh. "Sure. Of course. Just a mistake."

With a small shake of his head, he pulls the book toward his chest, accepting. "Bascomb?"

Spewing thanks, she nods. Her hand makes a tight fist around the address in her pocket. Dark fell while she was indoors, damp with it, chilling the evening air. A toothless grimy man with a stocking cap pulled close to his eyebrows extends his cupped palm toward her out of the shadows. Spare change? Acknowledging him with no more than the sideways flicker of a cold eye, Freddy walks on by, then reconsiders, retracks the half block and hands the hustler a nearly new five-dollar bill. The READ sign, urgent in the darkness, makes the transaction sanguine. "Pray for me," Freddy says.

The bum stows her bill in the pocket of his tattered pea coat. "Sure, lady, anything you say."

The building sits back from a commonplace street of forth-right fifties apartments, encircling its own dark garden full of shapely shrubbery. Hidden fixtures breathe a mist of light across the brick footpath that curves toward the door. Light from the door-side sconces falls on the black surface of a small pond from whose center a stone cherub, naked, rises on one plump stone toe. Freddy has a strong urge, frivolous and ir-relevant, to stop and look for carp in the dark water. Something in the architectural or horticultural arrangement of the court-yard seems to swallow up the sounds of traffic, so that her heels sound sharply on the bricks. In the chilly sky above her, she sees the glint of stars.

Freddy's nerves sing falsetto at a pitch so persistently high it makes her slightly nauseated. Long tendrils of ivy weeping down the dark brick walls, the leaded-glass windows, the corner towers of the building remind her there are odd pockets of old and rich in this raw new city. The rent here has to be four times her own. To combat an intimidation by wealth and privilege so innate she thinks it might actually be genetic, Freddy conjures up images of her father sober, her son happy. For a moment, too, she pictures a SWAT team, Ashford with a bullhorn, fling-ing ultimata at the tall brick turrets, and understands that this scenario is even more absurd than a single dark-haired warrior in a jumpsuit, armed with a mother's love.

As soon as she reaches the front door, before she has a chance to scan the panel of numbered buttons beside it, a throaty buzz purrs from its speaker and the handle yields to the pressure of her fingers. She has been watched. Inside, light bounces giddily back and forth between flame-shaped bulbs and mirrors and highly polished dark-wood walls. Caught in the ricochet, her pupils startle painfully, then narrow. The elevator is a dimly gilded cage. Rising slowly, Freddy thinks only of Chaz.

Guided by brass numerals, Freddy winds the plushy labyrinth to a cul de sac of hall and stands before the heavy door that proclaims itself 3D. Her breathing is as fast and shallow as if she'd climbed the stairs. Fear makes her feel so utterly alive that all the days and years before this moment seem like sleeping, like unremarkable hours passed in a dim dull drifting safety she would like to know again. If she did not believe her son was behind that gleaming door, Freddy would turn and run away, would burrow deep in some warm place and sleep and sleep. Chanting love inside her mind, invoking love, insisting upon it, Freddy raises her fist and strikes the door.

Almost immediately, as if the answerer did not need to be summoned but too had stood before it, the door opens, is opened and whatever Freddy did or did not imagine is supplanted by the tall elegant bespectacled woman who stands before her, by the smart restraint of her tailored gray dress, by the well-cut gray hair like a silver flower opening around a strong and handsome face. The voice that greets her—"Frederika, I have been expecting you"—is deep but plausibly female. "Won't you come in?"

The gestures are as polished, as gracious as the voice. This is the sort of older woman Freddy admires and would like to be, the kind of pulled-together presence that makes her feel, by contrast, hasty and half-baked. Entering, she reminds herself that this creature is a man, a witch, a murderer. "I came," she says. "Where is my son?" Her voice sounds as shrill and tinny as the song her nerves are singing.

With a sweeping gesture that bids her follow, the woman turns and leads her from hall to parlor, a large and formal room that easily accommodates the massive Victorian furniture and plentiful *objets*, that scales the full-size Oriental carpet with its Muslim vines and arabesques into an area rug, leaving naked expanses of polished hardwood floor. Freddy forbids herself to be intimidated by opulence. The woman settles on a leather love seat, unstops the cut-glass decanter before her on an inlaid tray. Into two stemmed glasses she pours an amber liquid. "Do sit and have some sherry."

Reluctantly, Freddy sits on the very edge of the proffered chair, accepts her glass. "I'd like to see my son."

The woman smiles, showing good teeth, lifts her glass and takes a tiny swallow before she answers. "Young Charles isn't able to join us just now, I'm afraid."

"Why not?"

"He's sleeping. He's slept a great deal these last few days."

"I'd like to see him," Freddy says.

Again, the velvet smile. "In due time you shall. For the moment, let us enjoy our sherry."

The woman's firm good manners, the form they impose on the encounter, dilute Freddy's power and sense of purpose. She wants the advantage of her anger. Is trying to find a way to claim it when the woman says, "Tell me about yourself, Frederika."

"There isn't much to tell. My life was going well until you came into it."

"I have been in your life for a very long time, my dear. I'm much more interested in hearing you account for yourself."

"Did Nick think you were a woman?"

Smiling, the woman says, "Nick thought I was his friend."

"Even after you stole his book?"

"There is a great seduction in being known. I understand that. Nick came to know me too." The woman shifts on the love seat. "Do drink your sherry. That's all it is. Our supper will be ready soon. Can you smell it?"

Now that she thinks about it, smell she can, the scent of spices rising from an unseen pot, nearer by, the sparkle of the sherry in her nose. Her ears awaken, too, and she becomes aware for the first time of a subtle symphonic soundtrack. Beethoven? She isn't sure.

"I asked about you."

"What do you want to know?"

"What do you live by?"

"I live by my art," Freddy says. "I live for my children."

"Not for yourself?"

Freddy has no sense of danger now, only a deep frustration. She says, "More than anything in the world, I want to see my son."

And the woman surprises her by rising, brushing the lap

of her dress smooth over what look to be long thighs. "Very well. Come with me." Freddy too gets up. The woman walks steadily on her tall heels. She produces a skeleton key from the pocket of her dress and stoops to unlock a door on the right at the end of a long, carpeted hallway. If she had some heavy object, Freddy might try to cosh her and escape. The woman is heavier by quite some than she and, though older, appears to be fit. Will so promising a moment come again?

The room is dark until the woman feels for a switch and turns on the overhead light. Chaz lies flat on his back in the middle of a large bed, all but his face obscured by covers. Freddy moves toward the bed. Behind her, the door closes. She hears the turning of the lock. The waxy pallor of her son's face frightens her. Even as a baby, Chaz slept on his stomach or on his side.

When she touches his forehead, the skin is cool. Her touch doesn't rouse him. If he breathes, it is too softly for the fingers she places under his nose to feel, or she is too distraught to feel his breath. Freddy peels back the covers. Beneath them, her child is naked. She puts her chin on the bed and watches his chest. Almost imperceptibly, it rises, falls. He is alive.

Freddy climbs up on the bed and gathers her baby in her lap. The unresisting weight of his body, its pale stillness remind her of something. What? They make the image of Pietà, Mary holding the dead Christ, a classic, chilling image she remembers from art history. To disrupt the composition, she strokes Chaz's hair, she says his name. If only he would respond. This sleep is deep and unnatural. Freddy wants him to know she has come.

It seems she too is prisoner now. With Chaz in her arms, she thinks of Paige, her sweet and prickly daughter. For the first time, Freddy wonders what will become of Paige if she should die. Jack has a father's right to her. Freddy studies the room, looking for what among the sparse furnishings might serve her for a weapon. Blankets and dresser drawers seem to be the only possibilities. She holds Chaz close and rubs his cool still legs. It was not her intention to come courting death. She had no intention but to find her son. Now she wonders what she thought would happen once he was found. The bait was so compelling she leaped and swallowed, with no more forethought than a trout. Netted, she reviews her regrets.

The woman who comes back is not the one who left. This woman is large and dowdy, with frayed gray curls, jeweled wings on her thick plastic glasses. This woman wears a shapeless dress the color of old wine and sturdy orthopedic shoes. Her voice, when she speaks, is rougher and more common than before.

"Satisfied? He's bare-assed because he wet himself and I haven't had the time to do a wash."

Freddy knows this woman; Chaz's description was remarkably exact. She looks for traces of the elegant woman in gray and finds none; even the way her wrinkles lie seems to have been transformed. This woman is more a Patniak than an Elsa. She plays pinochle and knows how to stretch her pension checks. "He's due to sleep awhile longer," she says. "Cover him up and come with me."

Freddy keeps her arms around her son. In a thin voice, she says, "What do you plan to do with me?"

"Feed you, for one thing," the woman says. "You're thinner now than at the funeral."

"You were at Nick's memorial?"

"You shook my hand. Don't you remember?" The woman grins at Freddy. "No? I didn't think so. We old ladies are so forgettable."

Sifting memories, Freddy stares at the ravaged face. Only the fine white teeth are the same, but the setting makes them improbable, so they seem like dentures.

"Come along now," the woman urges, her voice stern.

Freddy eases Chaz down on the bed, covers him to the chin. She leaves a kiss on his cool forehead. The woman leads her from the room, then locks it. Freddy follows dumbly, always wondering if this is the moment she should attack. The moment always passes. She is almost surprised to find the spacious living room unchanged. The woman looks less the tenant now and more the hired help. Even the way she takes up her glass is different, the gesture greedy.

"Actually," the woman says, "we've met more times than once. We've broken bread together. You've been a guest in my home."

Freddy assaults the disguise with vision and memory, searching for the smallest fissure through which the familiar might appear. She feels as she does in the course of those dreams where she's expected to take a test in a language she can't read. The search and all her will yield nothing. The woman chuckles at her bewilderment. "Finish your sherry," she says. "It's suppertime."

The sherry tempts her, but Freddy says, "No, thank you," and the woman says, "You think you can escape your father's fate." It strikes Freddy the woman means more than booze. "I hope so," she says.

The woman says, "We shall see. Are you hungry? *I* hope so. I've made a lovely stew."

When Freddy hesitates, the woman takes her firmly by the arm and guides her to a formal dining room, lighted by candles. The table is covered in white linen and set for two. The fluted white china is luminous in candlelight. The heavy silver gleams. Freddy sees the place settings contain no knives. Near the window, a magnificent gardenia bush sits potted on a carved stand. A dozen blossoms peer out like the faces of pale virgins from the dark foliage, their perfume sweet above the cooking smells.

The woman leads her to a place setting perpendicular to the table's head, pulls out her chair, snugs it up to the backs of Freddy's knees, seating her. "I'll just be a minute. Help yourself to bread and salad," the woman says. She disappears into the adjoining kitchen. Freddy unfurls a linen napkin and spreads it on her lap. Soon the woman returns, bearing two large, steaming bowls. One of these she sets before Freddy, then takes her own place at the table's head.

In the vapor rising from her bowl, Freddy detects the aromas of beer and rosemary, an odd but pleasant combination. Small pieces of shallot, potato, meat, and mushroom float enticingly in thick, ruddy broth and despite her ascetic resolution, Freddy finds she is hollow, in want of filling. The food will give her strength.

The woman dips a hunk of bread into her stew, bites with her strong white teeth. "I'm no poisoner," she says. "Eat up."

Freddy fills her spoon and then her mouth. The stew is robust but delicate, delicious.

"It's a new recipe," the woman says. "Belgian. What do you think?"

"It's very good." It is. Freddy eats ravenously. The stew fills her stomach with warmth and a sense of well-being. The woman pours Merlot into her own wineglass, then into Freddy's. Its color is so lovely in the candlelight that Freddy reaches out for it, unthinking. Her fingers close around the stem. It is hard to let go. She reaches for her water glass instead. The woman smiles. Freddy hopes there will be stew left for Chaz when he wakes up. He looked so pale and thin. She is ashamed of her own appetite. They eat in silence.

When she has eaten all her stew, the woman offers more. Freddy wants more but declines. In this shifting landscape, she needs to be alert. Perhaps she has eaten too much already. She no longer feels afraid. "The meat is so tender," she says. "Did you use veal?"

The woman shakes her head. "The recipe calls for organ meat."

"Normally I don't like it," Freddy says, "but this was good."

"I used your father's brain," the woman says.

It takes a few seconds for the words to mean, a few more to activate her gag reflex. Swallowing hard, she tries to quell it.

The woman says, "I loved Nick for his talent. For his mind. I got the notion that if I had his brain, I would have him."

All of Freddy's attention is dedicated to directing peristalsis, to keep it running in the usual direction. It is important to her to not be sick.

"It was silly, of course. A brain by itself is just a thing. The spirit does not reside in tissues."

Smiling at Freddy, the woman refills her own glass with Merlot and sips before she speaks again. "It was a custom among certain primitive tribes to devour the deceased," the woman says. "A sacred ritual. It was supposed to be a way to incorporate the virtues of the dead into the living. I rather like the idea, don't you? I always wanted to be as good a writer as Nick was."

A storm gathers at the back of Freddy's throat. Under the table, out of sight, she digs her fingernails hard as she can into her palms.

"My, but we're looking peaked," her hostess says, and then explodes into laughter too loud by half for the staid setting, stopping only when tears gather in her eyes, and she has to lift her rhinestone glasses to dab at them with her linen napkin. "Forgive my little joke," she says.

Freddy clutches her hands together in her lap.

"I was curious to see how you'd react," the woman says. "But I'm no cannibal. Here, drink your wine, it'll make you feel better. There's nothing more sinister than sweetbreads in my stew."

Freddy sips from her water glass. The fluid is cool and neutral. Inside, her pulse begins to slow.

"It would have been a perfect way to dispose of the evidence," the woman says. "But in the end, I thought of something almost as clever. Nick's not in the stew, but he is here with us now. See if you can guess where."

Bidden, Freddy scans the table, peers dumbly past the candles' flame, into the shadows of the dining room.

"No? I'll give you a hint. Why is the grass always greener in a graveyard?"

Freddy looks to the gardenia tree, its flowers ghostly in the candlelight.

The woman chuckles. "Lovely, isn't it? I always said Nick had a fertile brain."

The gardenias' perfume settles in Freddy's senses, conjuring hot southern twilight, forgotten proms. Touched, the waxen petals bruise. She struggles to regain her sense of mission. "Why did you kill my father?" Freddy says.

Candlelight dazzles the rhinestones on the woman's glasses. Beyond them, the eyes are deep and dark. "I had to," she says. "Nick wanted to claim authorship of *Hero Time*. The book is something of a classic, you know. It's sold well over the years. I offered to pay him every penny it ever earned, but it wasn't money he wanted. He wanted you and your children to know what he had done." The woman turns her eyes from the candle flame to stare at Freddy. "I told him you'd also know what else he'd done. I had the pictures. Nick said he was too old to care. He believed you'd understand." The woman cocks her head, locking her eyes on Freddy's eyes. "Would you have?"

Freddy rewinds her imagination, back, back, before. She was indignant and self-righteous. Would she have understood? Unexpectedly, she feels a rush of compassion for herself, for Nick. Unexpectedly, she can forgive them both. "Yes," she says. "I would have understood."

"We met for dinner downtown," the woman says. "Nick took me by surprise. I needed time to think. We went back to his house and set up the chessboard. I told Nick, if he won, I would write to the publisher and to the press, acknowledging that he had written *Hero Time*. If I won, we would both take the secret to our graves. He was just drunk enough to agree."

Freddy remembers the chessboard, Sandy's analysis. "But you never finished the game."

"There was no need to play it out," the woman said. "It was stalemate. We both could see that."

"There were no fingerprints."

"It was time-consuming, but I wiped every piece, after."

"If you lost," Freddy says, "would you have kept your word?"

"Who knows?" The woman laughs. "It didn't happen. I knew by then it was endgame. I told your father who my mother was. I told him he'd destroyed her."

Freddy feels a terrible sadness, a sense of waste. "Did you tell Nick you killed your mother?" she says.

"I told him everything. I told him it was really he who had killed Mother, as surely as if he'd pressed the pillow down. Nick said he was guilty of many things, but not of that. He said he was a young, poor boy. He'd worshiped Mother."

The sadness grows so big inside her it is the only thing she feels.

"Nick wept. I wept. He embraced me. Maybe now, he said, we could let the old wounds heal."

Nick was wise. Even now, perhaps there is hope. "But you killed him," she says softly.

"I gave him the chance to save himself," the woman says. "The same chance I'm giving you." The woman looks at her watch. "Your son should be awake now." Smiling at Freddy, she rises. "Wait here," she says.

The woman leaves the dining room, turns left into the hallway. Freddy stares at her wineglass. The wine is the color of garnets, beautiful. It promises to make her brave and strong and clever. It wants her to drink it. The scent of gardenias fills her nostrils, pools in her pores. At the very core of its sweetness, there is a tiny sting. The woman comes back, Chaz, swaddled in a blanket, in her arms. Chaz is rubbing his eyes. When he sees Freddy, he cries out. "Mommy."

"Hi, Sweet Potato." Freddy holds out her arms to take her

son, but the woman shakes her head. She puts Chaz down in the big armed chair at the far end of the table. "You need to be a very good boy, and very quiet, or I'll have to take you back to your room," the woman says.

"I love you," Freddy says. "You better mind." Chaz works one hand out of his blanket and puts his thumb in his mouth. Freddy longs to embrace him.

The woman goes to the long sideboard behind her own seat, pulls out a drawer, extracts a polished wooden case. This she sets on the table between her place and Freddy's. Sitting, she says, "For me, killing is less a matter of intention than inspiration. I never planned to kill my mother, or your father, or anyone else. When the time came, I simply knew."

Careful to keep her voice level, Freddy says, "How many people have you killed?"

"As with sex," the woman says, "numbers don't matter. One is a virgin, or one is not." She lifts the lid of the wooden case. Inside, a black revolver nestles on a bed of red velvet. "I assume you're a virgin," the woman says.

Freddy looks to Chaz. His eyes are big and bright. He sucks his thumb. At the other end of the table, the woman lifts the revolver from its case, inserts a clip of ammunition into the handle, then returns it to its velvet bed. "I told your father he could save himself," she says. "I put the gun in his hand and invited him to shoot me."

Freddy feels her nerves convulse, a great void where her stomach used to be. Suddenly it is very cold in the dining room.

The woman looks from her to Chaz. "Nick knew that if he didn't kill me, I would kill him. It wasn't that he couldn't do it, but that he wouldn't." She laughs. "I think I knew that."

Freddy knows what the woman will say next.

"I offer you the same opportunity."

Like the last chord of a concerto, her words hang, diminish slowly before they fade away. The challenge remains. Freddy feels the stalemate of her nerves.

The woman laughs. "You're pale."

"Who are you?" Freddy says.

The woman looks her in the eye. "Does it matter?"

"I don't know."

"I wonder," the woman says. She drains her wineglass in

one swallow, then sets it down. Freddy thinks she sees a tremor in her hand.

"If I show you," the woman says, "you'll have an advantage on your father. There's one thing Nick didn't know."

Freddy says nothing. She seems to be all pulse and synapse.

The silence stretches long before the woman says, "Very well." Swiftly she pulls the gray wig from her head, lays aside her spectacles, peels off a portion of her cheeks and chin. With a little popping sound her prosthetic nose comes off. She uses her linen napkin to wipe off the stage makeup.

The transformation is mesmerizing and terrible. Freddy's heart crashes once, hard, against her ribs. "Peter," she says.

Her mother's husband smiles at her. "Now you know."

"All your business trips."

"It has always amused me to live more than one life at a time."

Freddy feels sick on Elsa's behalf.

"I thought it would satisfy me to satisfy a woman Nick couldn't," Peter says. "There was a certain symmetry to it. Knowing as much about her as I did, I found your mother easy to win."

"You're a monster," Freddy says.

"I'm no less human than you are. Or than your son. At least your father understood that virtue is a choice."

Freddy fills up with love and pity for her mother.

"Nick was right," Peter says. "Your mother has a spine of ice. Neither love nor artifice could melt her."

Poor Elsa. Perhaps a daughter's love might warm her. She looks to Chaz and thinks he smiles at her, secretly, around his thumb.

Peter lifts the revolver from its cradle. Freddy hears a little clicking sound. Butt first, he extends the gun to her. "It's your turn now."

Freddy has never touched a gun before. She doesn't want to now. High seas swirl inside her. Beyond their storming, it is impossible to know what she feels. She takes the gun from him. It is cold and rather beautiful. She says. "Why are you giving me this?"

"To see what you'll do." Peter smiles at her. "I know you were raised to abhor violence. Your father's convictions were stronger than his will to live." He lifts his palm. "Why don't you aim, Frederika? It will only make our conversation more interesting."

Slowly, tentatively, Freddy raises the revolver. Looking down its barrel seems to magnify Peter's face until it is the biggest thing in the world, the only thing.

"You'll want to put your finger on the trigger," he coaches her.

"No," Freddy says. "I still don't understand."

"Killing is easy, but it has its price. If you shoot me, you'll understand that." Peter's smile stretches to the edges of the universe. "I've killed but never died. I'm not afraid. The only two people I've ever loved are gone."

Freddy supports the revolver with one hand while she feels for the trigger with the index finger of the other. Her touch is light as a whisper.

"Think what you can accomplish with just one bullet. You can avenge your father and widow your mother at the same time. For the rest of his life, your son will know his mother is a murderer. If you believe in damnation, you can achieve that too."

"Such a deal," Freddy says. She lowers the gun and lays it in her lap.

"Is that a decision?" Peter says.

"Tell me what happens if I don't kill you."

"Well," Peter says, "I will certainly kill you. Since he's seen my real face, I suppose I'll have to kill your son. I didn't intend that. I regret it." He looks at Chaz, huddled at the foot of the table. "He's a fine boy. He won my respect." Peter's eyes return to Freddy's. "Eventually I'll be inspired to kill Elsa, too, most likely from ennui." He laughs. "If you should choose to cross the line, you'll learn what I've known all of my adult life. It's exciting. An appetite that, once activated, becomes dreadfully difficult to deny. If you kill me, that appetite will be my legacy."

"It can't happen to everyone," Freddy says. "What about soldiers and policemen."

"What about them?"

Freddy does not decide to lift the gun, she simply lifts it. Some of Peter's smugness seems to fade. In her mind, Freddy reviews his crimes. Monster, witch, madman. He deserves hatred and she wills herself to hate him. He is scarcely human, an abomination. Peter's dark eyes stare at her. She feels a seed of anger split inside her, send down roots. Almost, she hates. And then, unbidden, she remembers the young child in the bathroom, the mother's ugly game. Tears blur her vision. Through their distortion, Peter's face is innocent and wronged. "I'm sorry your mother hurt you," Freddy says.

At the end of the barrel's dark canal, she sees his face contort, twist up in anger, baring the strong white teeth. "You fool. You bitch. My mother loved me." He lunges forward. To the end of her days, Freddy will not know if it is only she that pulls the trigger. Peter's face explodes.

After recoil, his body continues its forward thrust, landing briefly on her lap, then sliding down her legs to rest at her feet. Peter's warm blood seeps through the fabric of her jumpsuit. Tears that were a trickle become a flood. Freddy drops the revolver to the floor and sobs. Her body quivers. All she can see is red and blackness. If she isn't dead, she wants to be.

"Mommy?" A small voice reaches her out of the darkness. Blindly she turns toward it. Light from the candles hurts her eyes. Slowly her son comes into focus. He stares at her. Freddy gets up and goes to him. She kneels before his chair. "Forgive me," she says.

Chaz takes his thumb from his mouth and, with his right hand, reaches out to touch her hair. "It's all right now, Mommy. Can we go home?"

Home. The thought of home incites a ragged laugh. Freddy enfolds her son in her arms and carries him away from devastation, into the living room. Her glass is still full of sherry. Now she drinks it. "I have to call the police now," she tells Chaz. In what must be the master bedroom she finds a telephone. Numbers elude her. She dials the simplest, 911. When the police operator answers, Freddy says, "I've just killed someone. In self-defense." She gives the address and asks the woman to contact Lieutenant Ashford.

"Are you sure the victim is dead?" the operator asks.

Freddy says yes. In the living room, she sits beside Chaz on the leather love seat. "The police will be here soon," she tells him. "Then we can go."

"I was so scared, Mommy," Chaz says. He leans against her. In spite of his long sleep, he looks weary, his skin almost transparent. Freddy strokes his hair. After a while, Chaz says, "I'm hungry."

In its basket, the French bread is still slightly warm. Freddy butters the biggest piece for Chaz, then, stepping carefully, goes to the gardenia tree, picks off a blossom, and tucks it in her hair.

While Freddy listens for sirens, Chaz gnaws his bread. Once, between bites, he reaches up to touch the flower in her hair. "That's pretty, Mom."

His little fingers will mark the blossom, but Freddy doesn't mind.